WHERE HEARTS

ARE Free

BOOK THREE IN THE
DARKNESS TO LIGHT SERIES

Golden Keyes Parsons

THOMAS NELSON
Since 1798

NASHVILLE   DALLAS   MEXICO CITY   RIO DE JANEIRO

Published in Nashville, Tennessee, by Thomas Nelson. Thomas Nelson is a registered trademark of Thomas Nelson, Inc.

Thomas Nelson, Inc., titles may be purchased in bulk for educational, business, fund-raising, or sales promotional use. For information, please e-mail SpecialMarkets@ThomasNelson.com.

Publisher's Note: This novel is a work of fiction. Names, characters, places, and incidents are either products of the author's imagination or used fictitiously. All characters are fictional, and any similarity to people living or dead is purely coincidental.

Library of Congress Cataloging-in-Publication Data

Parsons, Golden Keyes, 1941–
  Where hearts are free / Golden Keyes Parsons.
     p. cm. — (Darkness to light series ; bk. 3)
  ISBN 978-1-59554-628-9 (soft cover)
  1. Huguenots—Pennsylvania—Fiction. 2. Pennsylvania—History—Colonial period, ca. 1600–1775—Fiction. 3. Indentured servants—Fiction. I. Title.
  PS3616.A7826W47 2010
  813'.6—dc22   2010023650

Printed in the United States of America

10 11 12 13 14 RRD 5 4 3 2 1

PROLOGUE

The familiar trembling slid its slippery fingers through Bridget's stomach and into her throat. Philippe galloped ahead into the meadow beyond the cornfield. She struggled to catch her breath. "D-don't go into the meadow. It is not part of Whisper Wood. It's dangerous!"

Ignoring her warning, Philippe urged the black gelding over the low wooden fence and plunged ahead. "The sow is probably down in the hollow by the river. Follow me."

Twelve-year-old Bridget halted her horse, and the mare reared as the girl slipped off. Her heart churned, and the heaving threatened to surface once again. "No, Philippe. Come back! It's ... it's sc-scary down there." She bent over and waited for the sensation to stop.

She could hear him thrashing through the brush on the riverbank as he searched for the sow and her piglets. Then he emerged from the

1

oak trees that lined the Schuylkill River, a wide grin spreading over his face.

"I was right. The sow has found a place for her piglets down on the riverbank and is burrowed in. I'll need to get the wagon and bring it back to—" He reined his horse in beside her. "What's wrong, mistress? Are you ill?" He dismounted and held the reins in his hands, staring at her.

"I don't like this place."

Philippe looked around. "I see nothing to cause you this kind of extreme alarm."

Tears formed in Bridget's eyes, and she brushed them away with the back of her gloved hand.

The boy dug into his tunic and pulled out a handkerchief. He handed it to her. "You never have a handkerchief when you need one."

She wiped her eyes. "I know. But you always do. After all, 'Clavell men are gentlemen.'" She mimicked his French accent.

"One can hardly call an indentured servant a 'gentleman.'"

"I don't think of you as a servant. I consider you my friend. Before you came, I had no one to ride with or talk to . . . no one close to my age anyway."

He chuckled. "I'm much older than you. You're still a child."

"Three years doesn't make you so much older. I'm almost thirteen." She sniffled and wiped her nose. "You've been with us almost a year now."

"Yes. And a long year it has been."

"Have you not been happy here?" She handed him his handkerchief.

Philippe fidgeted with the reins. "Your father has been more than fair and kind. I know I have fared well—better than most. But I'd rather be with my family."

"I understand. I would too." Bridget stroked the neck of her horse, then mounted. "I would like to show you a place that is special to me."

"We should get back to the house. Your father . . ." Philippe stuck the handkerchief into his tunic and mounted as well.

"My father trusts you to watch over me whenever we ride. He will not be worried."

"Are you certain you feel up to riding even farther away from the house?"

Bridget flicked her hand in the air. "I'm fine now." She spurred her horse. "This way." She urged the Narragansett into an easy canter and rode through the nascent cornfields. Before long the stalks would be taller than the horses' heads and bursting with sweet kernels. She led the way through the field until she could turn her horse across their own property toward the edge of the forest. Riding into the woods, she maneuvered her horse through the thick trees and then down the steep embankment to the river, downstream from where they found the sow and her brood. The spring rains had swollen the usually quiet stream into a bubbling, gurgling surge of white-capped cold water. She found the fallen logs that formed the perimeter of her cathedral in the forest. A gentle rocky descent afforded an unencumbered view of the bend in the river.

"This is my special place." She dismounted and placed her small foot, encased in a brown leather boot, on a fallen log. "Look. My favorite log rotted, but Father leveled this stump and smoothed it over to make a stool for me."

Half of an oak tree reflected the effect of a lightning strike; the other half remained healthy. Low-hanging branches formed a dome over the clearing.

Bridget pulled her riding skirt around her and sat on the stump, leaning against the standing half of the tree and using the log for a footstool. "I come here to be alone and think." She paused. "Listen."

"I don't hear anything." Philippe remained atop the large Percheron.

"Not at first you won't. But if you remain very still . . ."

The quiet of the woods enfolded them, and she closed her eyes. "I try to count how many animal sounds I can hear in the stillness— sometimes I hear the trills of cardinals and the fussing of blue jays, or the rustling of a rabbit or a squirrel. I've seen white-tailed deer and turkey in the autumn months." Her eyes popped open. "One time a black bear even walked by in the distance but didn't see me."

She ran her hand over the ground. Trout lilies and purple violets poked their heads up through the carpet of leaves. She plucked a violet and brought it to her nose.

Philippe got off his horse. "And you are not frightened here by yourself?"

"No, not here. I was at first, because . . ."

Philippe waited.

Bridget's horse nickered and pulled at her bridle. She wanted to graze. Bridget stood and led her down the embankment to the river for a drink. Philippe followed.

"Kimi." She patted the mare. "Her name means 'secret.' Did you know that?"

Philippe tightened the girth on his horse and turned to check Kimi's as well. "I . . . I guess I never really thought about it. Does she have a secret?" He chuckled.

"She's kept it well." Bridget ignored his joke. "I had named her

Lady, but . . . I changed it to Kimi. It's Algonquin." The horse nuzzled her hand. "Something terrible happened, Philippe. I made a vow to myself never to tell anyone, but now . . . now I want to tell you. I feel I can trust you." She pulled Kimi's head up, and they led the horses back to the log. "I can trust you, Philippe, can I not?"

"You can trust me, mistress."

Bridget sat on the stump, and Philippe sat on the mossy ground with his arms around his knees. The moistness of the early spring ground sent its musty odor into the air. Heads of mushrooms were beginning to peek through the ground cover of leaves by the log.

"This log was huge the first time I came across the tree, large enough to hide behind when"—Bridget paused and took a deep breath—"when that bad man was looking for me. I was only nine years old. I can still hear him crashing through the trees, shouting and swearing. I hid here for hours until the forest grew quiet again."

"What man?"

Bridget sighed. "I don't know. I didn't know who he was. And now I don't remember his face or what he looked like. All I can remember is his hair. It was light brown. His hat had blown off, and his hair was long, to his shoulders." She touched her shoulder and looked up the embankment. "I can remember the wind blowing his hair around his face . . ." Her voice trailed away.

"And Kimi—?"

"She returned to the house. That's how Father found me—she led him to me—here." Bridget smiled crookedly. "Isn't she a smart horse? Do you see why I love her so?"

Philippe nodded. "Why was the man looking for you?"

Bridget avoided his eyes. "I was riding in the cornfield, just as we did today. Father always cautioned me to stay close to the house,

5

but I rode farther out than I intended, all the way to the edge of our property. Suddenly I came to a fence. And then I heard a musket fire. A man was running toward me. His arms were stretched toward me and his eyes—his eyes were wild." She closed her eyes. "There was a second blast, and he fell. He fell right in front of me, and his back . . . his back just . . . it just exploded." She buried her face in her hands. "It was horrid. Blood splattered everywhere. As he fell he looked at me. His eyes weren't closed, they . . . were . . . st-stayed open. He r-reached his hand toward me as if pleading for help. But . . ."

A long moment of silence passed between them. Bridget could see the scene—as vivid as it was the day it happened—the helplessness she felt, the sheer terror and the smell of the blood. She could still smell the blood.

"Then what happened?" Philippe asked gently.

"A man holding a musket started into the meadow from the riverbank, but when he saw me he stopped. He began to curse and ran to his horse. He was young. I remember that. Kimi reared, and I thought I was going to fall off, but I managed to stay in the saddle, and . . . and she took off for the forest." Bridget paused to catch her breath, her eyes reddening with unshed tears. She felt her heart beat faster. "I could hear the man behind me and feared he was going to catch me, but suddenly Kimi stumbled down this embankment, and I fell off. I thought he would catch me for sure then, but he never saw where I was hiding. He rode right by me—so close I saw his face. Kimi ran away toward Whisper Wood, and he followed her. He never came down the embankment."

"Why did he kill that man? Did you see anything else?"

Bridget shook her head. "There was a small barge on the river at a dock. Men were unloading boxes."

"Yes, I saw that dock down there. What is it for? It's rather hidden."

Bridget shrugged her shoulders. "I don't know. All I know is what I saw that day. I was terrified that the man with the gun would find me. He knew I saw him." She wrapped her arms around herself and rocked back and forth. The tears brimmed over her eyelids and began to flow down her cheeks. "Oh, Philippe, that poor man. I didn't help him. He needed help, and I ran because I was afraid." She covered her face, and sobs convulsed through her body. "I . . . I didn't . . . h-help him."

Philippe leaned toward her. "There was nothing you could have done. You were a little girl. You have nothing to feel guilty about."

She shook her head as if trying to erase the memory. "You don't know what it's like to see a man die—murdered right in front of your very eyes. It was awful."

"I do know what it's like. I understand exactly."

Bridget took her hands from her face and stared at Philippe. "Wh-what do you mean? When did you—?"

"In France." Philippe stood and took a deep breath. He cleared his throat, and his newly deepening voice faltered. "I was only twelve, about your age, when the dragoons, French soldiers of the king, invaded our estate. Charles and my uncle Jean and I had to hide for several weeks in a cave my parents had stocked in anticipation of just such a possibility. My mother pleaded with the king to call off the soldiers, but he refused, and we escaped to Switzerland. On the way we happened upon a family in the forest who were being terrorized by . . . by another brigade of dragoons." He halted. A heavy hush hung in the afternoon air. "It was much like these woods—thick with underbrush, big trees—trees big enough to . . ." Philippe shuffled his feet.

"Go on . . . big enough to what?"

The boy reached up and touched a large overhanging branch. "Big enough to hang a person. The dragoons were going to hang the family because they were Huguenots—a man, a woman, and their son." Philippe looked at Bridget, and his eyes reflected the pain of the experience. He frowned. "The king ordered the conversion of all the Protestants, and if they wouldn't convert, they were shot, hanged, kidnapped, thrown in prison, or sent to the galleys, like my father." He turned away from her. "It was a terrible time. That's why we came here . . . to this country."

Bridget looked down. "What happened to the family?"

Philippe looked down at his hands. "We—my uncle, one of our servants, and I—we ambushed them and killed the soldiers. I killed one of them my-myself."

"O-ohh." Bridget let out a long breath. Empathy for him flooded through her.

"I had nightmares about it for a long time afterward. I still do sometimes."

Her voice rose barely above a whisper. "As do I—about what I saw. How did you . . . did you ever forgive yourself?"

"I don't know that I have completely, but it's better than it used to be. Maman and Uncle Jean helped me see that sometimes difficult decisions have to be made to save another life and for freedom. And that God's grace and forgiveness extends even to the most horrible of deeds that we commit."

"I . . . I don't think I can ever forgive myself. I did nothing to help that man. I never wanted anybody else to know."

Philippe handed his handkerchief back to her and sat down on the log next to her. "You did nothing to be ashamed of, mistress. You could not have helped the man. You did the right thing by escaping."

"Do you think so?" Bridget felt a glimmer of hope and relief from the burden of her guilt.

Philippe nodded. "I am certain of it. So it has been your secret all these years?"

"Yes. I didn't come back to the log for a long time, but one morning I gathered the courage to return. I was afraid it would bring back the terror, but it was just the opposite. It had offered safety and a hiding place before, so I began to come here often. After a few months my father fixed the stump for me." She hugged herself and rubbed her arms.

"Are you cold?" Philippe stood and offered his jacket.

"No, I'm not cold. Keep your jacket."

"Can you remember anything else?"

Bridget closed her eyes, playing the scene over again in her mind as she had time after time through the years, waking and sleeping. She shook her head. "I've tried, but I can't remember anything else."

"How many men? What kind of cargo?"

"I saw only three men, counting the one they killed."

"But you didn't see what they were loading or unloading?"

"No."

"And you never told your parents what you saw?"

Panic grabbed her. She gulped and stood. "No! And you mustn't tell anyone either. I'm frightened that man will come after me if I do. Please, you won't tell anyone, will you? You won't share my secret?" She began to tremble again.

"No, no, I won't. Your secret is safe with me. I told you that you could trust me."

Reliving the memory of that horrid day had overwhelmed Bridget, and she began to cry.

Philippe shook his head. "Don't cry."

She stepped toward him and laid her head on his chest, sucking in broken breaths. He hugged her around her shoulders in an awkward sixteen-year-old gesture of compassion, then gently but firmly took her by the shoulders and pushed her away. "Come, Mistress Barrington. I need to return you to the house."

She nodded and moved to her horse. "Thank you, Philippe, for listening—and for understanding. You are indeed a gentleman."

The young Frenchman chuckled and helped her mount her beloved Kimi. He gave the mare an extra stroke. "You shall get special care from me now."

The couple rode out of the forest, across the meadow, avoiding the cornfield, and back to Whisper Wood, their dreadful secrets like a spider's web, binding them to one another with invisible sticky threads.

ONE

Bridget pulled the lace curtain aside and peered through the diamond-shaped windowpanes. She watched from her upstairs room as the handsome Frenchman calmed a rearing red roan in the early morning fog. He dodged the flailing hooves with no more than a step sideways and stroked the neck of the nervous mare.

She tugged her hood over her head and pulled a blonde lock of hair out from under the folds of the soft blue fabric of her silk palatine. Not that Philippe Clavell would notice. Horses captured his attention; riding captured his attention; newborn colts captured his attention—but she did not. She had to admit, however, that his skill with horses was a most attractive aspect of this young indentured servant. He harnessed the team of mares to the carriage and led the rig around the corner of the house toward the front of the Barrington plantation that sat on the outskirts of Philadelphia.

It did not seem possible that six years had passed since her father had bid on him at the redemptioner's auction on the wharf that drizzly day. And though he'd carried her deepest secret all these years, the older the two became, the more he seemed to withdraw from her. They had not ridden together in months.

Bridget turned from the window and moved down the stairs to the front door. As she descended the steps from the porch to the circular driveway, Philippe appeared with the carriage. Her parents, Amos and Sarah Barrington, followed her, chattering about the day's outing.

Bridget loved going to Philadelphia to spend time with her best friend and childhood companion, her cousin Ella. But since Ella's marriage, their times to share confidences had become fewer and shorter. Bridget missed her.

The top of Bridget's head barely reached the tall Frenchman's shoulders as he opened the carriage door. He nodded and helped her into the cab, along with her parents, then climbed onto the perch and chucked the reins. Bridget was pleased that Philippe was their driver today. He executed impeccable, formal manners and exhibited a strength that gave her a sense of security in the noisy streets of Philadelphia.

"Look at the violets and clover. Aren't they beautiful this morning?" Sarah tapped her daughter on the knee and pointed out the window.

Bridget gazed in the direction her mother pointed and watched the wildflowers that covered the hills nod their colorful heads, shaking off the early morning dew. "*Mmm*, yes, beautiful."

"Do stop that squinting. You'll get wrinkles." Sarah sat back and looked at her daughter. "What is going on in that pretty head of yours this morning? You're awfully quiet."

"Nothing." She fidgeted with her gloves. "Has Philippe asked permission to go see his brother today?"

Sarah turned to her husband. Amos shook his head. "Not yet. Why should that be of any concern to you?"

She shrugged her shoulder. "No reason. No reason a'tall." She continued to stare out the side of the carriage, but her mood fogged over like the vapor that hovered in patches over the landscape. She didn't want Philippe to go visit his brother. As an indentured servant, he wouldn't be included in any of the family activities, but she could imagine what it would be like if he were . . . If only he could sit down to dinner with them, enter into conversation with the men, laugh at inside stories of the family. Family. Of course he wanted to go see his brother.

But still, selfish or not, she much desired to have him near. She was relieved when her mother began to prattle away about the arrival of Ella's new baby—the reason for their visit today.

"It's always nice to have a boy first. A big brother is . . ." Sarah paused, and her eyes misted over.

Amos patted his wife's hand as she searched for her handkerchief. "That was a long time ago, Sarah."

"I know, but I still miss him."

"So do I."

Bridget wished her mother wouldn't do that. Her heart twisted inside of her with compassion, but she felt awkward whenever the subject of her older brother came up. Somehow it made her feel inadequate or guilty, even though she had not even been born then. Asthma had taken his life when he was twelve. Then there had been a baby boy who was stillborn. But all Bridget remembered was being an only child. She never knew what to say during these conversations. At least the ride was only thirty minutes into town.

Philippe slowed the buggy in front of the Osbornes' house and guided the team through the mud to the hitching post alongside the wooden sidewalk. He jumped down, secured the horses, and opened the door of the carriage. Amos emerged with a grunt and helped Sarah maneuver out of the buggy. Philippe waited for Bridget to set her foot on the iron plate.

She held out her hand to him, and her eyes traveled over the new formal blue footman's uniform that Amos had requested Philippe wear today. It fit his tall, slender frame perfectly, the epaulets accentuating his broad shoulders. She looked into his face as she stepped onto the street, but he averted her gaze. "Philippe, I appreciate the expert job you do in driving us. Thank you." She took her father's arm as Amos clapped Philippe on the back.

"Your time to leave us is drawing near, my boy," her father said. "What are we going to do without you?"

Philippe smiled. "I am sure you will manage." The young man paused as he helped the Barringtons gather their belongings. "May I . . . may I have permission to visit my brother today?"

Bridget stared at Philippe and frowned.

"Of course." Amos glanced at his daughter and pulled a basket of baked goods from the carriage, handing it to his wife. "Be back here around three o'clock."

"Yes, sir. Thank you, *monsieur*."

Amos looked at the young man. "Your English has improved greatly, but one can definitely still detect the French accent."

Philippe nodded and untied the team to take them to the small stable in the back of the house. "I'll take care of the horses, and then I shall return before three, sir. Thank you, sir."

The Barringtons moved up the steps to the door of the house.

Bridget sighed. "I wish you had asked Philippe to wait here for us, Father."

"I would not deny the boy the chance to see his brother."

"He's not a boy. He's a man."

"Yes, of course. He's grown into a fine young man before our eyes. Come, ladies." He ushered his wife and daughter to the door and clacked the heavy knocker.

Bridget turned to watch Philippe head toward the back of the house with the carriage. He disappeared around the corner without so much as a glance in her direction.

PHILIPPE ADJUSTED HIS BAG, SHOVED HIS HANDS INTO HIS pockets, and walked at a brisk pace down the now familiar street. He hunched his shoulders against the morning chill. The yellow daffodils, red tulips, and white lilies of the valley in patchy flower beds struggled to announce the arrival of spring, but the mornings were still cool. The sun began to poke through the haze, burning the moisture away. It would take him about twenty minutes to reach the shop, but he didn't mind the walk. On these days when the Barringtons came into town to visit relatives and allowed him to go see Charles, he pretended that he was no longer a servant, but a free man. And that he would be soon.

Rounding a bend in the road, he spotted the Harbor Tavern & Inn. He opened the heavy door; the wood scraped against the floor, alerting the proprietor, who looked up from behind a large table set with steins of ale and rounds of bread. The smell of cinnamon wafted from a large brick oven where the owner's wife poked a long-handled peel into the interior.

A wide grin spread across the man's face, revealing stained teeth with a wide gap in the front. "Philippe! I was just thinking about you this morning. I reckoned it was about time for you to come around. Come in, my friend."

Philippe shook the man's large, beefy hand and nodded toward the door. "I would be happy to fix that for you."

"Ah, no need. It shifts and will likely not be scraping next time you visit. Have you come for your usual?"

"Yes. A round of cheese, some smoked ham, and a loaf of your wife's wonderful bread. Do you have rye today?"

"Sorry, but"—the man put his hand up in the air and laughed—"my good wife is baking apple pies this morning. Surely you would want one of those."

Philippe took a leather pouch out of his tunic, poured his wages onto the dark wooden table, and began to count the coins. "How much?"

"For you, I throw the pie in for good measure."

"*Ach*, Mister Clark. You are too generous. How can you stay in business if you don't charge your customers?"

"My customers, I charge. My friends, I can give a gift, if I choose, eh?"

Philippe chuckled and scooped the coins into his hand. "Very well. How much for the rest? And I think I would like two loaves of whatever kind of bread you have today, please."

"The same."

Philippe shook his head and counted out the money. "Any news in the city?"

"Nothing, except the Lenape seem to be moving north and west."

"Yes, we've seen the movement of the Indians past our place. No trouble, though?"

"Not that I know of. Some of the older folk are staying, but I hear the younger ones are moving to expand onto more land."

Philippe nodded. Amos had worked diligently to maintain a good relationship with the local Algonquin tribes. They traded goods and even worked for him on occasion. Philippe had heard tales of Indian uprisings in other colonies, but in Pennsylvania, all seemed to be peaceful—so far.

Philippe paid for his food, stuffed it into his bag, and stepped out onto the street. He headed at a brisk pace toward the foundry. Approaching the establishment, he noticed the sign that announced Zwicken's Foundry leaning against the front of the building. His brother emerged from the front door with a hammer in his hand and picked up the heavy, carved marker. The wind tousled Charles' hair, still red but growing darker as he matured. The young man looked up at the bracket and put the hammer down.

"Need some help?"

Charles whirled around and dropped the sign. It clattered at his feet as he ran to his older brother and pulled him into a smothering hug. "Philippe! I'm so glad to see you!" He pounded Philippe on the shoulders. "Don't you look fine! New uniform?"

"Yes, well, you know how Mister Barrington is. Likes me to look the part."

Charles looked down at his ragged breeches, his worn shoes and stockings. "Ha! Not quite like my employer."

Philippe winced. "Well, do you?"

"Do I what?"

"Need help with the sign?"

"Oh . . . uh, yes, please. I thought I was going to have to put on new hooks, but it appears to have simply swung out of the bracket. Grab that end of it, and I think we can hook it back on."

Philippe set his bag next to the shop window. He helped Charles heft the sign and rehook it. The heavy marker creaked as it swung into place.

Philippe motioned to Charles' tool belt. "Do you have pliers?"

Charles pulled out a pair.

"Let me lift you on my shoulders and you can press those hooks back together. Then it won't slip out again the next time it gets windy."

"Why didn't I think of that?" Charles cuffed him on the arm.

Philippe grinned and removed his tricornered hat. He bent down for Charles to climb on his shoulders, then slowly stood, raising Charles just high enough to reach the hooks. "Hurry. You're not as light as you used to be."

"Got it. Let me down."

Philippe lowered Charles and wiped his forehead with his sleeve. "It's warming up."

"Philippe, Clavell men are gentlemen. We use a handkerchief."

Philippe grinned and pulled a handkerchief out of the cuff of his jacket. "I remember saying that to *you* when the musketeers 'escorted' Maman and me to Versailles. You were pretty upset." He replaced the handkerchief, picked up his hat, and brushed his hair out of his eyes.

"*Oui.* I was." Charles wasn't quite as tall as Philippe but was more muscular. The gap of three years in their ages seemed to have narrowed now that they both were adults. "You look more and more like Papa every time I see you. Especially your hair—the way it falls across your forehead."

"I know." Philippe twirled his hat in his hands for a moment, then put it on.

"Philippe, do you know what bothers me?"

"What's that?"

"I can't remember what Papa looked like when I try to recall his face."

"You were pretty young."

"I was twelve. I should remember. But then when I see you, I see him. That makes me feel better."

"Don't feel guilty. I have trouble remembering as well." Philippe picked up his bag. "I brought food."

"You always do. Thank you. Can you stay awhile?"

"*Oui*, I don't need to leave until around two o'clock."

The door to the foundry opened, and a burly man with a bushy beard and huge arms filled the entrance. He boomed at Charles, "Anytime you feel like returning to work, Mister Clavell . . ." He glared at Philippe. "You again."

"Yes, sir. I'd like to visit with my brother for a bit today. I'll be happy to work."

Mister Zwicken eyed his uniform. "In that finery?"

Philippe lifted his bag. "I brought work clothes."

"*Humph*." He scratched his chin. "Very well. But if we lose any time on this job, you're on your way."

"You'll make up time with me working alongside Charles. I guarantee it."

Zwicken opened the door wider and shooed the brothers inside. The shop was already steamy and noisy. They walked to Charles' workbench in the back of the shop.

Philippe removed his jacket. "What 'job' is he talking about?"

"We have several dozen rifles to ready for the militia. They are required now to use flintlocks, rather than matchlocks." He handed one of the weapons to Philippe.

Philippe peered down the sight. "It's longer."

"Yes, and look into the barrel."

"Ah, there are grooves."

"Makes the ball spin—one gets a more accurate shot." Charles sat down at a table. "That's our current project. We'd better get to work. Get changed. Zwicken will be watching."

Philippe donned a work tunic. He suspected Zwicken mistreated his employees, but Charles never spoke of it. His brother worked hard and deserved better. Philippe didn't know how he was going to return to the family in central Pennsylvania a free man in a few weeks while his brother labored in these conditions. Where was freedom for Charles?

TWO

Bridget and her parents uttered the proper *oohs* and *ahhs* over the new baby in the wooden cradle. Ella beamed and rocked the cradle with her foot. David Osborne, the proud father, strutted around the room like a rooster and gathered with the men in front of the fireplace, discussing the latest news of the frontier.

"May I?" Bridget bent over to pick up the baby.

"I suppose that would be fine. We don't want to spoil him, though."

"I don't think his cousin holding him for a few moments is going to spoil him." Bridget picked the baby up in her arms and looked into his blue eyes as he blinked at her and jerked his fist into the air. "Do you think his eyes will stay blue?"

"I doubt it. Be careful. Hold his head. He's only a month old."

"I know how to hold a baby, Ella. Don't be so nervous."

"Well, you haven't had much experience."

Bridget smiled. Ella, with her dark hair and milk-white skin, looked more like Amos and Sarah's daughter than Bridget did herself. She knew what her cousin was insinuating: *You should be married by now with a baby of your own.* "I've birthed many a foal and puppy." She kissed the baby's forehead and nuzzled his cheek.

"Horses and dogs are hardly like a human baby."

"Oh, I disagree. They are very much like a human baby—helpless and weak and . . ." The baby began to search against Bridget's arm to nurse. "And always hungry." She laughed and handed the baby back to her cousin.

Ella blushed. "Please excuse me. I'll go upstairs and feed our little David Junior."

A rap sounded upon the door as Ella left the room. A servant stepped into the parlor. "Mister Edward Moorehead."

David bounded toward the visitor. "Welcome, Edward. Thank you for coming."

A delicately handsome man stepped into the room. He wore a chocolate brown riding habit lined in gold satin with gold braid on the cuffs and buttonholes over a shorter, dark green embroidered vest. Mister Moorehead removed his hat, revealing a well-groomed head of dark blond hair, and acknowledged his host.

David stepped in. "Let me introduce our aunt and uncle, Sarah and Amos Barrington."

Amos nodded. "Yes, we have met, at the last town council meeting."

"I remember."

"This is my wife, Sarah, and our daughter, Bridget."

Edward bowed slightly toward the women, then took Bridget's hand and kissed it. "I am indeed happy to make your acquaintance." He held on to her hand and looked directly into her eyes.

Bridget returned his gaze and slid her hand from his grasp. She nodded but felt her cheeks flush. She had been set up. Her parents were aggressively searching for a suitable marriage partner for her and had arranged this meeting without her knowledge or consent.

Bridget knew whom she wanted to marry. She just didn't see how her dream could become reality. She didn't even know if the object of her affections shared her feelings. How could six years have passed without an utterance? Bridget had danced around the issue, flirted, hinted. But Philippe never reciprocated, never gave her any indication of mutual feelings. The friendship that had been forged in their youth had faded into the background during their years of adolescence and young adulthood. Even the secret she'd told him—the one that still gave her nightmares—hadn't been mentioned again.

The words flowed easily enough between them when the conversation concerned horses. Philippe always took special care with her horse and gear. But occasionally she would catch a lingering gaze. And when their eyes met, even for a moment, there was a glimmer of . . . of a softness in his dark eyes. These glimpses gave her hope . . . mightn't the dreams she secretly harbored possibly be matched by feelings of his own?

Her parents would no doubt be less than enthusiastic that their daughter had fallen in love with a servant in their household. She fingered the small crucifix around her neck and prayed that the biggest hurdle of all—the fact that the Barringtons were Catholic and Philippe was Protestant—would not prove insurmountable.

An outburst of laughter from the men brought her back from her musing. The inane social chatter flitted around her. She remained in her chair and beat the air with her fan to cool her reddened cheeks. How could her parents do this to her without telling her? Or maybe it had been Ella and David's doing.

She looked aslant at Edward. She had to admit that he was actually quite handsome; too prissy for her taste, but handsome. He stood back on one foot with the other forward as if ready to execute a dance step. The fancy dark green vest accented his ruddy complexion. He turned his head and looked at her over his shoulder, and her throat tightened. He resumed his conversation with the men. They broke out in laughter once more.

"Do I remember correctly," her father asked Edward, "that you are not from Pennsylvania territory originally?"

Edward held an ornate gold-framed quizzing glass in front of his eyes as he looked at Amos. "That's correct. My family is from New York province, but I inherited some property here. Last year I decided to make the move and establish my household here permanently. My business interests and property have brought me in and out of Philadelphia for about twelve years now." He tucked the glass in his pocket, where a ribbon secured it. "Pennsylvania is the fairest among the colonies, in my humble estimation."

A murmur of consent spread through the room.

"Your occupation?"

"I have several business interests in town—an import-export concern, a tavern, a furrier, and a gunsmith and silver foundry. We also have a plantation that actually backs up to your property, Mister Barrington. It's primarily focused on purebred horses."

"Is that right? I thought the Archer family owned that piece of land."

"Cousins. I inherited it last year."

Bridget stood. "Would that be Zwicken's Foundry?"

Edward turned to Bridget. "Why, yes, it would be. You are familiar with our establishment?"

"Why is it called Zwicken's instead of Moorehead's?"

A condescending smile formed on Mister Moorehead's lips. "I am a 'silent partner.' Mister Zwicken owns a percentage and runs the place. Why is such a pretty head concerned about the dull business details of a foundry?"

Her father ever so slightly shook his head at her.

Bridget raised her fan and sat back down. "Oh, no reason. I've seen it on our trips to town. That's all." She paused. "Do you find it a profitable venture?"

"Bridget!" Sarah spoke up.

Edward flicked his wrist as if swatting at a moth. "I find it refreshing that the young lady has an interest in business. It *is* quite profitable." He addressed the men once again. "And, of course, I dabble in politics." The men chuckled and took seats in chairs around the fireplace, leaving the women on the other side of the parlor.

Bridget watched Edward Moorehead strut to his chair. He caught her eye as he sat in the circle of men and dominated the conversation. It seemed to her that he exuded pride and arrogance.

Ella had returned and placed the sleeping baby in the cradle. "He falls asleep nursing, then wakes up in an hour or so wanting to eat again. I am constantly feeding him."

"You have to thump his cheek to keep him awake long enough so he will nurse adequately." Sarah was eager to share her expert advice.

"Thump?"

"Just gently."

Bridget went to the window and looked down the street in the direction Philippe had walked. It was almost one o'clock. He wouldn't return for two hours, but she searched the street for him anyway, as the treatise on nursing babies continued and the men droned away about town politics. She wished she could just saddle a horse in the stable out back and ride through town.

The house sat close to the busy street, and the noise of the carriages, horses, and passersby carried inside the room. She was glad they lived in the country. She preferred the clean air and quiet evenings on their plantation.

The servant entered the room once again. "Mister and Mistress Bradley Effingham and Master William Effingham."

Bridget turned to see her cousin Bradley and his wife, Penelope, coming through the door with their three-year-old son.

Ella rose to greet her brother and sister-in-law. "You're just in time for dinner."

"Our timing is perfect then!" Bradley's loud voice boomed over the gathering. His quick smile and countenance always brightened Bridget's day. He wasn't necessarily handsome—his nose was too big, and his cheeks were scarred from a bad skin condition during his adolescent years—but his winsome ways made him a favorite at every gathering. He greeted Ella with a smothering hug and the men with slaps on the back.

William scampered toward Bridget with his arms open wide and eyes bright with excitement. He was still young enough to be wearing a dress, but he had hiked it up so he could run. "Aunt Gigi!"

She loved it that the boy called her aunt even though they were actually second cousins. She picked him up and twirled him around. Sitting down with William in her lap, she jostled him up and down on her knees. The child's laughter rose above the chatter and conversation around them. Each time she tried to set him down on the floor, he clambered back on her lap and begged, "Do it again, Aunt Gigi. Ride the horsey more!"

WHERE HEARTS ARE FREE

Out of breath, Bridget laughed. "That's enough for now, William. You are getting too heavy for me to do that for very long."

Penelope hung back, ceding the spotlight to Bradley and William. Bridget felt sorry for her at these family gatherings where everything was boisterous and loud. She seemed content to sit in a corner and fade into the background.

Still holding William, Bridget walked over to greet her cousin's wife. "I'm glad you came today. It's good to see you."

The corners of Penelope's mouth lifted in a demure smile, and she nodded. "It's good to see you too."

Bridget could barely hear her soft voice above Bradley's conversation with the men. She put William down. As soon as his feet touched the floor, he ran to Sarah and bounced onto her lap.

Bridget laughed and smoothed her skirt. "He's so like his father, isn't he? I wish I had all that energy."

Penelope sat in a chair beside a small tea table. She picked up a cup from a tray beside them. "I know. He looks like his father and acts like him as well. You'd never know he belonged to me."

Bradley approached the two women, bowed, and kissed Bridget's hand. "How's my favorite cousin named Bridget?"

"Stop it, Bradley. I'm fine."

He laughed and took her hand. "Aren't you ever going to get any taller? Are you going to stay a shrimp all your life?"

She chuckled. "I suppose so."

Bradley bussed her cheek and whispered, "Why have we been honored today with Edward Moorehead's presence?"

Feeling her cheeks flush once again, Bridget fanned her face. "You know as much as I do, but I'm guessing that David and Ella are trying to find a suitable match for me. It's embarrassing."

"Well, it *is* time, is it not, for you to be thinking about getting married?"

"Bradley! I didn't think you would take their side. Are you in on this conspiracy as well?"

"You're too beautiful to live out your life as a spinster. You can't simply ride horses on the plantation forever like a little girl."

"I'm only eighteen."

"I was eighteen when William was born."

"*Humph*, when I'm ready to marry, I'd like to do the choosing myself."

"Have anyone in mind?" Bradley elbowed her gently. "Perhaps we could at least give him a nudge, whoever he is."

Bridget smiled at her cousin. "I can handle my own affairs, thank you very much. When there is to be a choice made, I am perfectly capable of making that decision."

Bradley tapped his chin. "That choice wouldn't happen to be a certain Frenchman, would it?"

Bridget eyed her cousin and worked her fan. "Philippe? Why would you think that?"

Bradley chuckled. "One would have to be blind not to notice the way you look at him. If he himself hasn't noticed, he must be the most obtuse young man around."

PHILIPPE PULLED HIS WORK TUNIC OVER HIS HEAD AND stuffed it into his bag. "I wish I could stay longer."

Charles stood, holding the gun he was tooling. "I do too." He laid the gun down on the table and ran his hands over the stock. "These are beautiful guns, aren't they?" He brushed his eyes with the back of his hand.

"Don't, Charles. It just makes it harder for me to leave."

"I'm fine. And thank you for the food, especially the apple pie. I will enjoy that."

"Anytime." Philippe finished dressing and buttoned his jacket. He held his hat in his hand. "I'll come back again before . . . before I go home."

"How long is that?"

"A couple of months."

Charles looked at his brother. "I'm really glad for you, Philippe. I truly am. But I don't know if I can bear another three years here." He picked up the gun and sighted it. "I've learned a good trade, but . . . Zwicken is a hard taskmaster. There's no pleasing him. He's dishonest— a conniving swindler. And . . ." Charles paused.

"And what?"

Charles lowered his voice. "I think he's involved in selling guns illegally to the Indians. All these are supposed to go to the militia, but somehow they end up disappearing. I can't prove anything, but something's not right."

"Just do your work and don't do anything foolish."

"But—"

Philippe grabbed Charles by the shoulder. "Do you hear me? Just do your work. Your time will be up before long, and we'll all be together again." He gathered his brother to him in a fierce embrace. "Promise me."

"I promise." Charles' soft answer was not very reassuring.

Philippe released him, picked up his bag, and walked through the noisy shop into the afternoon sunshine. He turned and looked back, but his brother was already hunched over his workbench. Each parting was more difficult than the last.

He set off at a brisk pace. Mister Barrington demanded punctuality, and Philippe complied. His basic temperament to please and be obedient stood him well with his employer—and his employer's daughter.

THREE

Bridget and her parents emerged from the doorway of David and Ella's house and lingered on the porch to say their farewells. Philippe stood at the hitching rail with the carriage.

Stepping onto the porch, Bradley hoisted William to his shoulders and winked at Bridget. "Remember my advice, dear cousin." He looked toward Philippe and cocked his head.

Cradling the newest member of the family in her arms, Ella tugged on the baby's blanket. "What advice is that?"

Bridget laughed and tossed her head. "Oh, Ella, you know Bradley. Always sticking his nose in our business, thinking just because we're younger he can boss us around." She gave the baby a kiss on his cheek. "Take care of that little one."

Edward Moorehead lingered in the doorway. "It has been a pleasure to meet you, my dear."

Bridget nodded curtly. "Yes, thank you."

"Perhaps our paths will cross again soon."

"Perhaps."

"In fact, I plan to check on my property in your area within the next few weeks. May I call on you then?"

"Why, of course, Mister Moorehead," Amos responded. "We would be honored to have you in our home. Please plan to have dinner with us."

"That would be my pleasure." Edward took out his glass and peered at Bridget. "I hope you will be there when I come." His deep voice and cultured manners drew her in, despite her aggravation. She turned toward the carriage and caught Philippe watching them. She smiled as she turned back to Edward.

"Ah, I shall take that smile as a yes. I look forward to seeing you again soon."

"Good-bye, Mister Moorehead." Bridget extended her hand to Edward. He kissed it, then handed her over to Amos. She took her father's arm, and her mother took the other. As they approached the carriage, Amos helped his wife maneuver the foot iron, and then turned to assist Bridget. "Go ahead, Father."

The portly gentleman heaved himself into the swaying buggy. Bridget put her hand on Philippe's arm as he extended it toward her. "Thank you so much, Philippe." She spoke loudly enough for everyone to hear and gave his arm a squeeze.

She looked out the window at Bradley and waved. Her cousin grinned and bounced William up and down on his shoulders. Penelope stood in the open doorway and lifted her hand in farewell.

Amos smiled and tapped his cane on the floor of the carriage, signaling Philippe to get underway. "Edward Moorehead seems like an enterprising young man, don't you agree?"

Several seconds went by before Bridget answered. "*Enterprising* would indeed seem to be the proper term to apply to Mister Moorehead." She leaned forward. "Did you arrange for him to come today? Did you spin the web to lure the fly, or did David and Ella?"

"Bridget! You will not speak to your father like that."

Bridget looked down. "I'm sorry, Father. I don't mean to be discourteous, but that little performance embarrassed me."

Amos' usual pleasant countenance turned into a scowl. "Any decision that I make for my wife or my daughter is for the good of the household." He punctuated his words with his walking stick.

A few moments passed. Sarah dabbed at her eyes. Bridget looked out the window at the passing landscape shimmering in the long shadows of the late afternoon sun.

"David arranged it, with Ella's enthusiastic approval, and I agreed to it. So we were all a party to the meeting. And that's all it was, my dear. It was simply a meeting. No further obligation." Amos' voice had softened.

"Except you invited him to our home for dinner." Bridget set her mouth in a pout.

"Well, well . . . no harm in that. He is an acquaintance now, who will be in the area on business, and we have opened our home to practice hospitality, that's all."

Bridget snapped her fan and sat back.

"Besides, it's time you thought about getting married and starting a family. Your mother and I want you to—"

"To what? Marry someone I don't even know, just so I won't end up a spinster? I would rather be alone the rest of my life than consider someone . . . someone that I don't know or love. And, Father, he's so . . . old!"

Amos and Sarah both chuckled. Sarah reached across and patted Bridget's hand. "I would hardly call thirty or so *old*. He's just established and mature—a good combination for a husband. You would be well taken care of." Sarah smiled. "And he is quite handsome, wouldn't you agree?"

Bridget looked out the window as they moved out into the countryside. "In a feminine sort of way, I suppose."

"Your mother and I are getting older. You have no brothers and sisters. We want to see you married and settled in a good situation. You must be practical, my dear."

"I don't want to be practical. I want to marry someone I love."

Sarah scoffed. "Love! That is the stuff fairy tales are made of, not real life. Love won't put a roof over your head and food on your table."

"Is it impossible to have both? It seems to me that life is hard enough, but if you love your partner, surely that makes the journey easier."

"You learn to love the one you marry, not necessarily marry the one you love. Isn't that right, Amos?"

"I loved you from the first day I saw you, my dear." Amos smiled at his wife.

"I doubt that." Sarah shifted on the carriage seat. She looked at her husband of thirty years and patted his arm.

Amos looked at Bridget. "You seem to have some definite ideas. Do you have anyone in mind? Someone I could approach about the possibility of courting you?"

Bridget looked away and out the window again. "Perhaps. Perhaps there is. I shall think about it."

PHILIPPE HEARD THE VOICES OF THE BARRINGTONS RISE in the cab of the carriage, but he could not hear what they were discussing. He had heard them argue very little in the six years he had been with them, and he dismissed it from his mind as quickly as their conversation ended. His thoughts concerned Charles. His heart quickened at the prospect of settling on his own land, farming it and raising his own family, but the thought of leaving Charles in Philadelphia pained him beyond measure. Perhaps Madeleine and Pierre had finally saved enough money to pay out his brother's term early. Then they could go home together. He let his mind wander to the beautiful green hills of their property and what kind of house he would build . . . what he would plant . . . what kind of horses he would raise . . .

Philippe drove the horses through the iron gate and around the circular drive to the front of the Barringtons' country estate. The almost overpowering fragrance of the budding lilac bushes that surrounded the house greeted them.

Amos emerged from the carriage door before Philippe could open it for him. "Thank you, Philippe. We can manage. Take care of the horses and carriage."

"Yes, sir." Philippe turned and started to climb back onto the driver's perch.

"Philippe?"

The young Frenchman turned with one foot on the footplate to look into a pair of dusky blue eyes that drew him in every time he dared to look at her directly.

"Would you saddle Kimi for me, please? I have a couple hours of daylight left. I'll go change right now."

"Yes, mistress. I'll have her ready for you by the time you get to the stables."

The Barringtons bustled into the house, and Philippe pulled the carriage around to the stables. He called to one of the stable boys mucking out the stalls and handed the reins over to him. "Unharness the team while I ready Miss Barrington's horse for her, please. Start currying them down, and I'll be back to help you finish."

He strode into the interior of the stable and bridled the old Narragansett sorrel, Kimi—Bridget's childhood horse and still her favorite. He picked up her saddle and led the docile mare outside.

The sun had begun its descent, but Bridget had plenty of time for a good ride before dark. She hurried from the back of the house and down the stone steps, past the smokehouse and to the stable. She had put on her jacket, but held her hat in her hand. Stubborn golden strands of hair had escaped her blue hair ribbon and floated around her face in the gentle evening breeze.

Philippe lowered his eyes, checked the horse's girth, and helped her mount.

Pulling on her gloves, she smiled at him. "Thank you, Philippe. I'll not be gone long. I have some thinking to do, so I'll be down by the river." She stuck the stylish tricornered riding hat on her head and turned the mare toward the woods.

"Yes, Mistress Barrington."

Bridget halted Kimi and whirled her around to face Philippe. "How long have you been with us, Philippe?"

"Six years, mistress."

"And you were fifteen years old when you came, correct?"

"Yes." Philippe stared at her. The brightness of the late afternoon sunlight surrounded her head and lit up her hair like a halo.

"And I was twelve. After all these years, our close proximity in age, and being friends, do you think you could desist from calling me 'Miss Barrington' and 'mistress,' and simply call me Bridget—or Gigi?"

"I . . . I suppose so, if that is what you wish."

36

"That is what I wish."

"Very well." Philippe gave her a slight bow.

Bridget sighed. "Very well, what?"

"Very well . . . mistress . . . uh . . . Bridget."

"That sounds very nice coming from you. I . . ."

Her gaze lingered on him. He could feel himself blushing. She moved her horse even closer. What was she doing? Then she turned and spurred her horse into action toward the woods.

BRIDGET RODE THROUGH THE FIELDS TO HER CATHEDRAL in the woods. She needed to think and pray. Her family obviously was setting things in motion to marry her off to a very eligible and rich bachelor. Philippe would be leaving soon as well. If she was going to declare her affection for the Frenchman, it appeared now was the time.

She sat on the stump and held a rosary in her hands for a long time, moving from bead to bead. The quiet hum of the forest seemed to carry her along to her decision. She knew what she was going to do. In reality, she had reached a conclusion before she left the house. She was going to ask her father to approach Philippe about courting her. She knew it was probably fruitless, but she was willing to risk it.

She wanted Philippe Clavell to know that she had fallen in love with him before he rode out of her life forever.

FOUR

Castles and kings, courtiers, balls and queens—another life across the ocean.

Adriaen Clavell threw the slop out to the hogs. She wiped her hands on her soiled apron and watched the squealing swine fight for their share of the day's meal. She started into the barn. The young woman placed one hand on her swollen belly and twirled around in a circle, swinging the empty bucket in her other hand.

"Interesting dance partner you have there."

"Madeleine!" Adriaen stopped, almost bumping into her sister-in-law. "I'm sorry. I didn't see you."

The two were not technically sisters-in-law, but they thought of themselves as such. The young Dutch woman was married to the brother of Madeleine's first husband, now deceased. "I was . . . I was thinking about . . ."

She paused. Was the world of the royal palace of Versailles as dazzling as Adriaen had always heard? Had Madeleine in fact been the one true love of Louis the Sun King? She knew that Madeleine and her husband, Pierre Boveé, a former courtier, had met at a ball, but they rarely spoke of those days. Sometimes Adriaen felt as if there were a room in the house stacked with chests that contained fascinating and delicious secrets of their former life in France. But it was a room in which she obviously was not welcome.

It wasn't that the Clavells didn't love her. She knew they loved her deeply. It was that they had started a new life, and she was a part of that life—not the old one. They seemed to desire to forget the past completely. Still, Adriaen was curious to know more about their parents and the estate in Grenoble and . . .

Madeleine threw corn out onto the ground. "Here, chick, chick, chick!" She laughed at Adriaen, nearly fifteen years her junior. "You were in another world. Have you checked for eggs?"

"Not yet." She rubbed her tummy. "I was daydreaming about the world that you and Pierre came from. It had to be exciting, to dance at the balls and wear the beautiful gowns."

Madeleine hesitated for what seemed an eternity, then answered Adriaen in a voice barely above a whisper. "The gowns were beautiful, and the balls were spectacular."

Adriaen held her breath. "Please, do go on."

Madeleine cocked her head and looked away. "What I remember most about the balls was the myriad of colors in the gowns. Vivid blues, reds, greens—and gold—gold was everywhere. On the walls, in the paintings, on the furniture. The colors captured one's senses and . . ." Madeleine paused. "However, it was a world that appeared glamorous on the surface and lulled you into contentment, then pulled you under with an unseen hand and suffocated you. Your values, your life." She shook her head. "Sometimes one was not aware of the quiet encroachment upon one's morals until it was too late."

"But I love hearing how you and Pierre met at a *bal masque*. And how you appealed to King Louis to call off the dragoons, and—"

Madeleine's mouth grew tight. "And how François was sentenced to the galleys for his faith; and how he contracted consumption, which resulted in his early death, leaving me a widow with three children; and how Vangie was kidnapped; and how Pierre was thrown in the Bastille? It's easy to dream about the glamour and forget the reality."

Adriaen blushed. "I'm sorry, Madeleine. That was insensitive of me." She sat down on the end of the feed trough and fanned herself with her apron.

"How are you feeling this evening?"

"I'm feeling well, but the baby wears me out."

"Moving around a lot? It seems . . . are you sure you are only six months along?"

Adriaen laughed. "As best as we can calculate. Feels like he's turning somersaults."

"He?"

Adriaen nodded. "I think so. And Jean prays so."

Madeleine smiled. "God will give you what he wills. But I know that Jean longs for a son."

"It was terrible for him to lose both baby and wife in childbirth."

"Yes. It was a difficult time. I know Jean rarely speaks of it, but it crushed him." Madeleine patted Adriaen's hand. "I'm grateful he met you while we were in Amsterdam." She started toward the henhouse. "I'll go see if we have more eggs."

Adriaen pushed herself up. "I don't mind. Here, let me do that for you." She followed Madeleine into the domain of the clucking hens.

Madeleine held the basket and watched the young woman pluck the eggs from underneath the hens with a nimble hand. "I never have gotten the knack for that. The hens always seem to get angry at me. I'm afraid I am not a very good farmhand."

"I grew up doing this." Adriaen waved her hand over the landscape as they started for the house. "And nonsense. Look how you've brought the property to life. The vegetables flourish, and the flowers grow more prolific every day. You have a knack for growing things."

"God has sent abundant rain this spring, and your touch with the flowering bulbs you brought from the Netherlands is almost supernatural." Madeleine handed the basket of eggs to Adriaen, then stooped down and cleared debris from the blooming lilies of the valley, narcissi, and daffodils around the porch. She plucked a handful of daffodils and stood to watch Pierre in the corral, currying his beloved black Percheron. The stallion had survived the ocean voyage six years ago, but he was getting old. Pierre would be lost when Tonnerre died. The whole family would be devastated.

Adriaen knew about the time when Pierre and Jean rescued Vangie from the convent. Jean had told her about it, as had Vangie herself, who still called Pierre by the pet name Prince she had given him as a child. That Tonnerre would make the journey across the ocean with them, although the price was costly, seemed completely natural.

Adriaen shook her head. It seemed unconscionable that their horse made it off the ship without consequence, but Philippe and Charles had not. The family's money chest had been stolen on board, and the boys had to be auctioned off to redemptioners to pay the remainder of their ocean journey debt. Adriaen had heard Madeleine declare over and over again that she trusted God to take care of the boys, but she didn't know how the woman had been able to bear the separation from her sons these past six years.

Adriaen carried the eggs into the kitchen where Claudine—the children's governess in France, now simply a member of the household—was beginning preparations for the evening meal. Vangie sat in front of the fireplace with a quilt over her knees, washing an early crop of onions and placing them in a basket.

Madeleine followed her sister-in-law into the kitchen, got a goblet off the shelf, and poured water into it from a pitcher on the table. She stuck the daffodils into the makeshift vase. Claudine, who had taken over the kitchen duties since their arrival in the New World, stirred the bubbling kettle over the fireplace.

Vangie tossed several onions into the stew. "Those daffodils are pretty, Maman."

"Yes, aren't they?" Madeleine arranged the blossoms and stared into space as she fingered them.

"Maman? What are you thinking about?"

"What I'm always thinking about—the boys." Madeleine walked over to twelve-year-old Vangie and gave her a hug, then sat across from her daughter in another rocker. "I wonder if they are well. I wonder if they are hungry, if they are cold, if they are being treated well." Tears welled up in her eyes. "I don't worry so much about Philippe. I miss him terribly, but the Barringtons are kind to him. And he will be home in a few weeks." She laid her slender hand over her heart. "I can hardly wait. But I can't help but worry about Charles."

"I know, Maman." Vangie reached out and patted her mother's knee.

The child's skin was pale and transparent, and Madeleine worried that her youngest would never recover her health after the hardships she'd endured as a little girl.

"Don't we have almost enough money to pay out his debt?" Vangie asked. "Won't we be able to bring Charles home soon too?"

Madeleine smiled. "I hope so, *ma petite*. I hope so."

Pierre and Jean came onto the porch, stomping the mud off their feet. Jean opened the door and looked around the room. "Adriaen?"

"I'm right here." The young woman, holding a bowl of stew in her hand, stepped around from behind Claudine.

Jean strode to her side and put his hand on her belly. "Is the baby well? Active?"

Adriaen laughed and set the bowl down on the table. She reached up and kissed Jean on the cheek. "We are fine, my solicitous husband. We are just fine."

Jean tugged on her thick braid. "Wanted to make sure."

Pierre hung his hat on a peg next to the door. "I can hardly get any work out of him these days. All he wants to do is check on you and the baby." The former courtier walked over to Madeleine, who was setting plates on the table, and gave her a hug. "But can't say as I blame him. We've been married over six years now, and I'd rather be with my wife than anybody else."

Madeleine snuggled next to him. "Even Tonnerre?"

"*Hmm*, you may have some competition there."

Madeleine gave him a playful swat. "I've always suspected as much. Did you two wash up outside? Dinner is ready."

Pierre held up his hands and showed both sides to his wife. "Clean as a whistle." He scratched his cheek, where a full beard had replaced his fashionable goatee. "My beard needs trimming. It's getting a mite scraggly."

Madeleine reached up and stroked his beard with the back of her fingers. "I like it, and you're still most handsome and dashing."

Pierre made a mock bow and kissed her hand. "And you, my fair madame, are still the loveliest one at the ball." He held Madeleine's hand and spun her around as a roll of thunder rumbled in the distance. Pierre went to the window. "I thought those looked like rain clouds. I need to check on the horses." Turning back to Madeleine, he bowed again. "We shall finish our dance when I return, Madame."

"*Ach*, Pierre. Go on, but do hurry. Dinner is ready."

"I'll be right back." He ran out the door as raindrops began to pelt the roof.

Madeleine chuckled. "The horses always come first."

"He knows his business with them, that's a fact." Jean started for the door. "I'll see if he needs help." He turned back and pointed at Adriaen. "Don't go anywhere."

She laughed. "I shall be right here. But I think we may go ahead and eat."

Madeleine nodded. "The cornbread is ready."

Jean grabbed a poncho off a peg and ran out the door after Pierre into rain that had started to come down harder. "Be back as quick as we can."

"Vangie, come. Supper is ready." Madeleine pulled the quilt off her daughter's lap and extended her hand. "The stew has fresh carrots out of the garden in it. You love cooked carrots."

Claudine cut the cornbread, and the women gathered around the table. Madeleine and Vangie sat on one side, Adriaen and Claudine on the other, leaving the end spots for the men. They bowed their heads, and Madeleine spoke a blessing over the meal.

Vangie looked at her mother as Madeleine dished the steaming stew into a bowl for her. "Maman, I'm not feeling very well. May I be excused and go to bed?"

"Oh, Vangie. Try to eat a bit of something. It will make you feel better."

Vangie ducked her head and picked up her spoon, but the utensil dropped from her grip.

"Vangie! You're trembling." Madeleine touched her daughter's face.

"I feel a little weak. I just want to rest."

"Try to eat a few bites. That will give you some strength."

The young girl picked up her spoon again and ate two or three bites, then excused herself and pushed away from the table. Madeleine stood up with her, but Vangie shooed her away. "I'm fine . . . really, Maman. I'll see you in the morning. Good night." She made her way to the small room behind the fireplace that she shared with Claudine.

Madeleine sat down, and Adriaen reached across the table and patted Madeleine's hand. "She's just tired, Madeleine. She'll be fine."

"I'm not so sure. Nothing seems to make her better."

Claudine got up from the table. "I forgot the butter."

"Thank you, Claudine." Madeleine took the butter from her former servant. "You have been a loyal . . . a loyal part of our family for so many years. How old were you when you first came to be the children's governess in France? About twenty?"

"*Oui*, I was nineteen."

"You are still young. Do you desire to have a family of your own?"

"I think about it sometimes, but you all are my family."

"It's not like having your own children. If a young man should come along who pleases your fancy, we would be so happy for you."

Claudine blushed and fidgeted with her apron. "I'm an old maid by now, Madame."

"Nonsense. You're just reaching your prime."

"Madeleine, you're embarrassing her." Adriaen smiled as she passed Claudine the cornbread.

"Well, you never know what God is going to do. Don't dismiss the idea."

Pierre and Jean burst through the door, shaking the rain off their ponchos.

"It appears Tonnerre is going to be a daddy again tonight!" Pierre announced. "The black mare is ready to foal."

"It will be a long night in the barn," Jean added.

A thud and crash shuddered through the house at the same time that lightning struck nearby. Madeleine jumped up from her chair. "What was that?"

Jean looked outside. "Just a bolt of lightning a bit too close."

"No, there was something else." Madeleine ran toward Vangie's room, with Pierre and the others close behind her. "Vangie! Vangie!"

The young girl lay on the floor with a chair toppled beside her. "I . . . I got dizzy."

"Oh dear. Are you hurt?" Madeleine knelt beside her daughter. Blood oozed a bright red trail down the side of the girl's face. "You *are* hurt."

Pierre picked Vangie up and laid her on the bed. "Ah, *ma princesse*, what have we here? Looks like you bumped your head pretty hard."

Madeleine handed the lamp to Pierre and pulled the girl's dark hair aside. "Umm, yes, you have a pretty good cut there. Claudine, would you get some clean towels and water so I can clean this up, please?"

Pierre held the lamp closer. "Do we need to send for the doctor?"

Madeleine brushed Vangie's hair back and looked closer at the cut. "The bleeding is already slowing down," she said. "She will be fine." She kissed her daughter on the forehead and straightened up. "You gave us a scare, *ma fille*. You're going to have a bump and a headache in the morning."

"I'm sorry, Maman. I sat down to take off my shoes and dropped my book. When I bent down to get it, I . . . I just got dizzy."

Claudine handed Madeleine the cloths and water.

"What can I do?" Adriaen sat down on the bed.

"Hold her hair back while I wash off this blood."

Pierre held the lantern so the women could see. They finished and bade Vangie good night.

Adriaen saw Madeleine look at Pierre with a tight-lipped expression and concern in her eyes. She didn't blame her. Adriaen would be worried as well if Vangie were her child.

FIVE

The mare bore down and expelled the wet colt onto the straw. Pierre pulled the sac off and grinned at Jean. "It's a boy!" He rubbed the colt's face and stepped back. "Coal black, just like Tonnerre. A worthy successor to his father."

The newborn and the mare lay side by side in the straw, breathing heavily. Then the mare pulled herself aright and walked away, tearing the umbilical cord loose. She turned back and nuzzled her newborn.

Jean slapped Pierre on the back. "*Oui*, he looks good—fine lines." The thunder rolled in the distance. "And a fitting night for your new Tonnerre to be born."

"Yes, I think I shall call this one Tonnerre as well. This is the first colt we've had that looks just like him. I've been waiting on this one for a long time."

"What would you think if we called him by the English equivalent, just to avoid confusion? Thunder is a strong name in English as well."

"Good idea. I like that."

The mare nudged the colt. Spindly legs thrusting in all four directions, the colt attempted to stand and fell against the wooden slats of the stall. Chuckling, Pierre stood back and gave the two animals room.

"God's creation is amazing. I never grow weary of watching the process." He leaned over the railing and shouted down the darkened aisle of the barn. "Tonnerre, congratulations! You're a daddy again."

The Percheron poked his huge head over the gate of his stall across the way. He blinked and nickered. Pierre turned back to the foaling scene where the colt was attempting to nurse despite his wobbly stance. He patted the colt. "We shall be congratulating another new father before too long, I suppose."

Jean nodded and grinned. "We are becoming more and more hopeful as the days go by." He turned and unlatched the gate of the stall. "This baby . . . Adriaen . . . I don't know what I would do if . . . if I should lose Adriaen and the baby like . . ."

"But she's feeling well, *non*?"

"So far."

The pair started through the gate. The mare munched on fresh hay strewn in her stall as the colt suckled.

Pierre picked up the lantern and took hold of Jean's arm. "My dear friend, God has been generous and gracious to us in this new country of great plenty. I pray his mercy surround you during this time and that he bring you a healthy baby boy—as healthy as that young colt in there."

"I should be the more mature one in the faith, but I learn much from you." Jean handed Pierre his poncho and wide-brimmed hat. "I am glad God brought you to Madeleine and our family."

"The pleasure has been all mine." The Boveé smile glistened in the lantern light. "We'd best get back to our wives." His smile disappeared. "I want to check on Vangie."

Jean peered out the barn door. "Looks like Adriaen's back at our place. I can see a light in the window." The two men hunkered under their rain gear and made a dash for their respective homes—Jean up the hill to his and Adriaen's new little cottage, and Pierre to the main house that had been added onto several times during the first difficult years of pioneering.

Pierre ascended the steps to the porch, then removed his poncho and hat and shook the rain from them. He creaked open the door, entered quietly, and hung his wet things over the back of a chair to dry.

Madeleine sat in the soft glow of the fading embers of the fire, which she had already banked for the night. A candle flickered on the table beside her, and her head nodded on her chest. Pierre lingered for a moment, simply looking at the wife he so adored. Even in the dim light of the fire he could see a streak of gray beginning to appear in her dark hair above her forehead. It made her even more beautiful to him. The spinning wheel stood nearby, and she held a bundle of yarn on her lap.

He knelt beside her and tried to take the yarn from her hands.

Madeleine startled and woke up to smile at him. She smoothed her hair. "I guess I fell asleep. What did she have? Is all well?"

"She had a black-as-midnight colt that looks just like his father. We're going to call him Thunder."

Madeleine chuckled softly. "Oh, Pierre, I'm so delighted. That's wonderful. A successor for Tonnerre."

He stood and pulled Madeleine up with him. He took her face in his hands and kissed her lightly on her forehead. "How's my princess?"

"She's asleep. She's going to have quite a bump on her head in the morning." Madeleine looked up at her husband. "Pierre, our Vangie continues to weaken and decline. I fear—"

"*Shhh.* Nothing to fear. Our God is not going to leave us now. Vangie survived the ocean voyage and our early years here; surely she will get better now that our lives have gotten somewhat easier." He pulled Madeleine close.

"You would think so." Madeleine shook her head and shuddered. "I feared that none of us would survive that first bitter winter, much less Vangie. I was almost glad the boys were in Philadelphia. At least I knew they had shelter and were being fed."

"But we did survive and so did Vangie." He looked around. "Anything to eat? I'm starving."

"I'm sure you are. The stew should still be warm, and there's cornbread on the table." Madeleine got a bowl and spoon from the table and ladled leftover stew from the kettle hanging over the embers in the fireplace.

Pierre sat down at the table and broke a piece of cornbread into the bowl. "Jean's worried about Adriaen."

"That's natural. But I think she's doing well. She's not cramping like before. She is getting awfully large . . . Pierre? You seem preoccupied."

He had set his spoon down after only a few bites and was drumming his fingers on the table. He stood, walked to the window, and closed the shutters. "I saw Lenapes crossing our land today. A multitude of them."

Madeleine's eyes turned serious. "Where do you think they are going?"

"They were headed west. The locals say the tribe is not happy with the land acquisitions that Governor Penn has made with the Susquehannocks. They feel pushed off of their land."

"We can appreciate their feelings, can we not?"

"Of course, especially you. I had no land in France, but if we were to be forced off of our land here . . ." He returned to the table and sat down. "I cannot even imagine the anguish it must cause the families." He took Madeleine's hand. "Don't be concerned about it. The Lenapes have always been peaceable."

"I know. But I don't trust them. They are such a strange people . . . and what about those kidnappings and raids from other tribes?"

"We've traded successfully with them, and count them as friends. We've done nothing to give them reason to hate us."

"Except take their land."

He sighed and stretched. Madeleine gathered up the empty bowl and spoon, picked up the lantern, and headed for their bedroom. Pierre stepped out on the porch. All seemed to be quiet. He closed the door and set the latch.

BRIDGET CAME DOWN EARLY FOR BREAKFAST. HER MOTHER was nowhere in sight, and her father sat at the table going through a stack of papers as the head cook prepared the morning meal. Servants scurried about, busy with their daily chores.

The Barringtons always ate breakfast in the more informal keeping room rather than the dining room, which had been an addition onto the original house. Sarah protested from time to time, especially in the early days of building their plantation, Whisper Wood, but Amos' informal, casual nature finally won over her desire to "put on airs," as Amos called it.

"We are simply ordinary people who have done well. We will eat breakfast like ordinary people. Besides, I hate having to be so careful not to soil a tablecloth this early in the morning. We shall eat in the keeping room!"

Bridget had heard the speech over and over through the years, though not so much anymore.

"Is Mother not coming down for breakfast?"

"Oh, good morning, my dear. No, your mother is not feeling well this morning. I fear yesterday's trip wore her out. Seems it takes her longer to recover from our little outings these days."

Bridget sat at the heavy oak trestle table next to her father. A young domestic set a bowl of steaming cornmeal mush in front of her, along with a cup of cider. She reached for the molasses already on the table, along with the butter. She liked the mush, but what she liked even better was the morning after, when the cooks fried the leftovers into crisp rectangles in the big iron skillets. She would be sure to come down to breakfast tomorrow.

Amos was buried in his paperwork.

"Father, could we chat for a moment, or are you too busy?" She peered over his shoulder. "What are you working on?"

"The boundaries of the land here in Philadelphia. Maryland still insists that Philadelphia belongs to them, but Governor Penn is adamant that it was included in his land grant. It is almost unbelievable this disagreement is still going on." He looked over his spectacles at his daughter. "But you're not interested in that, are you?" He shoved his papers aside. "I always have time to chat with you."

"No. I mean, yes, I am interested, but that's not what I'd like to talk to you about." She sat across from him and put her napkin in her lap.

"Yes? What is it?"

"I'd like to discuss this matter of a suitor."

Amos removed his round spectacles and pushed back in his chair, resting his hands on his large belly. "Go on."

"Father, there *is* someone I would like you to approach about courting me."

"Yes? I am pleased that there is someone who has caught your fancy. Who is it? Someone we know?"

"It's . . . it is . . . well, you probably are going to be surprised. Shocked, even."

"Well, if you don't hurry up and tell me, I won't only be shocked, I'll be withering away from old age."

She giggled. "Oh, Father. No, you won't. It is someone we know well. Someone nearby." She looked out the door to the stables.

"Do go on, child."

"It's Philippe."

"Philippe Clavell? Our groomsman? Do you jest?"

"I do not jest at all. You and I know that Philippe is much more than simply a stable hand. We know he comes from an important family in France. He is a fine young man, and my feelings for him have continued to grow through the years he's been with us."

Amos rubbed his chin. "You have strong feelings for him?"

"I am desperately in love with him."

Amos stood. "I see." He took a piece of kindling from the fire and lit his pipe, then tossed the twig back into the flame. "And does Philippe know how you feel? Have you told him?"

She looked down at her hands in her lap. "No."

"That is as it should be. There are problems with your choice, my dear. For one thing, we are Catholic, and he is Protestant."

"That matters not to me."

"It may not matter to you, but I can assure you it will matter to *his* family." He stopped and encouraged his pipe, blowing puffs of smoke into the air. "But the more formidable hurdle will be your mother. She will not agree to this easily, if at all. She entertains high hopes for you—and marrying an indentured Protestant servant is not among them. The young man has no land, no financial means."

"But will you speak to her about it?"

Amos puffed on his pipe and returned to his seat at the table. "Let me think about it."

"Philippe will be leaving our household in just a few weeks."

"I am well aware of that fact."

"Don't delay, Father. If you don't speak to him, I will."

Amos put his spectacles back on his nose and stared over the rims at his daughter. "Young lady, are you saying that even if we disapprove and decide against allowing him to court you, that you will pursue it anyway? You would dare to defy us?"

"I don't know that he would even want to court me. He's never given me any indication that he is remotely interested. But I am saying that Philippe Clavell is my choice, and I want him to know how I feel before he leaves Whisper Wood." She looked down and swallowed. Her voice was soft and thick with emotion. "Would you consider speaking to him?"

"*Hmm.* This is most unorthodox. I need to consult with your mother. You know I like Philippe. He's an exemplary young man, but ..."

"But what?"

"Gigi, we cannot always choose our lot in life. This young Frenchman is a Huguenot, devotedly so, and we are Catholic—the very group responsible for the persecution from which he fled in France."

"But that wasn't us."

"No, but emotions run deep where convictions are concerned. And even if he consented, I'm almost certain his family would not. It would be too daunting an issue to conquer, I'm afraid." Amos reached across the table and took his daughter's hand. "My sweet Bridget. Your mother and I want the best for you. You don't realize from whence you have come."

"Why do you always say that? 'You don't realize from whence you have come.' What does that mean? I'm just a girl who wants to marry the man she loves, not some aristocrat or businessman who might provide wealth and a fine house for me." She stood and set her napkin on the table. "I have that now, and it's not enough. If I have to live here as a spinster after you and mother are gone, I will, but I do not wish to marry someone I do not love." She knelt beside her father and laid her cheek against his hand, spotted with age. "Please, Father. Won't you at least think about it?"

He sighed and nodded. "I shall."

Bridget rose and smiled at the man who represented all that was safe and secure and who had always been able to grant her every wish. She had no doubt that he would find a way for her this time as well. "Thank you, Father." She kissed him on the cheek, turned, and left him staring after her, puffing on his pipe.

Amos sat quietly at the table, tapping his pipe ashes into a small, shallow bowl.

"What was that all about?" Sarah entered the kitchen. She was dressed but had pulled a quilt around her shoulders like a shawl.

The old gentleman rose and pulled out a chair for his wife. "Sit down, dear. I didn't expect you down for breakfast this morning. Are you feeling better? Are you chilly?"

"I'm fine, just tired. And I am a bit chilled." She sat in the chair Bridget had vacated only moments before. "Is our daughter upset about something?"

"You could say that." He chuckled and patted Sarah's hand. "One never need guess what our daughter is thinking." He motioned to the servant. "Bring my good wife a bowl of mush to warm her."

Sarah shook her head. "Not yet. I'll just have some cider right now. That sounds good. So, do tell me what has our daughter in such a state."

"She has someone that she would like . . . Well, there is a young man for whom it seems she has strong feelings. She has asked me to approach him about courting her."

Sarah's eyes brightened, and she sat forward in her chair. "Wonderful! Who has caught her fancy?"

Amos shook his head. "Prepare yourself, my dear. You are going to be shocked."

"Well? Tell me who it is that is going to shock me. Has she acquiesced to accept Edward Moorehead's offer? Yes, I am shocked. What changed her mind?" Sarah stood, the quilt falling to the floor. "Oh my, we must make arrangements . . ."

"Sit down, my dear. You are jumping to conclusions and flying away with them on a racehorse of imagination. It is not Edward Moorehead."

"Who then? Our neighbor, young Thomas Bond? But I thought he was betrothed to Alice Adams from Baltimore."

"If you'll quit guessing, I will tell you. I simply want you to be prepared."

Sarah lowered herself into her chair and gathered the quilt into her lap. "Very well. I am prepared."

"It is Philippe."

Sarah's jaw dropped. "Philippe Clavell? Our stable hand? Our indentured servant?"

"Yes."

"Impossible. We would not, could not ever give our consent for that. He is a servant, and he isn't Catholic."

"I know, I know, my dear. I told Bridget that we would never agree to it. And I am certain that his French Huguenot family would vehemently oppose any sort of union between the two." Amos relit his pipe. "He *is* a fine young man, however."

"He is a servant!"

"Not by birth. Purely by circumstance. And he will be a free man in a few weeks."

"I'll be glad, then, that he will be gone, and we will have no more talk of a servant courting our Bridget. What can she be thinking?"

Amos peered over his spectacles at his disgruntled wife. "What makes a man, or a woman? Birth or circumstances? It's time we considered telling our daughter the circumstances surrounding *her* birth."

Sarah's mouth turned down at the corners. She gathered the quilt around her, and for the second time that morning, a Barrington female left Amos tossed about in the wake of her emotions.

SIX

Bridget shut the door to her room on the second floor and went straight to the large wardrobe by the window. She looked down on the kitchen garden where the servants had already been at work for hours. One of the housemaids struggled to the back door with pails of water hanging from a yoke slung over her shoulders. She slipped in the mud left by an early morning rain, but regained her footing. A rooster and his harem strutted between the smokehouse and the laundry dependencies. Other servants bent over rakes and hoes in the gardens.

There were other plantations in the area that sported grander grounds than theirs, but the Barrington estate pleased the eye with easy, natural lines. Bridget liked the bouffant sweep of the lilac and honeysuckle bushes—not so stuffy and formal. The far-reaching cornfields lay beyond the house and met the horizon at the top of a lazy hill in the distance.

She opened the dark wooden wardrobe's heavy doors and pulled on a drawer at the bottom. Thrusting her hand underneath a jumble of chemises and stockings, she pulled on the bottom of the drawer, revealing a false bottom. Wrapped in blue cloth and tied with a pink ribbon lay a leather volume. She gently tugged the book from its hiding place, then rearranged the clothing and shut the drawer. Sitting down in a chair at her desk in the corner, she opened a drawer that held hair ribbons, combs, and several keys. She selected a small one on its own ring, placed it in the lock of the diary, and opened the cover.

The aging brown leather had begun to dry and flake off. Bits of the musty cover floated onto her skirt. She brushed it away and leafed through the pages. Hurrying past and ignoring the first three-quarters of the epistle, she turned to the back.

April 25, 1686

It's out now. I revealed my feelings for Philippe to my father and asked him to allow Philippe to court me. He was not much agreeable to the idea. He says Philippe's family will not approve, nor will Mother. I believe Mother could be persuaded—eventually—but I don't even know Philippe's family. How they must have suffered at the hand of Catholics in France, but that wasn't me. That wasn't here in the New World. I don't care about Catholic or Huguenot. I don't care! I will convert. He is a man of faith, and I love God too. Isn't that what is important? My only desire is to be with the one that I love. I do love him, although he pays me no mind. He has no idea that I am desperately in love with him. I told Father that if he didn't move quickly, I would tell Philippe how I feel. I think I shall not wait at all. I shall let him know . . . soon.

She put the quill down and looked at the ink spots on her fingers. She spit on a handkerchief and rubbed at the stubborn black stains. The pages of the diary fell back to the accounts of the early years. She looked at her childish handwriting and quickly closed the book on those entries, locked it, and returned it to its hiding place.

Bridget pulled on the riding jacket that she had flung on a chair last night and picked up her hat. As she left her room, she noticed that her mother's bedroom door was shut. She stepped down the staircase without disturbing her. Her father no longer sat at the table in front of the fireplace. His papers had been put away. He had probably gone out on the farm to check the crops.

She walked through the cooking area where the cooks were cleaning mushrooms from the forest and baking bread for the week. She stopped and tore a piece off a hot loaf just out of the oven. A little girl about two years old played on the floor next to her mother, who sat beside the fireplace cutting the mushrooms in half and letting them fall into a pan on her lap. Blonde curls peeked out from under the toddler's pudding cap.

The young mother grabbed the pan of mushrooms and stood. "Oh, mistress. I did not know thee were ready to go out."

Bridget motioned to her. "Sit down, Abigail. I'm going for a ride." She laid her hat on the table and bent down to pick the little girl up in her arms. She tweaked the child's nose and gave her a kiss on the cheek. The little girl giggled and rubbed her nose. "She's gotten so big."

"I know." The young mother, about her own age, smiled. "And I'm expecting again. Did thee know?"

"I didn't. Congratulations. Children are a gift from God."

"Yes. They are a great joy, although hard work."

"You make it seem easy."

61

"I do? One day thee will have children, and thee will see. It may look easy, but it's not. They are constantly active."

The little girl wriggled down from Bridget's arms and dashed after a piece of mushroom as it bounced on the floor.

"Does thee see what I mean?" Abigail set her pot down and chased after the escaping toddler.

The child ran back toward Bridget, stumbling as she held her arms up to her, bumping her nose on the floor. Bridget swept her up in her arms and hugged the screaming child close.

"There, there, little one. You're fine. Let me see." She cooed and swayed back and forth. Pulling back to look at the tot's red, blotchy face, she dried her tears with her fingers. "See here." She kissed her nose. "Oh, it's all better now. Just a bit red."

Abigail reached for her daughter and smiled at Bridget. "I thank thee, mistress. Thee has a soothing hand with children." She wiped the toddler's face with her apron. "Ever since she's learned to walk, she's bumped and fallen all day long. The Lord truly watches over his little ones."

Bridget handed the child to her mother. "Yes, he does." She tugged gently on the little girl's hair. "I can't wait to have one of my own." She put on her gloves and started toward the door. *Yes, one of these days I will have children of my own, and their father will be Philippe Clavell.*

Bridget left the kitchen and hurried down the walkway to the stable, past the fragrant lilac bushes, their branches bending underneath the weight of the blossoms. Leftover raindrops glistened on the leaves. She pulled her hat on over her thick hair that she had simply tied back with a blue ribbon. The soft lowing of cows and the bleating of sheep created a rural symphony around her. Ever since she was a child, she preferred being outside with the animals and in the gardens or hunting with her father to sitting inside crocheting or embroidering or spinning as her mother wished.

Bridget didn't intend to ride alone this morning, but she wanted to appear as if she were going to. She had a much more important mission in mind. This wasn't the first time she had gone to the stable with the intention of confronting Philippe, but heretofore she never could muster the courage. Today, she was determined to make herself vulnerable to him once again. He had proven trustworthy in keeping her deepest secret all these years. She knew she could trust him with her heart. She had to make a move before her parents made arrangements to wed her to someone she didn't love, or before Philippe left Whisper Wood. She would wait no longer.

CHARLES WOKE THAT MORNING IN HIS ROOM IN THE BACK of the gun shop thinking of his brother's visit the previous day. He arose and rummaged through the sack of food Philippe had brought and removed the ham and bread. He sliced a piece of ham and put it between two pieces of bread, carefully replacing the cloth. The increasing light through the small window told him that dawn was imminent. He needed to get to his workbench. He wanted to light the fire and be at work before Mister Zwicken arrived. Gulping the tasty makeshift breakfast, he splashed water from a basin onto his face and tied his hair back with a leather strip. He dug in the sack again and found remnants of the apple pie left over from last night. He broke off two pieces and wrapped one in a napkin. Thrusting that one in his tunic, he carried the other in his hand, munching on it as he walked outside to draw water from the well.

Although technically drawing water was a chore that belonged to the kitchen staff, he usually drew the water for the cooks in the mornings. It allowed him to be outside for a few moments. The bucket clattered against the wet, cool stones as he pulled it to the surface, dipped a cup into the liquid, and washed the last of his apple pie down. He pulled a rag out of his pocket and wiped his mouth, and smiled as he recalled his exchange with Philippe yesterday.

Well, this isn't exactly a handkerchief, but it will have to do. Besides, I don't feel much like a gentleman anymore. Don't know that I will ever again.

He hefted the heavy bucket and walked into the kitchen below Zwicken's living quarters on the second floor. Water sloshed out of the pail as he set it down.

"Watch yer step there, young man. All that water is going to be on the floor rather than in the pot." The corpulent figure of the head cook bustled into the room from the adjoining pantry. Wisps of gray hair sprouted around her white head covering, sticking to her already perspiring forehead.

"You are up early, Goody Wallace." Charles liked the abrasive domestic, although most everybody else was put off by her brusque tone of voice. She had been at the foundry when he was brought to the household as a young boy and assumed the responsibility of looking after him. Widowed young, she'd come to the household and stayed.

"Couldn't sleep."

"Umm, I didn't sleep well myself." Charles picked up a towel and wiped up the spilled water. "My brother came to see me yesterday."

"*Humph.*" She hooked a black kettle over the fireplace. "Get that fire going, son. You'll be needing breakfast."

"I've already eaten. Philippe brought ham and bread—and this. I saved something for you." He pulled the apple pie out and handed it to her.

"What do we have here? Put it down on the table. Don't have time right now."

Charles laid the wrapped morsel on the table. "It's awfully good, and I know how much you love apple pie. Maybe you'll have time later to grab a bite."

"Go on. Get to work. I have my chores to do."

Charles went through the door leading from the kitchen into the dreary shop. He looked back over his shoulder as he rounded the corner and observed Goody Wallace picking up the pie and taking a bite. He chuckled to himself. He'd known she couldn't resist it for long.

As usual, he arrived in the shop before the rest of the employees. The early morning sunlight labored to penetrate the dirty windowpanes in the front of the establishment. Reaching to light the lantern on his workbench, he heard Zwicken arguing with someone in the next room. He hesitated.

"I don't care what you have to do," the second man said. "Just get these guns repaired and ready to ship downriver this week."

"I'm working my men hard. They are turning them out as fast as they can."

"See that you make that happen. Colonel Thorne is becoming suspicious; we have to give him something."

"Don't worry. You'll have your guns." The voices dropped, and Charles couldn't distinguish what they were saying. Then he caught the name. He moved closer to the door.

". . . I know what I'm doing. The Barringtons suspect nothing."

"I don't know, Moorehead, this makes me nervous. The body is buried on their land, and she saw—"

"She was a child. She has long since forgotten the details." Moorehead chuckled. "That body has fertilized their cornfields for years now. There's nothing left of it."

"I remember things from when I was that age. She saw us. And she saw the guns."

"I'm telling you she has no idea what she saw. I was with the Barringtons yesterday, and I am certain she suspects nothing. All these years, and nothing has ever come of it. Are you so dull you don't understand? If I can get close to the family, it will secure our safety as far as this unfortunate event is concerned once and for all. The man was a mere indentured servant—of no value."

A board creaked underneath Charles' foot, and the conversation stopped. Charles held his breath and moved quickly back to his bench. The office door opened and cast a thin beam of light into the shop.

"Oh, Charles, it's you. Well . . . glad you're here early. Get to work. We need this shipment right away."

Charles lit his lantern. "Yes, sir." He got the gun he had been working on the day before out of the case on the wall behind him and laid it on the bench. "I'll get right on it."

Zwicken closed the door, and Charles exhaled. His heart thudded against his ribs. Surely he had not heard correctly. A murder of an indentured servant? Zwicken and Edward Moorehead? At least he assumed it was Edward Moorehead, Zwicken's silent partner. And what of the colonel's guns for His Majesty's army? And the Barringtons? Charles shook his head as if to clear it. If it concerned the Barringtons, Philippe would be at least indirectly involved. The next time his brother came to visit, he would ask him.

Charles didn't know how much longer he could abide Zwicken. If the man were indeed a murderer, remaining in these horrible living conditions was intolerable. And the idea of being a participant in dishonest business practices sickened him. Now that he thought of it, last year Zwicken had returned from delivering guns minus one of the workers, a young Quaker. The stern shopkeeper had said the man had escaped. But in light of the overheard conversation, Charles wondered if he'd been murdered too. The notion of escape, always lying just beneath the surface of his mind, wriggled its way to the forefront this morning.

He watched Edward Moorehead ride past the front window in the brightening sunlight. Zwicken walked into the shop and stopped in front of Charles' worktable.

"I'm glad you're in early. Get a jump on this order. Thorne is getting impatient." Fingering a chisel in his hand, he eyed the young man. "Did you just get here?"

"Yes, sir." Charles looked up from his work directly into the eyes of his taskmaster. The two stared at each other for a brief moment. "I'll do my best to get the order finished today."

"You'll do better than that. You'll get it done."

"Yes, sir."

Zwicken turned and walked to the front of the shop. Charles had a good hour before the other employees began to arrive. He didn't fathom that they could produce what Mister Zwicken was demanding of them today. He would try, but the task was nigh on impossible. He started working on the gun in front of him. The requirement that every man in the colonies own a weapon was good for business, but kept Zwicken's foundry in turmoil trying to meet the army's need for material while keeping the rifles of townsmen in good repair.

His thoughts returned to the possibility of an escape. Where would he go? The first place Zwicken would look would be his family home. Or the Barringtons', where Philippe was.

Whether or not he attempted an escape, he had to talk to Philippe about what he had overheard. Random thoughts—some bizarre, some plausible—raced through his mind. He didn't know what he should or could do, but he must do something, and do it soon.

BRIDGET WENT PAST THE CHICKENS AND GOATS TO THE stable. She squinted into the dim light and heard someone within. "Philippe?"

"No, Mistress Barrington." An old black stable hand poked his head out from behind a gate.

She whirled around. "Oh, Eb. You startled me. Is Philippe about?"

"Sorry, ma'am. I didn't mean to frighten you. Philippe is out back checking the shoes on all the horses."

"Thank you." She looked down the long aisle of the stable out the back door, which stood open, and could see the horses gathered in the corral. Picking up her skirt, she walked through the dim interior and out into the sunlight. She spotted Philippe bent over, with the hoof of a chestnut gelding held between his legs. He rose and gave the horse a pat. Bridget watched him walk toward a black Percheron.

The horse nickered and nuzzled Philippe's hand. He smiled and patted the horse's neck.

"You have always been partial to that Percheron, haven't you?"

Philippe twisted his head around at the sound of her voice. He smiled at her. "Mistress Barrington. I didn't see you."

"What did you call me?"

"Umm, Bridget." He shifted his feet. "M-Ma'am, that just doesn't seem proper. I'm not comfortable . . ."

"But you seem glad to see me."

"Did you want to ride this morning?"

"Why do you like the Percheron so much?"

"He reminds me of a horse that belongs to my family. One of the best horses I've ever been around. Tonnerre was part of our rescue more than once in France and made the journey with us to the New World." Philippe's French accent covered the horse's name like velvet.

"Tonnerre. That means 'thunder,' right?"

"Yes, how did you know?"

"I don't know, I just did. The name suits the horse?"

"Very much so. He is a magnificent stallion."

"Tell me about your family."

"Pardon me?"

Bridget stepped closer to the young Frenchman. "Philippe, saddle up two horses and let's ride—together. Like we used to. I want to talk to you."

"But, mistress . . . Bridget . . . I have work to do. And it wouldn't seem proper."

"Let me take care of that. Father can spare you for an hour or so. Please, saddle up Kimi and the Percheron. I'll help you."

"I'll saddle Kimi for you, but I cannot ride with you this morning."

"For what reason? I'm giving you permission to do so. We used to ride together every day. I miss that. I want us to go to my special place in the forest—my cathedral. There's something I want to talk to you about. Remember when we went there once before?"

Philippe pulled Kimi's saddle blanket from the wooden railing where he had placed it last night after Bridget came in. His face was a blank. "Yes, but we were much younger then. Things are different now."

She looked up at the handsome young man, and she blinked tears away. "Are you refusing to go with me?"

"Mistress, I don't think it is best that we ride together to the woods. You are a young woman who . . ."

Bridget cocked her head. "You've never refused me before."

Philippe looked at her and shifted the blanket in his hands.

"I could insist that you go with me."

"Yes, mistress."

"Please call me Bridget."

Philippe turned his head and took a deep breath. "If you wish . . . Bridget."

"That sounds so very natural coming from your lips." Bridget placed her hand on his arm. "There is no need to saddle Kimi if you refuse to go with me." She looked into his dark eyes and the upturned quirk of his eyebrows. How many times had she seen that look on his face through the years? It always made her laugh. She smiled and reached up to touch his cheek.

He stepped back. "Mistress Barrington!"

"Please, put the blanket down." She moved away from him. "A young woman who what? You started to say that I was a young woman who . . ."

"I simply meant that you are a young woman and not a girl anymore. You are a young woman of courting age who will be . . . uh, who will be soon sought by suitors. And you must maintain a certain decorum."

Bridget waved her hand. "Oh, you are always so proper. But that is one of the things that I love about you."

Philippe stared at her. "Pardon me?"

Bridget took a deep breath. "Have you ever . . . do you ever . . ."

She bent down and picked up a piece of straw and twirled it between her fingers. "I mean, have you ever pictured us . . . together?"

"What do you mean?"

"You are correct when you say that my parents are looking for a suitable match for me. Someone to court me. But I don't want simply a 'suitable match.' I want the perfect match."

Philippe remained silent, his eyes downcast.

"Are you going to force me to reveal the innermost depths of my heart without any encouragement at all? That is not very courteous."

"Mistress Barrington . . ."

Bridget frowned at him.

"Er, uh . . . Bridget, I . . . I don't know what to say."

"Very well. I will be perfectly clear. Surely you must have guessed, Philippe . . . From the moment I saw you on the docks that miserable wet, rainy day at the auction, you have captured my heart. My infatuation with a quiet, young, handsome Frenchman who came to our household has steadily grown into something more. And when I told you my secret that day . . ." She looked down. "You were so kind and understanding. Now those seeds of love that have lain dormant all these years have blossomed into emotions I cannot contain any longer."

She reached out and took both of his hands in hers, and her tears began to fall on his tanned skin.

Philippe groaned and shook his head. He pulled his hands away from Bridget's grasp. "No, Mistress Bridget. You mustn't talk like this. You are the treasured daughter of a prominent citizen and must marry within your class."

"We are in the New World now. There is no such thing as royalty."

"But I am a servant."

"Yes, however, born into the French aristocracy and soon to be released from your servitude."

"And then I must return to my family. Besides that . . ."

Bridget waited a few moments. When he hesitated, she persisted. "Besides what?"

"I am Protestant, and you are Catholic. I simply could not . . ."

"If—if your heart is drawn to me as mine is to yours, we can overcome these obstacles."

Philippe shook his head. "No, mistress. I am afraid it is impossible."

Bridget felt tears begin to well up again. She wiped them away with her finger.

Philippe silently handed her his handkerchief.

She held the hankie in her hand and searched his face. "You still have not told me how you feel about me. I have lain my heart before you. It is yours to treasure or to trample. Is there any love in your heart for me, Philippe Clavell?"

Philippe returned her gaze and then took off his cap. "You have been . . . I have felt privileged . . . Your friendship has been a source of delight in what could have been a very lonely existence for me here. Our rides together when we were young, our caring for the horses during foaling, working in the gardens together . . . have all been pleasurable. But nothing more can come of this. I will be leaving in a few weeks. It would be best to forget anything that might have been."

"I see." Bridget brushed a lock of hair away from her cheek. "Merely 'pleasurable.' That's all?"

Philippe shifted his weight and replaced his cap.

"Well. I've certainly made a spectacle of myself, haven't I?" She sighed. "Please go ahead and saddle Kimi. I'm going for a ride—alone."

THE MARE TOOK OFF AND AS SHE DID, BRIDGET'S HAIR ribbon floated down and landed in the mud of the corral.

Philippe picked it up and inhaled. The fragrance of lavender filled his nostrils. He tucked the silky blue fabric into the pocket of his tunic where he usually carried his handkerchief and realized she had not returned the hankie to him. He watched her ride across the field, her blonde hair, loose from the ribbon, swirling in the wind. He picked up a bucket and went to his chores.

SEVEN

Amos greeted the domestics as he passed through the keeping room. The head cook bobbed a curtsy and plucked a pewter plate from the shelf above the fireplace. "Would Mister Barrington like a plate now?"

He looked around for Sarah. "Did my good wife eat yet?"

"Yes, sir. Almost an hour ago."

"Bring dinner to me in the parlor, please."

Sarah was waiting there for Amos. She looked up from her embroidery stand, her face twisted in a grimace.

He took a deep breath and placed his hat on a settee. "Good afternoon, dear."

"Good afternoon, indeed. Where have you been? And where is Bridget? Our noon dinner has come and gone, and neither one of you bothered to be present, nor let me know you would not be here."

"Since when, good wife, when I am working the farm, do I need to let you know whether I am going to be present for dinner? You know that I cannot ride the circuit and get back in time."

Abigail appeared at the door with a tray for Amos.

"Thank you, Abigail. Set it down on the table."

She set the tray down and scurried away.

"Now, my dear, what is really bothering you?"

"Where is Bridget?"

"That I do not know for sure." Amos buttered a piece of bread and looked at the plate of onion pie and marinated asparagus. "Eb said she went out riding early this morning after breakfast."

"She's been gone nearly all day. It's midafternoon."

"She's fine."

"How do you know?" Concern replaced Sarah's scowl.

Amos scooped up a spoonful of onion pie. "*Mmm*, that is good."

"Amos! How can you sit there devouring your dinner when your daughter has been gone for most of the day, and we don't know where she is?"

"She's a grown woman now and is one of the most capable young women I know. She's not going to put herself in harm's way." Amos put his plate down and wiped his mouth.

Sarah paused with her embroidery needle in midair. "Amos, I am upset with you. Why did you allow her—"

"Allow? I did not allow anything. She just left, on her own. She is understandably disturbed that we are not agreeable to her proposition to allow Philippe to court her." He took a swig of ale. "Gigi will come around, even though she has a strong will and a mind of her own."

"*Humph!* Which is very unbecoming at times." Sarah sat down and swatted her hand at him. "And I keep asking you, please refrain from calling her Gigi. She's a young woman now."

"It's hard to break a habit of eighteen years. And she's still my little girl."

Sarah glowered at him. "Go look for her."

"No, ma'am. She will come home when she has . . . *mmm* . . . come to a decision."

Sarah darted her needle up and down through the fabric in the embroidery hoop.

"You are worrying for nothing. We must trust our daughter. She's been raised properly. You taught her the catechism yourself, dear." Amos went back to his dinner. He chuckled. "You know, we were her age once. Have you forgotten what it is like to be young and in love?"

"Does Philippe feel the same as Bridget? Has he given her any reason to believe that he returns her affection?"

"That I do not know."

"We have not raised this child to be the wife of an indentured servant."

"We have raised this child to discern good character, and Philippe Clavell is a man of character and integrity."

Sarah's dark eyes grew intense, and the scowl returned. "I'm telling you, Amos Barrington, I'm not having it. I will not allow Philippe Clavell to court our daughter." She stood and walked toward her husband. She jabbed his chest with her finger, once slender and graceful, now knobby with the swollen knuckles of arthritis. "That is final!" She turned and left the room, her skirt swishing against the wooden frame of the door.

Amos sighed and returned to his dinner.

Bridget rode into the stable and dismounted.

Philippe emerged from the stable and grabbed Kimi's bridle. "I'll take care of her." He avoided Bridget's eyes.

Bridget stood with her riding crop in her hand. "Philippe, we can work this out. Please look at me." She caught hold of his sleeve.

He startled and looked over his shoulder. "Someone might see you."

"Let them see. I no longer care what people think."

"But you must, you have to. We must do what is expected of us."

"But why? Why must we always do 'what is expected'?"

Philippe started for the stalls with the horse.

"I'll help you."

"No." His firm reply surprised her. "No, you go on into the house and tell your parents where you have been. Tell them what we discussed and decided."

"What *you* decided."

Philippe pushed his cap back on his head. "You must tell them the truth about what I said. You know, Mistress Barrington, in some ways, you remind me very much of my mother—strong-willed, stubborn, determined."

"Is that a compliment—that I remind you of your mother?"

"Absolutely. Not only is she strong-willed and stubborn, but she is caring and compassionate and devoted to family, much like you." His eyes searched hers. "But her coloring and appearance are different from yours—she's taller and darker."

"I know. I saw her that day on the docks, and I've seen her on those occasions when she has come to visit you." Bridget paused. "She's very beautiful."

"As are you."

Bridget managed a smile and felt her cheeks redden.

"I have work to do." Philippe started toward the barn, then he turned. "Bridget, I think you should also tell your parents about . . . about what you saw all those years ago."

She shook her head. "Why bring that up after all these years?"

"I believe it's important."

"I'll think about it." She started on the path toward the house. As she got closer, she looked up at the steep-pitched gables. The curtain was pulled aside in her mother's room. She watched it drop into place. Taking a deep breath, she entered the house and prepared to meet her mother's barrage. She nearly ran into her father as he headed for the door, donning his black hat.

"Whoa, daughter! I was just coming to look for you. Where have you been? Your mother was concerned about your whereabouts."

"I've been out riding."

"You should have let us know where you had gone."

Bridget nodded and followed her father into the parlor. She heard the stairs creak, and then her mother appeared in the doorway. Bridget went to her and kissed her on the cheek. "Come on in, Mother. I'm sorry I worried you. I was just out riding. I would like to speak to both of you."

Sarah remained uncharacteristically quiet as she sat in her chair. Amos tossed his hat onto a nearby table and stood behind his wife. He pulled his spectacles out of the pocket of his waistcoat and put them on. Several moments passed in silence. Bridget removed her gloves, hat, and riding jacket. She brushed a leaf from her skirt.

"Well, daughter? We are waiting." Amos began to chew on his pipe.

Abigail appeared at the door. "I came for the tray."

Amos waved her away. "Yes, yes, I'm finished. Take the tray." They waited in silence again while Abigail gathered the dishes and left.

Bridget cleared her throat. "Mother, I've already talked with Father about this matter. But since then I have also shared it with . . . with Philippe."

Sarah blinked and continued to stare at her.

"I don't know any other way than to simply come out with it. I am in love with Philippe Clavell and would very much like your blessing and permission for him to court me. But . . ."

Sarah's countenance darkened.

"But what, my dear?" Amos' voice was soft.

"Oddly enough, Philippe agrees with you two. He will not agree to pursue a courtship. He feels you will not approve, nor will his family, particularly his mother. In his opinion, our stations in life are too far apart, and our religious issues cannot be overcome, in the face of what his family has endured from the Catholic persecution in France." Tears began to form in her eyes. "He does not wish to cause his mother any more heartache."

"Well! At least someone in this affair is being sensible." Sarah stood. "He is exactly correct. We would never give our permission. It is impossible."

"But can't we work something out? I don't care if he's Protestant. I'll convert."

"You'll do no such thing."

"What?"

"You'll not even entertain the idea of converting. We are Catholics and will remain Catholics."

"What does that matter? We've not been able to attend Mass regularly, no priest, no church. No way to go to confession in this colony that is completely intolerant to our religion. So isn't it in name only that we are Catholic? Isn't the most important thing that we love God, as does Philippe?"

Bridget turned to leave, but Amos grabbed her by the arm. "No, Bridget. We will settle this now. We'll not leave it dangling. You are correct. We have not been able to practice our faith as we would like here in this country. And perhaps that has been hypocritical of us. We have simply tried to live with tolerance in an environment hostile toward Catholicism. We are in the minority. The content of one's faith *is* indeed what is important. We've done our best to raise you . . ." Amos faltered and looked at Sarah. "My dearest, I think it's time that we told Bridget."

Sarah took out a handkerchief and began to sniffle. "Don't, Amos. This is not a good time."

"It's never a good time. It's not been a good time for eighteen years. Now is as good a time as will ever be. She needs to know."

"What are you talking about?" Bridget looked at her mother. "What is he talking about?"

Amos motioned to the settee. "Please, dear, sit down." He took her arm and sat down beside her. "You are aware that we lost two sons, dear Elijah when he was twelve, and our Henry was stillborn."

She nodded.

"What you don't know is that there were not only those two losses. Your . . . your mother had several miscarriages. Some were very early in the pregnancy; some were further along. And . . . well, we buried several of our unborn children."

Sarah had begun to weep quietly, stifling her sobs with her handkerchief.

"How many?"

"Nine, not counting the two sons who made it to actual birth. Two were girls; four were boys; the other three were too early to tell."

Bridget let out a long breath. "I . . . I didn't know."

"We didn't see any reason to tell you. They were difficult years. We buried them one after another in the same plot next to where your brothers are buried."

"The burial plot with no marker."

"Yes." Amos rubbed his chin and stood up. "Then you came along. We finally had a child that was healthy and beautiful. You must know that you have been the joy of our lives."

"And I was your last?"

Sarah looked at Amos. "There was one miscarriage after you came to live with us, then no more."

"Came to live with you . . ."

Amos and Sarah looked at Bridget as the young woman searched their faces. Amos wiped the lower lid of his right eye. Sarah held her handkerchief to her mouth. It was Amos who continued.

"My dear, your mother was not able to bear healthy children. During these years, one of our young indentured servants became pregnant. The father was another of our servants, a young man who was killed in a farm accident before they could be married. Unfortunately, the mother died shortly after she gave birth to the child, leaving the poor thing an orphan." Amos cleared his throat. "We decided to raise her as our own."

"Th-that child was . . . is . . . me?"

"Yes."

Bridget looked at Sarah. "You . . . you are not my real mother?"

Amos patted Bridget's hand. "My dear, Sarah is your mother. She has raised you from the time you were born."

Sarah's brow wrinkled in the anguish of the moment as she peered over her wadded-up handkerchief at her daughter.

Amos' voice grew tight. "Sh-she has loved you as if she bore you herself—more than most children are loved. We both have."

"Who was she? What was her name?"

Amos hung his head. "Is it imperative that you know all the details? Isn't it simply enough to know that we wanted you desperately and have loved you with a love that we didn't even know was possible?"

Bridget stood, her hands clenched at her side. "Suddenly, I don't know who I am. Where was my own mother from? Why was she indentured?" She looked from Amos to Sarah. "Who am I?" She clutched her hands to her face and began to cry. "You are telling me who I can or cannot marry, and now you tell me that I'm not who I've always thought I was. Tell me who my mother was! And what of my father? Who was he?" Her rising voice pierced the late afternoon sunlight filtering through the windows.

"Calm down, Gigi." The old gentleman gathered her in his arms. "Nothing has changed, my dear. You are still our beloved daughter, and we are your parents who have raised you and cared for you all your life. Nothing has changed."

She drew back and stared at her father. "My whole world has just changed—in one instant, one flash of a moment—and I am not who I thought I was." She saw the hurt pass through her father's eyes. She sat down and covered her face with her hands. Nobody spoke. Finally she took a deep breath. "Please, forgive me. I do not mean to be cruel. I know you love me. Nobody could have had a better home and parents. I have been pampered and loved beyond what anyone could desire." She smiled a little through her tears. "Probably a bit spoiled."

Amos cocked his head and smiled back at his daughter.

"And I love you. I see many things more clearly now—your protectiveness, your desire to marry me into a good family. Why I look so different from the rest of the family. But I have to know more. Please?"

Amos went to Sarah's side and cupped her elbow. "There will be plenty of time to talk about this later. Come, my dear. I'll help you to your room."

Her mother took her husband's arm, then turned and looked at Bridget. Her chin quivered. "I love you more than you'll ever know. You are the child of my heart." She opened her arms, and Bridget went into the familiar folds of her mother's embrace.

EIGHT

Philippe looked up at Bridget's window as he walked from the corral to the barn after finishing his chores. He was later than usual. It was getting dark. He could see the light from a lantern flickering behind the panes. The evening meal in the keeping room would be over. He had missed the noon dinner meal, and he was hungry. If he went inside to find something to eat, he would perchance run into Bridget—or worse, one of her parents. Sarah wouldn't be there, but Amos might be. Things would be awkward now, for he was certain that she must have talked to her parents as soon as she returned. How he wished he could talk to his mother and Pierre.

Philippe's stomach won out. He opened the door to the keeping room and peered in. Nobody about, but the kettle was still hanging on the lug pole over the fireplace. The tantalizing fragrance of whatever was bubbling in the black pot lured him in. He glanced around and seeing no one, he went in, grabbed a bowl from the table, and ladled out a thick pea soup. Bread was wrapped in a cloth on the table. He cut a piece and sat down to eat. Hearing footsteps behind him, he turned and looked over his shoulder.

"I wondered if thee would come in and eat this evening." Abigail carried a basket of potatoes, which she set down on the table. Her toddler hung on to her skirt.

"I was late finishing up. I'm glad you had something left. I was really hungry."

"Eat all thee wants. What's left is going into the slop jar." She went into the adjoining pantry.

Philippe ate in grateful silence, disturbed only by Abigail's return with a goblet of ale for him. He felt tired, more tired than he should.

"Ah, Philippe. I was hoping to see you this evening." The smoke from Amos' pipe trailed behind him as he entered the room. He puffed energetically to ignite the tobacco, then walked to the fireplace and threw his glowing kindling stick into the embers. Philippe stood, jarring the table and knocking over the ale. He sopped it up with the rag he was using for a napkin.

"Excuse me, sir. Clumsy of me."

"Sit down, sit down, son." Amos puffed on the pipe and sat down on the bench beside Philippe. "You know, Bridget talked to her mother and me this afternoon after she got back from her ride."

"Yes, sir."

Abigail walked out of the pantry and began to clean up the last of the dishes.

"Abigail, you can finish those in the morning. You take your sweet little girl and get her to bed."

The young cook looked at the two men. "But it won't take me long, and—"

"Go on, now. Philippe and I have some business to discuss. Those can wait until morning."

"Very well." Abigail picked her daughter up in her arms. "Good night, gentlemen."

"Good night." They watched the domestic leave for her room. "Now, as I was saying, Bridget discussed with us the fact that . . . the fact that she has feelings for you and would like me to give you permission to court her."

"Yes, sir, but you need to know that I understand that a relationship between the two of us is impossible, given our stations in life."

"Yes, she told us. She believes that is unimportant."

Philippe shook his head. "No, sir. Not only am I a servant, but the fact that I am Protestant, and she . . . your family . . . is Catholic . . . No, sir. It cannot be. My family would never approve."

"Do you have any feelings . . . any intentions whatsoever toward my daughter?"

Philippe hesitated. Then he looked directly at his master. "Mistress Barrington is a beautiful young woman, one any man would be proud to call his wife. Under different circumstances . . ." He paused. "But we do not live under different circumstances. We have enjoyed a youthful friendship through the years—one that filled the lonely places in my heart. But I have always understood we could be nothing more than friends."

Amos nodded and stood. "I have always appreciated that even as a young boy, you would look me in the eye and answer my questions directly and honestly. And if things were different, I would be proud to call you my son-in-law. But unfortunately, the situation in which we find ourselves is one over which we have no control. Youth and exuberance and the passion of young love sometimes forget that we all must live within the confines of society. Unfortunately, our society, at this time, dictates that any consideration of this sort is doomed for failure."

Philippe stood, and Amos put his hand on his shoulder. "Will you give me your word that this is a matter that you will neither encourage nor pursue?"

Philippe nodded his head.

"And you will not allow Bridget to pursue it either?"

"I will not."

"To facilitate our agreement, I am willing to make you an offer."

"An offer?"

"Your term with us is over in about six weeks. Is that correct?"

"Yes, sir."

"I am willing to release you now, as of this moment. I'll draw up the papers tonight before I retire, and you will be free to go home. I'll compensate you for the remaining six weeks, and you may pick one of the horses from the stable. You are a free man."

Philippe stared at his employer. "I–I'm . . . I'm free to go? To leave?"

Amos laughed. "Yes, son. I must admit, I hate to see you go, but you have served us well. You deserve to be a free man." The old gentleman looked down as he knocked his pipe against the inside wall of the fireplace. "There is one stipulation."

Philippe waited.

"You must agree to leave without seeing or speaking to Bridget. You must not leave her a letter—nothing, no contact."

Philippe exhaled. "You have my word."

"I will bring your papers down to the stable early in the morning with your wages. Then you may go."

"Mister Barrington, I don't know what to say. I'm very grateful for your generosity. And a horse as well? Any one I choose?"

"You've earned it." Amos chuckled. "I have a pretty good idea which one you will select—Legacy, the black Percheron?"

Philippe nodded. "If that is permissible."

"An excellent choice. You raised him yourself anyway. He needs to go with you. Oh, and pick out a saddle and bridle as well."

"I am overwhelmed, sir. You are much too generous."

"You'll remember our agreement?"

"Yes, sir." The two shook hands, and Philippe started to leave. Then he turned. "There is one thing that I would like to mention."

"What is that, young man?"

"Did Bridget tell you . . . did she say anything about the cornfield?"

"The cornfield? What about the cornfield?"

"Please, sir. There is something she needs to tell you, that I am not free to divulge. But she needs to tell you. It's . . . it is . . . I believe it is vital to her well-being. Please ask her about it."

"Very well. This all sounds very mysterious, but I shall do that."

"Thank you, sir. I shall see you first thing in the morning?"

"Yes, Philippe, first thing in the morning."

Philippe took the steps from the back door two at a time. His eyes filled with tears as he leapt and jumped over a log, cutting through the bushes to his quarters.

Free! I'm a free man!

He had been preparing for this moment for six years, but the premature conclusion to his time at Whisper Wood set his head spinning. He threw open the door to his small room and leaned against the wall, breathless. He looked around at his few possessions, but didn't know where to start packing. The Barringtons had provided nearly everything he "owned." He had purchased a few personal items with his earnings, but all the furniture belonged to the estate.

No need to be concerned about that. Once he got to the valley, it wouldn't matter. He wouldn't need anything once he got home . . . home! He was going home to his family. He sat on the edge of his bed, put his head in his hands, and began to heave sobs of relief, joy, release—all the years of frustration and longing to be free spilled out in a torrent.

After his tears were spent, he rose from the bed and got a bag out of a trunk, both of which the Barringtons had given him. He assumed he could take the bag. He began to stuff clothing and a few books into it. A coin fell out of one of the books—a *mereau*—the identifying coin of a French Huguenot. He hadn't needed that since being in the New World. He picked it up and put it in his pocket.

Suddenly the image of his brother's young freckled face and the dismal work conditions of the gun shop interrupted his celebration. Philippe groaned. Although he had been in town only yesterday, he would go back to see his brother before heading to the green, rolling hills of the Schuylkill Valley. Charles had to know that he was going home early.

He stepped out of his lean-to and looked at the stars. Tonight their brilliance seemed to echo his elation. Then he thought of Bridget. He thought of her gray-blue eyes searching his as she declared her love for him, unsure how he would respond. How brave she was, to take such a risk. He took her hair ribbon out of his pocket and felt the delicate fabric between his fingers, then glanced up at her room. Her lantern still shone; he watched her come to the window and look out. He stepped into the shadows and closed the door on the night and the reward that lay within his reach. The door resisted and creaked as he pushed on it. He felt a stab of sorrow, but he would keep his word to Amos. He would not see her again. This was best—a gut-wrenching departure, to be sure—but quick and clean. What other recourse did he have? Eventually she would heal. He prayed that one day she would be able to forgive him.

BRIDGET LOOKED DOWN AT THE STABLE JUST AS SHE HAD done yesterday morning when Philippe was hooking up the team to take her family into town. But it was dark now. She couldn't see anyone. She went to the armoire and took the diary out of its hiding place for the second time in one day. She didn't remember doing that for years, but this had been a most eventful day. She turned to the entry she had started that morning. Opening the inkwell, she found it almost dry. She dipped her hand into her water basin and let a few drops of the liquid dribble into the container. She swirled it around and watched the liquid turn dark. The quill lay where she had left it that morning. She wet the tip and coaxed a few extra strokes out of the leftover ink.

It's now the evening of the most important day in my life. I hardly know how to record the events of the last few hours. After writing my last entry, I went straight to Philippe to ask him to ride to the forest with me. He refused to go, so I bared my soul and told him how I feel.

But now my heart is heavy. It appears he does not return my affection. He agrees with my parents that it won't work—that we cannot find a way to be together. I am sure we could, but if Philippe does not return my feelings, what is the use?

And now my parents have informed me that they are not really my mother and father. I am the illegitimate child of one of their former servants! This is all too much to absorb in one day. Now I don't even know who I am.

I want to tell Philippe. Perhaps when he finds out that I'm adopted, he will be more amenable to courting me, especially since I am but a servant's child.

I do not know how this will work out. Whether or not I marry another, my feelings for Philippe will never change. I will never love anyone else.

Bridget closed the diary.

I want to go to him.

She looked down on the stable again. His light was still burning. She pulled a cape from the wooden peg by the door, then stopped.

In the morning I'll go to Philippe and explain everything. Yes. Things will be better in the morning.

She returned the cloak to the peg, rang for Abigail, and began to undress down to her shift. She looked out the window once more. *In the morning, my beloved, in the morning.*

NINE

Philippe rode in the increasing light of a gray dawn down the circular drive of Whisper Wood on his horse. He patted the gelding's neck. "Well, Legacy, looks like it's you and me now." He had tied his small bag of belongings behind the saddle, but his wages he had put in his tunic. He turned the Percheron's big head toward town and spurred the horse into a gallop. The young man held on to his hat as they sped by the trees; then he took it off and let the wind race through his hair—no restrictions or constraints. Legacy took the command instantly and ran easily. Philippe let out a *whoop* and plopped his hat back on his head.

He reined the horse into a relaxed canter and soon entered the city limits of Philadelphia. He didn't stop by the pub this time, but rode straight to the foundry, then turned down the alley between the shop and the shoe cobbler next door. Although the hour was still early, he could see the glow of a lantern in the interior of the shop.

He was certain that Charles would be at his workbench already. Philippe didn't want Mister Zwicken to know he was there. He didn't wish to encounter the unpleasant man, and he didn't want things to go ill for Charles.

He tied Legacy to a hitching post by the well and slowly opened the door to the kitchen. Goody Wallace had her considerable backside toward the door, bent over stirring what he supposed was mush or porridge in a black kettle hung on the lug pole over the fire. He let himself in.

"*Ahem* . . . Goody Wallace?"

The cook's arm jerked, slinging porridge onto the hearth. "Wha . . . what?! Mister Clavell! What are you doing here today . . . this early? You scared me half to death. I ought to flail you with this spoon for scaring me like that." She punctuated her words with the spoon thrust toward Philippe.

Grinning, he held up his hands. "I'm sorry. Please, please don't beat me with that spoon." He removed his hat, and his hair fell across his forehead. He brushed it back, running his fingers through it. "Is Charles already at work?"

"*Humph!* Weren't you just here day before yesterday?"

"Yes, ma'am, but something important has come up, and I need to speak to Charles—a family matter."

"Mister Zwicken is not going to take kindly to your showing up again today."

"I know. C-could I trouble you . . . could you fetch Charles for me?"

"What do you take me for—a messenger boy? I do not have time to be a courier for our employees." She slung the spoon around again, but started toward the door of the shop even as she spoke. "I have breakfast to prepare, and then dinner . . ." She waddled into the shop, muttering under her breath.

Philippe heard the cook rustling through the aisles between the workbenches, then the screech of a chair being pushed back across the wooden floor.

A moment later Charles sprang through the door, his eyes wide. "What are you doing here? Is everything well? Why have you come back today?"

Goody Wallace followed close behind him, still grumbling under her breath.

Philippe flashed a big smile at her and bowed. "Thank you, madam. You are indeed a fine lady."

"Oh bother!" She swatted at him. "Now get outside with you, so Zwicken doesn't see you. He will be in shortly for his breakfast. Don't be gone long. I'll cover for you as long as I can."

"Come, Charles. I'll explain everything."

The two brothers walked into the courtyard. "What's the news, that the Barringtons had to come back to town today?"

Philippe walked to Legacy and patted his face. "Do you see this fine specimen of a horse?"

"Looks like Tonnerre."

"Yes, he does. I think that's why I favor him so much. His name is Legacy—and he belongs to me."

Charles' mouth flew open. "He . . . you . . . you own him? How did that happen? How were you able to save enough money to buy him?"

"Mister Barrington gave him to me. But that's not the best news. The best news is that . . . and you must know that I give you this news with much ambivalence, my brother . . . I much desire that this could be your news as well."

"What? What? Quit keeping me in suspense."

"God has been gracious. Mister Barrington has released me from my term early. I'm free, Charles. I'm free to go home."

Charles began to pound his brother on the back, then grabbed him in a smothering hug. They laughed and cried at the same time, tears of happiness and distress mingled together.

"Come, let's go into my quarters." Charles motioned to Philippe, and they moved into the small room that opened onto the courtyard. "Tell me about it. What transpired to bring this about? Did you know nothing about this when you came into town day before yesterday? Well, speak up, man! I cannot stay gone long from the shop."

"I will, if you will give me a chance." Philippe laughed again. "No, I knew nothing about this until yesterday. But some things were revealed that changed the situation at the Barringtons.'" Philippe looked down at his hat that he held in his hands. "There is not only great joy in my being released—it is mingled with sadness."

The brothers sat at a crude wooden table. Uncharacteristically quiet, Charles looked at his brother. "Go on."

Philippe relayed the story of Bridget's profession of love for him.

"Do you return those feelings for her?"

Philippe looked out of the small, dirty window and replied with measured words. "I could have. It was tempting, but I did not allow myself the luxury of doing so."

Charles looked at his brother through furrowed eyebrows. He shook his head. "Are you being honest with me? They are Catholic."

"Precisely. I know that, and that's why I have guarded my feelings. I tried to make her see that it would never work." He chuckled. "She doesn't agree. She's a headstrong young lady, but no matter what she thinks, it never can be. And I . . . I would never hurt Maman by bringing home a Catholic wife. Mister Barrington approached me last night and offered to release me early, if I would simply leave and never contact her again."

Charles shuffled his feet and grabbed his brother's shoulder, pulling him to his side. "I am delighted for your early dismissal. And I am sorry for the disquiet you've encountered in leaving." He started for the door. "I must get back to work. Will you stay the night?"

"Yes, I hoped I could do that." He looked around the courtyard. "Where shall I put Legacy?"

"Put him in the stable. I'll tell Zwicken you are staying. He won't be happy about it, but when I tell him that you are leaving Philadelphia, he will be glad enough to accommodate you for the night."

"We'll go to the pub for supper tonight."

Charles smiled. "Very well." He started out the door, then turned to face his brother. "I am proud for you, Philippe, and I love you." He embraced his older brother once more, then went back to his work.

THE EARLY MORNING SUNLIGHT FILTERED THROUGH THE shutters and fingered the quilt on Bridget's bed. She squinted, rolled over, and pulled the covers up over her head. She tried to go back to sleep, but then remembered the events of yesterday. Her eyes flickered open as she stretched out from under the bedding and smiled to herself. It was going to be a good day. Things would work out. She was certain of it. She swung her feet over the edge of the bed and shimmied her feet into her slippers.

She walked to the wardrobe, stopping to peer through the window down to the stable, as was her habit, to see if Philippe might be in sight. He was not around that she could tell. She didn't ring for Abigail, but opened the heavy doors of the wardrobe and pulled out a blue dress with a white lace ruffle around the neckline. She knew that the dress accentuated her blue eyes. She laced up the white ribbons down the front of the bodice, and stuffing her hair up under a white linen cap, she pulled her cloak off a peg near the door and ran down the stairs.

The fragrance of cornmeal mush cakes frying and warm molasses tantalized her as she reached the bottom of the stairs. Abigail was doing the cooking this morning.

Looking up as Bridget came into the keeping room, the young domestic smiled. "Thee are up early this morning." Motioning toward the table, she said, "Thee's favorite."

Copper pots and utensils hanging over the table glinted softly in the sunlight. A large mold of butter and a pitcher of syrup sat on the table, along with the rectangular cakes that had already been fried.

"I have something I need to attend to. Where's Cook?"

"I told her I would do this. I know just how thee likes them— crisp around the edges. She's in the pantry gathering what she needs to begin preparation for dinner."

Bridget put on her cloak and picked up one of the patties. She dipped it in the syrup and started for the back door. "*Mmm . . . yum.* You do indeed know how I like these." Waving at Abigail as she went out the door, she called over her shoulder, "I'll be right back. Save some for me."

She gobbled down the crisp patty and ran down the path to the stable, licking the molasses from her fingers. She went into the dark stable, but saw no one at all—only horses in the stalls—all except the black Percheron. The back door of the stable had not been opened yet this morning. She unlatched it and pushed on it. It groaned open, but no horses were in the corral. Where was everybody? Even Eb was not around. They had to be working on something somewhere.

A young stable boy appeared, carrying tack, and started at seeing her.

"Where is everybody? Eb? Philippe?"

He shook his head. "I don't know, Mistress Barrington. I haven't seen anybody this morning."

"Thank you." Bridget walked toward the rear of the barn where Philippe's quarters lay. She approached the lean-to, hesitating. She had never gone to his room. She put her ear to the door and heard rustling inside. Smiling, she knocked softly. "Philippe? It's me, Bridget."

More scuffling, and the door creaked open. Eb's wide eyes blinked at her. "Mistress Barrington! What you doing down here so early?"

"Oh. I thought . . . well, I was looking for Philippe."

"Yes'm, but Philippe is gone. He done moved out. He left at the crack of dawn this morning."

Bridget pushed open the door to see for herself that the room had been vacated. She whirled around, took a few steps, then turned back toward the old servant. "What do you know about this, Eb? Where did Philippe go? Where did my father send him?"

"You needs to talk to yo' daddy about that. I don't know."

"Yes, I will. I shall do just that." She held her skirt and ran back up the hill to the house, tears blurring her vision. She burst into the keeping room, expecting to see her father sitting at the long table, puffing on his pipe and drinking his morning ale. But he was nowhere to be seen. "Abigail! Where is my father?"

"He ate very early this morning, then left. I'm not sure where he went."

Bridget plopped down on the bench and brushed the tears away. "They have sent him away. I know they have."

"Ma'am?"

"Nothing, nothing." She chewed on her lower lip. "But in reality—everything."

She retraced her steps and ran back down the path to the stable.

Where will Philippe go? To the Schuylkill Valley, of course. To join his family.

He couldn't have had much of a head start on her. It was still early. Perhaps she could catch up with him. She ran to Kimi's stall, grabbed a bridle and slung it over the mare's head, forcing the bit into the horse's mouth. She clutched the horse's mane in her fist and swung up on her horse bareback, turned Kimi's head northwest, and spurred the horse into a fast gallop. Then she slowed down.

No! He will have gone back into Philadelphia to tell his brother first. He wouldn't go without telling Charles. All I need to do is go into town to Zwicken's. He will be with his brother.

She whirled Kimi's head around and headed the opposite direction toward town.

She got around the circular drive and had started down the road when her father caught up to her. Even in his increasing years, the man still sat expertly astride his steed. He galloped alongside her, caught hold of Kimi's bridle, and pulled them to a halt. Kimi snorted and reared. Still holding on to the mare's mane, Bridget managed to stay on her horse.

Amos held the bridle and calmed the horse. "Where do you think you're going, young lady?"

PHILIPPE PULLED CHARLES UP BEHIND HIM ON THE BIG Percheron and rode down the alley to the muddy street. Zwicken had reluctantly given Charles permission to leave with his brother, with their promise to return in two hours. Darkness had already settled over the city. Random property owners, lighting oil lamps along the way, barely paid the two young men any attention as they rode toward the pub. Clouds covered the moon, and stretches of the street where no lampposts had been erected had only the soft glow of lanterns from within the buildings. However, the taverns and inns were well lit, and the brothers didn't have far to go.

Fragrant smoky aromas of meat mingling with fireplace smoke met them as they entered the pub. A slight hint of a spicy-sweet scent tantalized them. They made their way through the crowded pub and found a table in a corner.

"Philippe! What brings you back so soon?" The rotund proprietor clapped Philippe on the back and greeted Charles. "Good evening to you, young man. Haven't seen you for quite some time. You've gotten taller."

Charles grinned, and Philippe cuffed his brother on the head. "Hasn't caught me yet, however."

"No, but I can outwrestle you now."

"That's true." Looking at Charles, Philippe nodded. "He's gotten much stronger this last year."

"What can I get for you boys?"

"Just bring whatever you have tonight. I can pay for it. I've been released early from my redemptioner. I'm going home." Philippe grinned and took the bag of coins out of his tunic.

"That's wonderful news!" The proprietor looked at Charles, and the boy shook his head.

"Not I, but I'm thrilled for my brother. Zwicken allowed me to come celebrate with Philippe tonight."

"That was awfully kind of him." Mister Clark smirked and rested his fists on his hips. "Well! This is on the house tonight. Anything you would like."

"Do you have any of those apple pies left?"

"You are in luck. And my wife baked gingerbread today. We have the smoked ham, cabbage, turnips, potatoes, and pea soup. I'll bring you what we have."

"Wonderful. That's what I smelled when we came in—the gingerbread. Yes, that sounds good. And I *will* pay you this time."

"We shall see." Clark left and made his way through the crowd to the fireplace.

Charles leaned forward. "I have something troubling that I need to tell you. I don't know what action needs to be taken, if any. I overheard a conversation between Zwicken and . . ."

The barmaid brought a large platter of ham, cabbage, potatoes, and turnips and set it in the middle of the table. She placed two wooden bowls in front of the brothers. "This ought to do you for now. I'll bring pie and gingerbread after you're finished with this. More ale?"

"No, thank you, ma'am." Philippe took his hat off and laid it on the bench beside him.

"Ma'am, it is? Don't encounter manners like that very often."

Philippe smiled, as did Charles, as she walked away. Charles helped himself to the ham and vegetables. "Clavell men are gentlemen still, eh?"

"Indeed we are. Father would have wanted us to remain gentlemen, no matter our lots in life."

"I know. It's just that our life in France seems so far away now—another lifetime, literally. Were we really noble landowners? Did we ever own a fine estate? Was our mother truly the most beautiful woman in Dauphine Provence and once in the royal court of King

Louis?" Charles stopped, his spoon held in midair between bites. He shook his head. "I can hardly remember any of that." He held up a napkin, grinned at his brother, then wiped his mouth on it.

"Do you ever think about the fact that we really cannot go home?" Philippe asked.

"What do you mean?"

"Think about it. Maman and Pierre have made their home in the Schuylkill Valley. We have been in Philadelphia, indentured against our wills. That hasn't been home, because we weren't with our families. The only home we've ever known was at the estate in France, but it is no more and never will be again. Where is 'home' for you and me?"

Charles nodded. "Certainly not the foundry. You've been more fortunate, but I'm sure the Barringtons' plantation was not truly home for you either. But you also have already stated the obvious: home is wherever our family is—where our loved ones are."

Philippe fidgeted with his spoon. "Where our loved ones are." He set the spoon on the table and leaned back in his chair. "With Maman, Vangie, and Pierre, and Uncle Jean and the rest. The Lord is gracious."

Charles gave his brother a pat on the arm. "How is Vangie's health? Do you know?"

"If her health had worsened, they would have sent word. I assume she fares well. Now, what was it you needed to tell me?"

Charles took a deep breath and began. "I overheard a conversation between Zwicken and his partner, Edward Moorehead. Moorehead is putting the pressure on Zwicken for more and more guns, faster and faster, and shipping them downriver, even as the British quartermaster is expecting his deliveries. And then, from what I could gather, they spoke about an incident that occurred several years ago on the Barringtons' property. It sounded like . . . like they killed someone."

Philippe's eyes grew wide. "Did they say who it was?"

"An indentured servant. It could have been *me*. Something is terribly amiss here. It must not have ever been discovered. From what I could decipher, they buried the body on the Barrington property, and they were worried that someone might have seen." Charles paused. "And there have been others. One last year."

Philippe remained silent for a few moments, remembering Bridget's secret.

Charles finished his bowl of vegetables and ham and helped himself to another serving. "Well? What do you think? Should we do anything about this?"

"Just keep alert."

The brothers finished their meal and rode back to Charles' quarters at the foundry. They talked late into the night, knowing it would be the last time for a good while.

TEN

Bridget waited in the parlor in the slanted shadows of late after-noon for her father to return. She had not eaten all day. He had taken her back to the house after spoiling her attempt to catch up with Philippe and given her instructions to wait for him. After several vain attempts by her mother to coax her to talk, Sarah gave up and left her alone. At last Bridget heard Amos coming through the house, and her mother's undertone of concern as she encountered him in the hall.

"Gigi?" Amos entered the room.

"Father." Her voice was low and foreboding. "What have you done? Where is Philippe? What . . . have . . . you . . . done?" Her voice rose with each word until she was screeching at him. She ran to him and dissolved in tears as she pounded his chest with her fists.

"There, there, my dear. No need for such histrionics. Sit down." He pulled his hysterical daughter onto the settee with him.

She buried her face in her hands and sobbed. "Where has he

gone? Why have you done this? We could work things out. I know we could. We could have reached a compromise."

"And that's exactly what it would have been—a compromise. You are too valuable and too precious to live in a compromised situation all the rest of your life, simply because you—"

"Simply because I what? Fell in love with a wonderful man? Someone who would love me and take care of me and treasure me?"

"Take care of you? A former indentured servant who does not share your faith nor your feelings, from what I have gathered, and whose family would be against you as well? You are too young to realize the heartache that would bring to your lives. The blush of young love soon fades, and you are left with the harsh realities of everyday life."

Bridget thought of David and Ella, and Bradley and Penelope, and the grumbling she had heard among the young wives about their husbands. And although she believed her parents held a certain affection for one another, they were not exactly an example of passionate married love.

"Be sensible. You are thinking with your heart. You would be no different than anybody else and your relationship more difficult than most. If his family objected, which they most assuredly would, you would have to start from scratch on your own. How could he afford land? Certainly not with the wages I gave him."

"Is my dowry not going to be substantial?" She stared at Amos, narrowing her eyes. "You gave him his final wages and released him, didn't you?"

"I did."

"So he's gone home."

"Yes."

"That's simple. I know where his family is. I'll follow him. Perhaps Bradley would take me. You cannot keep me from him forever." Bridget stood. "And why did you not give him land? I know you've done that in the past for indentured servants. Philippe has been one of your favorites, and you did not give him land!"

Amos tried to take his daughter's hands, but she pulled away from him. "It's true. He was one of my favorites, but it's rather obvious why I did not set him up with land." He took his pipe out of his pocket. "I did give him the Percheron."

She spoke barely above a whisper. "I'm glad you did that." She blotted her tears with her handkerchief. "I will find a way for us to be together."

"You will not hear from him anymore, and you will not attempt to follow him again. He gave me his word that he would not contact you."

"You . . . you made him promise not to see me again?"

He tapped his pipe into an ash holder. "Philippe understands that you can never be together as husband and wife. He understands that a clean break right here at the outset is the easiest and best solution."

"Easy? You think this is easy? This is anything but easy."

"It may not seem like it now, but in the long run, my dear, believe me, it is the easiest solution. Philippe needs to be in the bosom of his family after six long years of being separated from them. Let him go."

Bridget fell silent. She twirled a curl round and round on her finger. In spite of her protests, her father's reasoning began to penetrate her emotions. She did not wish to cause Philippe any further anxiety. Glimmers of the dreadful truth began to settle in her heart—Philippe was gone. She would never see him again. "I shall always love him."

She tried to swallow a sob that came out in a gasp. "I . . . I shall never forget him."

Sarah entered the room as Amos embraced his daughter. "I know, I know, my dear. There is a part of your heart that will always remember him. He was your first love."

Adriaen walked up the steps of the porch with a full basket of eggs. She opened the door to the large keeping room and set the basket on the table. "The hens must be content these days. There are eggs everywhere in the coop." She laughed. "We'll need to make egg pie."

Madeleine took the basket and set it on the hearth. "Pierre will be glad of that."

"And spoon bread. Jean loves spoon bread."

Vangie came out of her room, a smaller bandage on her head than the day before. "Good morning, Maman, Adriaen."

"Good morning!" Adriaen's early morning exuberance brightened the room as much as the sunlight that flooded through the shutters she was opening. "How's the head? Healing well?"

"Yes, thank you." Vangie pulled her shawl around her shoulders and sat in the rocking chair beside the fire. "It still throbs now and then, but it is much better." She picked up the yarn she had been spinning the evening before and started to work.

"Vangie, eat something before you start on that." Madeleine ladled porridge into a bowl from a kettle that had been simmering over the fireplace. The men had already gulped their breakfast down with some cider and gone out to the early morning chores. A rabbit roasted on a spit over the fire.

"I've fallen behind. I need to get this done."

"That can certainly wait until you've had some nourishment. Come sit at the table."

"I'll just eat here by the fire. I'm cold."

Madeleine sighed as she spooned butter into the hot porridge and poured milk from a pitcher on the table for her daughter. "Molasses?"

Vangie nodded and stood, reaching for a cup of cider on the table. She took a step backward and seized the back of the rocking chair. The chair tilted with her, and she grabbed hold of her head.

"Vangie!" Madeleine dropped the bowl of porridge and dashed to her daughter's side, catching the frail girl before she fell. "Sit down! Sit down before you fall."

"I'm fine, just a little light-headed. I simply got up too fast." The two women helped her resume her seat in the rocking chair. "Really, I am fine." She looked at the porridge mess on the floor. "I'm sorry."

Adriaen had already begun to wipe it up. "No problem, child. This is easily taken care of. I'm glad, however, that your mother hadn't yet poured the molasses in it. Now that would have been a sticky mess." The young mother-to-be raised herself from the floor and sat on the bench by the table. "*That's* getting harder and harder to do."

"You should have let me do that." Madeleine spooned a second bowl for Vangie.

Adriaen gathered the dishes and began to help Madeleine get started on dinner. "Oh!" She clutched her expanding abdomen with her hands.

"Adriaen? Are you . . . is everything well?"

"The baby is turning somersaults again." She laughed. "He's kicking me."

"That's good. It means he is healthy." Madeleine eyed her sister-in-law. "It looks like that baby is dropping already. We may have a new arrival sooner than we expected." She began to take eggs out of the basket. "I don't have time to do the egg pie for dinner. Let's make spoon bread. That'll be good with the rabbit." She chuckled. "It was a long time before I could eat rabbit after our journey from Versailles through the woods back to Switzerland. That's about all Pierre and Philippe could catch in the forest. They did fish some, but . . ." She stopped in midsentence and starting cracking and separating the eggs.

"Go on, Madeleine. You know how we love to hear your stories."

"That was a long time ago—another life."

"Please, do continue, Maman."

Madeleine smiled. "What do you want to hear?"

"I like to hear about Papa."

Adriaen spoke up. "And how you met Pierre."

"You two are romantics." Madeleine pointed to the cornmeal barrel. "Adriaen, would you please mix up the dry ingredients while I separate the eggs?"

"Please, Maman, tell us about Papa. Tell us again about the first time you saw him."

The crunching of the eggshells punctuated Madeleine's words as she talked. "Very well. The first time I saw François was when he and Jean, and their father and their sister, escaped to our estate, fleeing from the dragoons . . . who had murdered their mother and other sister." Madeleine hesitated and looked toward the corner of the room, as if she were seeing the scene in her mind. "He had a bloody gash across his forehead and carried the limp body of his sister. She died shortly after they stumbled onto our property." Madeleine looked at Vangie. "Do you remember the scar across Papa's forehead?"

Vangie nodded and turned to Adriaen. "His hair covered it most of the time, but I remember it."

"And all because we Huguenots simply wanted to worship God the way we believed the Scriptures taught." Madeleine shook her head. "I fell in love with him immediately, and we married shortly after they came to the estate. And then Philippe was born; then Charles; and finally you, Princess. We were very happy for many years during the time that the Edict of Nantes offered the Huguenots protection, but for some reason . . . for some reason Louis began to get pressure from his advisors to take Huguenots prisoner if they wouldn't convert. They sent many to the galleys, where Papa ended up; and kidnapped children, such as Vangie, to monasteries and convents."

Adriaen jumped in. "Vangie, I've never heard you talk about being in the convent. Do you remember it?"

Vangie looked up at her aunt. "Well, I was so little—"

Madeleine interrupted. "Why don't we save that for another time, *ma petit chérie?* Adriaen and I need to be getting dinner started. Could you hand me the cornmeal, Adriaen?"

The two women cooked all morning, and Vangie returned to her spinning. Adriaen felt the need to sit down and rest frequently. She had not said anything to the family, but she had felt the baby dropping as well. It was too early, and she was frightened. Perhaps she was further along than they had calculated. Beads of sweat broke out on her forehead as the pain in her back tightened.

Heavenly Father, let this pain subside. It's too early for the baby to arrive.

She got up and continued to help Madeleine as the pain passed.

Jean and Pierre had gone out in the fields after the noon meal with their hired hand, Karl, to start cultivating the soil to prepare for planting. Peas and potatoes were already in the ground, as were the onion sets, but they needed to plant the greens and beets. Weeds were popping up every day along with the asparagus and rhubarb. Adriaen hurried with the dishes, so she could get into the garden.

Footsteps suddenly pounded on the porch, and Jean burst into the room. A grin spread across his face from ear to ear.

"My goodness, husband, what are you beaming about?"

"Come and see! All of you! Come, come outside."

Adriaen could hear shouting of men's voices and laughter from the barnyard. She looked out the door and saw someone on . . . was it Tonnerre? No, but it was a horse just like Tonnerre. It was Philippe! "Madeleine! Come—it's Philippe!"

Madeleine ran to the door, clutching her apron, and uttered a cry. "My son?" She stopped at the door and stared. An almost inhuman sob erupted from her throat as she gathered her skirt and began to trot toward him, breaking into a full run, chickens squawking and scattering in front of her. "Philippe, my son!"

Vangie rose and hurried to the door as well. She grabbed hold of the doorjamb.

"Steady there." Adriaen held on to Vangie's hand.

The men laughed and shouted, embracing the young man as he dismounted. Madeleine ran headlong into his arms, her hands clutching his shoulders over and over.

"My son, my son." She pulled back and caressed his face, kissing his cheeks, first one side, then the other. Then, still cradling his face in her hands, she asked, "Wh-what are you doing here? Charles? Is he well?"

"All is well, Maman. In fact, everything is wonderful. Mister Barrington . . . he . . . well, he released me early."

"Early? Praise God! Thank you, Lord! But why? Why would he do that?"

"Plenty of time to explain it all to you. It's a long story. But look!" Philippe pulled out his leather pouch. "He paid me, and best of all . . ." He pointed to Legacy. "He gave me the horse of my choice." Philippe rubbed the horse on his face, and the big Percheron nickered.

"This looks familiar." Pierre laughed. "He might be a threat to my Tonnerre."

"Not a threat but a good complement to carry on."

"We have a new colt out of Tonnerre. Looks just like him."

"Maybe we'll start a herd of Percherons."

"That's my intention," Pierre replied, and everyone laughed.

Philippe spied Vangie standing on the porch and went to her, picked her up, and swung her around. "You're almost too big for me to do that anymore. What's this?" He pointed to the bandage.

"Oh, it's nothing, really. I just fell down. It's fine."

The whole group chattered at once. They went to the barn to show Philippe the newest additions to their stock. Like a gaggle of geese, the family entourage went from one part of the farm to another showing off the improvements, new plantings, and fences since Philippe had last visited in the fall. Finally, and reluctantly, they all went to their chores, with Philippe helping Pierre in the stable.

Adriaen watched Madeleine peer outside every few minutes. "He's not going anywhere, Madeleine. He's home to stay."

Madeleine dabbed at her eyes. "I cannot get my eyes full enough of him. He's turned into a handsome young man, has he not?"

"Very handsome. You should be proud. Jean says he looks much like François?"

"He does . . . it's like I have a piece of François left. Tall and slender and strong. And his hair is exactly like François', dark and straight." She looked out once more. "I think I'll sit with Vangie on the porch and help her churn the butter. It is really quite pleasant outside this afternoon."

"Good idea. I'm going to work on those weeds in the garden. If we don't get them out now, they are going to overtake the new crops. Asparagus is going to be ready to pick within the next few days, the rhubarb as well."

"Adriaen, I know you—that hardworking Dutch heritage. Don't overdo it."

"I won't, but I also want to gather nettle to make tea for Vangie. It seems to strengthen her a bit when she is faithful to drink it." She smiled and waved at mother and daughter on the porch as she picked up the hoe from the side of the house and went to work on the pesky weeds, praying the tightening in her back would not return.

LATER THAT NIGHT, PHILIPPE TOSSED AND TURNED ON HIS pallet, too excited to sleep. Pierre and Jean had been working on a room on the back of the house, which they'd intended to have finished by the time Philippe returned home, but late winter snows had delayed them. They could finish it within a few weeks now that the weather had turned mild.

Bridget's face flashed before him. How angry she must have been when she found out that her father had released him. But he had given his word, and he would keep it. He would never see her again.

Then he thought of Charles, and the pain of leaving his younger brother wrenched his heart. The anguish in his younger brother's warm brown eyes as Philippe left him brought tears to his eyes. There had to be some way that they could gather enough money to pay out his release. He would speak to Pierre about that tomorrow. There must be a way.

THE SPRING MORNING HAD USHERED INTO THE PARLOR unusual warmth for the season. Bridget held the yarn between her hands as Sarah wound it round and round into a ball. Her mother droned on about their neighbor's daughter, who had become engaged to the mayor's son.

"It is a perfect match. The wedding will be a lovely affair, probably the biggest event of the year. Can you imagine what beautiful children they will have?"

"Stop it, Mother."

"Wh . . . what? Stop what?"

"Stop hinting at the fact that I'm not married and am getting almost beyond the point that anybody is going to be interested in marrying me."

"Why, I was doing nothing of the sort. I was simply relaying the news of our neighbors."

"I'm going outside for a bit of fresh air." Bridget set the yarn down on a footstool. "It's stuffy in here." She walked onto the front porch. Large potted plants graced the portico. She went to the steps and sat down.

Abigail stood up from the flower beds, her face red from exertion.

"Oh, hello, Abigail. I didn't see you down there." Bridget smoothed her skirt.

"I came out to pick some flowers for the parlor and started pulling weeds. Once thee starts, it's hard to know where to stop. Is there anything that I can do for thee?"

"No, nothing. I just needed some fresh air." Bridget looked at the young mother; the evidence of the new life inside of her was beginning to bulge beneath her dress.

The servant returned to her knees digging in the soil, and Bridget cleared her throat. "Abigail?"

"Yes?"

"Are you—are you in love with your husband?"

Abigail's head jerked up, and she stared at her mistress. "Am I in love with my husband?" She leaned on the trowel in her hand to push herself up. "Why would thee ask that?"

Bridget shrugged her shoulder. "*Mmm* . . . just curious."

The servant looked down at her hands covered with dirt. "My husband is a good man and a good father."

"That's not what I asked you."

"He treats me well and isn't given to much wine like some of the other men on the plantation."

"That's not what I asked you either." Bridget held her breath. "I want to know if you are in love with your husband."

"I have grown to love him."

"So you were not in love with him when you married him?"

Abigail looked down and over at her toddler who played with a shovel in the dirt beside her. "Well, no, not exactly. I had only seen him at church."

"You are Quakers."

"Yes. Our parents approved our courtship and arranged the marriage. It was agreeable to me. I liked him."

"I see." Bridget looked out over the gardens at the lilacs and yellow jonquils bursting with color. "Was there anyone else, any other young man whom you would have rather married, but it wasn't possible?"

Abigail shook her head. "No, ma'am. Zachary was the only one who asked to court me."

"Are you happy with . . . with the arrangement? Has it been a satisfactory one?"

"Oh yes, Mistress Bridget." She wiped her hands on her apron. "Certainly there are adjustments in any marriage, but we have done well . . . I think."

"You have a lovely family."

Abigail smiled and touched her swelling belly with her hand. She wiped her brow with the other, smearing dirt on her forehead.

Bridget looked at the young girl's plain but beautifully made dress, with the white crisscross kerchief tucked into the apron. The girl's dresses were always of lovely color and impeccable. Bridget stared at her servant's open, innocent face that glowed with the anticipation of birth that mothers-to-be seemed to possess. Abigail wasn't what you would call pretty, but her countenance exuded a natural, healthy beauty.

Bridget leaned down toward her. "Come here, please." She wiped the dirt away from the girl's face with her handkerchief, then returned to the porch and sat in a rocking chair. The young servant caught her toddler by the hand and went around the corner of the house. Bridget picked up a fan and began to stir the breeze with it. A girl about the same age as she, content in an arranged marriage, about to have her second child. She sighed again.

She thought of Philippe. She thought of him every day, and the pain of his departure tortured her. She was trapped, with nowhere to turn. Even if she could travel to the Schuylkill Valley to see Philippe, she would meet with opposition not only from his family but from Philippe himself. And she couldn't stand the thought of being rejected by him. Philippe had given his word. He would not deny his honor. Her father had secured a tidy knot on the arrangement.

The door opened, and Sarah stepped out onto the porch. "May I join you for a moment?"

"Of course, Mother."

"I instructed Abigail to bring some buttermilk for us."

Bridget continued to rock and fan. "You know I don't care for buttermilk."

"It's something cool to drink. Today is warm for May."

"Yes. But did you come out here to talk to me about the weather?" Bridget's comment sounded harsher than she intended.

Sarah flustered and began to beat the air with furious flaps back and forth with her fan. "I do have something I need to tell you."

Abigail arrived with a pitcher of buttermilk and two goblets on a tray. She had washed and re-gathered her hair underneath her plain white head covering.

As soon as the servant left, Sarah poured the white, creamy liquid and sat back in her chair. She picked up a goblet and took a sip. Bridget left hers on the tray.

"Your father ran into Edward Moorehead in town earlier in the week." She avoided Bridget's eyes and swirled the milk around in her goblet. "He asked if he could . . . if it would be possible . . . he asked permission to come see you this week to discuss the possibility of courting you."

Bridget's stomach turned over, and her heart thudded against her chest. "And what did Father tell him?"

"He agreed."

Tears sprang to Bridget's eyes, and she shook her head. "No, Mother. Please don't make me do this."

Sarah's demeanor softened, and she reached for Bridget's hand. "Child, give him a chance. At least, allow him to call on you. You may grow to like him."

Bridget pulled her hand away and hung her head as the tears dripped onto her skirt, spotting the fabric. "There is no comparison between Edward Moorehead and Philippe."

Sarah stood. "It has already been arranged. He is a perfect match for you—a man of means, handsome, and well thought of. He is enchanted by you, and he is Catholic. He will be here in time for dinner and will remain for the afternoon. Go to your room now and change. I'll send Abigail to help you." She picked up the tray and turned to Bridget. "You'd best banish Philippe Clavell from your head and heart. To hang on to the idea of marrying him will only cause you heartache. Be content with what your father and I feel is the best for you." She pushed the door open with her hip and went into the house.

How could her parents do this to her? She would run away, that's what she would do. The sun began its ascent toward the midday sky. A few clouds floated lazily by, and a bird hopped along, pecking at the ground. A slight breeze ruffled the tops of the trees enclosing the circular drive to the house. Soon Edward Moorehead would be riding up that path. There was no place for her to run. Where could a woman go by herself? If she went to Philippe, he would send her back. She could go to David and Ella's, or Bradley and Penelope's, but that could only last for a season. They were in favor of the courtship, and besides, that would only put her in closer proximity to Edward Moorehead in Philadelphia. She was hedged in as surely as Whisper Wood was hedged by the trees surrounding the plantation.

She went into the house and climbed the stairs to her room, the room that had been hers from the time she was a little girl. Her dolls sat in a row in the wooden cradle that her mother had rocked her in. Her mother . . . which mother?

Bridget shook her head and went to the wardrobe, removing her diary from its hiding place. She sat down on the bed and unlocked it. One by one she began to rip out the pages. The only sound in the room was the tearing of the brittle pages and intermittent sobs. Page by page, she tore the epistle of her journey from childhood to young womanhood into pieces.

A few embers from last night's fire flickered beneath the ashes. She blew on the embers and coaxed the flame back into life, then slid the first page into the fire. *My life as I have known it is over.* Again and again, each page followed the next into the consuming blaze. *I will . . . I will do what my parents ask of me, but I will never be truly alive again, as I was with Philippe. I will appear alive on the outside, but my heart and my spirit will be dead and brittle. Like these pages.*

Bridget sat beside the fireplace and watched them curl and crinkle and disappear into smoke. *I will bury who I really am, because my desires seem not to matter. I will walk as a shell of a woman. Perhaps when I have children, I will revive somewhat, but . . . it will be a bitter reminder of who I wanted their father to be.*

Sighing, Bridget rose and resigned herself to the destiny that her parents had fashioned for her. The days of recording her dreams in a diary were over. It was time to grow up.

She looked at her writing paper and quill. She would write a letter to Philippe and tell him that she had decided to acquiesce to her parent's wishes and agree to a courtship. She would marry and proceed with her life. That's what he wanted, wasn't it? She penned the letter quickly.

Philippe,

I am writing you this letter to say that I have decided that you were right. Although I will always care for you, there seems to be no way to obtain our parents' blessings. And being the man of character and integrity that you are, it appears that we will not try to hurdle that obstacle.

Bridget stifled a sob and wiped a tear away from the page, smearing the ink.

My parents have arranged a courtship with a man I hardly know, but Mother says perhaps if I get to know him, I will learn to like him. His name is Edward Moorehead, an entrepreneur from Philadelphia. I have met him once before, at my cousin's house, and consider him a prideful snob. You may remember the dandy who came out on the porch as we were leaving the last time you drove us to town.

I wish you prosperity, love, and happiness, my dear Philippe.

She hesitated. How should she close? Simply . . .

Forever,
Bridget

She sealed the envelope and placed it on the table outside her door for a servant to pick up and post. Abigail appeared at the top of the stairs.

"Come in, Abigail, and help me get dressed." She walked to the wardrobe, removed her best dress, and began to ready herself for Edward Moorehead.

Bridget peered across the table at Edward as they finished the blueberry buckle. The early afternoon sun glinted on the silver pieces adorning the table. Edward's grooming was perfect, as it had been when they first met.

He is a prissy thing, Bridget thought, and sighed. Today he wore varying shades of blue—a dark blue jacket with gold trim, a light blue vest and white cravat. His breeches were even blue, navy. His hair was tied back with a navy ribbon.

Sarah had hardly drawn a breath through the entire meal between bites and trying to keep the sagging conversation propped up. Bridget toyed with her food and sent most of it back to the kitchen. Her stomach cramped underneath the stays that drew her waist in as tiny as possible. She caught hold of the large ruffled flounce of ecru lace on her sleeve and held it in her hand so it wouldn't drag through the butter as she reached for her glass of claret.

Cook bustled in and out of the dining room as they progressed through the meal, frowning at the small amount of dinner Bridget ate.

Amos pushed back from the table and pulled his pipe out of his pocket. "Edward, shall we adjourn to the parlor?"

"Certainly." Edward stood and set his chair back in place. He bowed slightly at the waist. "Ladies, I hate to leave such lovely company, but I believe Mister Barrington and I have a most important issue to discuss." He smiled at Bridget. "May I speak to you after your father and I finish our conversation?"

"Yes, of course." It was Sarah, not Bridget, who answered.

"Bridget?" His eyes found hers.

"Yes, Edward. I shall be outside on the porch."

Bridget stood and picked up her fan as Amos and Edward moved into the parlor. Sarah remained at the table, sipping her wine and watching the servants clear the dishes.

Bridget went out the door and sat in the porch swing. She moved the swing back and forth gently, fanning herself and listening to the low punctuations of the men's voices, interspersed with chuckles, through the open windows. The perfume of the lilac blossoms filtered through the air. Her toes barely touched the floor as she swung her legs to keep the swing moving. Maybe if she kept the swing moving, the men would keep talking and . . . she closed her eyes and listened to the hum of bees in the lilac bushes.

Abigail stuck her head out the front door. "Mistress, thy father would like thee to come to the parlor."

Bridget snapped her fan closed and rose from the swing, sending it careening from side to side. She stopped the swing with her hand and walked into the house. Taking a deep breath, she started down the hallway and turned into the parlor. The two men stood by the fireplace looking at Amos' guns hanging above the mantel. Edward had taken a musket down and was examining the stock. He swung around with the musket in his hands as Bridget came into the room.

Bridget gasped and stepped back as the musket swung in her direction. "Oh!" She stared at Edward. Her hands began to tremble.

"Oh, my dear!" Edward's voice of velvet immediately soothed the atmosphere. "I frightened you. I humbly beg your pardon." He replaced the musket above the fireplace and hastened to her side. He took her hand and helped her to sit down, then knelt beside the chair. "You are trembling."

"You . . . you startled me."

He took her hand and kissed it. He looked at her and smiled.

"Please don't be frightened. We were merely looking at the stocks on your father's muskets. And I was telling him of a master crafts-man employed at my foundry. It will soon be *our* foundry, as . . . well, perhaps it would be more proper for your father to make the official announcement."

Bridget searched his eyes. His concern appeared to be genuine.

Amos approached the couple as Edward rose, still holding Bridget's hand. His hands were soft. Amos slapped Edward on the back. "My dear, Mister Moorehead has asked permission to court you, and I—we—have given our enthusiastic approval."

Sarah had appeared in the doorway. She began fluttering her fan. "Oh yes. Our very enthusiastic approval."

ELEVEN

Philippe sat on the edge of his bed and listened to the rooster's announcement of dawn's arrival. He smiled, pulled on his breeches, and opened the door of his new room that he, Jean, and Pierre had built onto the back of Pierre and Madeleine's house. He liked the fact that it had doors leading both outside and into the main house. He walked out to the well to draw a bucket of water for his washbasin. The sun had turned the sky into a rosy canopy, coloring the green hills. He had not been this happy and content since before the dragoons invaded their estate in France.

He removed his hat and looked toward the sky. *I am forever grateful, my Father, for your goodness to me. Your mercies are new every morning. Thank you for allowing me to come home. I pray for the Barringtons and am so very thankful for how well I was treated there. And I pray for Bridget. May she be well.*

Summer was well upon them, which meant long days in the fields and the garden, picking ripe fruits and vegetables and then storing them for the winter. It was harder work than he had experienced at Whisper Wood, but it was different being free and working one's own land. His mother and Pierre had designated a plot of land for him down by the river and one for Charles across the valley when he came home. Philippe couldn't wait to start clearing his plot, but his help was needed this season at the main house. He didn't know how they had managed without his assistance before now.

He returned to his room, splashed water on his face, and pulled his hair back with a leather strip. Rubbing his chin, he leaned into the mirror. He wouldn't worry about shaving today. He picked up the unopened letter from Bridget lying on his washstand. A post rider had delivered the message two days ago, but Philippe could not yet bring himself to open it.

Father, I pray for Bridget, that she will find comfort by turning to you. I pray that you will grant her the faith to trust you. Please reveal yourself to her.

He put the letter in a drawer in his dresser and went into the house for breakfast.

Vangie turned from stirring the kettle over the fireplace and smiled at her big brother. "It's so nice to see you coming through that door every morning."

"Sometimes I am nearly overwhelmed that I am here . . . free and finally . . . finally with . . ." He gave his sister a hug without finishing his sentence. She smiled and patted his arm.

He looked around the keeping room. "Where are Maman . . . and Pierre, and Claudine? Where is everybody?"

"Pierre is in the barn already, and Maman and Claudine are up at Jean and Adriaen's." Vangie giggled. "After the false alarm a few weeks ago, I think the baby is really coming this time."

"Isn't it too early?"

"Not so much, I don't think. Maybe a little. I think they expected it next month, but she was getting so big. Maybe they misfigured." She spooned him a bowl of porridge. "Sit down and eat. Pierre will need your help. Jean's no good to him today."

Philippe hurried through his breakfast. He picked up his ale and took it with him to the barn.

Pierre looked up from where he sat on a milking stool. "Ah, glad you're here. We're shorthanded this morning."

"Yes, I just heard." The splat of the milk hitting the bucket set up an early-morning rhythm that spoke security to Philippe. He liked the predictability of the every-morning ritual. It was like the rising of the sun—one could depend on it no matter what. He picked up a milking stool, greeted Karl, the hired hand, and went to the end of the line of cows.

Pierre called to him from around the rump of a Holstein. "We're almost finished with the cows. Would you go outside, please, and milk the goats?" He grinned at the young man.

Philippe sighed. Pierre knew he preferred milking the cows to coaxing milk from the skittish goats. Milking had not been one of his regular chores at the Barringtons', but he certainly knew how to milk. Everybody pitched in with all the chores here on their own place. It still startled him to see Pierre in the role of a farmer. To him, Pierre was, even now, a dashing courtier. Especially on those occasions when he'd kiss Madeleine's hand and in jest execute a sweeping bow.

Philippe picked up a feed bag and started outside. "Guess I should have gotten out here earlier, eh?"

"Thank you, son. I'll switch off with you tomorrow."

Philippe hung the feed bag on the stanchion. *Son.* He liked it when

Pierre called him that. The man had stepped in as graciously as the head of their family as anyone could have wanted. Not that Philippe would ever forget his own courageous father and the values and integrity he had instilled in his children. He would always be indebted to his father for that, and he was grateful now for Pierre as well.

This was a new chapter in his life—of that he was aware with every step he took in the fields of this green valley, with every new skill he learned, with the breaking of every new dawn of his freedom.

THE SUN CLIMBED INTO THE NOONDAY SKY, SENDING ITS blistering heat onto Philippe's strong back. He removed his shirt and worked in the garden alongside Karl. The weeds grew in between the vegetables with dogged persistence. The fence to keep the deer out needed repairing.

Pierre took care of the horses and fed the chickens and hogs, Adriaen's usual chores. Claudine scurried back and forth between the two houses gathering more towels and washbasins. Philippe looked up once to see Madeleine standing on Jean and Adriaen's porch, wiping her brow. She waved to Philippe and shook her head. No baby yet.

After he finished in the garden, Philippe repaired a break in the corral fence. He put his shirt on as the shadows lengthened into late afternoon. Then he split wood and stacked the logs against the house.

Vangie came out of the house struggling with a big black kettle and started up the path to Jean and Adriaen's.

Philippe jumped to her side. "Let me carry that for you."

"Thank you. I like having a big brother around again." She smiled at him. "I thought maybe they would like some stew for supper. Wait a minute, and I'll go back into the house and fetch the cornbread."

She seemed stronger than Philippe had seen her since he got home. She rejoined him quickly.

"You seem to be feeling well."

"I am. Better than I have in months. Maybe it's because you're back—or perhaps it's Adriaen's nettle brew."

He carried the kettle with one hand and held on to her arm with the other as they walked up the hill. The sun was slipping to the horizon in a gentle haze of pink and blue as they stepped onto the porch.

"Shouldn't the baby be here by now?" he asked. "Does it always take this long?"

"I would think so. Maman says that sometimes with a first baby it takes a long time." Her thick dark lashes fluttered on the milky white skin of her cheek. "I don't really know much about these kinds of things."

Philippe nodded. Just as they opened the door, they heard a scream that began low and rose to a tortuous pitch. Vangie's eyes grew wide. Philippe hung the kettle over the fireplace and looked around the room. Jean was pacing back and forth in front of the bedroom door with tears brimming in his eyes.

He wiped his face with a rag, went to Philippe, and embraced him. "It's been too long. It's been way too long. The baby should be here by now." He shook his head. "I'm so frightened, I can't even pray. I can't think what to say except 'Jesus, Jesus, Jesus.'"

Philippe held his uncle. "That is prayer enough."

Claudine emerged with bloody cloths and picked up clean ones. "Vangie, can you fetch more clean rags, please?"

"I'll go." Philippe went out the door as Adriaen screamed again.

"PUSH, ADRIAEN, PUSH!"

Adriaen could hear Madeleine instructing her through the haze of pain. She thrashed her head back and forth on the wet pillow. How long had she been bearing down? An hour? Two hours? All day? All sense of time blurred with the crush of each contraction. She'd known birthing a baby would be difficult, but she never dreamed the pain would overtake her like this. Here came another wave. She grabbed hold of the edge of the headboard and pushed as hard as she could. Blood spurted everywhere.

"What's wrong, Maddy? What's wrong? Why won't . . . why won't . . . ?"

"Try to rest between labor pangs. I can see the baby's head. He's almost—"

Another contraction interrupted Madeleine, and Adriaen felt like her body was being turned inside out. She squeezed her eyes shut and bore down again. Suddenly she felt a release and opened her eyes. Madeleine held a tiny, grayish-blue baby in her arms.

"It's a boy, Adriaen." Madeleine's voice was controlled—too controlled. She began to swing the baby back and forth and swat his little behind. Silence.

"Please, please, little one, breathe. Breathe!" Madeleine gathered the baby boy in her arms and jiggled him up and down. She spanked his bottom again. Still nothing. "Oh, Father, be merciful. Spare this babe."

Adriaen held her breath and, trembling, leaned up on one elbow. Then Madeleine hit his bottom hard again. The baby gasped and—then let out a cry. Madeleine laughed and began to cry at the same time.

"He's alive, Adriaen! He's breathing. He's going to be fine. You have a baby boy."

Adriaen exhaled and began to weep. "Let me see him. Let me hold him." She reached out her arms to hold her son.

"Just a minute, let us take care of the cord. Then you can have him." Claudine and Madeleine set about cutting the umbilical cord and cleaning the baby.

Adriaen crunched the quilt up in a ball in her fist. Another wave of pain overtook her. "Madeleine, something's not right. The pain returns!"

"That's just the afterbirth." Madeleine continued with her attention on the baby.

"No, something's wr-r-r-o-n-n-g!" Adriaen emitted another scream that pierced the room and beyond.

The door flew open and Jean came into the room, his eyes wild. "What's happening? I can't stand being out there. Adriaen?"

Madeleine thrust the baby into Jean's arms. "You have a son." And then she went to the end of the bed again and raised the quilt. Her eyes widened. "There's another one! I can see him. Claudine, come help me." Madeleine went to Adriaen's side and stroked her forehead with a wet cloth. "You've got to push again, Adriaen. You have twins! No wonder you were so big."

Adriaen groaned and tried to sit up.

"Can you do it? You've got to push another one out."

"I must do it." She nodded. "I can do it." She looked at Jean and reached out to him.

Her hand trembled as he came to her side and clutched it. He cuddled the little bundle in his other arm. His voice was hoarse. "Look, my dearest. We have a son." Tears spilled over the rims of his eyes and ran down his cheeks. "We have a son."

Adriaen looked at her husband and her new son. "He's so little.

He's so . . . ah-h-h-h . . . !" She clenched Jean's hand, her nails biting into his skin, and began to moan. Then the moan turned into another scream.

Claudine took the baby from Jean. "Push, Adriaen. You've got to push."

Madeleine looked up at Jean. "The baby is turned wrong."

"What does that mean?"

"Buttocks are coming out first instead of the head."

"Is that all right? Can he make it? What about Adriaen?"

"I don't know. I'm not a midwife, but I've heard that sometimes you can turn the baby around into position. If we don't get him out soon, I fear for both."

They stared at each other. "I can't . . . I can't lose Adriaen." He seized Madeleine's shoulders. "This cannot happen again. You must do something!"

"Pray. Go tell the others, and pray. I'll do the best I can."

Jean left the room. Adriaen heard voices in the other room being lifted to God in prayer. She grabbed hold of Madeleine's arm. "Do what you have to do to save the baby."

"I'm going to do what I have to do to save both of you."

Another labor pang wrapped its viselike claws around Adriaen's torso and compressed until she thought she was going to pass out. Then it subsided. She tasted blood and realized she had bitten her lip.

Madeleine stood alongside the bed and pulled Adriaen's gown aside to reveal her abdomen. "I'm going to try to turn the baby around. Tell me when another wave is coming." Madeleine looked up. "God, I can't do this. I don't know what to do, or how to do it, but you do. You know exactly what to do, so guide my hands. Please save this baby

131

and spare Adriaen's life as well. Please, Father. I'm begging you—spare these lives."

Adriaen nodded her head. Madeleine placed her hands on her sister-in-law's abdomen and began to attempt to turn the baby around. "I think he's moving." She went to the end of the bed and looked. "He's moving. He's moving."

"Here it comes."

"Try not to push this time."

"I can't . . . I can't help it." She grabbed hold of Madeleine's hand and rode out the pain.

Madeleine checked and groaned. "He flipped back around. He's still bottom first." She breathed in a long deep breath. "Let's try again." She began to press harder and harder on Adriaen's abdomen, trying to goad the baby to turn.

As the next labor pang began to build, Adriaen felt something different. "Another one, Maddy, but something's different. Something's different . . ." A groan began low in Adriaen's throat and finally erupted in a scream as she pushed as hard as she could.

"He's here! He flipped around. He's here. Oh my! He's a she!" The little one began to cry and turned pink immediately.

Again Jean burst into the room, slamming the door back against the wall. "Is she well? Is my Adriaen . . . ? Is she . . ."

Adriaen had slumped, panting, back on her pillow, and Jean gathered her up in his arms.

"Oh, Adriaen . . ." He wiped the perspiration from her face. "You are alive." He buried his head in her shoulder and wept. "I was so scared. I couldn't have . . . have gone on"—a sob interrupted him—"without you."

Adriaen caressed his cheek, then turned his face toward Madeleine and pointed. "Look what we have."

Jean wiped his eyes and looked at Madeleine, who held the bloody little girl in her arms.

"She's not cleaned up yet, but congratulations, Papa. You have a daughter as well."

"A daughter? We have a little girl too?"

"We do, my fine husband. You are now a father twice over." Adriaen sank down into the mattress and closed her eyes. "I didn't think I was going to make it."

"But you did. A jewel among women, my wife is." Jean looked around the room as Madeleine and Claudine finished cleaning the babies. "Isn't she? Isn't she the bravest woman in the world?"

"She is, indeed." Madeleine looked at her pale, spent sister-in-law. "Jean, why don't you take the babies to show everyone and give us time to clean things up?"

Jean nodded and took the two tiny bundles in his arms. He looked around and grinned at the birthing scene. "God is good and merciful, is he not?"

"He is. Now go on, and I'll call you back when we get things in order here."

Claudine opened the door for the new father. Squeals of excitement from Vangie could be heard as Madeleine closed it again.

Adriaen opened her eyes. "Is everything as it should be? There seems to be too much blood."

Madeleine touched her shoulder. "We need to deliver the afterbirth, and that will seem like copious amounts of blood. A first birth is always messy. I can't tell exactly, but it looks like you tore when your son came out. I'm afraid you are going to be very sore, and you will bleed for several weeks."

Adriaen laid her head back on the pillow and tried to rest. The two women cleaned the bed the best that they could and changed Adriaen's gown. Her body throbbed with pain and was numb at the same time. She felt almost too weak to sit up, but she wanted to hold her babies. "Let Jean back in. I want my babies."

"Can we get you anything?"

"Thirsty. I'm so thirsty."

Madeleine stuck her head out of the door and motioned for Jean to come back in. Vangie held one baby and Jean the other. "Bring the babies in, Jean. And, Vangie, would you get Adriaen a cup of fresh water, please? And get some wine as well."

Jean brought both babies in, still grinning, and laid his son in the new mother's arms. Adriaen bared her breast and let her son begin to suckle. She smiled at her husband as he cooed at his daughter. "What shall we name them?"

"Well, we had picked a boy's name . . . William Freedom." Jean smiled. "Is that still agreeable with you?"

"I like that. I have an idea for our daughter. What would you think about Liberty Nicole?"

"After my mother, Nicole. I like it. I like it very much. Freedom and Liberty. Good New World names. The Clavell heritage continues."

Madeleine stood at the door. "May I call the others in?"

"Give me a minute to let Liberty nurse. Then by all means, let them in. Claudine, would you pull my hair back please? I'm sure I look a mess."

Jean chuckled. "Women. Always concerned with how they look. After what you've been through, why do you care?"

"Because I want my handsome husband to continue to find me fair."

"I will never stray far from your side, my wonderful wife . . . and now mother of my two children."

The others shuffled in quietly and gave Adriaen hugs and congratulations. The babies blinked and looked around with glazed eyes.

Pierre and Madeleine stepped out on the porch. She sidled up to her husband and sighed. "New life. What a miracle! I feared for a bit that the babe—babes—were not going to make it. Adriaen as well." She looked up at him. "Do you regret that we never had any children of our own?"

He looked into her dark eyes and caressed her cheek. "Honestly?"

Madeleine nodded.

"Sometimes. Of course, I love Philippe and Charles and Princess as if they were mine. But when I see a proud couple with a new baby, sometimes I . . ." He hugged his wife close to his chest. "But I don't regret a thing. I have you, and that is enough for me."

Philippe leaned against the outside door of his room and looked up at the stars. Supper had been late, but the family had finally settled down. The lights were still burning in Jean and Adriaen's cabin. From time to time he could hear a baby cry. Claudine had stayed with the new family; Pierre and Madeleine and Vangie had retired.

Philippe wasn't sleepy. He had been nine when Vangie was born, but he was too young to be aware of the life-and-death struggle his mother went through to bring her into the world. He empathized with Jean better now and realized why losing his first wife and baby had changed him. No wonder his uncle had been so paternal toward him and Charles and Vangie. The family relationships the Clavells shared suddenly took on layers of meaning that he had not understood before. It was as if a new page in a book had been turned.

Philippe walked around the house and surveyed the land under the eerie glow of the full moon. He was overwhelmed with God's goodness to their family. A verse from the Psalms came to him: *What is man that thou art mindful of him?* He felt very small in the grand scheme of things.

As he walked, his thoughts drifted to what might have been—children, a home, a family. He found himself wishing that God would allow Bridget to be part of his destiny. But she was Catholic. It could never be. What if she converted? He shook his head. He was chasing rainbows. He had made the break, and it could never be. He walked back to his room and went to bed.

TWELVE

The family gathered at David and Ella's to celebrate Edward and Bridget's engagement. The courtship had droned on through the summer like the never-ending hot, humid days, filled with visits from Edward and chaperoned rides in the country. He had finally proposed in late October.

The first snow of the season came early that November and covered the ground with a beautiful blanket of white. The table glistened with the Osbornes' best china and crystal that had been carried across the ocean from England when they came to Philadelphia. Bridget looked around at her family—laughing, eating, and toasting with a continual clinking of glasses. Everybody seemed thrilled—everybody except the bride-to-be.

Edward leaned toward her and took her hand. "You are awfully quiet tonight. You look ravishing, by the way. Your blue dress matches your eyes perfectly." He touched her sleeve. "I prefer you in blue, so

I hope your wardrobe contains plenty of blue gowns. If not, we will remedy that once we are married." He looked into her eyes and gave her a smile.

He genuinely was a nice-looking man, if one had a disposition toward a polished, slick appearance.

"Thank you." Bridget pulled her hand away, then noticed Edward's expression cloud. "I'm a bit . . . overwhelmed by this whole thing."

"You mean, becoming engaged, or the big family gathering?"

"Becoming engaged. I'm used to our family gatherings."

"And there will be more such gatherings." Edward's countenance cleared. "We are going to be the couple everyone desires to have at their affairs. And you will be the most beautiful lady of all. I am unbelievably lucky to have you as my fiancée."

"Oh, Edward." Bridget pouted. "You know I'm not very comfortable with that kind of social calendar. I'd rather be on the farm, riding my horse."

Edward smiled indulgently. "You will get used to it. And you will certainly still ride. My stable is full of exquisite horses."

"None like my Kimi."

Edward sat back and picked up his wineglass. "My dear, you can ride whatever horse you desire to your heart's content." He took a sip of wine and smiled, but his eyes remained cool. "That is, until we are expecting our first child. And that, I'm hoping, will be right away. I don't want to wait too long to become a father."

Bridget felt a shiver run down her spine. The wedding date would arrive sooner than she desired. The banns would be read for three Sundays beginning that very week, but her heart still resisted the idea.

Bradley stood, tapping his glass for attention, and the room grew quiet. "Ladies and gentlemen, I wish to offer a toast to the happy couple. May they enjoy wedded bliss, such as my good wife and I do." He looked at his wife, who ducked her head and blushed. "And may they need a cradle nine months from the wedding night—if not sooner!"

Boisterous laughter rolled over the room. Sarah swatted at her nephew. "Bradley, behave yourself!"

Bradley threw back his head and bellowed his characteristic laugh. "I have another announcement to make. We cannot loan the new couple our cradle, for Penny and I will be needing it for our newest arrival in about six months." The room broke into applause.

"Congratulations!"

"Good news!"

Penelope blushed an even deeper shade of pink.

Bridget shook her head and smiled as the dinner conversation swirled and eddied around the table. She was happy for her cousin. Bradley and Penny were good parents, and she could picture them having many children through the years. Nearly every one of her friends had needed a cradle sooner than nine months after the wedding, including Bradley and Penelope, but she was determined that would not happen to her. Edward Moorehead would need the blessing of the priest to claim his rights as a husband and not one second before.

Edward put his arm around her shoulders, playing with the lace ruffle on the shoulder of her dress. She stiffened, and he moved his arm to rest on the back of the chair. Her skin crawled at his touch. She wondered if all women felt this way if they were not in love with their prospective husbands. She couldn't imagine living the rest of her life avoiding her husband's touch.

Edward turned his head slightly in her direction. His attention lingered at the bustline of her gown. "What deep thoughts are running through that pretty head of yours? You seem in another world."

"I was thinking about our wedding and our . . . married life together." She looked down and then into his eyes. They were rather interesting eyes—hazel with a dark brown rim around them. They seemed to change colors with whatever he wore. And he took great care in his wardrobe. Of that fact she was very aware. Something about his eyes . . . she searched his face for several seconds.

He tilted her chin with the tips of his fingers. "I am looking forward to a lifetime of drowning in the blue ocean of your beautiful eyes." He reached into the pocket of his vest. "I have something for you." He pulled out a small box.

Bridget took the box and stared at him.

His eyes softened as he smiled at her. "Go ahead. Open it."

She opened it and gasped. Lying on black velvet cloth was a dazzling gold brooch, inset with diamonds. "O-o-h, Edward."

At that moment, as she looked into his eyes, he seemed like a little boy who wanted only to hear a word of praise.

"It . . . it's lovely."

"Do you like it? It was my mother's."

"I do like it. I like it very much. Thank you."

Edward took the brooch from the box and pinned it on the bodice of her dress. His fingers lingered a bit too long, closing the window of warmth she'd briefly felt.

THE CELEBRATION LASTED LATE INTO THE NIGHT, BUT Bridget rose early the next morning. She had experienced difficulty sleeping ever since Philippe left. She didn't always get out of bed, but she awoke early most mornings, then tossed and turned until daylight. She'd slept more fitfully than ever last night. Sharing Ella's bed and hearing Davey's little unfamiliar baby noises during the night added to her sleeplessness. It wasn't the same as it had been when they were growing up, sharing secrets at night and giggling until the wee hours whenever Ella visited at Whisper Wood.

Bridget didn't want to get up and wander through the house and wake everyone else, so she scurried barefoot across the cold floor and added a log to the fire. Then she got back into bed and pulled the down comforter up around her neck. The room was freezing.

It must have snowed all night, and soft flakes were still coming down—lightly now. She loved how still the earth seemed when it snowed. She dozed off and awoke as the sunlight began to filter through the curtains. Ella and the baby were gone. This time she put on her robe and slippers. The fire was crackling and had chased the chill from the room. A servant knocked softly and entered.

Bridget waved toward the fireplace. "I got up earlier and put a log on the fire. It was so cold. You might want to add more wood."

"Yes, ma'am. Is Mistress Bridget ready for breakfast?"

"Just some hot cider for now. Thank you. Where is Ella?"

"Downstairs feeding the baby. They've not been up long either."

Edward had gone to his own house last night. Bridget was glad she didn't have to face him first thing. She didn't look forward to seeing him later in the day either, when he and Amos planned to finish the dowry arrangements. Opening the door, she looked across the hallway to the room her father and David had slept in last night. It seemed to be vacant. She closed her door and walked to the window in the hallway that looked out on the street. Horses and buggies were *clip-clop*ping along in the snow, and people hurried along the rickety walks with their heads down and mufflers snuggled around their necks.

She returned to her room. The servant set a tray on the table with cider and sorghum cake, and then busied herself with her chores. The snow had nearly ceased, and the sun poked through the cloudy sky, brightening the room. The few remaining falling snow crystals created dazzling prisms of light as they danced in the air.

Bridget felt lazy and once again pulled the covers around her. "I don't want to get up."

"Yes, ma'am. Is there anything else that I can do for you?"

"No, thank you. You may leave the tray for now."

As the servant went out the door, Bridget heard the front door slam shut and male voices downstairs. She recognized the voice of Edward Moorehead and groaned—so early. Pulling the covers up over her head, she squeezed her eyelids tight like a little girl, and hot tears seeped through them. Turning over, she stuck her head out from under the covers. A rush of cool air hit her flushed face, and she sat up. She fought back tears.

How am I going to go through with this when my heart is knit to another? To pretend to love does not produce love. Or does it? Perhaps, as Father and Mother say, one can learn to love. Perhaps I am wrong. I know I will be well provided for. We will have a prosperous life. I pray I am wrong. Please, God, please let me be wrong.

ON THE OTHER SIDE OF PHILADELPHIA, CHARLES TRUDGED through the snow from the well into the kitchen. He set the water bucket on the table, blew into his hands, and stamped the snow from his boots. Goody Wallace spooned up a bowl of gruel and set a stein of hot cider on the table.

"'Tis a cold morning, Goody Wallace."

"Yes, and you're tracking mud and snow into my kitchen."

"I'm sorry." Charles smiled.

"How much longer do you have here?" Her voice softened.

"Three more years until I'm one and twenty." Charles finished his bowl of gruel and held it out for more. "Since I was so young when I came here, I will have served longer than most by the time Zwicken releases me. My family is hoping we can strike a bargain with him and pay out the rest of the redemption money."

"*Humph!* Fat chance of that happening. He has too good a worker in you—skilled and compliant. Nobody else has your kind of talent to make the wooden stocks fit the guns. Yours are a work of art."

"In reality, we've more than paid back the money for our passage. It's not fair for him to keep me."

"Fair has nothing to do with it. When you have money, you make the decisions. We poor folk are beholden to those who hold the purse strings."

"Don't I know that? When we were in France . . ."

"Young man . . ." Goody Wallace waved her spoon at Charles. "You're not the son of a rich landowner in France anymore. If you were, you wouldn't be in this predicament." She took his emptied bowl for the second time. "At least you get your fill every day and have a place to sleep. Some don't fare that well. Now get to work."

The bench squealed as Charles stood and pushed it back from the table. "I'm grateful for the good food that you put on the table, Goody Wallace. Don't think I'm not, but I'm not sure that I can—"

She faced him with her fists on her hips, the spoon jutting out crazily. "That you can what? Don't you be thinking of doing anything stupid." She thrust the spoon down into the kettle of gruel.

He took a last swig from the stein and handed it to her. "Don't worry." Then he gave her a peck on her forehead. "Thank you."

"*Pshaw!* Go on now!" She shooed him away.

Charles started into the shop.

"Charles?"

He turned back toward the cook.

"Should it come to that—I don't want to know." Her wrinkled eyes reddened. "I wouldn't blame you, but I don't want to be privy to any of your plans. Understand me?"

Charles nodded, then broke into a smile. "Why, Goody Wallace, if I had plans to do anything drastic, the only clue you'd have would be that some of your good biscuits would be missing. I wouldn't leave without tucking some of those into my bag."

She waved her spoon at him again. "Did you hear what I said, Clavell?"

"I heard you." He grinned and left her standing in front of the fireplace. He picked up a packing crate and carried it to his workbench to ready the latest batch of gun repairs for transport. He just needed to check the stocks on a couple of the flintlock rifles, and the shipment was ready to go.

Standing instead of sitting at his station, he polished and trimmed the wood. He could detect the slightest imperfection as he passed his fingers over the smooth finish. He savored how a perfectly weighted gun felt in his hands. Some customers preferred to make their own stocks, but those who knew the fine craftsmanship of Charles Clavell paid Zwicken a high price to obtain one of his.

Other employees drifted into the shop and exchanged greetings. One of the men had stirred the fire, and it was crackling. "Hey, Charles, you fell down on your job. The fire was getting low."

"Sorry, I was talking to Cook." Charles slapped his colleague on the shoulder. "You did such a fine job, I should turn it over to you permanently."

Zwicken's shadow darkened the doorway from his office into the shop. "Cut the chatter, men, and get to work. We have a shipment to get out today."

The men scattered to their workbenches. "Didn't know Mister Sunshine was in the office," Ben grumbled under his breath. He was a newly indentured servant and recently married; Charles knew this because Ben's workbench sat next to his own.

Zwicken paused and looked over his shoulder. "What's that?"

Charles spoke up. "Nothing, sir. I just said that I was glad we finally had the light of sunshine today. Makes it easier to see the finishing details in the wood."

"*Mmm.* Like I said, cut the chatter and get to work. Since the sunshine makes your work so much easier, you should put out twice the work today, eh?"

"Yes, sir."

Zwicken closed the door and left the men to their labor.

Ben exhaled. "Thanks, Charles."

"Zwicken is not an easy man to work for. He's a hard taskmaster, and if he suspects any insubordination . . . well, you're in trouble. Just do your job and try to stay out of his way. At least we have shelter and good food."

"I don't know how you've managed all these years. I'm chafing to get out of here after only a few months."

The two young men polished the stocks on the rifles as they talked.

"At least Dorcas and I were bought by the same household. I would have been half crazed if she had been purchased by another employer."

"You do what you have to do." Charles picked up an armful of rifles and started placing them in the crate. "My brother was released from his employer a few weeks ago and joined our family in the Schuylkill Valley. I've served six years. I yearn for the day I can be with them as well."

Ben shook his head. "I don't know if I can do this."

"You can do it. For the sake of your wife and future family, you must do it."

The two young men worked side by side all morning and into the afternoon. Before sealing the crates, Charles threw his arms toward the ceiling and stretched. "Let me see if Zwicken wants to inspect the shipment before we seal them up. Take a break."

He paused at the office door and knocked. He could hear voices. "Enter."

Charles pushed the door open and saw Edward Moorehead sitting across the desk from Zwicken. "Excuse me, sir. Do you want to take a look at the rifles before we seal the crates?"

Zwicken made a circle with his fingers from his mustache around his chin. "No, I trust you, Clavell. Go ahead and close 'em up." He motioned toward Moorehead. "Congratulate my friend. He has become betrothed to a most desirable and beautiful young lady."

Charles smiled and nodded. "Yes, indeed. And who is the fortunate recipient of your proposal?"

Moorehead looked at Charles through his quizzing glass. "Unusual manners for a servant."

Zwicken chortled. "*Sir* Charles grew up minor nobility in France, and he's never outgrown thinking himself a gentleman. Though I must say his refined courtesies come in handy sometimes."

"*Humph*. A bit uppity if you ask me. If you are, as you say, minor royalty, what are you doing as an indentured servant in our shop?"

"I didn't say. Mister Zwicken did." He looked at his employer, then back at Edward. "I was only twelve when we crossed over. My mother's jewelry chest, which contained most of our money, was stolen on board ship. It contained the remainder of our passage money."

"How sad." Moorehead replaced his glass in his pocket. "No one you would know."

"Sir?"

"My fiancée is no one you would know."

Zwicken smirked. "Oh, but you are mistaken, my friend. His brother works for the Barringtons. You've probably seen him—the tall, dark servant, Philippe."

"Ah, yes." Edward looked at Charles from head to foot. "You don't look much like brothers."

"I know. We hear that frequently." He cleared his throat. "You have become engaged to Mistress Barrington?"

"I have. Just completed the details of the dowry arrangements this morning. I am to take Miss Barrington and her parents for a sleigh ride this afternoon to see my house and holdings here in Philadelphia, and to meet my dowager aunt." He chuckled. "Now, Auntie Margo, she's the real chief of affairs, if the truth be known. The Barringtons have been to my home, of course, but have not seen the extent of my . . . my true wealth."

Charles maintained his composure and gave a slight bow to Moorehead. "My congratulations. Excuse me, I need to get back to work." He turned to go. "When is the happy occasion?"

"We shall marry at Christmas."

"Again, my congratulations."

Zwicken shuffled some papers on his desk. "Load the crates and deliver them to Mister Moorehead's this afternoon."

Edward stood and slung his cloak around his shoulders. "Yes, you may arrive before I do. If so, proceed to the back of the house and unload them onto the wagon. My valet was to have it ready to receive the crates."

"Yes, sir." Charles closed the door and started back to his workbench. His knees had turned to water, and he sat down. Christmas. Only a few weeks away. Mistress Barrington had no idea she was betrothed to a swindler and murderer.

THIRTEEN

Bridget, cloaked in a blue woolen cape trimmed in white fur, hood, and muff, took Edward's hand as she descended from the carriage at his impressive Tudor-style home on the opposite side of Philadelphia from David and Ella's house. Amos and Sarah followed, with Sarah chattering about the snow and the lovely shutters on the windows and the upcoming wedding. The three windows on the second story looked like a set of eyes and a nose to Bridget, with the matching gables serving as eyebrows. The house seemed to be a silent guard watching the comings and goings on the street. Small balconies jutted from the windows. The front door, in the middle between two windows, opened onto a small porch with rounded steps leading to the ground.

Bridget did not care for the close proximity of the house to the street. She preferred the long circular driveway bordered by the lush trees and open fields at Whisper Wood. The houses in town made her feel confined and restricted. The spindly masts of ships docked in the harbor behind the house were lined up like schoolchildren awaiting their assignments.

However, nice hemlocks did border the front of the house and shouldered the snow like a fur cape. Pin oaks stood along the street and jutted their scrawny limbs into the sky as if begging the sun to warm them. A lone streetlamp sat in front of the house.

Edward instructed his servant to take the carriage to the back of the house to the small stable. Then he ushered the Barringtons up the steps and into the large foyer.

Dark, Bridget thought. *It is depressing and dark, although quite elegant.*

A highly polished wooden staircase wound gently to the upper floor. Bridget's eyes followed the lines of the stairs, and she strained to see what lay beyond them. She had attended a ball here shortly after Edward began to court her, but she had seen only the bottom floor of the house.

A tall, slender, stoic valet took the Barringtons' wraps and motioned them into the parlor. The diamond brooch unveiled at the neckline of her dress glinted in the candlelight, and Edward noticed. "It suits you," he said quietly, then touched her arm. "I'll give you a tour of the house later."

She looked at the multiple bookcases filled with volumes, the tapestry hangings on the walls, and the tall windows, festooned with heavy draperies. Soon she would be the mistress of this imposing household. The place definitely needed a woman's touch.

"If you will excuse me for a moment, I need to attend to a matter." Edward had not removed his outer garments. "Make yourselves comfortable. I'll only be a moment." He turned and disappeared down the hallway.

Bridget circled the room, picking up a book here and there, fingering the draperies.

"Bridget, mind your manners." Sarah sat on the edge of the sofa, rigid and upright.

"This is to be my house soon. I'm simply making note of things I want to change." She pulled the draperies back and fastened them on the large brass hooks on the sides of the windows, letting in what little light was available through the snow clouds. "The first thing we are going to do is get some light in this gloomy place."

"*Ahem.*" The valet stood at the door with a young maidservant carrying a silver tray with tea and scones. He looked at the windows.

Bridget moved to the second set of windows. "You may set the tray on the table. Thank you."

The servants exited the room.

"Now, isn't that better?" She traced her finger over a shelf on the bookcase. "Except that now it shows all the dust." She brushed her hands together. "Oh well, that's what housekeepers are for, right?"

"It would behoove you to be gracious as you move into the role of mistress of this house. It will not sit well with the servants for you to begin to change routines immediately." Amos chewed on his pipe. "You must be wise. It will go better for you in the long run."

Bridget nodded. "Of course, you're right, Father."

Sarah poured tea for them. Bridget went to the window with her teacup in her hand and looked out. "But it feels like a dungeon in here. I simply wanted to bring some light into the room."

A wagon turned into the alley that ran beside the house and headed toward the harbor. A young man with red hair sticking out from under his cap drove the wagon, which was loaded down with several crates. Another young man sat beside him on the driver's perch. The crates were labeled *Zwicken's Foundry*. She craned her neck to watch until the wagon turned the corner to the back of the house.

Zwicken's Foundry. A redheaded servant. That's Charles! That's Philippe's brother!

Bridget set her cup down on the tray with a clang and ran from the room, down the hallway in the direction Edward had gone, stopping at the entrance to the kitchen.

The maid looked up and bobbed a curtsy. "May I help you, mistress?"

"Uh, yes. Where did Master Moorehead go?"

The maid pointed to the door at the rear of the kitchen. "He went outside to check on a shipment."

"Thank you." Bridget cracked the door open and looked out.

Dark clouds had blotted out the sun, and it had begun to snow again. Edward, holding a sheet of parchment, stood with his valet beside the wagon, as if he were checking off items as the two young men began to unload the crates onto another wagon. The redhead stepped toward Edward with a pad in his hand.

Bridget stepped onto the landing. "Edward?"

Edward's head swiveled around abruptly. "Bridget! Do get inside. It's begun to snow again, and you have no wrap. You'll catch your death."

"Are you coming back for tea?" She stared at the redheaded boy, who looked up at her, his soft brown eyes focusing on hers. He smiled hesitantly. It was Philippe's smile.

"Yes, but I need to check these goods. I shall be right there. Now, back inside with you."

"Very well. Do hurry though." She disliked the condescending manner in which he spoke to her, as if she were a child.

"I shall be in shortly."

Bridget returned to the kitchen, but tiptoed to watch out the window. She was desperate for news of Philippe. Had Charles seen him? Somehow she must talk to him.

The young man with Charles finished unloading the crates, and Edward and Charles headed up the steps to the kitchen. She remained at the window and watched as they stamped the snow off their boots and entered the warmth of the house.

Edward looked at her with surprise as she helped him off with his cloak. "Why, thank you, my dear. Now, if you will excuse us . . ."

Bridget looked at Charles as she hung Edward's cloak on a peg. "Do I know you? You look awfully familiar."

Charles gave a slight bow. "I don't think so, mistress, but the pleasure is mine."

Edward took the inventory list from Charles. "Bridget, this is Charles Clavell. He is one of Zwicken's best craftsmen at our foundry."

"Clavell! Why, of course. You are Philippe's brother. I'm Bridget Barrington—Philippe was one of our favorite indentured servants for many years. You're the brother he always went to visit when we came to town."

Charles grinned and took off his cap. "Yes, Mistress Barrington, I am that Charles Clavell."

"How does your brother fare? We . . . he is sorely missed at our estate. I fear we've found no one as good as he with our horses." She searched Charles' eyes. "My father has not been able to replace him."

"I'm sure he is well. We had a good visit the night before he went to the Schuylkill Valley to be with our family. He . . . he caught me up on everything . . . everything concerning his departure . . . but I've not seen him since."

Edward looked up from the inventory list. "Well, if you two have caught up on the state of the world, my dear, may we finish our business dealings here, please?" He turned to pick up a quill on a table beside the door that served as a desk and scribbled something on the bill of sale. Edward's caustic tone ended the conversation, but not before Bridget had discerned the double meanings tucked into Charles' sentences.

"Wait here a moment, Clavell. I have something I need you to take back to the foundry." Edward ducked into a small adjoining room.

Charles turned to Bridget, his eyes darkened. "It is urgent I speak with you."

She caught her breath. What could this mean? "How?"

"Come to the foundry, if you can . . ."

Edward came back into the room with a handsome rifle in his arms. "The stock on this just doesn't feel right. You are the expert. Fix it for me." He looked at Bridget. "You may go back into the parlor. I'll be joining you shortly."

"Of course." She turned and left the kitchen, her heart thudding in her chest. Why did Charles need to speak with her? Did he have news of Philippe?

"You look as if you've seen a ghost." Sarah rose and started toward her daughter.

"It's nothing, Mother. I merely stepped outside without a cloak, and it rather took my breath away." She moved to the window and looked out on the alley.

The now-empty wagon made the turn from the back of the house and slowly rumbled down the alley toward the street. As it drove by the side of the house, Charles looked up and into the window where Bridget stood. She smiled and nodded. He tipped his hat and chucked the reins. The empty wagon jostled over the ruts in the alley and disappeared quickly into the increasing snowfall.

FOURTEEN

Edward returned to his guests, blowing into his hands. "I'm afraid we are in for a storm." He looked around the parlor at the open draperies. "Do you prefer the draperies open, my dear?"

Bridget flirted with him. "You have such a beautiful home here, why hide it in the shadows?"

"You are right. You see, you have already begun to bring lightness to this household. I knew you would be good for this lonely bachelor. Open they shall remain then, except at night, of course." He walked to the windows and closed the draperies.

"Lonely bachelor, indeed. Not from what I've gathered. I've heard you are quite popular with the ladies." She dared a rebuttal with her eyes.

"Bridget!" Sarah wrung her hands, and Amos looked up from his pipe.

"Oh, *pshaw*, Mother. I'm just teasing him. Every man likes to think that he sets all the young ladies' hearts aflutter, doesn't he?" She laughed and tossed her hair behind her shoulder.

Edward turned from the window toward Bridget and smiled. He took out his quizzing glass and looked at her. "Naturally, my dear. But I'm afraid you have heard only rumor and gossip. I spend many a long night in this dreary house alone, except for my aunt, Dame Margo . . . and Stuart, of course. You are going to be as refreshing as springtime to this household." He reached beside the drapery and pulled the bell cord for the servants. "The storm is worsening. I don't think we should take the sleigh out again if the weather continues to deteriorate."

The valet entered.

"Light the lanterns. My beloved likes light. We shall accommodate her. Her every wish is your command—anything her heart desires. Is that understood?"

The valet bowed slightly. "Yes, sir."

Edward extended his arm. "Now that business has been taken care of, I would like to introduce you to my aunt. I moved her with me here from New York. Her room is upstairs. She never leaves it, but she is eager to meet the young lady who has stolen my heart." He started toward the stairs, motioning for Sarah and Amos to follow them. "Stuart, I would like an early supper. The Barringtons will be spending the night with us. I don't want to get back out in the weather. Instruct Sophie to see that the guest rooms are in order."

"Very well, sir."

"Thank you. I'm afraid our tea has gotten cold. Would you see to it that it is refreshed, and have Sophie bring it to Dame Margo's room while I show the Barringtons around? We shall take tea with her. That will be all." Edward dismissed the servant with a flick of his wrist.

The servant picked up the tray and disappeared around the stairs and down the hallway.

"Has ... umm ... Stuart been with you long?" Bridget watched his long stride take him toward the kitchen as they ascended the stairs.

"Ever since I was a child. I wouldn't know how to get along without him."

"He's rather somber."

"You'll get used to him. He's very efficient and is a genius at anticipating my every need."

"How does he feel about having a new mistress in the house?"

"Never thought about it. He will do whatever I ask him to do." Edward put his arm around Bridget's shoulders as they reached the first landing. "Don't worry your pretty head about that. You will fit in fine here. And you shall have a maidservant all to yourself."

"I would like to bring Abigail with me."

"I suppose that could be arranged."

"She's married and has two children—one a baby."

"We have room, if your father can spare them." Edward turned to Amos.

"They are a good family, and I would feel good about them coming with Bridget to your household." Amos cleared his throat. "But, Gigi, don't you think it best for Abigail to stay at Whisper Wood? It is a good place to raise children; they will have room to play there."

Bridget sighed. She knew her father was right.

"Don't fret, love," Edward said. "We shall arrange for Sophie to attend you. And I shall make sure you have everything you need." He motioned to Amos and Sarah. "Come. Let me show you the rest of the house, then we'll go meet Auntie Margo. I think you will be pleased at your daughter's new residence."

Sarah and Amos exclaimed at the beauty and fine craftsmanship of the house as Edward showed them around. He proudly announced which room would be Bridget's, adjacent to his bedroom with an adjoining door. The canopied, curtained bed boasted beautiful ivory linens and furniture that was lighter wood than the darker tones of the other rooms. Edward walked to the bedside table and lit a lantern. A lovely vanity sat beside the tall, diamond-paned window with a large wardrobe on the other side of the bed. An upholstered chair with a heart-shaped back matched the vanity.

Bridget walked to the chair and sat in it. "What a charming room."

"I'm glad you are pleased with it." Edward beamed. "We've been working on it to make it fit for a new bride. I'm afraid it was a rather stodgy room initially. Come, my dear." Edward ushered them back into the hall.

He did not show them his harbor holdings because of the bitter cold, but the house sat not far from the docks, and he spoke glowing reports of how good the business of exporting and importing had been for him.

Finally they approached a set of arched, dark, ornately carved double doors with brass handles that sat at the opposite end of the second floor from the bedrooms. Light shone from beneath the doors. Edward knocked on the door. "Auntie Margo? I have someone here I want you to meet."

"Enter."

Edward smiled at Bridget and held the door open as the Barringtons eased into the stuffy room. The room, dimly lit with lanterns, fairly glowed red. Everything in the room was red—red draperies, red bedcover, red upholstered chairs, red walls—and on a red chaise sat a rotund woman in a red dress and red shoes, fanning herself with a red fan. Two red dogs scurried back and forth and began to yip at them.

"Quiet." The stout lady leaned up and patted her lap. The dogs jumped onto the chaise, circled, and curled up at her feet. She smiled, showing blackened teeth, her eyes disappearing into her full cheeks.

"Auntie Margo, I would like for you to meet my fiancée, Bridget."

The Barringtons inched into the room.

"Yes, yes. Come, come closer, so I can see you, my dear. I want to see if my nephew has finally had the good taste to choose wisely for his bride." She cackled. "Thought he never would get married, this one."

Edward nudged her elbow. Bridget moved to the side of the chaise as Dame Margo looked through her spectacles at her. "Oh my. She's a young one, isn't she?" She looked at Edward and cackled again. "You neglected to mention that, nephew."

"I didn't think it was relevant."

"All the more time to have lots of babies. We need to get about extending our heritage, don't we, dear? Particularly since I never married."

The dowager reached out a wrinkled hand. Bridget took it and moved even closer.

"I don't see so well, my dear." She reached up and touched Bridget's hair. "Blonde. You two will make a good match. Sit. Sit." Dame Margo motioned to Bridget to sit in a chair next to the chaise.

"Auntie Margo, may I present Mister and Dame Barrington, Bridget's parents."

"Yes, how do you do? Please find a place to sit."

Sophie entered with the tray of tea and scones and set them on a table at the foot of the chaise. Edward motioned for the maid to serve the tea.

"Now, how do you feel, my young Bridget, at becoming the mistress of this household?"

"How do *you* feel at the prospect of having a new mistress of the Moorehead household?"

"Ah! Ah! A young woman with spunk! No wonder my Edward has fallen for you." Dame Margo clapped her hands together like a child. "How delightful. We are going to get along just fine."

As they left the dowager's room, Edward took Bridget's hand. "Magnificent, my dear. You won her over. Not many people do. If you pay her a bit of attention every day, you will get along splendidly. Just take care never to get on her bad side. Once you do, there's no turning back." He kissed her hand.

They moved into the large dining room and ate a light supper of stew, bread, and cheese, served by Stuart and Sophie, but Bridget noticed other servants coming and going. "How many servants do you . . . do we . . . have, Edward?"

"Eight house servants and fifteen or so in the stable and on the docks. Then at the country estate I've lost count. I think I have ten house servants and thirty or more slaves working the fields and the stables. I probably won't have a chance to show you that piece of property before the wedding, but we shall go out in the spring. It's a bit more rustic than this house, but I have a feeling you will feel more at home there."

"You have slaves?"

"I treat them well. It takes quite a labor force to keep the farm running. As I'm sure your father understands."

"Yes, but we don't have slaves, we have servants."

"What's the difference?" Edward reached over and patted her hand.

Withdrawing her hand and placing her napkin on the table, she retorted, "Don't patronize me, Edward. I may be young, but I'm not stupid. Servants eventually gain their freedom. Slaves remain in bondage forever."

Edward patted around his mouth with his napkin. "My slaves are content. I provide well for them—they have a place to live and food to eat. Families are together."

"They are still slaves."

A barely detectable pall of darkness slid across Edward's face, then vanished as quickly as it had appeared. He smiled. "Come, now. Let's not ruin a perfectly nice evening by getting into a discussion about slavery. It's a necessary fact of life, distasteful though it may be at times. You'll adjust to it. Let's adjourn to the parlor."

Edward stood and ushered the Barringtons into the adjoining room. The discussion was over. Bridget sat in a chair, nonconversant for the rest of the evening, and the others ignored her ill humor. Amos and Sarah asked Edward pertinent questions about his holdings and assets, and discussed the upcoming wedding.

Finally Bridget stood and covered her mouth as she yawned. "If you will excuse me, please, I would like to retire."

Edward and Amos stood as well. Edward picked up a lantern. "I shall accompany you."

"That's not necessary."

"Not necessary, but my pleasure."

Amos motioned to Sarah. "I believe we shall do the same. It's been a long day."

The little group wound their way up the massive staircase, the lantern casting a circle of dim light. Amos and Sarah said their good nights and went into their room.

Edward walked Bridget to her room at the end of the hall. "Sleep well, my love. I'm right next door . . . if you should need anything."

"I believe I have everything I need."

Edward leaned in to kiss her and she turned her head, causing the kiss to land impotently on her cheek. He set the lantern on a large table beside the door, then took her in his arms, turning her face to him, and kissed her gently on the lips. This was not their first kiss. He had stolen brushes across her lips in the carriage or as they sat on the couch when Amos and Sarah turned their backs for a moment.

Bridget pushed against him and leaned back to look in his eyes. She did find the kiss rather pleasant, but she continued to hold him away from her.

He leaned toward her again, this time pulling her against his body. He grabbed her chin and jerked her face toward him, and his expression turned into a scowl. "I am your husband-to-be. You'll not ever push me away—especially not in my own house." He kissed her again—his mouth came down on hers hard and demanding.

Struggling against him, at last she managed to wrench herself free. He seized her wrist and twisted her arm around to her back. The buttons on his jacket scraped against her cheek as he yanked her against his body. The residue of tobacco on his clothing and the stale wine on his breath made her stomach turn. Tracing her face with his finger, his hand wandered down the side of her neck and then trailed across the low neckline of her bodice to the brooch. Her skin prickled. He wound his fingers in her hair with the other hand, forcing her to look up at him. He stared at her and moved toward her again.

Bridget pushed back from him with her forearm. "Stop right there. We're not married yet, and you'll not have any privileges until the priest pronounces us man and wife."

Edward still held her head in his hand. He looked her over—from her eyes down to the front of her bodice—and then slowly released her. A slow, grim smile lifted the corners of his mouth. "You're a feisty one, aren't you? You're a filly that needs to be broken in . . . and I'm just the one who can do that. Yes, with great pleasure, I will do that."

He opened the door to her room and let her in. Then he picked up the lantern and disappeared down the hall. Bridget locked the door behind her and checked to be sure the lock on the door into Edward's room was latched. She pulled a table over in front of it. The cruel, insistent kiss of her husband-to-be burned on her lips. She wiped her mouth with the back of her hand and fell into the heart-shaped chair and wept—wept for what was and for what might have been.

FIFTEEN

Sophie knocked softly on Bridget's door. She rattled the door handle. Bridget jumped out of bed and went to the door. "Just a minute, please." She looked at the table in front of the door leading to Edward's room. "Uh, could you bring me some hot cider, please?"

"I have it right here, mistress."

"Just . . . just a moment." Bridget pushed the table away from the door and grimaced as it scraped against the wooden floor. She unlocked her bedroom door. "Come in. Uh . . . I'm used to locking my door at night."

The maid nodded and hurried into the room. She set the tray of hot cider and porridge on the table and went to the fireplace to stir the ashes. As she coaxed the embers into a flame, the young girl tucked her hair from around her face back into her cap, and Bridget noticed a reddening bruise on Sophie's cheek.

Bridget frowned. "That's a nasty-looking bruise."

"It . . . it's nothing. I stumbled into a . . . a door last night."

"*Hmm.*" Bridget looked around the room. "Is there a robe I may use?"

"In the wardrobe."

She found a robe in the large armoire and belted it around her. It puddled around her feet. She looked out the window at the snowfall. The street and trees stood stiffened with the icy lace. Were they going to be able to get home today? She would insist that they at least return to David and Ella's. She didn't like being in the big, cold house. Rubbing her wrist where Edward had gripped her last night, she looked at her skin and realized it was bruised and tender. She wiped her mouth again where he had forced his wet, searching lips. She felt like throwing up. What was she to do?

Sophie left the room and went downstairs.

Bridget peered out of the door, held the skirt of the robe in her hand, and tiptoed to her parents' room. She knocked on their door, and Amos threw the door open, greeting her with his usual fatherly, smothering embrace. Bridget went into his arms and began to sob.

"What's this?" Amos held her at arm's length and wiped her tears. "What are these tears from the bride-to-be?" His comment made her cry all the harder.

"He . . . he . . ."

"What? Who, he?"

"Edward. He . . . he k-kissed me last night. It was horrible!"

Amos began to laugh. "Why, my dear. For the prospective groom to kiss his soon-to-be bride is perfectly normal. What was so horrible about it?"

"You don't understand. Look!" She showed him her wrist. "He hurt me. He forced me."

"He forced you to do what?"

"To . . . to kiss him. I didn't want to kiss him."

"Nothing else?"

"No . . . well, he pulled my hair when he forced my head back."

"Did you resist him?"

"Of course I did. We're not married yet."

"You mustn't resist him, my child. A verbal agreement has been made, and you are as good as married. Resisting him will only lead to heartache." Amos motioned to a settee. "Come, sit down."

Bridget stood back from her father, astonished at his reaction. Sarah sat up in the large four-poster bed, where she had been listening with the breakfast tray on her lap.

Amos puffed on his pipe. "Sarah, have you had a talk with our daughter about the manner of men?"

"Well, yes, rather."

"Rather? What does 'rather' mean?"

"Well, generally, but I didn't think it necessary to go into detail."

Amos looked at his daughter. "My dear, men are . . . men have . . ." He coughed. "Please, sit down here with me."

"I don't want to sit down."

"Very well." Amos shuffled his feet. "The fact is that men sometimes can be boorishly insistent that their women meet their physical needs."

Sarah interrupted from her place in the bed. "And it is the wife's duty to satisfy those needs."

Bridget scowled at her mother. "I know that. I'm not a child. And Ella has told me . . . things. But we're not married yet, and I don't intend to give anything away until we are."

"If you are resisting a mere kiss, I'm sure Edward is wondering what else you will resist after you are married."

"A gentleman would have respected my wishes. Philippe wouldn't have—"

"Philippe is not a consideration. You are engaged to become Mistress Edward Moorehead, not Goodwife Bridget Clavell." Amos' words cut through Bridget like a knife.

"Philippe comes from good lineage, and you know that." She'd never known her father to be openly condescending toward their servants.

"His bloodline may be distinguished, but his station is not." Amos slammed his hand down on a table. "And I will not discuss that young man anymore. I repeat, he is not a consideration!" He glared at his daughter and lowered his voice, measuring his words. "You will become the willing and cooperative wife of Edward Moorehead. Discussion is over." Amos turned and went to the window. "The snow has stopped."

BRIDGET LOOKED AT THE DISPERSING CLOUDS AND approached the sleigh. The fresh, unspoiled snow shimmered in the morning sunlight, and the blue of the sky seemed washed sparkling clean by the moisture. Edward came to her side and assisted her into the sleigh, then stepped back to allow Amos and Sarah to bundle up in the open carriage.

"I wish you wouldn't insist on returning to your relatives so early today. I would love to show you around my holdings down at the harbor, and with the weather clearing . . ."

"Thank you, Edward, but we must be on our way. I would like to get back to Whisper Wood before dark." Amos helped Sarah into the sleigh.

THE AIR BETWEEN BRIDGET AND EDWARD HAD BEEN charged with tension that morning. She'd barely spoken to him. She took breakfast in her room, and then, after dressing, had gone to see Dame Margo to say her good-byes. Even the elderly woman's dressing gown was red.

"Oh, you're leaving so early? I had hoped we would have time to chat. Well, perhaps another time. We will have to make plans for the wedding, won't we? I just know you two are going to be very happy."

The old lady had gone on and on. Bridget didn't have to worry about holding up her end of the conversation. After only a few minutes Bridget had bade her good-bye and had left the stuffy room to go outside to the sleigh.

"I HOPE YOU WILL FORGIVE ME FOR NOT ACCOMPANYING you this morning. I have a business appointment down at the docks in a little under a half hour." Edward looked at Bridget. She avoided his glance.

"Of course, my boy." Amos leaned across Sarah. "This early snow caught us unprepared and put a snarl in all of our schedules. Thank you for your hospitality."

Edward nodded his head and reached for Bridget's hand. She allowed him to take it, but she did not return his grasp. She glared at him as he lowered his voice and spoke aside to her. "I apologize if my behavior last night was offensive to you." She simply stared at him. He kissed her hand, although it was gloved. "I shall come to Whisper Wood soon, so we can finalize our plans."

"Very well."

He stepped back and bid them good-bye. The sleigh gave a slight lurch, then settled into a smooth rhythm on the snow. Edward waved at them as the sleigh pulled away from the imposing house.

Sarah stuck her hands in her muff. "Bridget, you are not behaving properly. You are pouting like a child who has been denied a sweet. You must grow up and act like an adult."

Amos nodded. "Put what happened last night out of your head. The man apologized, for goodness' sake. Give him some grace. He simply was overcome with his . . . uh . . . affection for you."

"No, Father, it was not affection—it was cruelty that comes when one's desires are denied."

The trio fell silent, the only sound being the sleigh *swoosh*ing along in the snow. As they made their way through the streets, Bridget spoke up. "I want to go by Zwicken's Foundry on the way."

"What for?" Amos shifted his weight under the blanket.

"I'm curious about it. That's where the gun shipment came from yesterday, and I want to . . . to start learning about Edward's businesses."

Amos sat up straighter. "That's my girl." He spoke to the driver. "Take us by Zwicken's Foundry, please."

"Yes, sir. I'll have to make a slight detour, but it won't be much out of the way."

THE SLEIGH PULLED IN FRONT OF THE FOUNDRY AFTER about ten minutes. The sign, covered with snow, swung in the slight wind that had begun to pick up. All three Barringtons got out of the sleigh and headed for the door.

Sarah stopped. "Oh, look, there's a cobbler next door. I think I'll go in and see what he would charge to make shoes for us for the wedding."

Amos chuckled. "Go ahead, my dear. I'll join you in a moment. We won't be long."

He opened the door to the foundry. The jangle of a bell attached to the top of the doorjamb announced their arrival. A disheveled man with a large belly ambled from his office to the worn, wooden counter. He growled a greeting. "Anything I can help you with?"

"Yes, are you the owner?"

"I am. I am Leo Zwicken." He picked his teeth with a piece of straw.

"I am Amos Barrington, and this is my daughter, Bridget Barrington."

Mister Zwicken's demeanor softened immediately. "Oh yes, yes. Edward's fiancée." He came around the corner of the counter and shook Amos' hand, and bowed slightly to Bridget. "I am pleased to meet you." He shifted his weight. "What can I do for you today?"

"Well, Edward told us about the foundry, and Bridget here assisted him with receiving a shipment of guns yesterday. We wanted to stop by and see the place, since after they are married, this will be of interest to them as a couple."

"Yes, of course."

"May we look around?"

"Yes. Well, directly behind me is the shop where most of the work is done. You can see that we are very busy."

Amos followed Zwicken into the interior of the shop. Bridget looked around frantically. She spotted Charles in the back of the shop, bent over his workbench. Amos and Mister Zwicken moved in the opposite direction.

Bridget walked toward Charles and stopped in front of him. He looked up, startled. "Mistress Barrington!"

"Quickly, I don't have much time." She nodded toward her father and Zwicken. "What did you need to tell me? Do you have a message from Philippe? Is he well?"

"Philippe is fine. My concern is for you. Edward Moorehead is—"

Charles opened his mouth to speak, but across the room, Amos beckoned to Bridget to join him.

"Hurry!" Bridget whispered. "What is it I need to know?"

Zwicken and Amos began walking toward the two young people.

"Edward Moorehead . . ."

The two men approached them. Charles hesitated.

Zwicken began to laugh. "Well, have you two made your connection?"

Amos cocked his head and pointed at Charles. "You're Philippe's brother, aren't you? The one he always visited when we came to town."

"Yes, sir. I am Charles Clavell." The boy inclined his head respectfully. "I met your daughter yesterday when we delivered the guns to Mister Moorehead's house."

Amos turned to his daughter. "Is that why you wanted to come by here today?"

"No, Father." Bridget sighed. "As I said, I was curious to see the shop after meeting Charles yesterday and seeing the large gun shipment." She paused. "Mister Zwicken, that shipment of guns—where are they going?"

"*Humph*. How should I know? I simply make them, repair them, and deliver them. I don't know what all of my customers do with them."

"But Edward is your partner. Surely you . . ."

Amos interrupted her. "Dear, that's none of your concern." He moved toward the entrance. "Come, we need to join your mother next door. We've taken up enough of Mister Zwicken's time."

"But I haven't had the . . . the privilege to look around the establishment."

"There will be plenty of time for that after you become Mistress Moorehead. Come, now. Your mother awaits." Amos began to usher her to the front door.

"My gloves . . . I left my gloves on Charles' workbench."

"I'll get them. You go ahead to the sleigh and meet your mother."

"But, Father, I can—" Bridget hesitated at the door.

"I said, go on to the sleigh. I'll be right there."

Reluctantly Bridget walked out the door and into the startlingly frigid air. Her hands began to tremble, and she stumbled into the sleigh. Her mother emerged from the cobbler's shop carrying a package. Turning her head away from her mother as she climbed into the sleigh, Bridget took a deep breath, but the trembling would not stop.

Sarah and Amos settled themselves in the sleigh opposite her and tucked blankets around their legs. Bridget's hands trembled, making it difficult to pull on her gloves. Zwicken stood at the door of the foundry with his hands resting on his belly and watched them leave.

"You're trembling. Are you cold?" Sarah fussed with Bridget's blanket.

"Yes, yes, I am. It was so warm in the foundry, and then the cold air. I guess I got chilled."

"Put your gloves on and stick your hands in your muff."

Bridget finally managed to get her hands into her gloves, grateful for the cover of the cold weather. Tears stung her eyes and froze on her cheeks as the wind whipped around them. She put the muff up to her face to protect it from the wind. What was Charles trying to tell her about Edward? What did he know? She was glad Ella's house was not far away. The icy atmosphere between the Barringtons and their daughter was matched only by the temperature of the ride.

FROM HIS WORKBENCH, CHARLES WATCHED THE SLEIGH pull away from the front of the foundry. He sighed and went back to work. He needed to talk to Philippe. His brother had always spoken well of the Barringtons; he needed to know that Bridget was headed for a disastrous marriage. But Philippe was gone—gone home. And Charles was still in Philadelphia. For now.

SIXTEEN

In reality, Charles hadn't formulated a plan, but the plot had lain beneath the surface of his mind for so many years that when he made the decision to go, he knew exactly what he was going to do. He awoke early and lit a candle. Nothing about his predawn activities would cause suspicion. It was his habit to be up and about before the rest of the household. He stuffed his extra change of clothes in a knapsack and took a pistol out of the drawer in his small table. He had retrieved the weapon from the trash heap when the owner had brought it in for repairs and Zwicken declared it irreparable. Charles disagreed and had worked on it at night until he got it in working order. A small bag of ammunition went into the knapsack as well.

He arranged the quilt and pillow on his rope bed so that it would appear he was still asleep, then he went to the door and looked back at the bed as if he were coming in from the outside. It looked like someone was in the bed.

The young man wound a muffler Vangie had knit for him last Christmas around his neck and pulled his cap down around his ears. He pulled on his tattered gloves and stepped into the brittle cold, shivering as he broke the ice in the well and drew up a bucket of water. He pushed open the door into the keeping room and set the bucket of water beside the fireplace for Goody Wallace.

The banked fire winked at him through the ashes. He took the poker and stirred the embers into life, placing a large log in the back and smaller ones in front.

That should suffice until Goody Wallace gets up.

He pulled a tin of biscuits down from the mantel and emptied them into a napkin. A round of cheese went into the bag as well. That would have to do. He set the empty tin on the table. He paused at the door and looked around the kitchen. Then he went out into the frigid morning, closing the door behind him.

He tromped through the fresh snow the few blocks to the Harbor Tavern. Walking had warmed him up by the time he got there. The sun was just beginning to lighten the sky. Charles knocked on the heavy wooden door. He could see a halo of light coming toward him. Mister Clark cracked open the door, squinting into the dim light as he held up a lantern. Charles could see into the room where Goody Clark already was hard at work, bending over the table kneading bread. The heavy, sweet odor of yeast escaped through the open doorway.

"Clavell! We're not open yet, but come in, come in! Have you come for bread or a meal? Is something amiss at the foundry?" Mister Clark opened the door and ushered Charles in. He set the lantern down and finished lacing his vest. "Well? What can I do for you, son?"

Charles shrugged his knapsack off his shoulder and dropped it on a table. He dug into it and pulled out a small leather drawstring bag. "I beg a favor of you. I need a horse." He held up the purse. "I have saved my wages. I can pay."

The proprietor looked at Charles through his bushy furrowed brows. "This isn't a livery. I don't sell horses."

"I realize that, sir, but I need a horse . . . and I . . . I need a friend . . . and I didn't know where else to turn. I . . ." Charles gestured and took a deep breath. "Can you help me?"

Clark rubbed his chin. "This would be a horse for you, not for Zwicken?"

"That's right."

He motioned to Charles to sit down as he sat across from him. "I do have an older mare that was my daughter's before she passed away a couple of years ago. I simply haven't been able to get rid of it. She's old and not the fastest steed around, but she's steady and dependable."

Goody Clark looked up from her dough board. Mister Clark turned around on the bench. "Goodwife, would you be agreeable to sell Star to Mister Clavell here?"

The rather plain-looking woman brushed her hands together, sending flour into the air, and then wiped them on her apron as she walked toward the men. Most of her hair was hidden by her white head covering, except for a mass of auburn parted in the middle before the ruffle of the cap took over. A redhead, like himself.

"Why do you need a horse, Charles? Is Zwicken sending you on a mission? Why does he not provide you a horse?"

The bench scraped on the wooden plank floor as Charles stood. "No, ma'am." He looked from the woman back to her husband. "I am going home. I'm leaving. Zwicken should have released me from my servitude by now, and I . . . I need to go home."

The couple looked at each other. Goody Clark put her hand on her husband's arm. "We could not possibly sell Star to you."

Charles' shoulders slumped.

"However, we could give her to you, as a gift."

His head shot up, and he punched his fist into his hand. "You would? Oh, that is truly a miracle, and so very generous of you!" He danced a little jig. "Thank you, thank you!"

"On one condition."

"Anything, anything you say."

"That you treat her like royalty. She is a queen of a horse."

"Absolutely. You know my family breeds and trains horses in the Schuylkill Valley. She will receive the best of care."

"You'll be needing the gear to go with her?"

"I'm afraid so."

"I can give you her bridle, but the only spare saddle I have is a side saddle."

"I can ride bareback."

"I can give you a blanket."

"Thank you, Mister Clark. I don't know how to thank you."

"I consider myself a good judge of character. I have observed sterling quality in both you and your brother. You are both fine young men who ought to be with your family. And Zwicken is a crook—in my opinion." He put his arm around his wife's shoulders and stood up straight. "We consider it a privilege to assist you, Charles Clavell."

"I shall be eternally grateful."

"Now, come with me, young man, and we'll get Star. Good wife, gather some food."

"I have biscuits and cheese."

"How long a journey do you have?"

"Depending on the weather, three days or so."

"Biscuits and cheese is not enough. Put in some ale, smoked ham, and dried fruit." He waved his hand. "And whatever else we can spare."

Mister Clark looked down at Charles' feet. "Do you have heavier hose and boots? You need more protection against the weather."

Charles wriggled his foot inside his worn buckled shoe. "This is all I have."

"I can help you there too, I think. Come with me."

"How can I ever repay you?"

"No need. God has been generous to us, and we can afford to be generous in return."

"I . . . I probably need to hurry. I don't know how soon Zwicken will discover I'm gone."

"Yes, come, come!"

The two men exited the back toward the stable as Goodwife Clark went to work packing her baked goods.

A BAY WITH A WHITE BLAZE ON HER FOREHEAD, THE OLD mare performed exactly as Mister Clark said she would. She paced steady ahead through the snow—wasn't skittish or obstinate, easy to handle. As he was riding bareback, Charles was grateful for that. He came to a stream frozen around the edges, but still gurgling over the rocks in the middle.

No bridge. I think there used to be one here, but it must have washed away.

Charles halted, got down, and looked up and down the banks. "Well, Star, I think we can make it. It doesn't appear to be very deep. Are you up to it, old girl?"

The horse turned her head and blinked at him. He adjusted the blanket, grabbed hold of her mane, and clambered back on.

"It's either that, or go back and try to find another crossing. We'll make better time if we can get across." He patted the mare's neck. "Let's go."

He inched Star to the muddy edge of the bank. She backed up and balked, and Charles patted her neck again. "C'mon. You're only going to get your hooves wet—and cold."

Slowly Star stepped into the icy stream. She snorted and bobbed her head up and down but obeyed Charles' gentle urging. "Good girl. Keep going."

The water lapped around the horse's legs but stayed shallow.

As they emerged on the bank on the other side of the creek, Charles jumped down and let the horse shimmy the water from her coat. He wiped her down the best he could with one side of the blanket. "Good girl. You're a good girl." He walked beside her for a bit, then remounted after she dried off.

The snow glistened and glittered as the sun bounced off the hills. Thick woods ambled back and forth across the scene, coming close to the road at times, and then retreating to its secure underbrush haven.

Charles knew Zwicken would come after him once the man discovered he was missing. A light cover of snow lay undisturbed in the ruts in the road, but the sky was clear. It wouldn't warm up much, but no more snow for today, at least. He urged the mare with his heels. "Let's put some miles between us and town while we can."

As DARKNESS BEGAN TO FALL, CHARLES LOOKED FOR A place to camp for the night. He probably could ask for shelter at one of the farms along the way, but he didn't want to leave a trail. He had passed only one wagon on the road, a young father with two little boys. Charles had simply waved and moved past them.

He moved into a stand of trees and found branches to make a crude lean-to for the night. He watered Star from a small stream nearby, then quickly lit a fire with the tinderbox he had brought from Zwicken's. He pulled out the cheese, ham, and biscuits and munched on them. Burrowed under the branches and saddle blanket, he fell into a fitful sleep.

Something cold hit him in the face. He sat up as he brushed snow from his nose and saw a sliver of light slip through the trees. The mare nickered at him.

"Well, good morning, Star. I guess we best get stirring here." He dug in his knapsack and pulled out one of Goody Clark's oatmeal apple cakes. "This is good, even cold. Here, have a bite." He fed some to the horse and then gave her some feed that Mister Clark had sent with him.

He bridled the mare and then threw the blanket over her back. He turned the horse's head north and rode toward another stand of trees. "Looks like we might locate water over there." They had started out of the trees when Star stumbled and went down. As Charles fell off, he looked up and saw the big mare come down on top of him and roll over him.

He must have blacked out for a few moments. The next thing he remembered was looking around for the horse and realizing he was lying in a snowbank. Star stood a short distance away, the reins slack and the blanket on the ground. A sharp pain pierced through his chest. He couldn't catch his breath. He tried to sit up, but the pain forced him down. Yellow fuzzy spots covered his vision . . .

He forced his eyes open to see a head of dark hair with a feather protruding from it hovering over him. The Indian brave stared at him.

Lenape.

Charles pushed himself up on his elbow and grabbed his side as the pain stabbed him again. Two other braves stood to his left with the horses, including Star. They had fur cloaks around their shoulders and carried bows and arrows—and rifles—flintlock rifles. They had to be a hunting party this far west. Strings of beaver pelts hung from packs on their horses. And those rifles—those were rifles from Zwicken's—rifles that Charles himself had fashioned. Rifles that were supposed to have been shipped to the militia. He would know them anywhere.

The Indian brave held a knife in one hand and reached out the other to help Charles get up. Charles groaned. "Do you speak the king's English?"

The Indian stared at him. Charles eyed the knife in the brave's hand. He tried French. "*Parlez-vous français?*"

The brave didn't take his eyes off him, but sheathed his knife and nodded his head.

Charles continued in French. "So, you've traded with Frenchmen? It's been good for you?"

The Indian nodded and replied. "Very good. You are French, yes?"

"Yes, but been here for six years. My family lives up the Schuylkill Valley. I'm . . . I was traveling home, and my horse stumbled."

"Snow keep you from being killed—soft." The Indian pointed to the snowbank with his rifle.

"Yes, you're probably right. Nice rifle you have there."

"The best." The Indian held it out as if testing the balance. "Come. We will take you to our village."

"No, no, I think I'm fine. I need to get home." He tried to draw a breath, and the fuzzy yellow spots began to reappear before his eyes. He slumped to his knees.

"You are not well. We take you to our village."

The pain jabbed at his side again, and Charles acquiesced. The Indians quickly made a litter from tree branches and his saddle blanket. Strong arms lifted him onto the litter and covered him with a fur robe. Charles looked at the sun and realized they were traveling southeast—exactly the opposite direction in which he wanted to travel. But he was too weak to resist.

ZWICKEN STORMED INTO THE KEEPING ROOM WHERE Goody Wallace stood cutting up potatoes into a black kettle hanging over the fire. His voice teetered on rage. "Where's Clavell?"

The cook kept her eyes on her work and shrugged her shoulders. "How should I know? He must be ill." She pointed to the empty tin of biscuits. "He came in earlier and got some biscuits." She put down her knife and wiped her hands on her apron. "I'll go check on him."

"He's never sick. Get him in here. We've an order that needs to be shipped to the militia today." Zwicken turned and stomped back into the shop.

Goody Wallace took a shawl off the coatrack beside the door and went down the rickety steps into the small courtyard behind the shop, past the well to Charles' room.

I know what I am going to find. Blast you, Charles Clavell! How am I going to cover for you without bringing Zwicken's wrath down on my head?

She pushed on the door to the small room. Enough light shone through the window and the open entry for her to see what appeared to be someone still in the bed. She looked over her shoulder and went into the dim room, closing the door behind her. She walked to the bed and touched the quilt. Of course he was gone. It was a dummy. She left the room and returned to the warmth of the kitchen.

Muttering under her breath, she pulled the shawl closer around her shoulders. "I'll cover for you as long as I can. Run, Charles, run. And God be with you." A tear traveled down the crisscrosses of her wrinkled cheek. She brushed it away with the tip of her apron and hung the shawl back up on the peg. Then she waddled to the fireplace and resumed cutting potatoes.

ZWICKEN DISCOVERED CHARLES' EMPTY ROOM AND BED shortly after lunch. Goody Wallace gritted what teeth she had left and tried to ignore the curses and toppled chairs as he ranted throughout the foundry. Intimidated servants tried to stay out of his way as he questioned one after another, especially Ben.

Zwicken jabbed Ben in his chest. "You were friends with Clavell, were you not?"

"Y-yes, we are friends."

"Were, not are. He's gone. Did you know about his plans? Where is he? Do you know where he went?"

"S-sir, I knew nothing of this. He said nothing to me." Ben looked over Zwicken's shoulder at Goody Wallace at the door of the keeping room. Almost imperceptibly she shook her head.

"Well, your sorry excuse of a 'friend' has left you with double work to do. Get busy on this shipment for the militia. It still must go out today!" He blustered into his office and kicked a chair, sending it careening toward the wall. The workers stared after their master's tantrum. He slammed the door to his office shut, sending dust billowing into the air.

EDWARD MOOREHEAD TIED HIS HORSE TO THE HITCHING post in front of Zwicken's Foundry. He stomped the snow from his boots as he entered the dark shop, accompanied by the proclamation of the jangling bell against the door. He looked up at the flimsy contraption. The clatter annoyed him. He would speak to his partner about it. The dismal shop needed updating and cleaning, brightening up. Perhaps Bridget would take on that task after they married.

He smiled to himself at the thought of his naïve, virginal fiancée being completely his to possess. He was glad he had delayed getting married until now—only a few more weeks until the wedding, and she would be Mistress Edward Moorehead.

He hurried to the office and went in without knocking. Zwicken's eyebrows were knit together in a dark frown, his lips set in a thin line as he looked up at his partner.

"I started to say 'Good day,' but it does not appear to be that for you, my friend."

Zwicken shook his head. "C'mon in."

"What has you so disturbed? Business is good, no?"

Zwicken nodded. "Business is fine, but one of my indentured servants is missing."

"Get another."

"This one cannot be replaced. He knows our business almost

better than I do. I've had him six years. No one can make wood stocks for the guns like he can."

"Six years? That must be Clavell. Six years is a long time."

Zwicken grumbled. "I can keep him until he's one and twenty; he's only eighteen."

"Three more years? I don't blame him for escaping. I've kept my hands off the day-to-day operation of the foundry for the most part, but my advice to you is—let it go." Edward sat in a wobbly chair in front of his partner's desk and began to shuffle through invoices. "How long has he been gone?"

"A couple of days already. I thought he was sick. So did Goody Wallace."

Edward took out his quizzing glass and picked up a bill. "Did all these guns get . . . delivered?"

"Yes. Did you send your shipment on its way?"

"Of course." Edward continued to rummage through the papers on Zwicken's desk. "The exchange of pelts exceeded my expectations this time. Beautiful coats."

"*Hmm.* Clavell was the redhead who made the delivery of guns to your house last week."

Something in the recesses of Edward's mind began to agitate him. "Yes, I know who he is. My fiancée knew who he was as well. His brother had been in the service of their family. I think she said that her father recently released the older brother to go home."

"No question about it. That's where Clavell has gone. His brother being freed put the notion in his head, and he's gone to be with him. I'll simply go after him."

"Zwicken, I said let the boy go. Try to collect some money from him, perhaps, but after serving six years . . . well, he's going to be more trouble than he's worth at this point." Edward stood. "I need to be going." He motioned outside. "At any rate, you won't be going after Clavell today. It's snowing again."

Zwicken went to the window, wiped it with the side of his fist, and peered out. "So it is."

Edward swiped his hand across the gritty shelf of the bookcase. "Everything is filthy in here. I realize it is a foundry, but you need to clean this place up."

"Don't tell me how to run my business."

"*Our* business." Edward stared at his partner and pulled on his gloves. "Don't you forget who owns the major part of the shop. I could put you out of operation in a heartbeat."

Zwicken sat on the corner of his desk and folded his arms across his ample belly. "True, but I don't think you will do that. There's too much—shall we say—too much at stake?"

"*Humph*. I would come out the victor if you decide to turn on me, and you know that is the truth. I have a reputation in the community that would back me up—not you."

Zwicken went behind his desk. "No need for us to quarrel."

"Very well." Edward went to the door and turned. "And, by the way, that bell on the door annoys me. Take it down." He strode out the door.

SEVENTEEN

Bridget stood on the footstool while the dressmaker cut a swath of fabric from the bottom of the robin's-egg blue dress and struggled to pin up the hemline. She shifted her weight from one foot to the other. The dressmaker sat back on her haunches with straight pins poking out of her mouth like porcupine's quills and frowned up at the bride-to-be. She removed the pins and stuck them on a pin cushion bracelet that encircled her wrist. "This dress will not be finished by Easter, much less Christmas, if you don't stand still."

Sarah turned to look at her daughter from the linens that she and Ella were folding. "Bridget! Do stop fidgeting."

"I'm tired of trying this thing on. It's too heavy and pretentious. Can we not do something simpler?"

Sarah pushed herself off the couch and walked to where Bridget faced the three-sided mirror. "You are well aware that Edward wishes you to wear the dress his mother wore when his parents married in

England." She smoothed a ruffle on the sleeve. "Besides, it's a very becoming color for you."

Bridget cocked her head and looked at herself in the mirror. Her mother was right—the color *was* good on her, but the fussy dress overpowered her diminutive figure. "I feel lost in it, but I suppose if that's what Edward wishes . . ."

The woman went back to work and finished the hem within a few minutes. "There! That should be all I have left to do." She got up from the floor with a groan. "I'm getting too old for this. Altering a dress is sometimes more difficult than simply making it in the first place. But it will be beautiful, and you will be a beautiful bride." She went behind Bridget and began to pull the buttons out of the loops.

Bridget felt tears begin to well up in her eyes. She tried to wipe them away without anyone seeing, but the dressmaker caught sight of the telltale droplets in the mirror. "What's this? A weeping bride? That's no good."

"It's nothing. I'm just tired."

"Here, step out of this. I'll have it finished by next week—Thursday or so."

"That will be fine. Thank you." Sarah handed the dressmaker her cloak. "We'll come by your shop for the final fitting."

Ella rang for a servant to show the woman to the door.

"Really, Bridget, I would think you could control your emotions at least until the hired help is out the door. No one knows what gossip might be spread all over town. I can just hear it now . . . 'Edward Moorehead weds reluctant bride.'"

"That wouldn't be gossip. That would be the truth." Bridget pulled on her robe and sat in the window seat. "It's beginning to snow again. Maybe the weather will be too bad for the dance at Edward's tonight."

Sarah shook her head and left the room.

Ella joined her cousin in the window seat and jostled Davey on her knees, but got back up quickly. "*Brrr*, it's too cold by the window. Come over here with me, Bridget, by the fireplace."

"I'm fine here."

"Oh, Bridget. I hate seeing you so sad. I want the old Bridget back."

The girl turned to her cousin with tears brimming on her eyelids. "The old Bridget is being slowly choked to death by a marriage of convenience. And I don't know that she will ever be back." She stood. "I need to rest. Please tell Abigail to come wake me after an hour and assist me in getting dressed." She walked across the hall to the room where she was staying and closed the door.

LIGHTS GLIMMERED FROM EVERY WINDOW IN EDWARD'S house, and evergreen boughs draped over everything from the lamp-post to the hitching rail. Bridget stepped out of the carriage with her parents and stared at the beautiful decorations.

Sarah commented, "Edward's mother was Dutch, wasn't she? They certainly are festive in their celebration of Christmas."

They walked up the steps, and Stuart opened the door before they could knock. Several other guests had already arrived. The fact that new lamps were scattered throughout the ordinarily dark hallway did not escape Bridget. After Stuart took their wraps, he led them past sumptuous tables of food and drink. Edward had spent a considerable amount on this affair.

Edward came toward them smiling, his arms outstretched. "Good evening and welcome!" He bent low over Bridget's hand and kissed it tenderly. "My love," he murmured. As always, his clothing was perfectly matched. He sported a burgundy habit over a gold vest with matching burgundy breeches. His hair was powdered tonight and pulled back with a burgundy ribbon. He kissed Sarah's hand and shook Amos', then again took Bridget's hand and tucked it under his arm. "You look ravishing this evening, my dear. I don't think I've ever seen you in white. Ivory velvet, very elegant—simple, but elegant."

"I like beautiful fabrics, made simply with good lines." She tapped the diamond brooch at the high neckline with her fan. "This goes well with the white, don't you think?"

"Ah, yes, perfectly gorgeous." He leaned down to whisper to her. "I would prefer a lower neckline to that one. However, what is not seen can sometimes prove to be very provocative." His eyes glinted.

Bridget chose to ignore his suggestive remark.

He escorted the trio into the large drawing room, which had been converted into a ballroom. Edward signaled the orchestra, and the musicians began to play as he and Bridget entered. He executed a perfect bow and led her out to the ballroom floor to begin the evening with a country dance.

After three dances in a row, Bridget escaped to a corner, fanning herself vigorously.

Edward followed. "Are you well, my dear? Too much for you?"

"I would like something to drink, please. It's the stays. I'm not used to wearing them."

"Yes, of course. Wait here. I'll get something for you. Hot or cold?"

"Some claret would be nice."

Edward nodded and walked to one of the large tables set with pastries, cheeses, and drinks.

A large, imposing gentleman in British military dress came through the archway from the hall, holding his tricornered hat in his hands, his cape still around his shoulders. Deep wrinkles set in leathery skin around his mouth could be laugh lines or stern etches of authority; Bridget couldn't discern which. His hair was tinged with gray at the temples, and he showed signs of a receding hairline.

He looked over the festive crowd and, upon spotting Edward, started toward the refreshment table. He walked in front of Bridget and nodded to her, then looked directly at her with eyes that were as blue as the winter sky. He seemed to take in every detail as he walked through the guests, acknowledging various ones on his way.

Edward greeted him and set the two glasses of claret down. He began to gesture broadly with his hands and appeared to be agitated. The soldier's voice rose above the music, and Bridget caught the word *shipment*. She walked over to the table and stood by Edward's side. He took her elbow.

"Bridget, may I present Colonel William S. Thorne. Colonel Thorne, this is my beautiful fiancée, Mistress Bridget Barrington."

The colonel smiled, bowed elegantly with a sweep of his cape, and took her hand. His smile took over his face. The wrinkles were laugh lines. His hands were cold and huge, but he held hers gently. "The pleasure is all mine, I assure you." He looked at Edward. "You've done yourself proud here, my friend." His thick London accent sounded almost foreign to Bridget.

Edward beamed.

Bridget bobbed a slight curtsy. "Thank you, Colonel Thorne. I hope I didn't interrupt something important, but I wanted to meet the very distinguished gentleman with whom my intended seemed to be engaged in a discussion much too serious for the occasion. Please forgive him."

"I'm afraid I must take the blame for that, Mistress Barrington." Colonel Thorne raised his eyebrows and chuckled. "Not only is she gorgeous, she is outspoken as well."

Edward smiled and rubbed his chin. "Yes, I am finding that out."

The colonel took a glass of ale from a tray extended by Sophie. "My apologies, Mistress Barrington. You are entirely correct. I should not have come with business tonight." He raised his goblet. "I should have come with best wishes and congratulations. When is the happy date?"

Edward answered, "Christmas, right here."

"Ah, but a few weeks away."

Edward turned to Bridget. "My dear, would you excuse me for just a moment while I tend to this little matter?" He handed her a glass of claret, then turned to Colonel Thorne. "If you will, Colonel, let's go across the hall to the parlor."

The two men exited and closed the door behind them. David and Ella were dancing, and Amos and Sarah chatted with friends on the opposite end of the room. Bridget eased around the wall and then slipped into the hallway, wishing now that it was dark as it usually was. She blew the lantern out beside the parlor entrance and stood by the door. With the background of the music and chatter of the guests, she could hear nothing. She pressed her ear against the crack of the door, but all she could make out was the low murmur of the men's two voices. As she turned away, the parlor door opened suddenly and the men emerged.

"Bridget! What are you doing out here in the hall?"

"Oh, you startled me." She motioned toward the stairs. "I . . . I was going up to see Auntie Margo while you were engaged with the colonel. And I didn't know whether I should ask your permission or not, and I was . . . I was—"

"You were . . . what?"

"I was going to knock and ask you, and then I decided not to disturb you. I was just headed upstairs." She felt her cheeks flushing. She was glad she had blown out the lantern.

"You do not need my permission, my dear. In fact, Auntie Margo told me to ask you to come see her this evening. I hadn't gotten around to doing that."

Colonel Thorne put on his gloves and tipped his hat. "I must be going. Once again, it has been a pleasure meeting you."

"Yes, thank you, Colonel Thorne. I do hope you'll come again sometime." Bridget nodded. "Oh, Edward, do have Sophie relight that lantern. It seems to have gone out. You know how I like things nice and bright." She scurried up the stairs.

Stopping on the first landing, she slipped into the shadows and listened.

"You'll have your full shipment of guns, Colonel. I do not know why you've not received the correct number, but I'll take care of it." Edward's voice was not cordial.

"See that you do, Moorehead. It would not be wise to tamper with the king's militia." He stepped out the door and said something else, but Bridget could not hear. Edward closed the door and swore.

Bridget turned and hurried to the dowager's door. She knocked softly on the large double doors, which were slightly ajar.

"Who is it?"

"It's Bridget, Auntie Margo."

"Oh yes! Come in, come in."

Bridget pushed open the door into the hazy room and was greeted by the little balls of yapping fluffy fur. The dowager patted the cushion of the chaise beside her, and the dogs scampered to her side. Bridget had expected to find the elderly woman in her dressing gown, but Auntie Margo had on a red brocade dress, laced up the front with black cord.

She waved Bridget in. "I'm so glad you came up to see me. Is the ball going well? I suppose it's not really a ball, but as close to it as we get here in the colonies. Oh, I would love to see it—all the lights and decorations. The only decoration I have up here is this little bit of mistletoe Sophie brought to me." She pointed to a sprig of the greenery tied onto the base of a pewter candlestick with a ribbon. "And I stuck some in my hair." She chuckled, touching her white hair that frizzed around her face. "Probably looks silly on an old lady, but it makes me feel a bit festive."

Bridget looked at Dame Margo's attempt at a tiny bit of Christmas cheer in her gloomy room, and her heart went out to the old lady.

"And the music—oh, how I would love to hear the music. I've had the door open a bit, so . . ." She paused for a breath. "Listen to me rattling on. Come, pull up a chair next to me. Don't you look ravishing tonight!" She clasped her hands to her chest. "Ah! You have on my sister's brooch. Edward told me he gave it to you. That was her wish—that Edward's wife would have the brooch."

"Thank you. It is lovely, isn't it?" Bridget took the old lady's wrinkled hand. "And you are dressed in a beautiful gown as well."

"It makes me feel as if I'm part of the celebration, although I'm stuck up here—with my little friends." She brought one of the dogs onto her lap.

"Why don't you come downstairs and just sit and watch?"

"Oh no. I could never do that. Once I got downstairs, I'd never get back up here."

"Nonsense! We could help you. Between David and Edward and Stuart, we could get you down. You can walk some, can you not? I've seen you at the window before."

"Yes, with a cane. It's my knees. It's so painful to walk that it's just easier not to."

Bridget stood. "You do whatever you need to do to ready yourself. I'm going to get Edward and David." She went out the door and ran down the stairs, her mouth set in determination.

Edward should have seen to this prior to the guests arriving. She should have been already seated, ready to receive company.

She entered the drawing room to see Edward fawning over an attractive brunette. Bridget walked straight to him. "Edward, I need to speak to you, please."

He turned and stared at her. "Of course, my dear. In a moment. By the way, have you met Mistress Martha Schilling? Her husband owns several of the ships in the harbor, among other interests."

The darkly handsome woman faced Bridget and turned her lips up. Her smile revealed bad teeth. "Charmed, my dear." Then she turned back to Edward.

"Yes, I'm sure." Bridget disliked the woman instantly. "Now, Edward. I need to speak to you now."

Edward sighed. "Very well. What is it?" He bowed to Mistress Schilling, took Bridget by the elbow, and walked her to a corner of the room.

Bridget pulled her arm away from him. She put her fan in front of her mouth. "First of all, Edward Moorehead, I am not a gnat to be swatted away, especially when you are making a public spectacle of yourself with another woman." She looked around and closed the fan. "But we shall deal with that at a more appropriate time. Auntie Margo wishes to come downstairs and be a part of the occasion."

"What?" Edward gaped at her. "She never comes downstairs. That's impossible."

"She never comes downstairs because no one offers to help her. She's not an invalid, but she soon will be if she continues to be a hermit in that room and simply lies on that chaise or in her bed." Bridget touched Edward's arm. "Edward, she got herself dressed in a beautiful gown and put a sprig of mistletoe in her hair. She wants to come to the party. Please, between you and David and Stuart, I think we can get her down here. I'll ready the settee for her to sit in. She will love it. Please, Edward?"

Edward looked at the face of his fiancée and softened. "Very well. Get the settee ready, and we'll bring her down."

Edward and David left the room, and Bridget began to pull the settee to the side of the entrance.

Sarah approached her daughter. "What are you doing? Rearranging furniture in the midst of a dance?"

"Edward is bringing Auntie Margo downstairs."

"Really?"

"Yes. Here, help me get this over by the door." They easily scooted the settee close to the entrance. "Mother, I went up to see her, and she was dressed like she was coming to the dance. It broke my heart for her to be sitting up in that room all alone with her dogs, and no one paying any attention to her." She walked out into the hallway. "Here they come. See, she is doing fine."

The two men on either side of the old woman held on to her

arms as she slowly descended the stairs. Stuart went in front of her. They had maneuvered past the top landing and were now at the lowest one—only ten more steps to go.

"One moment please, gentlemen. Let me catch my breath." Dame Margo looked down at Bridget and grinned. "Looks like I'm coming to the party!" She wheezed and puffed for a moment. "I'm ready now."

They slowly descended the steps and seated her on the settee. She took out a handkerchief and wiped the perspiration from her forehead. Then she flipped open her fan and began to fan vigorously.

Bridget brought her a glass of ale and sat with her. "Are you comfortable? Can I get you anything else?"

"Would you check on my doggies? They are not used to being left alone."

"Of course. Do you want them down here with you?"

"Oh, could I? Edward, could we? They'll just sit in my lap. I'll make sure they behave."

Edward spoke up. "I'll get them." He ran up the stairs and returned quickly, placing the two dogs on Dame Margo's lap. One started to bark, but the old woman shushed the dog, and the animal nestled into her skirt and blinked at her mistress. Couples stopped by and introduced themselves, commenting on the dogs.

Edward and Bridget stood by her side. Bridget bent down to speak to her. "Do you need anything?"

"The only thing I desire right now is to see the two of you dance together. You make such a handsome couple."

Edward knelt in front of her. "Will you be content here?"

"Of course. Sophie's around, and . . . Bridget, why don't you send your mother over to chat with me, dear?"

Bridget motioned to her mother, and Sarah made her way to them.

Edward took his aunt's hand. "Please forgive me, Auntie. I was most insensitive. I should have realized that you would want to attend the dance. Men can be such dullards at times." He looked at Bridget. "And as for my bride-to-be, I'm learning that she doesn't take no for an answer."

Edward turned to Bridget, offered her his arm, and led her to the dance floor. She stared at this man whom she was to marry within a matter of weeks. He smiled at her. His eyes seemed full of love for her now, not lustful or angry. She was learning that Edward Moorehead exhibited two personalities—one cruel and harsh, the other sensitive and kind. And she never knew which one would surface.

On the other hand, Philippe's behavior was always gentle and respectful. He could be firm, but never with anger or harshness. Her heart wrenched every time her thoughts turned to him, and she ached to be with him. She knew who the true Philippe was, but which was the real Edward—she didn't know.

EIGHTEEN

Despite the freezing temperature, Philippe removed his jacket and tossed it on top of the split wood he had stacked in the bin next to the house. He pushed his hat back on his head and wiped the perspiration off his forehead with a handkerchief. He looked at the piece of cloth and stuck it in his jacket pocket and remembered the handkerchief he had handed to Bridget to wipe her tears away the last time he saw her. He remembered those blue eyes filled with tears—tears he had caused.

Pierre, Jean, and Karl trudged through the snow from the barn, interrupting his daydreams. Pierre stopped and patted him on the shoulder as the other two men went inside. "Time for dinner." He looked at the stack of wood. "I honestly don't know what we did before you came back home. You handle an axe rather well."

Philippe grinned. "Just wait until Charles gets home. This will be the most productive farm in the whole colony of Pennsylvania."

"Can't argue with you there. We are blessed, are we not?"

"Blessed beyond measure." Philippe laid the wedge and splitting maul down and stuck the axe in a big log.

Pierre looked at the large stack. "Keep working on the wood this afternoon. It seems we always underestimate the amount of wood we will go through each winter."

Philippe nodded. "I'll work on it until I have to quit for milking." He picked up his jacket and chuckled. "Didn't need this for long." They stomped the snow off their boots on the porch as they walked toward the door.

Pierre had started into the house when he paused and nodded toward the road. "Looks like we have company." He shaded his eyes with his hat. "Doesn't look like any of our neighbors."

Philippe's heart started to pound. "Those are Zwicken's men," he said. "I recognize them from the foundry. What are they doing out here?"

Something's happened to Charles! No! Not that.

He walked out to meet the men, the older one riding a large dapple gray gelding that matched the man's own salt-and-pepper hair. The younger man sat atop a chestnut with a white face and white socks. He looked to be about Philippe's age.

The older man cleared his voice and coughed several times before he spoke. "We are looking for the Clavell family."

"You have found them. I am Philippe Clavell. I recognize you from Zwicken's, do I not? Has something happened to my brother?" Philippe grabbed hold of one of the horse's bridles.

Jean appeared in the doorway, followed by Madeleine, wiping her hands on her apron.

"Whoa there, Clavell. You tell me. That's what I came here to find out." The older man got off his horse. "Your brother has turned up missing, and Zwicken is convinced that he is here."

Madeleine stepped up behind Pierre. "Oh dear. Charles . . . ?"

Pierre put his arm around his wife's shoulders. "We have not seen Charles. He is not here."

Philippe stood with his hands on his hips. "You are correct, he would have come here, but he has not. Something must have happened to him. How long has he been gone?"

"Can't say for sure—probably a week or so." The older man who was speaking for the two cleared his throat. "I hate to ask you this, but may we have a look around? Zwicken will ask if we searched. If we can assure him that we did, it will go easier for us."

Philippe's angular jaw jutted out, and he glared at them. "We are men of our word. There's no need to search."

"It will do no harm for them to take a look." Pierre extended his arm toward the barn and the smokehouse. "Look wherever you like. Philippe, show them around. Then please, join us for dinner before you start back. Or spend the night if you wish. You must be weary. I know my wife joins me in the invitation."

Madeleine's voice betrayed her concern. "Of . . . of course."

Her son's betrayed his outrage. "Pierre!"

"These men are not our enemies. They are simply doing their job."

The older man spoke up again. "I, for one, am willing to take you at your word, but if you don't mind, we'll have a look around the barn. We knew Charles. Liked him. Really can't blame him for taking off. But Zwicken hates losing his best craftsman. Clavell knew how to fashion a gun stock better than anybody in the whole colony. Zwicken's gonna miss him for certain." The two men and Philippe started toward the barn. "You are correct in your assessment, my friend. If your brother is not here, where is he? For I can assure you that he is no longer in Philadelphia."

PIERRE AND PHILIPPE WALKED THE MEN TO THEIR HORSES after dinner. Pierre motioned toward the barn. "Are you sure you don't want to bed down here tonight before starting back? It's plenty warm in the barn."

The older man began to cough, and the younger one answered. "No, we need to get as far as we can this afternoon while the weather holds."

"Yes, we thank you for your kindness. We did not relish having to do this."

Philippe walked down the steps from the porch. "If . . . if you should see . . . anything . . ." He couldn't finish the unthinkable.

The men reined their horses around. "We will make sure we get word to you if we should hear anything. Does the post rider come out here?"

"Every month or two."

"Very well. Again, Mister Clavell and Mister . . . Bovée, is it?"

"That's right."

"Again, thank you for your hospitality under these awkward circumstances."

Philippe's countenance turned grim as he watched the men ride away. He looked at Pierre and expressed what had hung heavy in the air, unsaid . . . afraid that articulated, it would become fact. "We've got to go look for him. He must be hurt . . . or . . ."

"*Oui.* We'll head out first thing in the morning."

PHILIPPE BROUGHT LEGACY AND TONNERRE AROUND TO the front of the house. The two black Percherons pawed the snow, eager to be on the road. Madeleine and Pierre came to the door. She looked up at him, and he whispered to her, then stepped out on the porch, pulling on his gloves. The younger man handed the reins over to him and nodded.

"Wait a moment, please." Philippe walked to his mother and gathered her in a tight embrace. She wiped tears away with her apron. "Maman, we'll find him. I promise you, we'll find Charles. Pray. Pray like you've never prayed before." He turned and went to his horse and mounted. *I don't know that I can keep that promise. I don't even know where to begin.*

Both men's faces reflected their somber mood as they started down the path to the road.

"How do you think Maman truly is? Will she fare well with us away?"

"She trusts God. But she's concerned about us as well as Charles ... afraid that she could lose all three of us."

"We won't let that happen."

"No, we won't." Pierre looked straight ahead as they moved onto the road.

"Where do we even begin?" Philippe felt his emotions beginning to take over. "What if ... what if ... ?"

"Don't let your imagination run away with you. Here's the impression I keep getting—surely Charles knew that this would be the first place Zwicken would look for him. Perhaps he's hiding out somewhere until he feels it is safe."

"But where would that be? Where would he go?"

"I don't know, son." Pierre turned in his saddle to face Philippe.

"This is when we need to exercise our faith and declare that we trust our God. He is in control of our destiny. He has Charles in his hand. He will take care of him. And not only that, he will guide us as we look for him."

"But what if he had an accident on his way here and couldn't get help?"

"God loves Charles as much or more than we do. If our heavenly Father cares for the lilies of the field and the sparrows of the air, don't you think he cares for us?"

"I don't need a sermon. I know all of this."

"Ah! Forgive me. I don't mean to preach. But think about how God took care of us at Versailles. He will make a way for Charles too. And, in the event he has chosen to allow Charles to go home to be with him . . . well, his will be done."

"I feel in my heart he's not gone. Is that simply hope, or is that assurance from God?"

Pierre smiled at the young man. "Hope is of God as well, and I agree with you. I don't think Charles is gone either. He's out there somewhere."

"Where shall we start?"

"I think we should travel the route to Philadelphia. Maybe we'll spot something that will give us a clue."

"Zwicken's men would have seen something. They were looking for any sign of Charles."

"Maybe not. They were bent on getting here as quickly as they could. They easily could have passed by a significant clue." Pierre looked up at the morning sky. "I don't like the looks of those clouds. We're liable to run into snow before the day is out. Then any clues that are out there will be covered up. Come on, let's get moving."

They rode in silence for the next hour. Philippe mulled over the statements of confidence that each had declared—and desperately clung to the thread of belief that Charles would be found well. Pierre took one side of the road and Philippe the other, searching for any sign that Charles had been there. Philippe walked Legacy off the road a couple of times to explore snow that had been disturbed, but it never turned out to be anything but animal tracks. They saw nothing that would make them think Charles or anyone else had met with foul play along the road.

The snow started late that afternoon. Philippe held out his hand and watched the silent descent of the deceptively beautiful crystals.

Pierre pulled his hat down around his ears. "We need to find shelter. We can make it to the Saunders farm within the half hour if you're willing to risk it. That'll be better than spending the night out here." Dervishes of snow swirled in the increasing wind, making it difficult to see one another. "The road will be covered soon, but we can follow the ruts until we get to the Saunderses' fence."

The wind began to blow with increasing intensity. Philippe shouted above the howl. "Let's give it a try."

The two men hunched over their saddles and urged the horses forward. Pierre and Tonnerre went in front as the big Percheron picked his way along the road, bending his head against the wind. Philippe and Legacy followed close behind in their tracks. Once Tonnerre stumbled in a hole in the road, but gained his footing straightaway.

"Make a way through this storm for us, Father God. Make a way. Make a way. Make a way." Philippe repeated the prayer over and over as they inched along. His fingers were numb around the reins, and he knew they needed to find shelter soon.

"There's the fence!" Holding his muffler up around his face, Pierre turned and shouted again, "We've made it. There's the fence!"

"Thank you, Father." Philippe nodded, and they turned into the path to the Saunderses' cabin.

Pierre pulled up to the hitching rail, jumped off his horse, and ran onto the large porch that wrapped around the cabin. He pounded on the door with his fist. "Hello! Hello, Saunders family! It's Pierre Bovée."

The door opened almost immediately, and a large man with a long beard stepped out. "Mister Bovée! What are thee doing out in this weather? Come in, come in."

"Actually we—Philippe and I—need a place to spend the night. We have reason to believe that Charles has tried to get home and didn't make it. We are out looking for him."

"Come in and warm up and eat some supper. You must be freezing. We've just finished our meal, but there's plenty left." Mister Saunders pulled his hat and jacket off a peg beside the door. "Jeremiah! We have company. Come help with their horses. Rebecca, we have friends we need to feed. Make ready two plates."

"Thank you, Mister Saunders, we are so grateful. We'll help you with the horses. These two are special." Pierre started off the porch with Mister Saunders.

"Beautiful mounts. Does thee have any more Percherons? I'd be interested in a team for plowing. They are strong."

"We do. We are raising them, and we just had a black colt exactly like the stallion here." The men had to yell at each other to be heard above the wind.

"I'd be interested." The older man turned as he and his son led them around the cabin. He cupped his hands around his mouth. "Stay close to the fence. It will lead us to the barn. This blowing snow can be deceptive. A man can get lost and freeze to death between his barn and his house." The men chatted as they fed and watered the horses and bedded them down in the barn, then crept along the fence to return to the warm cabin.

An older woman, wearing the traditional Quaker dress and head covering, stood beside the table putting plates and goblets down for the unexpected visitors. Her face broke into a large hospitable smile as they entered. "Welcome! Thee are welcome in this house. I've cabbage and potato stew ready, and pickled eggs. And plenty of biscuits."

"Thank you for your hospitality, Goody Saunders. We are most grateful." Pierre removed his hat. "This is our older son, Philippe."

Philippe removed his hat as well and nodded. "My pleasure."

"He has just recently been released from his servitude in Philadelphia. We are so glad to have him home."

Goody Saunders ladled out the stew and motioned toward the table. "Sit, sit. Would thee prefer ale or cider? Or I have milk and water."

"Ale for me. What would you like, Philippe?"

"Ale, as well, please."

"Yes, Abigail told us that Philippe had returned home." Goody Saunders poured ale for the two while Jeremiah stoked the fire.

"Of course. You are Abigail's family. I knew her folks lived here in the valley, but I didn't make the connection." Philippe sat down at the table and looked at Jeremiah. "I can tell you are her brother."

"That's what everybody says."

"Jeremiah, I do believe you are going to be taller than your father." Pierre stood beside the young man and measured him with his hand as the adolescent rose up from the fireplace. The young man smiled and ran his hand through his head of thick light-brown hair.

Pierre scooted onto the bench and motioned to Mister Saunders. "As the head of this household, would you pray for us? We need God's guidance in our quest to find Charles. We know that he left Philadelphia about a week ago. But other than that, we have no idea where he is, or if he . . . if he is . . ."

"Of course, I would consider it a privilege to offer up prayers for you." Mister Saunders stood at the head of the table and began to pray in a confident deep voice.

Philippe felt the presence of God descend upon them.

"Our Father, we acknowledge who thou art and that thou art always good to thy children. We beseech thee, O Father, to guide these two men in their search for their loved one. Thou dost know where he is. We do not. We are praying that thee would keep him safe and from harm. Send someone to help him if he needs help. Send aid if he is afflicted. Protect these two as they search for him. And, Lord, I'm asking thee to tell the snow to cease. Thou dost command the wind and the waves. Surely that includes the snow, so I'm asking thee to do that for us tonight so that the search can continue in the morning. If Master Charles should be out in this storm, please lead him to shelter—lead him to safe shelter. And . . . oh yes . . . bless the food that these two are about to enjoy." He chuckled and stroked his beard. "Amen!"

"Thank you, Mister Saunders. I believe God heard that prayer." Philippe picked up his spoon. *I wish I knew how to pray like that. This is a man who knows how to touch God.*

"God hears all our prayers. I feel a sense of peace in this matter. I believe thee will find thy brother sooner than thee may think."

"God told you that?"

"It is simply an impression, my boy. God speaks to his people. Trust him."

PHILIPPE SAT UP FROM HIS PALLET IN FRONT OF THE FIRE-place. The wind whistled around the eaves of the cabin and found its way through the cracks in the walls. He listened, but all was quiet, except for Pierre's snoring—and the wind. He lay back down and folded his arms underneath his head. A huge log lay on the back of the grate in the fireplace, glowing and radiating heat. As the log burned it shifted and scraped against the grate. That must have been what he'd heard. He closed his eyes and turned over, pulling the quilt up around his chin.

There it was again. He was sure he heard something this time. He stood and listened. He heard a horse nicker and snort.

Mister Saunders came through the bedroom door pulling on his breeches and snapping his suspenders over his long underwear. "Must be the night for visitors. There's a lone horse in front of the cabin." He unlatched the door and creaked it open. Snow blew into the room, and in a heap on the porch lay a redheaded young man, unconscious.

NINETEEN

W hat have we here?" Mister Saunders picked the man up out of the snow in his strong arms and carried him to the settee. "This young man is half frozen. Someone get the door, please."

Philippe pushed the door shut against the storm and stared at the midnight visitor in disbelief. "It's Charles! It's my brother!"

Pierre jumped up and pulled on his boots. He bent over the young man and felt his reddened cheeks. He looked at Philippe. "We need to get him warm."

"Yes, but not too fast. We need to warm him up gradually." Mister Saunders started removing Charles' wet clothing. "Look, he's wearing a fur robe. He's been with the Indians. That's a blessing. He has some kind of binding around his chest. It seems to be dry. We'll leave that be. Goodwife! Hurry! Bring quilts."

Goody Saunders rushed into the room, her nightcap askew,

pulling on a robe. Going to the opposite side of the room, she opened a large armoire and removed several quilts from the neat stack. She covered Charles with two of them and placed two more beside him. "I'll heat water and cider."

Charles moaned.

Philippe sat on the edge of the couch, taking his brother's hand. "Charles, it's Philippe. All is well. You are safe now."

Charles turned his head from side to side, mumbling incoherently. Philippe looked up at Pierre. "Will he . . . will he make it?"

Pierre and Mister Saunders looked at each other, and Pierre took a deep breath. He patted Philippe's shoulder. "We'll just have to wait and see. I am confident that God will restore him to us. I don't think he brought us this far to leave us deserted. After all, Mister Saunders prayed that he would be able to find shelter tonight, and he did. God led him here."

Jeremiah climbed down from the loft. "Who is that?"

"Jeremiah, this is Philippe's brother. Put on your clothes and take his horse to the barn."

The boy dressed and looked outside. "The wind seems to have died down. And the snow is stopping. I can see stars." Jeremiah turned around and smiled at Philippe. "I hope he will recover." Then he went out the door.

Philippe looked back at Charles, who was beginning to stir.

Charles opened his eyes and tried to speak. His voice came out in a raspy whisper.

"*Shhh*, don't try to speak. We're here. You're safe."

Charles lapsed back into unconsciousness.

Mister Saunders spoke up. "We need to get him warm. He's suffering from exposure."

Charles continued to mumble. Philippe leaned down with his ear close to his brother's mouth. "H . . . hands. My . . . my hands."

Mister Saunders touched Charles' hand. "Frostbite." He brought the lantern closer. "*Hmm*, yessir. They look frostbitten for sure. See how these three fingers are dark? We'll just have to see. We'll do what we can. Good wife, bring a bowl of warm water."

"Here, Mister Philippe, see if thee can get him to drink this." Goody Saunders handed Philippe a mug of sweet, hot cider and went to check on the teakettle. Philippe sat Charles up, coaxing the warm liquid down his throat.

Goody Saunders brought a large bowl of warm water and a towel.

"Make sure the water's not too hot, just warm." Mister Saunders stuck his finger into the bowl. "Just right."

His wife sat down beside Charles with the bowl in her lap. "Young man, this is going to be painful, but we need to get thy hands thawed out and warmed up." The woman gently guided the half-conscious boy's hands into the water. He moaned and yanked them out.

"Come now, thee must leave them in. Let's try again."

Charles' eyes rolled back in his head, and he passed out.

"That's probably best. This way he won't be in so much pain." She replenished the warm water a couple of times, and then dried his hands off and wrapped them in clean cloths. "We need to keep them covered. If God should choose, perhaps we'll be able to save the fingers."

"I'm going back to bed." Mister Saunders turned toward his bedroom just as Jeremiah came in, stomping snow off his boots. "I think we've done all we can tonight."

"I'll stay up with him." Philippe had not left Charles' side, and he didn't intend to.

The Saunders family retired again for the night, and Pierre returned to his pallet.

Philippe slept very little, rousing each time his brother stirred and moaned. Overwhelming love rose in his heart for his sibling. He scooted Charles over on the couch and molded his body into his. His mind flew back to France when they were hiding in the cave from the dragoons, snuggling together to stay warm.

I will never allow Charles to be taken back to Philadelphia. A tear hung in the corner of his eye and then trickled down his cheek. He pulled the quilt over Charles' shoulders and wrapped his arms around him. *They will have to get past me to get to my brother ever again.*

Philippe awoke as the two Saunders men went out the door to do the milking. Goody Saunders clanged a large kettle against the fireplace and set plates on the table. "Good morning, Mister Philippe. How is Mister Charles this morning? Did thee get any sleep at all?"

"I think I slept a little off and on." He stood and looked down at his brother. "I don't know how much sleep he got. He seems to be in much pain." He picked up a mug of hot cider. Pierre joined him at the table.

Philippe leaned on his elbows toward Pierre. "Do you think we can we take Charles home today?"

"We'll have to see if he can ride."

"You know my brother will say he can, but I don't think he will be able to hold the reins with his hands encased in those bandages."

"Either one of our horses can carry double easily. Charles can switch off riding with each of us."

Charles raised himself up on one elbow. He managed to croak, "Did I hear my name?"

"You're awake." Philippe jumped up and went to his brother's side. "How are you feeling?"

"I . . . I'm not sure. Where are we?"

"The Saunderses' cabin. You made it to the Saunders farm."

"Well . . . uh . . . what are *you* doing here?"

"Looking for you." Philippe chuckled. "He's fine. Same old Charles."

"How did . . . how did you know that I . . . would be here?"

"We didn't, but I guess God did. You might say that he guided us all here."

Charles laid his head back on the pillow. "Philippe, I need to talk to you, right away."

"Whatever it is can wait. Let's take care of you first."

"But we don't have much time. And you need to know—"

Philippe held up his hand. "Wait, first fill us in. Where have you been for a week? And where did you get a horse?"

Charles smiled. "Mister Clark gave her to me. She belonged to his daughter. She's old, but she has been wonderful—except when she stumbled and rolled over me."

Pierre brought a mug of hot cider for Charles. "Here, drink as much of this as you can."

Charles reached for the mug, looked at his hands, and shrugged his shoulders. Philippe took the cider and helped his brother sip it.

"So that's why you have bindings around your chest. Cracked some ribs?"

"I think so. A Lenape hunting party found me after Star—that's my horse's name—fell."

"Mister Clark has been a good friend."

Charles coughed and groaned, gathering his hands against his chest. "My hands hurt."

Goody Saunders turned from her breakfast preparations. "That's a good sign. That means the skin is not dead. The fingers are coming back to life."

"Do you think you can travel today—riding double?"

"I can ride myself." The boy pushed himself to a standing position. He struggled to take in a breath. He looked at his brother and then at his bandaged hands and grinned. "Maybe."

Pierre looked up from his breakfast of smoked sausage, porridge, and biscuits. "The sooner we get Charles home, the sooner your mother's mind and heart can be put at ease. We could be there by this afternoon. The whole family—together at last."

"Home." Charles sat down at the table. "We will finally be home, Philippe."

"It's been a long time coming." Philippe patted his brother's leg. "But it appears that we truly are going to be able to have a home again."

"We must talk. There's something I need to tell you. It's why I left."

"What is it? What mysterious bit of information caused you to risk your life to escape?"

"It concerns Mistress Barrington."

Philippe's heart began to thud. Why was Charles bringing this up? He stood. "Why should news of Mistress Barrington concern me?"

Charles looked around. "Goody Saunders, is there somewhere we could talk privately?"

"Of course. Use our bedroom if thee prefers. Thee may close the door."

The brothers went into the small bedroom. A plain chest of beautifully polished wood sat at the end of the bed. A candle in a pewter holder flickered on a small wooden table beside the bed. Darkness still hung over the early dawn sky. Philippe closed the door as he heard the Saunders men coming in from their chores, stamping snow from their boots on the porch. The brothers sat on the chest and faced each other.

"You told me to get word to you if I heard anything else about Moorehead and Zwicken's illegal practices," said Charles quietly.

"I did. What have you heard?"

"Bridget is to marry Edward Moorehead at Christmas. He knows it was she who witnessed that murder all those years ago; she saw them unloading guns on the river. He's been diverting sales of guns from the king's militia to the Indians for fur pelts—the militia is being shorted the guns they have been promised and paid for. And listen to this—the Indians who picked me up were carrying Zwicken guns. Bridget is unknowingly right in the middle of all of it; by marrying her, Moorehead effectively silences her."

He paused; Philippe sat stunned, a myriad of emotions playing across his face.

Charles cleared his throat and continued. "In our last conversation at Mister Clark's pub, you told me Mistress Barrington had expressed affection . . . love for you, but that you did not return her feelings." Charles looked down at his bandaged hands. "Brother, you weren't very convincing. Your feelings for her swim in your eyes at the mention of her name."

The thought of Bridget sliced across Philippe's heart with new pain. "Her parents have arranged this. She doesn't love him. She loves . . ."

"We know she loves you, but do you love her? Do you truly care about her? She is in danger, Philippe. Moorehead is not only arrogant and dishonest, he's a murderer." Charles stood and waved his bandaged hands in the air. "Here, help me take these bandages off."

"But—your fingers."

"They are fine. Help me remove the bandages."

"Calm yourself for a minute, and I'll get Goody Saunders to look at your hands." Philippe paced back and forth. "What do you think I should do?"

"Do you love her? Be honest with me. Are you in love with Bridget Barrington?"

Philippe stood at the window and looked out at the snow-covered landscape. He ran his fingers through his hair. Conflicting emotions of love and denial born of habit collided in his heart. "I . . . I don't know. I've never allowed myself the luxury to nurture the feelings. But even as I speak, I feel the love begging to be set free in my heart." He walked toward the door. "I'd like Pierre to be part of this." He looked out into the keeping room. "Pierre, could you come in here for a minute, please?"

Pierre entered the room and looked from Charles to Philippe. "Is there something I can help with? Is there strife between the two of you?"

Charles spoke up. "It's not strife between the two of us; it's what is between Philippe and Bridget Barrington."

Pierre leaned against the door and looked at the brothers. "I think you had better explain."

So Charles told Pierre the whole story, including the conversation he overheard at Zwicken's. Philippe filled in with what Bridget had seen as a little girl.

"So Mistress Barrington could be in a dangerous situation?"

"Yes."

Pierre looked at Philippe. "What do you say to all of this? You are a grown man. What are your feelings toward Mistress Barrington? Is she important to you?"

"I've never allowed myself to consider it, Pierre; she's Catholic."

"So am I."

"Yes, but . . . you converted."

"God came to me in the forest that day in France, and I knew he was real and was with me. That experience began my spiritual journey. It's a matter of following Jesus, not of with which church one affiliates. And in this country, we do not have to fear—"

"But Maman . . . she would never accept . . . I could never bring home a Catholic wife."

"Aha! So you *have* thought about it?"

"Well, fleetingly. But—"

"I assume you eventually wish to be married and have a family and settle on the land we've purchased for you. When you picture that, whom do you see in the role of your wife?"

Philippe cast his eyes downward, and he whispered, "Mistress Bridget Barrington."

"And she loves you?"

Philippe nodded his head. He pulled a blue hair ribbon out of his pocket and looked at Charles and Pierre. "She put all of her pride aside and declared her love to me the day before I left. That was what caused Mister Barrington to release me early." He began to pace. "Refraining from taking her in my arms and expressing to her the love I also felt for her took every bit of resolve I could muster, but I simply didn't see any way that it could work out. I felt that the easiest path would be to not become entangled, but to just leave. She dropped this as she rode away from the stable the last day I saw her." He stuffed it back in his pocket. Long-buried feelings began to rise in his belly. "What a fool I've been! Now she's in danger. Things might have turned out differently, if only I'd told her that I loved her. She would never have agreed to marry Moorehead." He clenched his jaw to repress the emotions that threatened to overtake him. "Now it's too late."

Pierre took Philippe by the shoulders. "No, it's not. She's not married yet. Go after her. Don't let anything stop you. You'll never regret it, even if you fail. But if you don't at least try, you'll live with the sorrow of it the rest of your life. I've never regretted going after your mother. Even with my imprisonment in the Bastille and my father's death and all the danger we encountered, I've never regretted it for a moment."

Philippe took a deep breath. "I'll need to go right away. We're only two weeks from Christmas."

"I suggest we take Charles home, then regroup and go to Philadelphia to find your Bridget and bare your soul to her."

"What about Maman? She will never agree."

"I think your mother, in the end, will be reasonable. Express your heart to her, and she'll open hers in return. I'm sure of it."

"Very well. I would like to be able to talk to Mother about Bridget."

"Then I will step in and try to smooth things over." Pierre scratched his jaw through his beard. "Believe it or not, your mother is mellowing somewhat as she gets older. If God is in this, he will speak to her about it as well."

Charles stood. "You're not going to Philadelphia without me."

"You're in no shape to be making another trip."

"Give me a couple of days, and I'll be right and ready to go. My ribs already are much better, and . . . let's get these bandages off."

"Be patient. We'll have Goody Saunders change the dressing, and then we'll prepare to go. It's early, and the sky is clear. We can be home by late afternoon."

DUSK WAS SETTLING AS THE PAIR OF BLACK PERCHERONS, leading an old bay mare, plodded down the hill to the bridge over Bushkill Creek. They took the sharp curve up to the Clavell cabin. As the house came into view, every window in the house glowed with lanterns and lighted candles, as did the windows farther up the hill at Jean and Adriaen's cabin.

The door flew open, and Madeleine, with a shawl drawn around her shoulders, stepped out on the porch. She brought her hand to her cheek as she watched Charles slide off the back of Legacy and walk, smiling, toward her.

"Oh, Charles, Charles. Where have you been? And whatever happened to your hands?" She took his hat off and ruffled his hair and kissed his cheeks over and over.

Pierre and Philippe, carrying their packs, joined them with hugs and kisses and laughter.

"I didn't expect you back so soon. We determined to burn candles and lanterns in the windows each night as a vigil to welcome you home. Where did you find him? Oh . . ." She couldn't quit kissing and hugging both of her sons.

Jean and Adriaen, each holding a baby, and Vangie and Claudine appeared at the door, smiling. Vangie ran into Charles' arms. "They found you. I prayed and prayed that God would lead you to each other."

"You will not believe how he answered your prayers."

Jean handed his bundle to Claudine and pulled on his jacket. "I'll get the horses to the barn."

"Thank you, Jean. And hurry. We have a story to tell—and another adventure to prepare for."

They went into the house of lighted windows, the family complete and together at last in their home in the New World.

TWENTY

Philippe stuffed the letter from Bridget back in the envelope. He felt miserable that he had acted upon presuppositions and been lured from the girl that he loved by the promise of freedom and a horse. Although a formidable chasm loomed between them caused by their religious differences, he had not even prayed for God to open the doors for them to be together. Bridget had appealed to him through her letter one last time before the tentacles of tradition had wrapped around her, and he hadn't even bothered to open it. Now she was in danger.

Philippe looked back at Charles, who was still asleep, and stepped quietly through the door from his room to the cabin. "Where are the others?"

Claudine looked up from kneading dough in the bread bowl and wiped her forehead with the back of her hand, leaving a trace of flour. "Vangie has gone up to Adriaen's. Madame is in her bedroom."

"Thank you." He walked to the open door of his mother's room and stood quietly for a moment, watching her fold quilts and place them in a trunk at the end of the bed. She was humming a Huguenot hymn.

"Maman."

She startled, and then smiled. "Oh, I didn't hear you, *mon cheri*. Have you already finished with your chores? Nothing's wrong, I hope."

"No, all is well. But—"

"But, what? Something *is* wrong."

"I need to talk to you. And be at peace. All is fine. There is simply something I wish to discuss." He motioned to her. "It's a beautiful morning. Let's go for a walk."

The men had told his mother about Charles' escape from the foundry and his rescue by the Indians, but nothing about Bridget. Philippe needed to tell her.

She looked out of the window at the barren trees spreading their skeletal fingers over the sky on the wintry hillside. "It's so cold—"

"Yes, but the sun is shining, and there's no wind. I want to show you something." He motioned with his hand. "It's been a long time since we've taken a walk together—Versailles, in fact." He grinned. "Come, get your cloak."

She walked to him and brushed his hair out of his eyes as she had brushed François' out of his eyes years ago. She patted his cheek. "So like your father. Very well." She put the last quilt in the trunk and followed Philippe out of the bedroom. "Claudine, we are going for a walk."

"A walk, Madame?" She looked up at the couple.

"Yes, my impulsive son wants me to go on a walk with him . . .

and has something to show me. I'm most curious." Madeleine put on her cloak and got her muff out of a chest beside the door. "We shan't be long."

Claudine nodded, picked two loaves up with the peel, and shoved them into the oven.

They walked into the radiant morning and crunched down the path to the road. Philippe waved his hand over the landscape. "It's not the gardens of Versailles, but in its own way, I think, it is even more beautiful. I feel free and alive in this valley."

"Yes, I agree." They walked down the road toward the creek. "Where are we going?"

"There's something I want to show you down here by the water. Do you miss France, Maman? Versailles?"

"Sometimes I miss being a 'lady.' I miss dressing up for a ball or a ballet. I miss our estate." She looked at her son. "It really was a lovely manor, wasn't it? I remember the gardens in the spring, and Henri grooming our horses. Loyal Henri. He and Therese took good care of us, didn't they?"

They both fell silent. Their former life seemed but a dream now.

She took his arm. "But I would not go back. Our family is complete, now that you and Charles are home. Jean and Adriaen have their babies. It's perfect now, isn't it, Philippe? We've had our share of heartaches, but it has been worth everything we've sacrificed."

Philippe didn't answer. They approached the bend in the road that led down to the creek. "Watch your step here." Philippe took her elbow and guided her off the road to the bank of the creek where a path had been cleared.

"You've already been here."

"I came down a couple of days ago to check the bridge. That's when I noticed something." They stood on the bank, and he pointed toward the water. "Look, it appears to be frozen, but if you observe carefully, you can see the water running underneath it. Later in the winter, of course, it will freeze over solid. And look here." He turned and led her upstream a bit to a small waterfall. "Look how the ice is trying to cover the rocks, but the water keeps bubbling to the surface. It will eventually freeze over, but in the spring, when it begins to warm up and the conditions are right, it will run again."

"What are you trying to say?"

He looked down at his feet and scuffed around in the snow with his boot. "Maman, everything is *not* perfect. I need to tell you something. I . . . I . . . there is a young lady that has . . . that I have . . ." Nervousness crept up the back of his neck. He stammered, and then hesitated and looked at his mother. *This is going to be every bit as hard as I thought it was going to be.* "This is very difficult, Maman."

"There is someone you'd like to marry?"

"Yes, there is."

"I'm delighted. Tell me who it is."

Philippe took his mother's hands and looked directly into her startling blue-green eyes. "It is Mistress Barrington."

Madeleine pulled away from him, but he continued.

"It's like winter has come to my soul, and is trying to freeze over the bubbling emotions that lie hidden beneath the surface. However, they are still there, and have not died—will not die."

"You will recover as time passes."

"Perhaps, but time will not completely ice over my love for her. Just as it would not for you and Pierre."

"Philippe, she is Catholic."

"Pierre was too."

"Has she converted?"

He snapped a twig off a tree and turned it round and round in his hands. "Can we not trust that God has come to Bridget, or will come—just as he came to Pierre?"

Madeleine turned her back on him. Her hood fell around her shoulders, and her dark hair tumbled out from under her white head covering. She rubbed her forehead, then shook her head. "Don't do this to me, Philippe. I cannot approve such a match."

"Cannot, or will not?"

She stared at him. "Do you want me to betray everything we have risked our lives for? Everything that we came to this country for? Your father died because of his faith. Can we do no less?"

"We came to this country to escape King Louis and for the privilege of living free. Give me that same freedom—the freedom to choose to marry the woman I love. Our hearts are free here."

Madeleine stared at her grown son, now a man. "And if I do not give my approval?"

Philippe looked back at the river. "I'm not willing to live the rest of my life with my feelings for Bridget frozen inside of me, ready to bubble to the surface at any time. That would not be fair to any other woman—one that you might choose for me." He looked back at Madeleine. "Bridget is engaged to be married at Christmas to a man of questionable character—coincidentally, Zwicken's silent partner at the foundry. She witnessed a murder when she was nine years old, and the murderer was the man to whom she's now engaged. Maman, this is too complicated to explain now. Mistress Barrington has no idea how dangerous her situation is. I have made up my mind. I'm going after her."

Madeleine remained silent for a long time. Then she looked at her son. "I am very sorry for Mistress Barrington's plight. I'm sure she is lovely, and I certainly do not wish her any ill will, but that doesn't change the fact that we are Huguenot, and she is Catholic." She looked down at her hands enshrouded by her muff. "You intend to pursue this with or without my approval?"

He nodded slowly. "I greatly desire your approval. If God will be gracious to me and grant me favor, I hope to reach her before she marries this despicable man." He swallowed. "I am going as soon as I can gather my things."

Madeleine blinked away the tears that sprang to the surface.

"Don't cry, Maman." The young man stared at her tears. "This is something that I must do. I know this is right. Please, can you not trust me?"

"I know this must sound harsh to you, but I will not give my blessing for you to marry a Catholic. That's final."

"I am sorry, Maman. I do not wish to cause you pain, but I am going after her. I would like your approval, but I . . . I will not require your permission."

Madeleine turned her back on him and began to trudge through the snow back to the road. The two returned to the house without speaking. As they reached the small gate in the fence that surrounded the house, Madeleine turned to her son. "Your willfulness in this situation grieves my heart. Go tell Pierre that I need to speak to him, please."

"Maman, will you at least pray and ask God to show you if you might possibly be wrong?"

She looked up at him with tears shimmering in her eyes. She nodded. "I will. I give you my word that I will."

Philippe found Jean banging away on the blacksmith anvil near the front of the barn. The muscles rippled beneath his shirt as he lifted the hammer in a clanging rhythm. Philippe nodded and walked on past until he came upon Pierre mucking out stalls in the back.

"Pierre, Maman would like you to go to the house. She needs to speak with you." He looked directly into Pierre's dark eyes. "I'm going to Philadelphia to get Bridget."

Pierre leaned on his shovel. "You told her?"

"Yes."

"Did she agree?"

"Not exactly."

"You're not going without me." Philippe whirled around to see that Charles had joined them. The cloths were off his hands, but he had put on gloves.

"Impossible. If you show your face in Philadelphia, Zwicken will put you back in the foundry." Philippe reached out. "How are your hands?"

"I won't lie to you, they are tender, but as long as I keep them protected, I think they will be fine." Charles grinned. "And as far as Zwicken is concerned, he will have to catch me first."

Pierre spoke. "Charles, you know that your mother and I have been saving money to buy out your contract. We've almost enough now, and we will somehow find the rest. We will eventually pay Zwicken what is due him."

"But—"

"We will honor the contract. You will be able to walk into Philadelphia with your head held high thereafter, and will not have to avoid Zwicken for the rest of your life."

Philippe clapped his brother on the shoulder. "We need to get to Whisper Wood before the Barringtons go to Philadelphia. We'll leave in the morning."

"This is not going to be easy for your mother, but I will try to reason with her." Pierre leaned the shovel against the stall and started for the cabin.

PIERRE STOOD IN THE DOORWAY OF THEIR BEDROOM, removed his gloves, and pushed his hat back from his forehead.

Madeleine did not look at him as he came into the room and sat on the bed.

"Maddy, what are you thinking about?"

She didn't answer for a moment, but stared into the flames in the fireplace. "I was thinking about our estate in France." Her eyes were dry, but her voice faltered.

"I wish I could have seen it before the king's dragoons burned it."

"I do too, Pierre. It was a lovely country home. Not too pretentious, but elegant and comfortable at the same time. And our stables and horses were the best in the province. Henri did a masterful job with the horses." A catch in her voice caused her to hesitate. "We were very fortunate." She still would not look at him.

"Blessed, I'd say." Pierre knelt in front of her.

She spread her hands and looked at them. "I used to be the most beautiful woman at the ball. I had the most beautiful gowns, and I was the desire of the king—the envy of the other ladies of the court."

"I know that, my dear. I witnessed it for myself. You were the most striking woman I had ever seen. Every man in court knew when you entered the room."

"My hands used to be soft and beautiful. Now they are rough, reddened, and dirty—always grime around my nails. Even when I scrub them with a brush, the—grime—won't—come—off." She accentuated the last few words by rubbing one hand and then the other. "It just—won't—come—off."

Pierre took her hands and kissed them. "Your hands are still lovely, and you would still be the most beautiful woman at the ball . . . if we were to have a ball." He chuckled. "I haven't heard of too many balls going on around here, however." He stood and pulled her into his arms. "But if there were balls, I would reserve every dance with you and dance the night away as if we were still young." He began to sway to music heard only in his head.

Madeleine followed him as he executed expertly even now the steps to a *menuet*. He stepped back and kicked the rocking chair, sending it careening into the wall. They laughed and embraced.

Madeleine righted the chair and sat down, breathing hard. "Well, we're *not* young anymore, but you are still my favorite partner."

Pierre leaned against the fireplace and stroked his beard. "You mean I outrank the king?"

"By far." She went into his arms and smoothed his beard with her fingers. "My hero. Where would our family be if you hadn't risked your life for ours—more than once?"

"Where would *I* be if God hadn't brought you into my life? I would still be searching for him." He paused. The room grew quiet except for the sizzling of the fire. Pierre kissed his wife. "Maddy, I was Catholic, remember? And you loved me."

"Yes, but you had come to faith before—"

"—before what? Before we fell in love? Before François died? I hardly knew what happened to me when God came to me in the forest that day. I had to learn what it meant to trust in Jesus by faith. I had to learn to walk in belief. I had to learn the Scriptures and how to rejoice in the Lord. Give the girl a chance. How do we know that she doesn't already know God?"

"But she was raised Catholic."

"Let's find out more about her before we close the door. Let's trust Philippe's judgment."

"He rejected her and came home without her."

"That's because he knew how you would react. And . . ."

". . . and I've reacted exactly as he thought I would?"

Pierre cocked his head at her and smiled.

Madeleine turned her back. "You knew about this, didn't you? I want you to talk him out of it."

"I didn't know until yesterday, but I cannot do that."

She whirled around and stared at her husband. "You what? What do you mean, 'I cannot do that'? You will not stop my son from making the biggest mistake of his life?"

"Calm down, Maddy. I will not try to stop him, because I happen to agree with him."

"You . . . you agree with him? I did not think I would have to fight you on this as well. You are the head of this family, but . . ."

He motioned toward their bed, and they sat down. "You are letting your emotions color the situation. This is not a dragoon threatening to imprison, torture, or kill your son—or anyone in your family. This is a young woman, who happens to be Catholic, who is in love with your son. All they want to do is to be together. Perhaps God brought her to our family for a purpose—both in her life and in ours. Perhaps—as it was in my case—perhaps our family has been appointed to encourage her in her spiritual journey. How can you rule that out?" He pleaded with her. "I know you have strong convictions—obstinate, some would say—and I admire you for that. That courage has saved us more than once. But this time . . ."

Tears gathered in her eyes. "This time . . . what?"

"This time I think your convictions are misplaced. I think you need to trust your son's judgment. He's a grown man. He has been a good son and does not want to inflict further anguish on you, but *he* is in anguish. Do not let the pain of your past cause future pain for your son. I fear it will drive a wedge between the two of you."

"He *is* a good son, isn't he? I couldn't have asked for a better son. François would have been so proud of him." She dried her tears with her handkerchief.

"I've talked to Jean and Charles. I would suggest you talk to the woman yourself. We are all in agreement that you should tell Philippe to go get Mistress Barrington. Please pray about this. If we wait too long, Mister Barrington will have married her off to this man of most questionable character. Maddy, we can trust God in this. I know we can."

In a sudden rush, tears began to stream down her cheeks. "We've come too far to go back. We've sacrificed all that we had and are in order to live our faith out in freedom. I cannot have the cloud of Catholicism hover over our household again. I simply cannot give my approval, Pierre. I cannot do it." She fell into his arms and heaved broken breaths onto his shoulder.

Pierre tilted her chin toward him with his finger. "I think you are making a mistake. Sometimes we can be so wrong in our righteousness. I fear you will live to regret this decision."

TWENTY-ONE

Abigail placed the wedding dress on the bed along with Bridget's other gowns. She organized her mistress' jewelry according to occasion with each corresponding gown. Bridget stood at the wardrobe and opened the drawer containing her shifts and stockings. She ignored the secret compartment that had held her diary as she emptied the drawer. A small case sat at her feet into which she placed her things. On top she laid a carefully folded man's handkerchief, and closed the case.

The last two weeks had been filled with making plans for the wedding. Sarah bustled in and out with news of the season and parties that they would be attending. "We shall go to David and Ella's for the night, then to Edward's in the morning. It will be the most festive Christmas we've ever had."

On her last trip into the room, she brought the shoes that had just been delivered by the cobbler. Bridget looked at the door as her mother scurried out. *She's almost gleeful, and I feel as if I am preparing for an execution.*

Zachary brought in a large trunk from the attic for her gowns.

"Thank you."

"Is there anything else right now, Mistress Barrington?"

"No, not at the moment."

Abigail looked up at her husband and smiled. Bridget's heart constricted as she observed the affection that passed between them. Their newborn lay sleeping in a cradle next to the fireplace.

Abigail stood back and counted the gowns. "Thee has six gowns and three everyday dresses, your two cloaks, plus your riding habit. And, of course, the wedding dress. Three pairs of shoes, the wedding shoes, your riding boots, two hats, gloves. I have coordinated the jewelry with your garments."

Bridget's traveling dress lay on the chair in front of the vanity with her cloak and muff. "Thank you, Abigail. You take such good care of me. You have always taken good care . . ." A broken sob caught in her throat. She looked at her servant and companion as tears filled her eyes. "What am I going to do without you?"

"Thee has been a good mistress." She looked at Bridget as her eyes reddened as well. "I wish I could go with thee, but God has willed that we stay here . . . with the baby and all."

Bridget dabbed at her eyes with a hankie. "I'll have Sophie, of course, but that's not the same. I'll have to get used to her ways, and . . ." She smiled. "And she'll have to get used to mine." She took off her robe. "Help me get dressed, please, and then you may start packing the trunks. Everything looks acceptable."

"I've been expecting you." Edward sat at a desk in the parlor of his house, scribbling with a quill. He did not look up as his valet ushered Colonel Thorne into the gloomy, musty interior. "One moment, Stuart."

The colonel remained just inside the doorway. The moments ticked by as only the scratching of the quill interrupted the silence. A log fell off the grate in the fireplace and scattered embers onto the hearth. Stuart picked up a fireplace shovel and lifted the log back into place. A tea tray rested on a table beside Edward's desk, but he did not offer any of the contents to his guest, nor did he propose that he be seated.

"*E-hem.*" Colonel Thorne cleared his throat.

Edward scooted his chair forcefully as he stood. "Please forgive me. I needed to finish this letter and send it on its way." He folded the papers in his hand, sealed them, and handed them to his valet. "Post these immediately."

"Yes, sir. Right away."

Edward motioned toward two wingback chairs. "Please, sit down." He and the colonel sat across from each other. Edward leaned back in his chair and crossed his legs. "It seems we have encountered a bit of a problem here, haven't we?"

The older man nodded slowly. "It appears so. Zwicken's shipments of guns seem to have come up short on a regular basis."

"Yes. I assure you I knew nothing about this. I only recently discovered that he had been pilfering from the business for years. Very clever man. I never suspected."

"I find it hard to believe that a businessman as adroit as yourself could be swindled in this manner." Colonel Thorne sat on the edge of his seat looking as if he would rise at any moment.

"Zwicken's is only one of several business ventures I own. I trust my managers. Obviously, in this instance my confidence was misplaced."

"He has been with you for years, has he not?"

"Yes. He became too complacent in our association and decided I would never find out. The letter I just posted contains papers dissolving our partnership. The foundry will no longer be Zwicken's. I suppose I shall have to take it over until I find another manager." He fidgeted with the cravat at his neck. "I assure you, sir, I fully support the Crown's army. I was appalled when I discovered that your troops were being shorted their guns."

"We can expect full restitution?"

"Absolutely."

"Where are the guns? Did you find that out?" Colonel Thorne stood with his hand on his sword.

Edward stood with him. "As I said, I will take care of the matter. Your soldiers will have their guns."

The colonel stepped so close to Edward that he could smell the lingering odor of tobacco on the officer's breath. "It would not be wise for you to continue testing our patience on this. There could be consequences."

Edward stood his ground. He took out his quizzing glass and looked at the colonel. "Consider the matter taken care of and closed."

"We understand each other?"

"We do."

"To make sure that we do, Mister Moorehead, I am assigning one of my officers to oversee the operations at the foundry for the time being. And Mister Zwicken will not be allowed on the premises."

Edward stared at the colonel, and his jaw worked back and forth. "You have my word that I will take care of the situation. Zwicken lives upstairs above the foundry."

"He will have to move out. We are conscripting the property. It now belongs, at least temporarily, to the Crown."

Edward nodded his head slightly. "Very well. We bow to the

authority of the Crown." He motioned toward the door. "Now if you will excuse me, Colonel, I have a dinner engagement with my fiancée. You know, I'm to be married at Christmas."

"Ah yes, the lovely lady I met here a few days ago. She's quite young, isn't she?"

"Yes, I've waited a long time for the right one to come along. Am I not a fortunate man?"

"I would say so." The colonel put on his hat. "I would say 'lucky.'"

Edward walked with the colonel to the hallway. "Stuart. Show Colonel Thorne out, please." He watched through the window as the soldier left and mounted his large brown gelding.

Edward climbed the stairs to his room and rang for Sophie. He removed a fur cloak made from silky, shiny beaver pelts from the wardrobe and laid it on his bed. "You will be a vision of loveliness in this, my darling. No one in Philadelphia will have any finer."

"Sir?" Sophie appeared at the door, and her soft voice barely rose above a whisper.

"Yes, wrap this cloak for me. There's a box in the corner, and the matching muff and hat are still in the wardrobe. See that Stuart puts it in the carriage for me." He smiled at the maid. "I'm dining with my fiancée tonight. Do you think she will like it?"

Sophie looked down. "Any woman would like such a cloak. It's beautiful."

Edward stepped toward the young woman and caressed her cheek with the back of his fingers. "This is a gift fit for the future mistress of the house, but have I not treated you well? Are you not satisfied with your position here?"

"I . . . you have treated me well." The maid moved away from him and picked up the cloak, running her delicate hand along the fur.

"After I'm married, your chief duty will be to attend Mistress Barrington. But that doesn't mean that you can't still pay special attention to me every now and then."

"Of course." Sophie held the cloak up between herself and Edward. "I'll get this packed."

"You've plenty of time. Come here." He reached for her arm, and she resisted for a moment, only a moment. He motioned to the bed with a nod of his head.

She obeyed him and sat on the edge of the bed as he walked to the door, unfastening his vest as he went. He closed the door softly. "This will be the last of our delightful afternoons together before I'm a married man. Our little trysts will have to be more ... shall we say ... discreet?"

The heavy draperies were already closed, shutting out the afternoon sun. He blew out the candle on the nightstand, and the room was plunged into darkness.

THE BARRINGTONS ARRIVED IN PHILADELPHIA AROUND three o'clock in the afternoon for the overnight stay with the Osbornes. As Bridget walked into the foyer, she found a note on the hall tree from Edward.

> My Dearest,
>
> I cannot bear the minutes until I see you again. Please allow me to call upon you the evening of your arrival. I have a special gift I want to bring to you.
>
> As ever yours,
> Edward

Her heart fell. She had been looking forward to one last free evening with Ella and her family. Instead, the servants were scurrying around making ready for a guest for the supper meal.

Bridget brought in only a small satchel for the night and took it up to Ella's room. Ella was finishing her preparations to spend a few days at the Mooreheads' prior to the wedding. "I never imagined how much more paraphernalia one has to pack for one small infant, even if only for two or three days."

Bridget grunted as she lifted Davey Junior and rested him on her hip. "He's not so small anymore. He's almost nine months old now, isn't he?"

"Yes, and before we know it, he will be a year old. He's already trying to pull up and walk."

Bridget buried her nose in Davey's mop of dark hair. "*Mmm.* I love the way a baby smells when he's just had a bath. When did the note come from Edward?"

"A couple of days ago. There were two—one for you and one for us, asking permission to call. Of course, I sent word that it was perfectly permissible, and we would look forward to having him join us for supper."

"Of course."

"That was less than enthusiastic. Doesn't sound like an eager bride-to-be." Ella stopped her packing and sat down on her bed.

"Nothing has changed."

Ella took Davey from Bridget. "I'm so sorry for you, Gigi. Sorry that you are entering this marriage with such dread, but you are going to have to resolve yourself to it and make the best of it. Who knows? Perhaps you will fall madly in love with Edward on your wedding night." She giggled and sat Davey at her feet on the floor.

Bridget glared at her cousin. "I can hardly stand to think about it." She turned on her heel and walked out of the room.

Her hands folded in her lap, Bridget sat in the Osbornes' parlor watching the servants light the candelabra on the mantel and the lanterns on tables around the room. The candlelight glinted on the polished dark wood of the furniture.

Strange, how differently things look in the shadows than they do in the light. One can hide for only so long. Then the light comes, and all is revealed. I cannot hide in the parlor or at Whisper Wood or in my dreams of Philippe forever.

"It's rather chilly in here. Would you mind putting another log on the fire, please?"

The male servant stoked the fire and threw the last of the firewood into the fireplace. He left and returned with an armload of logs to replenish the supply.

Sarah and Amos joined Bridget in the parlor to wait for Edward's arrival. "There you are. We were looking for you." Sarah began her nervous chatter as she paced around the room straightening pillows and chairs and anything else that did not need straightening. "I cannot believe that it's almost upon us—the wedding, that is. My, it seems like yesterday that we first met Mister Moorehead, here in this very room. Who would have thought then that we would be looking at a Christmas wedding. Why—"

"Where did you think I would be?"

"What?"

"You said that you had been looking for me. Where did you think I would be? Where else could I have gone? Out on the streets of Philadelphia? No, I have obediently prepared myself to receive my fiancé—the man that you all have chosen for me—as a dutiful daughter should. And I am waiting for his arrival, prim and proper here in the parlor."

Amos sat next to Bridget, the legs of the chair groaning as he eased his weight onto it. "You have no cause to be rude to your mother. You should consider yourself fortunate to have such a prosperous and enterprising fiancé—who, in addition, obviously cares for you."

"And is most handsome, even dashing, I would say." Sarah toyed with her fan. "That's an added blessing."

Bridget looked away toward the window and touched the brooch at the neckline of her dress—*her* dress, made of brown brocade. The lace around the neckline matched the lace on her head scarf and the large flounces on the sleeves. *I may have to bend to my parents' wishes as to a marriage partner, but I don't have to follow his desires as to what I wear . . . yet.*

She watched Edward's stylish carriage pull up in front of the house. He descended, and a footman followed him up the steps with a large package. "Edward's gift for me appears to be quite large." She watched from her chair and waited for the servants to introduce the arriving guest.

David and Ella came down the stairs as the servant opened the door. David ushered Edward in. "Come in. We have all been eagerly awaiting your arrival."

Ella clapped her hands. "Oh my! What do we have here?"

"A wedding present for my beloved. Something I hope she will make use of beginning tomorrow and for a long time to come." The Osbornes' servant took the box from the footman.

Amos and Sarah rose and met Edward as he entered the parlor.

"Good evening, Mister Moorehead." Amos' deep voice rose above the others.

Sarah touched the box with her fingers. "Whatever could this be? Bridget, Mister Moorehead has arrived, and look at this huge package he has for you."

Edward gave his hat and cloak to the servant. He walked immediately to Bridget and took her hand and kissed it. "I have been counting the minutes until your fair face would brighten my day again." He motioned the servant to put the box on the floor at Bridget's feet. "I have a wedding present for you, my dear."

Bridget looked at the box and then at Edward, who had knelt down in front of her beside the box. "Why, Edward, the brooch was quite enough."

"Nonsense. That was a betrothal gift. This is a wedding present. Shall I cut the string for you? Sophie wrapped it special for you."

"Yes, please."

Edward stood and asked for a knife. He wore a forest green jacket with matching green breeches and a tan vest. A long cravat with lace edging, in the French style, hung loose. David returned with a knife and handed it to Edward, who cut the strings and stepped back. "Now. You open the box."

Bridget bent down and had to stretch both arms wide to grasp the top of the box. She pulled on it, and it hung on the corner. Edward reached down and helped her. As she raised the cover, Sarah gasped, and Ella stared wide-eyed at the fur pelt. Bridget stood and pulled the cloak out of its container as she rose. "Edward. I am stunned." She swirled the cloak around her shoulders. She pulled it up around her face and nuzzled her cheek into the fur. "It's so soft. This is much too extravagant, but it is beautiful. And I will love wearing it. Thank you. However . . ."

"However, what, my dear? Is there something amiss?"

"It does seem to be a bit too large."

"Easily remedied. We'll take it to the furrier shop we own down-town. He will simply need to remove one of the pelts." Edward stood back and observed the garment, which indeed did overpower Bridget. He motioned to the box. "There's a matching hat and muff, as well."

Bridget picked up the muff and then returned it to the box. "They are lovely. Thank you." She removed the cloak and returned it to the box. "I believe supper is ready?"

EDWARD CLIMBED INTO HIS CARRIAGE AT THE END OF THE evening with the Barringtons and the Osbornes. Snow had begun to fall and grew heavier as they plodded through the streets of Philadelphia to his house. His jaw moved back and forth as he clenched his teeth.

I will not be treated as an unwanted appendage or a servant by my fiancée—simply someone to provide for her and bring her gifts. The rhythm of the horses lulled him into a tipsy cloud that had begun with the fourth glass of ale. *I've had too much to drink.* He doubled up his fist and hit his knee with it. *Miss High-and-Mighty will regret treating me with anything less than the utmost respect. After we are married, I will teach her a thing or two. Yes, after we are married . . . after . . . however, perhaps she needs to learn that lesson beforehand.*

TWENTY-TWO

Philippe awoke during the night, sat on the edge of the bed he and Charles shared, and looked outside. Snow. Snow so heavy it had begun to drift against the side of the house. He arose and walked to the door, pushed against it, and peered through the slight opening toward the barn. It was completely hidden behind the blanket of snow descending from the dark sky. He lay back down.

Why, God? Why, when I need good traveling weather, do you send the snow? He closed his eyes and fought his disappointment. *My dear Bridget, I will try to get to you in time. But I cannot control the weather. Only God . . . only God controls the weather. Only God.*

He turned on his side, away from Charles. His brother moaned and mumbled from time to time in his sleep. Philippe wondered if he'd always done that or if it was simply because he was in pain.

If Bridget and I are meant to be together, won't God make a way? As he made a way for us in France and through the snow to the Saunderses'?

And for Charles to get there as well? Is there a reason he sent the snow to delay us? For Charles' hands to heal? To avoid some danger of which we are unaware, but he knows? We don't know, do we? But you do.

Philippe's midnight musings turned into a prayer. *Father, once more, you are requiring us to trust you. Build my faith. Help me to be patient and rest in your arms. I place my faith in you. Help me to get to Bridget as quickly as I can.*

His mind began to fill with visions of the girl he now knew he loved—her smile, her laugh, her dusky blue eyes. He chastised himself again for rejecting her. Almost tangible pain rose in his heart. *Father, if you give me the chance to claim her as my own, I will never reject her again, for any reason. Never again.*

PIERRE STOKED THE FIRE IN THE KEEPING ROOM AND brought the flames to life. Claudine scurried to the fireplace from the small room she shared with Vangie, pulling on her white cap. "I'm sorry, *monsieur*. It's so dark outside; I didn't know what time it was."

"All is well, Claudine. My timepiece says it's about six o'clock. We've had quite a snowfall during the night."

"I'll have breakfast for you soon." She set about putting a kettle of water on the fire and bringing out skillet biscuits from the night before. She cut slices of smoked venison and cheese on a board and set them on the table. "Porridge will be ready as soon as this water gets hot."

The door to Philippe and Charles' room scraped open, and the two brothers ambled into the keeping room. Philippe looked at Pierre with a quirk of his eyebrows. "Looks like our trip is going to be delayed."

"That it does." Pierre reached out for Charles. "How are your hands feeling?"

"Better every day. The tips of these two fingers are still numb." He held up the fourth and fifth digits of his left hand.

"You need to be diligent to protect them from further injury. They will be quite sensitive to the cold for several weeks."

Charles nodded. "I know. I'll be careful."

The men, their faces reflected in the mellow glow of two lanterns at the trestle table, discussed the brothers' options.

Pierre rubbed his chin. "Have you thought about where you are going to stay? And the possibility of running into Zwicken, Charles?"

"I'll be watchful. Zwicken doesn't leave the shop during the day, and every night he goes to the Boar's Head and drinks himself into a stupor. We'll cut a wide swath as far as he is concerned."

Philippe propped his leg on the bench. "We can stay at the Harbor Tavern & Inn. I believe it's far enough from the foundry. I've never been to Moorehead's, but you have, Charles, correct?"

Charles nodded. "Yes—making deliveries."

Pierre leaned back in his chair at the end of the table. "This reminds me of when I set out to look for your father. I had no idea where he was in all of France, or whether he was even alive. But God guided me every step of the way, and he will guide you as well. However, I didn't have snow to contend with—only King Louis' wrath."

Madeleine came into the room. "You are talking about Louis?"

"Only indirectly, my dear." Pierre motioned for his wife to join them.

"In a moment. I'll help Claudine finish up."

Vangie emerged soon from her room, drawing a shawl around her shoulders. "I didn't hear you get up, Claudine."

"The dark skies and snow have thrown our clocks off." Claudine smiled as she dished up the porridge, and Madeleine set it down in front of the men.

Vangie sat down next to Charles and snuggled up to him. "I'm so glad you are home."

"You're growing up too fast." He chuckled and pulled on one of her braids.

She looked out the window as the sky started to lighten. "It's still snowing."

Philippe kept his head down and began to eat his porridge.

Madeleine put her hand on his shoulder. "Surely you are not going to try to leave today, are you?"

He continued to eat. "God will make a way when it is time."

FIVE DAYS LATER, AFTER THREE FULL DAYS OF SUNSHINE, THE brothers decided to start for Philadelphia. They appeared at breakfast with their packs ready, awaiting the first sign of sunlight. Charles carried the fur robe the Indians had given him. They sat at the table to eat breakfast with Pierre and Vangie. Madeleine was missing.

"Is Maman . . . ?"

Pierre, slathering a piece of bread with apple butter, shook his head. "This is difficult for her—to watch both of her sons leave again, and on a mission that she does not approve of."

CHARLES SAT ATOP A LARGE PERCHERON MIX. HE ADJUSTED his gloves over the wrappings with which Claudine had bound his fingers. Philippe threw his knapsack over the back of Legacy. Each of the brothers carried a rifle, a knife, and a pair of snowshoes. And in Philippe's vest pocket lay a blue hair ribbon, tied into a soft, loose knot.

Philippe turned toward the house as Vangie came out the door and handed each of her brothers biscuits, smoked venison, and cheese wrapped in cloth and a flask of ale. "There are dried apples in there as well."

Philippe looked into the dark Clavell eyes of his sister and chucked her chin. He bowed to her. *"Merci, mademoiselle."* Then he kissed her hand and hugged her. "Now get inside. It's too cold out here for you. You're already shivering."

She smiled and walked back onto the porch. Pausing in the doorway, she waved and then went inside.

Pierre handed Legacy's reins to Philippe. "Be alert, and be wise. I pray Godspeed for you on this mission." Then Pierre walked over to Charles and put his hands on top of his. "I pray quick healing for these hands, Father."

Philippe looked at the clear sky. "Could you pray for good weather, as well?"

Pierre laughed and tipped his hat. "That I will do. Now be on your way. Be especially attentive to the rivers and streams. They will be dangerously rapid after this snow. Don't try to cross unless you know—"

"I know." Philippe smiled as he mounted Legacy. He paused and looked toward the house.

"Don't worry about your mother. The past is still too real in her memory. She still sees her sons being captured by an enemy. How can she put her stamp of approval on that? But I am confident that with time and prayer she will see that God is bigger than Protestants and Catholics and dragoons and the king of France." Pierre handed Philippe a bundle wrapped in cloth and tied with twine. "She made hoecakes for you to take, and there's some extra money in there as well." He waved his hand. "Go on about your mission, and bring your Bridget home, if God allows you to arrive in time, and she agrees. We shall be waiting with open arms—all of us."

Philippe nodded, and the Clavell brothers headed for Philadelphia.

LEO ZWICKEN TOSSED EDWARD'S LETTER OF DISMISSAL ONTO his desk. He leaned back in his chair and put his feet up on the desk and chuckled. *He cannot dismiss me. I know too much. He wouldn't dare. This is just for show.*

The bell over the door jangled, and loud voices rose above the noise of the foundry. Taking his feet down and rising, Zwicken made to leave his office, but stopped in the doorway, shocked. British redcoats stood across the front of the shop.

"What is this? What is going on?"

A lieutenant stepped forward with a paper in his hand. "Are you Leo Zwicken?"

"I am."

"You are hereby notified that this property is being conscripted by the Royal Crown of England. Mister Leo Zwicken will no longer be allowed on said property until further notice."

"Impossible! You cannot do this. I am a partner in this business, and my quarters are upstairs."

"I have my orders, sir. I am to escort you off the property."

"Off the property? This is *my* property!" Zwicken pounded his fist on a table.

The lieutenant stepped forward with his hand on his sword. "Please, Mister Zwicken. Let's do this peaceably. We are authorized to use force if we must."

The workers in the shop had stopped their work and were staring in disbelief at the scene. Goody Wallace stood at the door between the shop and the kitchen with a mixing bowl in her arms and a spoon in her hand, her mouth agape.

Addressing the workers, the lieutenant motioned with his hand. "Continue with your work. We have orders to keep you busy, and you will be paid as usual." He took Zwicken by the elbow.

Zwicken wrenched his arm free, tore off his apron, and threw it on the floor. "Would you allow me to gather a few things from my quarters?"

"Of course. You will be escorted."

Zwicken stormed through the shop, into the kitchen, and up the stairs with a soldier close behind him. The two returned a few minutes later; Zwicken hefted a large bag. He started back into the shop, but the door was blocked by another soldier.

"I'm sorry, sir, but I cannot let you enter the shop."

Zwicken blustered and bellowed, "What? Can I not even get my hat out of my office?"

The soldier turned and shouted to one of the workers. "Fetch Mister Zwicken's hat!"

The hat was duly retrieved and handed over solemnly. Zwicken grabbed it and stormed out of the kitchen, down the back steps, and out to the stable to get his horse.

AFTER THREE DAYS OF CLEAR WEATHER, PHILIPPE AND Charles rode into Philadelphia late in the afternoon. The sun slid into the horizon, and the evening air settled like an icy shell in between the shops and stores lining the streets.

"We need to get to the inn," Philippe said.

Charles pulled out his money bag and grinned. "I have money."

Philippe shooed his hand away. "Keep it for now. I'm sure we will need it later. I have my wages from the Barringtons, and Pierre gave me a few coins as well."

The brothers pulled up to the Harbor Tavern & Inn and rode around to the side. Philippe stepped onto the walkway, then turned to Charles. "Remain here while I make certain there is no one inside who might recognize you."

He walked around the corner to the entrance and pushed open the door, which was still scraping across the floor. He stepped inside and looked over the sparse crowd. He saw no one that he recognized, but neither did he see Mister Clark. He stepped down the two steps into the dining room, then he spotted the proprietor with his back to him toward the side of the room wiping a table. Philippe walked up behind him. "Mister Clark?"

The innkeeper jerked his head around. "Why, Philippe. What are you doing back in Philadelphia?" He began pounding Philippe on the back with his free hand and laughing, then his countenance sobered. "Your brother? Did he make it home? Is he . . . ?"

"*Shhh.*" Philippe put his arm around the rotund man. "Charles is fine and waiting outside. And my family thanks you for your help to him. We can never adequately repay your generosity. Now"—Philippe looked around the room—"we need a room for a couple of nights."

"Of course. I have plenty. Most people are home with their families this time of year." He looked at Philippe and raised his eyebrows.

"I shall explain everything. And we *will* pay." Philippe smiled.

Mister Clark nodded. "Go get Charles. I'll see that your room is ready."

Philippe went outside and got Charles and tipped a young groomsman to take care of their horses. They came back in and found a table in a back corner in the shadows of a carved post. The aroma of limes, lemons, oranges, and spices mixed with warm rum filled the room.

Goody Clark smiled at the brothers and set a bowl of the steaming brew in front of them. She looked at Charles. "I'm glad to see you made it. Star got you home?"

Charles grinned. "She did. She is a queen, just as you said. She is safe and warm in the stables on our homestead. Thank you for coming to my rescue. The horse was an answer to prayer."

She laughed and flicked her wrist. "I'm glad Star has a good home. I'll bring your supper right over."

Philippe ladled out mugs for themselves. "You'll like this. The Barringtons used to serve lime punch at Christmastime at Whisper Wood. I always got a cup before Abigail carried it out for the guests."

Charles removed his gloves and fur robe. He encircled the warm mug with his hands. "That feels good."

"How are your fingers?"

"Better!" He wiggled the two digits that had been affected the most. They did look better. "They are still a mite sensitive, but better." He took a swig of the punch. His eyes sparkled. "That *is* good."

"Don't drink it too fast. You'll get light-headed quickly on it."

Charles took another sip and put the mug down on the wooden table. He began to help himself to the plates of smoked bacon, ham and tongue, stewed oysters and eels. Pickled beets, onions, and eggs sat in smaller bowls around the table, along with cooked cabbage, potatoes, and turnips. Large rounds of bread and cheeses sat on breadboards at each end of the table. "What are our plans, big brother? What do you propose we do now?"

Philippe took off his hat, setting it on the bench beside him, and filled his pewter plate, avoiding the oysters. "Never developed a taste for those." He helped himself to the bacon and ham and vegetables. "We'll ask God for direction. He will show us what to do next."

TWENTY-THREE

Bridget offered her hand and curtsied as Edward introduced her, her parents, and David and Ella to his older brother, Jacob; his wife, Faith; and their children. Three girls and two boys, close in age, all in their early or middle adolescence, dutifully curtsied and bowed. Jacob and Faith were acting as host and hostess for the wedding, as Edward's parents were deceased.

Jacob and Edward looked astonishingly alike. However, Jacob's good looks were definitely more masculine than Edward's. He dressed much the same, their build was the same, their voices identical, their hair the same color. But Jacob was less flamboyant and appeared to be more humble than his brother. There could not have been more than two years' difference in their ages.

"I'm so pleased to meet you, Jacob—and Faith. I am shocked at the similarity between you two." Bridget looked from one to the other.

"I must say I agree." Sarah pulled the hood of her cloak down and looked around the massive foyer.

Ella giggled. "You'll have to be sure you don't get them mixed up, Bridget."

"No danger in that." Edward clapped his brother on his back. "Actually only fifteen months separate us, but he is the elder."

Jacob grinned at his brother and cuffed him in return.

Faith, a delicate beauty with strawberry blonde hair and turquoise eyes, motioned to the Barringtons. "I'm sure you would like to freshen up from your trip. We'll send our servants for your luggage. When you have rested, I'll show you where the wedding is to be held, and we'll talk about the arrangements."

Bridget walked upstairs to the room she had occupied once before; she took off her cloak and laid it on the large four-poster bed. Faith took the others to their rooms, her parents again occupying a room down the hall. She tried the adjoining door to Edward's room and locked it. The bed was elegant, obviously English, but she had not noticed previously that the other furniture in the room was all Dutch. A large ornate cupboard with painted pomegranates and quinces on the doors stood in the corner. That piece had not been in the room before. Bridget ran her hand over the wood.

Faith stood in the doorway. "That's a Dutch *kast*, a closet for storing linens and household goods. It is usually handed down from generation to generation as a dowry gift."

"It is exquisite."

"It will belong to you. It is Edward's, handed down from my mother's grandparents, who were Dutch. Our father's side was English—that's why we are Catholic." Faith smiled, reached out, and took Bridget's hands. "I look forward to getting to know you. I hope we will be the best of friends. Edward has always . . ."

Bridget waited. "Always what?"

"Oh, nothing. We just were beginning to wonder if he would ever get married. When he moved to Philadelphia, away from all the eligible young women in New York, they were heartbroken. He could have had any of them he wanted, but . . ." She hesitated. "Well, we are so thrilled he has chosen to marry you. We never thought he would find marital bliss."

Bridget looked away. *Marital bliss. Only when I think of Philippe is that term applicable.*

"Forgive me. I'm sure you'd like to get your things unpacked and arranged. After that, we'll talk."

Bridget turned to her future sister-in-law. "Thank you. However, I would like to say hello to Auntie Margo first. Would that be possible?"

"Oh yes, of course. She has been anticipating your arrival with great eagerness and would be disappointed if you didn't stop by her room."

"Would you send Sophie up to unpack my things while I'm visiting with Auntie Margo, please?"

"I'll go tell her right now. I shall look forward later to showing you what we plan to do to decorate the room for the wedding. I hope you'll be pleased."

"I'm sure it will be beautiful. Thank you." Bridget walked into the hallway. Despite the evergreen boughs and wreaths that decorated the railings of the staircase and windows, everything seemed dark and foreboding.

Is my mind coloring the sense I have about this house? It feels so . . . oppressive to me. Is that my imagination? Or is it real? She shook her head and walked to the other end of the hall. She knocked softly on the door.

"Enter."

Bridget stepped into the room and caught her breath. "Auntie Margo! I've never seen you . . . well, you've always been on your chaise every time I've come."

Dame Margo turned from her wardrobe and opened her ample arms, tottering a bit. "Bridget! Oh, my darling child. I've been awaiting your arrival with great anticipation."

Bridget walked into the woman's embrace. Dame Margo patted and hugged and kissed her cheeks, and then hugged her again. Indicating a chair, she urged Bridget toward it as she eased her ample weight into the vanity chair. "Sit down. I *do* get up to dress and look out the window occasionally. I was just about to ring for Sophie to help me dress."

"She's unpacking my things." Bridget stood. "I'll go get her for you."

Dame Margo waved her hand. "No, no. Just send her in when she's finished. I want to talk to you." She patted her lap for the dogs, who were reclining on the chaise, to come to her. "Do you like dogs, my dear?" The two fluffy balls of fur jumped up on her lap.

"I love animals."

"One can tell a great deal about a person by the way she treats animals."

Bridget nodded. An uneasy silence inched its way into the conversation—the kind of silence that occurs between people who do not know each other well. Bridget cleared her throat and shifted her weight in the chair. "Have you been well, Auntie Margo?"

"As well as can be expected—after I recovered from your party." She chuckled. "Oh, I loved every minute of it, and I plan to come down for the wedding."

"Wonderful. I'm so glad. You need to get out of this room more often, and after Edward and I are married, I will see to that."

She reached over and patted Bridget's hands. "You are a dear child. And you . . . are you well?"

"Yes, as well as can be expected."

Dame Margo narrowed her eyes and scrutinized Bridget. "One would think a bride-to-be would be very well—very well indeed." She stroked her dogs' heads, first one and then the other.

"Yes, one would."

"We are delighted that you are going to be part of our family."

"Thank you."

"Our Edward needs someone like you."

"What do you mean?"

"He has been a bachelor for so long—waiting for the right match. I feared he would never marry. Many a lovely lady was interested, but he was so busy with all the businesses—gone all the time. Then when his father passed away . . . well, he just never married. A man needs a good woman." She pursed her lips. "I hope you are as happy to become a Moorehead as we are to have you."

"Yes, of course." Bridget rose. "If you'll excuse me, I need to rest a bit. Sophie should be about finished unpacking my things. I'll send her to you now."

"By all means. Thank you for coming to say hello to an old woman."

"You are one of my favorite people, Auntie Margo." Bridget bent over and kissed the dowager on the forehead, gave the dogs a pat, and went down the hall to her room for a nap.

HER HAT BLEW OFF AS KIMI GALLOPED IN THE OPPOSITE *direction from the men. Her hair, swirling in the wind and hindering her vision. The blast of a musket. Blood splattering all around her. Pounding, pounding, pounding of the hooves echoed in her ears, then softness as they galloped onto the mossy floor of the forest. Dark shadows enveloping her, and murky fingers reaching out for her. Tree branches thrashing around her head and scratching her arms. Down, down, tumbling over and over, dirt in her face and mouth; Kimi snorting and whinnying as she runs away . . . to Whisper Wood. Home. Whisper Wood.*

The man, the man with the long hair, looking, looking, looking for her. She tries to scream, but nothing comes out. He taps along the trees with his musket—tap, tap, tap . . .

BRIDGET BOLTED UP IN THE BED. HER HEART BANGED SO hard against her chest she could hardly breathe. She glanced around the room, and for a moment she didn't know where she was. *Tap, tap, tap.*

"Mistress Barrington?" The door slowly creaked open, and Sophie stuck her head in. "Mistress Barrington. Are you ill? You were moaning."

Bridget clasped her hand to her chest and exhaled. "Oh, Sophie. Come in. I'm fine. I was having a nightmare and . . . I was trying to scream, but I guess moaning was all I could manage." She sat on the edge of the bed and rolled her head from side to side, rubbing her neck. "I didn't intend to sleep so long. I guess I was more tired than I realized." *And anxious and miserable.*

"Are you ready to get dressed for the evening?"

"Yes, please. I think I shall wear the purple *robe à lànglaise*, with the lace head scarf."

"Yes, mistress." Sophie put the purple dress on the bed, then unpacked the beaver cloak. "This is very beautiful."

"Edward said you wrapped it up for him. Thank you."

Sophie looked away and removed the muff and hat from the box.

"It's too large. We are going to have to have some panels taken out of it." Bridget smiled. "I'm not very big."

The servant motioned to the small case. "That case was locked. Did you want me to unpack it for you?"

"No, thank you. Those are just some personal things."

Sophie closed the shutters on the darkening evening sky.

"Master Edward said you like the sunlight to come into the rooms." Sophie ducked her head. "I do too."

Bridget turned and looked at the domestic, not so much older than she. "I'm glad to have your assistance, Sophie. I miss my Abigail. Are you happy working for Mister Edward?"

"Yes." Her voice was so soft Bridget could hardly hear her.

"Do you wish to remain in his service? I would like you to stay."

"Master Edward pays well. And I have no place else to go." She avoided Bridget's eyes. "I . . . the household needs a mistress." She gathered her skirt and looked as if she were about to bolt from the room.

Bridget caught hold of her arm. "Wait, please—"

Sophie didn't move. There was something in her demeanor, Bridget thought. Something sad, something . . .

"Yes, mistress?" Sophie's words broke the spell.

"I—I need to dress for supper." Bridget shook her head.

Bridget stared in the mirror at her reflection as Sophie tightened the stays and laced up her dress. *You poor thing. Nowhere to go, nowhere to turn.*

The women worked in silence, each captive to her own thoughts.

"That's all, Sophie. Thank you."

The maid curtsied and went out the door. Bridget sat in the heart-shaped chair, unlocked the small case, and took out the handkerchief. She smiled. *Philippe Clavell is a gentleman, but Edward Moorehead is a . . .* She didn't know what to call him. She stood, tucked the handkerchief into her sleeve, and went downstairs.

Evergreen boughs, mistletoe, wreaths, berries, and fruit decorated every wall, window, and doorway.

"Why, I've never seen such lavish Christmas decorations. Would you just look at all of this?" Sarah exclaimed over and over as they went through the house.

Faith waved her arm at a window completely surrounded by greenery. "Well, the Dutch are known for their extravagant month-long celebration of Christmas. We go all out—businesses close; we feast all month; and *Sinterklaas* comes on Christmas Eve."

The inane chatter around the supper table rattled in her head until Bridget thought she would scream. She toyed with her food.

Edward turned toward her with a glass of claret in his hand. "You are so very quiet tonight, my dear. What is troubling you?"

"I am simply weary from the trip."

"Will you feel like going to our furrier shop tomorrow for a fitting on your cloak?"

Faith spoke up. "Edward, they are closed for Christmas."

"Could we get Johannes to open up for us?"

"I'm sure he would."

"Good. Send a message to him to meet us at the shop first thing in the morning—say nine o'clock? We are to meet with the priest at ten. That is, if he has had a safe trip from New York."

Edward took another sip of wine and reached for Bridget's hand. She pulled it away and folded her hands in her lap underneath her napkin.

Edward leaned in and whispered through clenched teeth, "You will never, ever pull away from me." His eyes glinted. "Am I clear about that? Give me your hand—now."

Bridget slowly slipped her hand from under the napkin and put it on the table. He put his glass of wine down and placed his hand over hers. "You are trembling."

"Y-yes. I told you that I am very tired. May I please be excused?"

Edward pushed back his chair and stood. "Of course. I'll see you to your room."

"No, thank you. I'll see myself to my room. Please send Sophie up."

"Yes, of course, my dear. Sleep well. I'll see you in the morning."

"Yes, nine o'clock—to the furrier."

He sipped on his claret and watched her climb the stairs.

TWENTY-FOUR

Bridget sighed and leaned her head against the large wooden back of the rocking chair. Her hands gripped a handkerchief that she wrapped and unwrapped around her fingers. She stared at the orange flames in the fireplace as Sophie encouraged the fire with bellows to burn hotter. Bridget put the handkerchief in the pocket of her robe. "Sophie, would you hand me my shawl, please?"

Sophie picked up a pink shawl from the bed and handed it to Bridget, who pulled it around her shoulders.

"This is a lovely room, but it is cold."

"Yes, mistress, it is." The young maid, her white cap tied neatly under her chin and her apron tied perfectly, continued with her evening tasks—turning down the bed, hanging Bridget's gown in the wardrobe, bringing fresh water. She had brought a glass of claret and put it beside the bed.

A knock came on the door, and Bridget turned in her chair. Sophie hastened to answer.

"I wanted to say good night, dear." Sarah swept into the bedroom, followed by Amos. Her father seemed to be limping more than usual. "We won't have the privilege of bidding you good night every evening after the wedding. You will be in your own home."

"We won't be too far away, and we will visit frequently." Bridget gave her parents a good-night hug and kiss. "Father, you are leaning heavily on your cane tonight."

"These old bones are simply a little creaky. I shall be good as new in the morning."

Sarah drew her shawl around her. "This room is chilly."

"Sophie, would you please make sure they have plenty of blankets on the bed and that their fire is blazing strong?"

Sophie curtsied and closed the door as she left.

The old couple turned to leave.

"Mother?"

"Yes, dear?" Sarah turned.

Amos stopped with his hand on the door latch.

"You too, Father." Bridget clutched her hands in front of her. "Thank you for loving me and being such good parents. No one could have had better. I could have ended up on the streets or in an orphanage if you hadn't taken me in."

"Oh, my sweet darling." Sarah rushed to her daughter and embraced her. "You have been the joy and delight of our lives."

Amos stood aside and watched mother and daughter with a smile on his face. Bridget went to him and snuggled in his arms.

"What would I have done without my papa?" She looked up at both of them. "I love you very much. I know you have tried to make the best decision for me. I will do my best to be content and make you proud."

Sarah patted her daughter's hands. "We know you will." She turned to her husband. "It's late. You need to put this old lady to bed."

Amos chuckled. "I've been doing that for forty years. I suppose I can manage one more night." He turned to Bridget and smiled. "Good night, dear. Only two more days, and your life will be altered forever. We shall see you in the morning."

"Remember, Edward and I are going to the furrier shop early in the morning and then to see the priest. I'll not see you until dinner."

"Very well."

"Good night."

Bridget opened her eyes. Ghostly moonlit shadows floated across the room through the slats in the shutters. It had to be the middle of the night. She searched for the glass of claret beside her bed. It was empty, and her throat was dry. Her head was throbbing. She sat on the edge of her bed and searched for her slippers. Pulling her robe from the back of a chair, she lit a lantern and walked to the door. Easing it open, she stepped into the hallway. She tiptoed down the unfamiliar stairs with the goblet in one hand and the lantern in the other, thinking she would go to the kitchen.

Instead she turned into the parlor to see if there might be claret left in the flask on the table where the men had gathered after supper. She raised the lantern and looked around the room. There was the flask on a small table beside the settee. She set the lantern down and shook the container. *Ah!* She could hear liquid sloshing. The flask clinked against her goblet as she filled it. She sat on the couch and touched her forehead with the cool flask. It soothed the headache somewhat. She drank about half the goblet, then stood to return to her room.

What was that? A creak in the floor. Bridget froze, listening. Whirling around, she gasped to see a shadowy figure in the doorway.

"I thought I heard someone in here. I went to the kitchen to find the ale to take to my room. You went up-shtairs much too early." Edward slurred his words. He moved toward her.

Bridget gathered her robe around her and stepped behind the sofa. The soft glow from the lantern cast sinister shadows on their faces. "You're drunk."

"Maybe. Probably!" He chuckled. "But not drunk enough to be unaware of your beauty." He swayed and caught hold of the back of a chair. "I would like a good-night kiss." He snickered. "A man needs to give his fiancée a proper good-night kiss, does he not?"

Her heart thudded against her chest. She attempted to maneuver past him, but he blocked her path to the door. She lowered her voice. "Get out of my way, Edward. Go to bed and sleep off the effects of your drunken evening."

Suddenly Edward seemed completely sober. He did not move, but continued to block her escape. "That will not do, unless you come to bed with me." He lunged for her and grabbed her arm, pulling her to him. "That will not do at all. I want a proper good-night kiss—now." He gripped her wrist and wound his other arm around her waist. "A tiny waist. I like that. I like that very much." He rubbed his body against her.

Bridget twisted and tried to push Edward away as he half carried, half dragged her up the stairs and into her room. He closed the door behind him with his foot. She broke loose from him for a moment, but he grabbed for her and caught her by her hair.

I—I cannot scream and awaken the whole household. I don't want my parents to hear. He is very soon to be my husband. This is between the two of us.

Edward pushed her down on the bed, pinning her arms above her head with one hand and her torso with his knee. He brought his other arm across her neck, choking her. "It will be best if you don't fight me. That would complicate things, indeed."

The silver, luminescent shimmer from the moonlight offered too much light. Bridget wanted to hide herself in darkness. She closed her eyes. She didn't want to see Edward's face. She continued to struggle against him.

"I'm telling you, it's better if you relax," Edward growled. "You might even find yourself enjoying it."

His arm across her throat began to cut off her air. The smell of liquor on his breath, mingled with the sickeningly sweet musky odor of his cologne, turned her stomach as he descended on her. Bile rose in her throat.

This can't be happening! Her eyes popped open.

His face above her contorted into a rigid mask. He was strong, unbelievably strong. How could he look like such a dandy and be so strong? Why could she not get away from him? Sophie's face with the bruise flashed in front of her. She heard herself gasping for air, and it sounded like someone outside of herself. She felt as if she were watching the violent, abominable scene from the corner of the room.

Pain . . . searing pain. Ripping, tearing, shoving pain.

She was riding through the cornfield, dashing for the woods. Kimi, hurry, hurry! Take me away from here. If I . . . can . . . just . . . If I could just get to my sanctuary in the woods—then he won't be able to hurt me. Then the hurting will stop. I'll hide beneath the log, and he won't be able to find me. If . . . please don't do this, Edward. Please . . . don't . . . Philippe, oh, Philippe. This is not how it was supposed to be. Please, stop . . . stop. Will it ever end?

The pain was almost unbearable. She pushed against him and heard someone whimper—whimpering, pitiful sobs. And she realized that it was she.

Edward finally got off her and refastened his breeches—his fancy breeches. She tried to get up and felt a dampness running down her legs. He stood over her and smirked, daring to extend his hand to her. She ignored it.

She could not bear to look at him, and a palpable loathing and rage rose up in her. "You!" she hissed. "You'll not get away with this. Do you think you can treat me like so much rubbish to be used and thrown aside, like one of your servants?"

He stared at her.

"Oh yes, I've seen the bruises." She pulled her robe up around her neck and stood on legs that trembled uncontrollably. "Well, I'm not Sophie." She staggered to the fireplace, picked up a poker, and started swinging it at him.

He ducked, quietly laughing at her efforts. Reaching out, he took the poker from her. "You are being much too dramatic, my dear. What's a man to do when his fiancée teases him, then changes her mind? I simply claimed what rightfully belongs to me a bit early. And Sophie has merely been a means to satisfy a man's desires."

Bridget backed up from this man who was to be her husband, clutching her robe around her. "What despicable, immoral, decadent behavior."

Edward returned the poker to the hook with the rest of the fireplace tools. Then he stood with one hand on his hip, while he searched among his pockets for his quizzing glass with the other. "My dear, you are overreacting. Surely you are aware this is a common practice. Not a second thought is given to it. The men talk and jest about it at social gatherings, and the women pretend as if they are unaware." He replaced the quizzing glass. "As for you, my dear . . . we are to be married shortly. We simply . . . took the liberty to consummate the union a bit early."

"This was no consummation to our marriage," Bridget whispered defiantly. "You took me against my will!"

Edward grabbed her by her wrist and pulled her to him once again. He drew his face down to hers until she could feel his breath on her skin. He snarled at her. "You belong to me. You are no longer Mistress Bridget Barrington, but Mistress Edward Moorehead. You will service me when I desire." He released her and straightened his vest. "Obedience to me will be accompanied by many benefits: anything your heart desires that money can buy—houses, land, horses, clothing—fur cloaks." The corners of his lips turned up in a sneer. "You do like your fur cloak, do you not?"

"You may have been able to buy your way into this marriage, but you will never have my heart or my love or my respect. Those cannot be purchased with money." Suddenly the fight went out of her. She sagged onto the bed. *No, don't cry. I don't want to give him the satisfaction of seeing me cry, but the tears . . . the tears . . . they won't stop.*

The tears flowed down her cheeks and dripped off her chin. She reached into the pocket of her robe and wiped them away with Philippe's handkerchief.

"No need for tears, Bridget."

"Get out." Her voice came out hoarse and soft. "Get out and leave me alone. Give me the dignity to clean myself up and get some rest."

He walked toward the door and paused before he went out. "Yes, of course. Do clean yourself up—you look a mess. And make sure your appearance is presentable in the morning."

He walked out and closed the door behind him as if nothing had happened. But Bridget would never be the same. Just as her father had prophesied earlier in the evening, her life had been altered forever. She wiped the tears away from her cheeks, folded the handkerchief, and stuffed it back into her pocket.

TWENTY-FIVE

She heard Sophie bring in the breakfast tray and set it on the table. The young maid opened the shutters, but Bridget kept her eyes squeezed shut. A few moments went by, then Bridget swung her legs over to the side of the bed and groaned. She grabbed her stomach and staggered to the chamber pot, retching into it.

"Oh dear, mistress, you are ill." Sophie grabbed a towel and rushed to her.

Bridget leaned on the servant and then slumped into the rocker. "No, I'm not ill." Her chin began to quiver and tears sprang to her eyes.

Sophie's glance about the room stopped on the bed, where the sheets displayed a bloody discharge. The servant exhaled. "Oh."

"What time is it?"

"Near seven o'clock."

"Help me clean up and get dressed. Do away with the sheets and find clean linens somewhere. I do not want anyone else to know. I will not give Edward Moorehead the satisfaction of seeing me b—broken." She put her hand over her mouth and suppressed the sob that had begun to rise in her throat.

I will not, I will not, I will not allow my grief to show. I will hide, as I did in the forest, until the danger goes away. Nothing can hurt me if I hide.

Sophie brought warm water for Bridget to clean herself. Bridget moaned as she washed.

"Mistress?"

"Yes."

"It's not so bad after the first time."

Bridget looked at her servant and knew her suspicions were true.

"What gown does Mistress wish to wear?"

Bridget continued to regard Sophie thoughtfully, until the maid shifted nervously.

"What gown—"

"How long have you worked for the Mooreheads?" Bridget asked slowly.

Sophie paused. "Almost five years now."

"May I ask you a question?" Bridget sat down in the heart-shaped chair.

"We must get you dressed."

"It will only take a moment."

The girl hesitated.

"Please." Bridget touched Sophie's hand. "That bruise I saw on your face awhile ago . . . You didn't stumble into a door, did you?"

The maid touched her cheek with her fingertips, and for a moment remained perfectly still. "Mistress—"

"You are safe with me. Did Mister Edward do that to you?"

Sophie looked at her with beautiful gray eyes that reflected deep hurt. "Please."

"You don't have to remain with the Mooreheads. My father would give you a job where you won't be abused or hurt. Are you married?"

Sophie lowered her eyes and shook her head.

"You have confirmed my suspicions about my fiancé. I need to ask you one more thing. Is Edward . . . does he take advantage of you?"

A tear spilled out of one of the maid's eyes and trickled down her cheek. She brushed it away with the back of her hand, then abruptly turned away from Bridget.

Bridget put her hand on the girl's shoulder. "You need say no more. I assure you once more, you are safe with me. Now would you help me dress, please?"

You are safe with me, Sophie, but am I safe with Edward? What other secrets am I going to find hidden in the closets here in this house? Poor Auntie Margo. She must know what a scoundrel Edward is. Or perhaps she doesn't. How can I go through with this marriage?

Sophie silently busied herself with the basin and towels, and Bridget steeled herself to go out with her fiancé, to make polite conversation, to smile as if all were well.

Is this the way other people live their lives, with lies and secrets simmering beneath the surface of superficial, courteous behavior? Bridget sighed. *Is this truly acceptable—for a man to have a mistress?*

She didn't like it, but she didn't know what she was going to do. If she confronted Edward, she knew he would deny it and then take it out on Sophie. She couldn't tell her parents. They wouldn't believe her. She was trapped.

"What gown does Mistress wish to wear?"

If I wear the brown dress, I'll look like a brown wren, a poor, pitiful little wren. If I wear the red Watteau, I'll appear strong and in control.

"I'll wear the Watteau."

Sophie smiled shyly. "And the matching *fontage*—from Paris?"

"No, I think I'll wear the beaver hat and carry the muff, since we are going to the furrier to have the cloak altered."

Sophie assisted Bridget into her dress and coiffed her hair, setting the beaver fur hat on top of her curls. Bridget put on the cloak and looked in the mirror. "Yes, much too big, but I'll wear it today to get an idea of what needs to be done to it."

"Is there anything else Mistress needs?" Sophie stood at the foot of the bed. She looked so innocent. One would never guess that she was a woman who serviced a man as his mistress.

Bridget removed the cloak and sat in the rocker. A magnificent silver candelabrum on the mantel glinted in the morning sunlight. "My father was right, you know. My life will be altered forever after Edward and I are married. Would you mind if I told you something shocking?"

"Pardon, mistress?"

"I mean, I know your secret, and it is safe with me. May I tell you one of mine?"

"Mistress, 'tisn't proper."

The old rocking chair creaked as Bridget rocked back and forth. "I don't care. I am weary of propriety and tradition and courtesies. It is because of those very things that I find myself in this position. My parents made what they felt was a good decision for me. They believed that Edward was a good match—wealthy, respected in the community, a good businessman."

"Yes'm." The domestic wiped her palms on her apron and hesitated between her new mistress and the door.

"The truth is that I do not want to marry Edward Moorehead—ever. I am in love with another, a man who has rejected me."

The maid's eyes grew wide, and she rested her hand on her chest.

"It's true." Bridget smiled a sad smile. "I declared my love to another man, and not only did he not return the feelings, he walked away from me forever." She looked down at her hands.

"Mistress—"

"I told you that you would be shocked. Oh, I will marry Edward, because it is what my parents wish, as the man I truly love is gone. So . . . I am trapped. What's a woman to do without a husband? We must take advantage of the proposals that come our way, mustn't we?"

Sophie looked down. "I'm sorry, Mistress Barrington."

"I am too." Bridget stood and walked to the young servant and took her hand. "You probably understand my dilemma better than anybody else."

The empty rocking chair creaked back and forth on its own, the only sound in the room. Then Bridget smiled. "Take my wool cloak downstairs with you. I'd like you to accompany us today."

Sophie curtsied. "I'll need to get my things."

"Go on. I'll be right down."

Sophie gathered the linens and went out the door. Bridget turned and looked at herself in the mirror. She didn't look any different than she did yesterday, but her heart had been forever changed. A wall of stone had been erected around it, and she would never allow Edward Moorehead to penetrate it. She resolved to live her life behind that protective wall and never again come out.

She walked to the door and raised her head high. She opened it and descended the massive staircase. Edward stood at the bottom of the stairs, waiting for her. She looked him square in the eyes and clenched her jaw.

"Good morning, my lovely bride. You look stunning this morning." He kissed her hand. "I trust you rested well."

He is acting as though nothing happened last night. Was he so drunk he remembers nothing? I'll not give him the satisfaction of reminding him.

"I slept rather fitfully, thank you very much. In fact, I woke up nauseated, but I feel much better now. Sophie's a dear. She attended to me well."

"I am happy to hear that."

"Yes, I have asked her to accompany us to the shop. I could use her help with the fitting."

"I asked Faith to accompany us." Edward put on his hat. "In fact, she's already in the carriage."

"She's most welcome to go as well. I simply would like Sophie's company today. We are getting to know one another."

"Of course, whatever your heart desires. Your wish is my very command." He assisted Bridget into the heavy beaver cloak. "Shall we?" He extended his arm, and she placed her hand on it.

She turned her head to look behind her. "Coming, Sophie?"

"Yes, mistress."

The couple exited, with the young domestic following behind.

EDWARD'S CARRIAGE PULLED UP TO THE FURRIER'S SHOP A little before nine o'clock. The shopkeeper, watching through the window for the owner, unlocked the front door as they descended from the carriage. Six large, paned windows lined the front of the shop. An ornately carved sign swung over the front door, which fronted on a corner and proclaimed VANDERVOORT'S FINE FURS. The business sported evergreen garlands around the door and windows. Gables atop the roof had wreaths hung in them.

Bridget looked at Edward. "Vandervoort's?"

"My mother's maiden name. She was Dutch."

"Of course. Faith told me a little bit about your Dutch heritage last night." Bridget gathered the voluminous cloak around her and stood as tall as she could to keep the garment from dragging in the slushy snow.

The shopkeeper greeted them as they moved into the shop. "Welcome, Mister Moorehead. And a Merry Christmas to you, sir."

"Yes, Johannes. Thank you for opening up for us." He pointed to Bridget. "May I present my fiancée, Mistress Bridget Barrington. We are to be married day after tomorrow."

The wiry, bent-over old man peered at her over his glasses. "Yes, so I understand."

"As you can see, the beaver cloak I had you make for her is much too big. Can it be easily remedied?"

"Let me see. Would you mind stepping up on this little stool, please?"

Bridget took Edward's hand and steadied herself as the tailor examined the fit. He looked on the outside of the cloak, and he looked on the inside. He put it on her, and he took it off of her. He removed some stitching from the lining and examined the underside of the pelts. Faith, meanwhile, ambled around the shop looking at the hats and jackets on display. Sophie stayed close by Bridget's side.

"I can fix it, but I am afraid the task will not be simple. It's not only too large, which is easily dealt with, but it is too long—in which case I need to take some off at the shoulders, not from the hem. It is going to require almost remaking the whole garment."

Edward sighed. "So I assume that it is impossible to get it before our wedding."

"Your assumption is correct. It will take a month or more to repair."

"Very well. Do what you need to do and let us know when it is ready."

Bridget motioned to Sophie to bring her the woolen cloak, and Edward helped her with it.

"I shall have to get used to how very diminutive you are." He circled his hands in front of him. "With a tiny waist about this big—that I like very much." He gave her a slight smile.

Bridget looked up at him. He *did* remember. She looked away and walked out ahead of him and leaned against the carriage. Edward lingered behind, talking to the shopkeeper.

Sophie came to her side. "Can I get anything for you? Are you feeling ill again?"

Bridget's breath had quickened, and she felt faint. "I'm just feeling a little weak. Could you find me something to drink?" She entered the carriage and sat holding her forehead in her hand, propped up on her elbow.

Faith stepped in. "Are you feeling unwell?"

"Just a little faint. Sophie went to locate something for me to drink."

Sophie brought a goblet of water, followed by Edward. "Sophie tells me you're not feeling well."

"Thank you, Sophie. This will suffice." Turning to Edward, she narrowed her eyes, ever so slightly. "I'm fine, Edward. I didn't have much of an appetite this morning. Something nauseated me during the night."

Faith interjected, "We're going to be late for your appointment with the priest. Are you well enough to proceed with our plans, Bridget?"

"I am fine, really. I'm going to be just fine."

THE GROOM BROUGHT THE CLAVELLS' HORSES AROUND TO the front of the inn. Philippe dug into his coin bag and paid him.

"Thank ye kindly, sir, but that's not necessary."

"Maybe not from your standpoint, but from mine it is. We appreciate your service to our horses. We'll be around for two or three days."

"Yessir. Thank you, sir." The boy stuck the coins in the pocket of his tattered jacket.

Charles led the way. They headed north, then turned down a side street. He pointed. "We need to cut across and go east for a bit. Then we'll turn back north in a few blocks."

Philippe nodded and tipped his hat to an old gentleman locking up his furrier shop. "Merry Christmas."

He looked up at the young man and nodded his head in return. "And a Merry Christmas to you, my boy." He got in his buggy and drove off as the Clavell brothers headed for the Mooreheads.'

THE FARTHER NORTH THEY RODE, THE FEWER HORSES AND buggies they encountered until they were almost the only ones on the road. The road was muddy and slippery. A carriage drove past them, splashing mud, and pulled into a driveway a way down the road.

"That's the house," Charles said, nodding. "That could be them."

The carriage went through an iron gate that clanged behind them as Philippe and Charles rode by.

"That *was* Bridget!" Philippe said softly.

"And Edward."

"Yes, and Edward."

Charles kicked his horse, and they rode past the house into a stand of trees and bushy cedar on a vacant lot next to Edward's house. They dismounted and tied their horses to a large oak tree. They could see the back door from where they stood.

"What do we do now?" Charles took a drink from a wineskin.

"I've got to figure out some way to get a message to Bridget without Edward finding out."

"Any ideas?"

"No. Pray for God to show us what to do."

A maid came out and threw scraps out the double Dutch door to chickens that huddled around the back stoop. A groomsman was unhooking the carriage from the team of horses.

"Stay here. I'm going to go closer and see if I can look in the windows."

"What for?"

"Maybe there's somebody here who would be sympathetic and take her a message from me. *Shhh!* Stay here."

Philippe moved toward the house. The windows were too high for him to peer into. He went around to the side. Climbing onto a rain barrel, he could just barely peek into a window. The family was sitting down to dinner; he could see Bridget and Edward, another couple he did not recognize, the Osbornes, and Amos and Sarah. He slid off the barrel and ran back to Charles. "That's the dining room, and they are eating dinner. The Osbornes are here, as well as Mister and Mistress Barrington. Maybe Ella will help us."

"Let's wait for them to finish dinner, then pray for a way to get a message to Bridget."

After several minutes passed the back door opened again, and a different maid emerged. She set something in a bowl on the back porch and called, "Kitty, kitty, kitty."

"That's Sophie!" Charles exclaimed.

"Who?"

"Moorehead's maid. I know her."

Philippe looked up. "Thank you, Heavenly Father. There's our message bearer. How well do you know her? Would she recognize you?"

"Probably so. I've seen her when I made deliveries."

"Would she take a message for us?"

"I don't know. She's always seemed so sad and downtrodden. Maybe."

"Good. Go to the back door and ask to see her."

"Have you lost your senses?"

"Probably, but do it anyway. Just go ask for her. The maids and cooks won't pay any mind."

"Very well. What shall I tell her?"

"Simply tell her to get a message to Bridget that I'm here, and I need to see her right away. Go on."

Charles stepped out of the stand of trees, glanced around, and walked to the back door. He shaded his eyes and peered in through the window. Philippe saw him motion to someone from inside. Sophie stepped out onto the porch as Charles removed his cap. Sophie looked in his direction, and then nodded her head. She returned to the kitchen. Charles sat on the porch steps and put his cap back on. Fortunately the sun was shining, and there was no wind today.

The door opened, and Charles jumped up. The maid talked to him for a minute, shaking her head. Charles gestured with his gloved hands, and she shook her head again. The maid closed the door and went inside. Charles walked toward his brother.

"What did she say? Did she give Bridget the message?"

"Yes, she gave her the message."

"Well? What did she say?"

Charles shook his head and quirked his mouth.

"Come out with it. What did she say?"

"She won't see you, Philippe. She said that she's getting married day after tomorrow and for you to go away. She refuses to see you."

"I don't believe it. I don't believe she doesn't want to see me." Philippe sloshed back and forth in the soft snow.

Charles threw his hands up. "All I know is what Sophie told me."

"Go back up there and tell Sophie to tell Bridget that unless she agrees to come out here and speak to me, I'm coming in. I shall demand to see her."

TWENTY-SIX

B ridget peeked out the leaded window casement of her room after dinner. The rest of the family had gone upstairs for afternoon naps, or were helping Faith work on decorations for the wedding. Edward and Jacob had taken a servant and gone down to the harbor to talk to one of their ship's captains. She saw Philippe and Charles toward the back of the house standing in the snow.

Philippe. My beloved Philippe. She watched him pacing back and forth, his tall, slender frame and broad shoulders pitched forward in determination. Her heart fluttered even in its battered state. *How I long to fly into his strong arms.*

Someone knocked on her door. Bridget remained at the window, staring out on the gardens.

Sophie spoke softly. "Mistress Barrington, Mister Philippe is insisting that he see you."

Bridget walked to the door and cracked it open enough to speak to the servant. "Tell him to go away. I do not want to see him. I cannot see him."

"But, Mistress Barrington. He's come all this way."

Bridget leaned her head against the door. "I cannot, Sophie. Surely you can understand why. Send him away."

"Please reconsider, mistress."

"Send him away."

"The man will not be dissuaded. He says if you refuse to see him again, he will come in and demand to see you." Sophie wrung her hands. "I don't think that would be wise."

She sighed. "Very well. Tell him I . . . I'll be out in a minute." She closed the door as Sophie turned and hurried down the stairs. She splashed water on her cheeks and retied the ribbon around her braid. She moved out into the hallway and looked both ways. Seeing no one, she stepped silently down the stairs, through the keeping room, past the cooks chopping vegetables and rolling out piecrusts, and went out onto the back porch. Philippe stood just on the edge of the trees, his hands on his hips, watching her. Her knees began to shake at the sight of him. She gripped the railing of the back steps and edged down.

Oh, Father, help me go through with this charade. Glancing over her shoulder, she picked up her skirt and ran toward the trees.

She wanted to run straight into his arms and beg him to rescue her from the nightmare that had become her life. Instead she pasted a smile on her face and took a deep breath. She extended her hand to Philippe for him to kiss. "Why, Philippe Clavell, what a pleasant surprise. I did not expect to ever see you again."

Philippe stepped forward and bowed slightly, but instead of kissing her hand, he took her by the arm. He stared at her. "Come over here with me. I need to talk to you . . . alone." He glanced back toward the house. "Where is Edward?"

"He and his brother went to check on one of their ships down in the harbor." Bridget hunched her shoulders under her cape, turned her back, and brushed a tear away.

They walked a few feet away from Charles and stepped behind a bushy cedar.

"Bridget. Something has changed. What has happened?" He took her gently by the shoulders. "Or is it that you have decided that you do not love me after all. Have you regretted confessing your undying love for me? Have I come after you in vain?"

She swallowed hard and forced herself to look directly at him. *Why now? Why did he wait until it is too late to confess his love for me?* "Oh, Philippe. You were right. We were good friends, and my infatuation with you was just that—infatuation. We are from two different worlds and need to live our lives as dictated by our families. Mine with the man my parents have chosen for me, and yours with someone that your family would approve of." Her voice caught in her throat, and she turned away. She pulled the hood of her cloak over her head. Her knees felt like water.

"I don't believe you. Turn around and look me in the eyes." He tilted her chin up. "You are trembling." He tried to gather her in his arms, but she pushed him away.

"I'm simply cold." She stepped back and looked up at him. "I . . . I do not love you. I thought I did, but it was foolish infatuation, conjured up in the head of a child. I am to be married day after tomorrow."

He took hold of her shoulders. "You cannot marry this man."

"I most certainly can and am going to."

285

"You don't understand. You are in danger. You don't realize it, but you are in a compromising situation."

"Whatever are you talking about?"

"I have never forgotten the . . . the secret that you told me about that day in the woods. About the man with the musket?"

"Have you betrayed my trust? You were never to tell anyone."

"Charles overheard it in a conversation between Edward and Mister Zwicken."

"Mister Zwicken at the foundry?"

"The same. Bridget, what you stumbled upon that day was a smuggling operation, illegal sales of guns that were supposed to go to the military. The man who was murdered had probably threatened to go to the authorities. The man who killed him was . . ."

"Are you going to tell me that was Edward?"

"It was. Charles heard him talking about it, and about marrying you in order to silence you. Charles has proof that he is still stealing guns from the British Crown. He's seen Lenape with guns from Zwicken's."

Bridget listened, feasting her eyes on her beloved's face. Her head was swimming. She felt angry; she felt betrayed; she felt frightened. A roaring began in her ears that wouldn't stop. Everything went dark around her, and she felt as if she were looking at him through a tunnel.

Philippe's voice seemed to be detached from him. "Come away with me now. I love you. I should have told you that day at Whisper Wood, but I didn't dare believe it myself. I didn't see any way that we could be together." He took her hand, kissing it over and over. "Don't even go back to the house. Come with me, now."

She shook her head slowly. "I can't. It's too late."

"What do you mean, it's too late? You haven't said your vows, have you?"

She shook her head. "No, but it's too late. Please go." She turned toward the house, then whirled around, facing him. She took a deep breath. "Thank you so much for coming all this way, Philippe. I am truly flattered." She ran to the house, climbed the stairs to the back porch, and went inside.

PHILIPPE WATCHED HER GO INTO THE HOUSE, STILL NOT believing what she had told him. He shook his head. "Come, Charles. We might as well leave."

"What just happened here? Did she hear what you said? Does she understand—"

"I don't know. She obviously doesn't love me after all. It seems we made the trip for naught." He caught hold of Legacy's reins. "I can't believe it. I don't believe it."

"What are we to do?"

Philippe got on his horse. "Go home, that's what."

"Right now?"

"First thing in the morning."

BRIDGET HELD ON TO THE DRAPERY AND WATCHED FROM HER room as the Clavell brothers rode away. She felt as if her heart were being ripped out. She stood on tiptoe and watched until she could no longer see the handsome brothers astride their splendid mounts. She curled her knees up in the rocker in front of the fireplace and pulled her shawl around her. The fire needed attention, but she ignored it.

Was what Philippe told her about Edward true? Her fiancé was a dishonest man, a cheat, a thief . . . and a murderer? Then it hit her with a force that almost knocked the wind out of her. Edward was not only the one who had shot the man that day at the edge of the cornfield; he was the man who had chased her into the forest and from whom she'd hidden, trembling and fearful for her life. That day at Whisper Wood when Edward had turned toward her with the musket in his hands . . . something deep within her had recognized him. And she was *marrying* him!

She stood and for the briefest of moments thought of trying to stop Philippe; thought of falling into his arms and being whisked away—but that was a fantasy. She would have to go through with the wedding. Even if she revealed what she had learned, who would believe her? Edward would deny it. Her mother and father would think she was simply trying to get out of the marriage. More than ever, she was trapped. She could never speak of this again to anyone. For the second time that day, she resolved to bury her feelings and go on with what was expected of her.

CHARLES AND PHILIPPE RODE BACK TO THE INN IN SILENCE. The afternoon sun warmed them, and it almost didn't feel like winter. Charles had laid his fur robe across the back of his saddle.

Tomorrow was Christmas Eve. They reined in at the front of the inn and left their horses with the same groom. The inn was almost empty.

Mister Clark greeted them. "How about tall steins of ale, my good men?"

Charles tossed his fur robe onto a bench. "Ale would be most welcome." He took off his cap and tried to smooth his unruly hair.

Mister Clark set a pitcher of ale on the table along with two steins. "Your faces tell me that the result of your visit was not what you expected."

"You're correct. Not what we expected at all. We'll be leaving in the morning to go back home."

Philippe removed his jacket and hat and straddled the bench facing Charles. "Thank you, Mister Clark." He watched the innkeeper walk away, sat with his head down, and started tracing the wood grain on the table with his fingers. "Something's not right here. Let's say she doesn't love me. Very well. I am the unfortunate loser, but why would she not listen to us about Edward and his questionable past?"

"Perhaps she thought we made that story up to persuade her to come with us."

"But she's the one who saw him when she was a little girl. Surely a flicker of recognition is stirring in her memory."

"Maybe she has come to love him and doesn't believe he could have done all those things."

"She does not love him. I know she doesn't, despite what she may say. It's something else. She's afraid. She's fearful of him for some reason."

"But if she's afraid of him, Philippe, why wouldn't she leave? He wasn't there. It was a perfect time for her to leave."

Philippe shook his head. "I don't know." They sat in silence drinking their ale.

He looked at his brother. "I cannot do it, Charles. I cannot leave her here. Whether she loves me or not, I cannot leave her to marry that man. He will destroy her."

"I understand your feelings, Philippe, but I don't see that there is anything else we can do, short of kidnapping her."

Philippe looked at his brother and grinned. "Maybe not kidnap her, but perhaps we could offer her a bit of strong encouragement to accompany us on a little trip." He pulled his hair back. "I'm going back out there . . . tomorrow night. You may come with me or not, but I am going. I'm going after her."

"Just try to go without me."

"Tomorrow night is Christmas Eve. If what I have heard about the Dutch celebrations at Christmas is true, there will probably be guests in the house, lots of celebrating, and much drinking. We'll need to wait until the hour is late. We'll talk to Sophie again earlier and find out where Bridget's room is. After the house gets settled in for the night, we go get her. Simple!"

Charles poured himself another glass of ale. "What if she's staying with her parents?"

"In that house?" Philippe shook his head. "Edward Moorehead would not put Bridget up with her parents. He would furnish a room for her."

"Very well. What if we go up to her room during the festivities and simply wait for her there? There will most likely be so many people around and so much activity, we'll never be noticed. We could get word to Sophie to take us up the back way."

Philippe nodded. "That might work."

Darkness was settling in, and more travelers entered the inn. The brothers continued to make plans over supper, then went to their room.

THE MOOREHEAD FAMILY AND GUESTS ATE A LIGHT SUPPER, and Bridget, Ella, and the Moorehead daughters helped Faith hang more wreaths and fruit in preparation for the wedding. The girls all had blonde hair and blue eyes. Bridget could have passed as a blood relative. The oldest daughter, Martha, at fifteen was not that much younger than she was, but Bridget felt much older.

Faith climbed down from the chair she was using as a stepstool and took a sprig of mistletoe from Bridget. "This is the last bit of it." She tied a red ribbon around it and placed it on a hook over an archway.

Bridget smiled. "I like your Christmas traditions."

Cousin Ella straightened a wreath on a window. "Oh, I agree. This is so much fun."

"The Dutch do like to celebrate. We celebrate the birth of our Savior all month long."

The women joined the rest of the family in the parlor. Bridget looked around at David and Ella and her parents, who were playing a game of whist. She sat in a small, upholstered chair next to her mother. Edward was drinking and talking too loudly with Jacob, in a lively discussion over a fence issue. She watched him get up and pour more wine into his goblet. He looked her way and smiled, then returned his attention to Jacob.

She felt caged. She wanted to leave; to get away from her family and the Mooreheads; to go to bed and escape through the numbness of sleep. She rose slowly and eased out of the parlor while everyone's attention was diverted elsewhere. She went soundlessly up the stairs, into her room, and locked the door behind her. She made sure the door to the adjoining room was locked as well.

The linens had been changed and her nightclothes freshly laundered, lying folded on the bed. Just as if nothing at all had happened last night. Philippe's handkerchief, which she had left in the pocket of her robe, lay neatly folded on top. She picked it up and returned it to the robe pocket. She didn't ring for Sophie, but washed up quickly, changed, and blew out the lantern. She curled up on the bed on the opposite edge from where Edward had taken her virtue. Someone knocked on her door, but she did not answer.

She thought about Philippe, and the longing to feel his arms around her became a palpable pain. Her arms ached. Sending him away was the hardest thing that she had ever done.

She pulled the comforter around her shoulders and closed her eyes, but sleep did not come. Arising from the bed, she pulled the comforter off the bed and threw it across the back of the rocking chair. She put several more logs on the fire. Every time she closed her eyes she saw Edward's face as he threw her down on this very bed last night; saw his face as he ravaged her; saw his face as he chased her through the woods when she was a little girl. He had stalked her, and now, at long last, he had conquered her. She would never be free of him. Her nightmares had become her reality.

TWENTY-SEVEN

Someone was knocking at her bedroom door. Bridget looked outside. It was morning, gray and overcast. She uncurled her legs and got out of the rocking chair and went to the door, dragging the quilt with her. "Who is it?"

"It's Sophie, mistress, with your breakfast."

Bridget unlocked the door. "Come in. You may set it on the vanity. Thank you."

Sophie moved a silver hand mirror aside and set the tray down. "Are you ready for your breakfast yet?"

"In a minute. Would you build the fire back up, please? I fear I'm chilled." She wound her hair into a loose bun and nestled back down in the rocker.

Sophie bent over and picked something off the floor. "You lost your handkerchief."

"Thank you, Sophie." She took it from the servant and folded it in the palm of her hand. "I never want to lose this particular hankie."

"It is special?"

"It belongs to the man I loved."

"Oh, I see," Sophie said softly.

With tears threatening to spill over onto her cheeks, Bridget looked at the servant. "I am most miserable. This should be one of the happiest days of my life—the day before my wedding and Christmas Eve—and I am completely miserable. But not only that, I am frightened of this man. He is . . . a bad man."

Sophie kept her eyes on her task at the fireplace and said nothing.

"I'm sorry. I shouldn't be voicing my concerns to you. Forgive me."

"Is there anything else Mistress needs?"

"Not right now. Thank you."

Sophie walked to the door, then turned to face Bridget. She spoke so softly that Bridget could not understand her.

"Excuse me? I did not hear you."

The maid gripped her hands in front of her. "I said, don't make him angry. As long as you do what he says, and don't make him angry, you will fare well enough." She opened the door and was gone.

I don't want to fare well enough, tiptoeing around, fearful of awakening the ire of my husband. I want to love my husband and have children with him. I want to hear joy and laughter ring throughout the house.

Bridget fell to her knees in front of the heart-backed chair and wept. *Oh, God, if you are up there and you care about your children, would you please deliver me from this marriage and this man?* Her shoulders heaved as she broke out in sobs. *I cannot bear this. How did my life change so quickly? Help me.*

She laid her head down on the chair and cried for what seemed like an hour. Each time the tears began to subside, they would burst forth again. She couldn't seem to stop them.

God in heaven, make a way of escape for me. If you are real and truly care for me . . . A sob erupted from her throat. If God was loving, why did he allow Edward to ravage her?

If you are a loving heavenly Father . . . I have no place else to turn. Won't you rescue me? I'm begging you. Please, please, please . . .

After dinner at the inn, Philippe spoke with Mister Clark. Charles waited outside with the horses. Eventually Philippe came out to the hitching rail, his jaw set.

"What did you tell him?"

"I asked him to hold our room for tonight and to please keep it private; that we would be back late, and would have a lady with us."

"What did he say?"

"He asked me if he could depend on my integrity as a fellow believer in the faith, and I assured him that he could. I didn't go into any details, but I did tell him that it was a situation that involved danger. He shook my hand and bade us Godspeed."

Charles nodded and mounted his horse. Philippe brought Legacy around and got in the saddle. The two brothers rode north again through the streets toward the Moorehead house.

They arrived in the late afternoon and rode again to the side of the house in the shelter of the trees. The temperature began to fall as the sun eased below the horizon. From their vantage point they could see carriages arriving, guests spilling out, calling to one another and laughing.

As soon as it seemed apparent that most of the guests had arrived and it was fully dark, Philippe elbowed Charles. "It's time. Go find Sophie."

Charles stepped out into the clearing.

"Wait a minute. Do you have your knife?"

Charles grinned and pointed to his boot.

"Very well. Just in case. Go on."

Charles ran across the clearing and walked up the steps to the back door. Philippe could hear an orchestra playing inside. The door opened, and Charles went into the house. Then in only a few minutes, he stuck his head outside and motioned for Philippe to come. Philippe checked to be sure the horses were tied securely. Their rifles were stuck into leather holsters on their saddles.

Philippe slipped in and glanced around the enormous kitchen. Sophie stood just inside the door, talking to Charles. She pointed to a narrow spiral servant's staircase behind him. "Follow me."

The brothers followed the servant up the stairs, which led to the second-floor landing. Sophie put out her hand. "Wait here. Let me check and see if the way is clear."

She walked into the hallway, then went to a door and knocked. She opened the door and looked in, then motioned for the Clavells to come. "This is Mistress Barrington's room. Mister Moorehead is in the adjoining room. Make sure that door is locked, and lock this door as well after I leave." The maid held her hands clasped in front of her. "Shall I tell Mistress Barrington that you are here?"

Philippe and Charles looked at each other.

"Do you think she will come up to her room during the evening, or will she not be back until the guests leave?" Philippe asked.

"I would say that she will not be back to her room until the guests leave."

"Don't tell her until she's about ready to retire. Then be sure she is alone."

"Yes, Mister Philippe."

"Thank you, Sophie." The maid turned to go, but Philippe spoke again. "I'm curious. Why have you been so willing to help us?"

She looked away. "Mister Moorehead is a cruel man. Mistress Barrington has been kind to me, and . . ."

"Please go on."

"I may be speaking out of turn, but I believe she loves you, Mister Philippe." She nodded toward the vanity, where his handkerchief lay folded. "That is her most prized possession. Mister Edward lavishes her with furs and jewelry and promises of wealth, but that handkerchief is what she treasures."

Philippe felt his pulse quicken. He had forgotten about the handkerchief he'd given her the day before he left Whisper Wood. He pulled Bridget's hair ribbon out of his pocket and smiled.

"You two need to be together."

Sophie turned and slipped out the door.

Charles looked over the room. "At least we can be comfortable while we wait." He walked around and looked at the furniture. He ran his practiced hands over the wood of the *kast*. "Beautiful pieces."

Philippe checked the locks on the doors. "Yes, very. And I can smell Bridget's lavender perfume." He picked up logs from the pile of firewood and got the fire roaring. "Look, even every window in here is decorated for Christmas."

The brothers settled in to wait out the evening. Charles tumbled onto the bed and fell asleep. Philippe sat in the rocker and stared into the flames.

Father God, I'm asking for your guidance. Tell us what to do, when to go, when to stop. Break down Bridget's defenses and open her heart to me. She's so fearful and hurt. Make a way of escape for us.

PHILIPPE WOKE WITH A START. THE CANDLE HAD BURNED low on the vanity. Someone was knocking on the bedroom door. He shook Charles awake, moved to the door, and put his ear to it.

"It's me, Bridget."

He opened the door and pulled her in, then gathered her in his arms. "Let me hold you, my love," he murmured.

She pushed against him, resisting for a moment, then crumpled into his embrace and started to weep silently. "Oh, Philippe, how I have longed for you to hold me. I have dreamed of feeling your arms around me."

Charles cleared his throat. "*Ahem.* I'll just be right over here." He moved to the corner of the room.

"If you truly feel that way, if you love me, let me take you away from this. Your rescue is at hand."

"But I cannot. I am ruined, soiled—no longer worthy of your love." They both spoke in undertones.

"What are you talking about?" Philippe looked surprised. "You are the purest, most beautiful woman I know."

Bridget looked up at him and continued to cry without making a sound.

"What is it? Calm down. I'm here." He looked at Charles and shrugged his shoulders.

"Edward took me against my will," Bridget whispered forcefully. "He was drunk, and he . . . he ravished me. I cannot be your wife. You deserve someone pure and clean and beautiful. I feel ugly and dirty."

Rage like Philippe had never felt before rose in his belly. "*Arrgghh!*" He turned from Bridget and shook his fist in the air. "We tried to get here sooner, but the weather prevented us. This is *my* fault, not yours.

If I had told you at Whisper Wood how I felt about you, none of this would have happened."

She shook her head. "I cannot, I cannot."

"*Shhh-shhh*. Yes, you can. I want *you*. You are not ruined. God can make all things clean." He brushed her tears away with his fingers and wished he could erase her pain as easily. "You are beautiful. It's you that I love, and we will find a way." He leaned down and kissed her softly and gently on the porcelain smoothness of her cheeks.

She began to tremble. "I . . . I need to sit down."

Philippe helped her to the edge of the bed. He enfolded her in his arms and simply held her, caressing and kissing her forehead and cheeks. He touched her lips tenderly with his fingers and then softly kissed her. "Did he injure you? Are you hurt? Let me look at you."

"No!" Bridget hid her face in her hands. "I'm so ashamed." Sobs overtook her.

"*Shhh-shhh*." He took her hands from her face and turned her toward the window.

A light flurry of snow had fallen earlier that afternoon. The moon lit up the new snow, covering the ugliness of the old, dirty melted snowfall as if nothing had soiled the landscape previously—the mud in the gardens covered by the lacy flakes, the trees flocked with new white shawls, the road surrendering to the overlay of pure white.

"Look out there. You are as pure and beautiful as that new snow outside. God's mercy will cover you. You are not at fault; you were attacked. I will make it up to you. I am as much to blame as he is."

She kept her eyes downcast. "Don't blame yourself. You had nothing to do with it. It was all Edward and my parents' insistence, and—"

"Look at me, Bridget. Look at my eyes."

Her eyelids fluttered, then she slowly looked at him.

"Never avoid my eyes," he said gently. "We can conquer whatever comes our way in the years to come if we confront it together—even something as heinous as this."

She nodded as the tears began to fall again. He turned and got the handkerchief off the vanity and gave it to her. "I think you have something of mine."

She smiled up at him. "Yes, I do."

"Clavell men are gentlemen."

"What?"

"Just a Clavell byword." He smiled and took her face in his hands. "I love you with an eternal love. Nothing that has happened or will happen can change that," he whispered. "God has given you to me. I know that now, and I want to take care of you for the rest of our lives. I want to keep you safe and secure within my arms and my love." He kissed her again on the lips and then stood. "Pack your things, and as soon as it is safe, we will leave. We will find someone to marry us, and we are going home—home to the Schuylkill Valley. I would like to challenge Mister Edward Moorehead. I want to thrash him within an inch of his life, but to do so would jeopardize our escape."

"But what about your mother, your family—"

"They will love you, just as I do. Hurry and get your things. We will stay at the Harbor Tavern tonight, then head out in the morning for home."

"Philippe, are you certain?"

"I've never been so sure of anything in my life."

"I need to tell someone that I'm going."

"Sophie knows."

"That is unfortunate for her. I've seen bruises on her where Edward has beaten her."

Philippe winced.

"I think I need to tell Ella. She will understand and be supportive. I'll go get her. They are probably not asleep yet."

BRIDGET WENT OUT THE DOOR AND AROUND THE CORNER TO David and Ella's room. She could hear men's voices from the parlor. She supposed the men had stayed up, smoking and drinking. Then she heard Faith laughing. Of course! It was Christmas Eve. They were filling the wooden shoes for *Sinterklaas*. They would have to wait longer until everyone was asleep. She knocked softly.

Ella, already in her nightgown and cap, opened the door. "Oh! Bridget. You are still dressed."

"Yes. Can you come to my room for a bit? Is little Davey asleep?"

Ella turned and looked at the baby tucked in a small bed and covered with blankets. "I think so."

Bridget smiled. "I guess I need to talk to a married woman on the eve of my wedding."

"Of course you do. Let me get my robe. Davey will be fine." She followed Bridget to her room.

Bridget looked down the hall, then turned to her beloved cousin before she opened the door. "I need to prepare you. There is a bit of a shock behind this door. I need your support and understanding."

Ella looked at Bridget and cocked her head. "Gigi. You know you always have my support."

Bridget opened the door and quickly ushered Ella inside. The

Clavell brothers stood in front of the fireplace and turned as the women came into the room.

Ella gasped and her hand flew to her mouth. "Philippe! Wha . . . what is going on here?"

"*Shhh.*" Bridget held her finger up. "Ella, this is Philippe's brother, Charles," she whispered. "Sit down. This is going to take some time."

Bridget told Ella everything. Philippe and Charles interjected their perspectives and findings along the way. Ella sniffled and wiped her eyes from time to time, asked a few questions, and listened.

"So, now that you know the whole story, what do you think?" Bridget asked her.

Ella took a big breath. She looked at her cousin and then at Philippe, who stood at Bridget's side holding her hand. "I think . . . I think you are most blessed to have someone who loves you as much as Philippe does and is as brave as he."

Bridget looked up at her beloved and smiled.

"And I think Edward Moorehead is a cad. I think this is going to cause an uproar of the largest magnitude. And I think you should get your things packed and leave as quickly as possible."

"Will you cover for us?"

"What do you want me to do?"

"The wedding is scheduled for tomorrow morning at eleven o'clock. Try to prevent anyone checking on me for as long as you can. And I would like you to reassure my parents that I am safe, and I will contact them as soon as I am able to do so." Bridget paused. "There's one more thing. Philippe, I'd like to take Sophie with us. I know my father would let her work at Whisper Wood. I fear for her when Edward discovers I am gone."

Philippe nodded. "She can ride double with Charles as long as she doesn't bring too many things."

A knock came on the door. Bridget froze and squeezed Philippe's hand. He motioned for her to go to the door.

"Yes?"

"It's Edward, my dear. I saw your light still on. May I come in?"

She spoke through the door. "Oh, Edward. Well, Ella is here, and we are chatting. We are in our nightclothes."

He chuckled. "I don't mind." He tried the doorknob.

Ella spoke up. "Well, *I* do!"

"It's the last time Ella and I can be girls together before our wedding," Bridget said. "We are not dressed to receive gentlemen. You understand, don't you, my love? I'll see you at the ceremony in the morning. Good night."

She heard him shuffle his feet.

"Very well. But this will be the last time you will ever lock me out of your room."

Philippe stepped toward the door, but Bridget put up her hand.

She heard Edward walk away toward his room. Her mouth turned dry. She turned to her little group of conspirators and gulped. "We must make haste."

TWENTY-EIGHT

The moon slid from behind the clouds and shone through the casement window of their room at the inn, splashing silvery beams on the couple as they snuggled in each other's arms in front of the fireplace.

Charles turned over in the bed and leaned up on one elbow. "Do we need to make a bundling board for you two?" He chuckled. "Are you going to stay up all night?"

"Go to sleep, little brother. You have no need to be concerned."

Sophie's soft breathing from a pallet on the floor assured them she was already asleep.

Charles lay on his back with his arms folded behind his head and sighed. It was not long before he began to snore.

Philippe caressed Bridget's face with his fingers and whispered, "Moonlight only makes you more beautiful."

She took his hand and kissed his palm—rough from his years

of breaking and training horses, and now from the hard work on the farm. "I love your hands. I've admired them for years, you know."

"No, I didn't know."

"I observed you as you harnessed our teams to the carriage, and as you helped mares foal in the spring, and as you repaired a fence—so strong and well-defined, yet tender. They are handsome hands."

"I didn't know hands could be handsome," he teased.

"Yours are."

"I think they must look like my father's, from what Maman tells me." He spread them out in front of him in the moonlight.

"Tell me about your father. Tell me about your life in France. I want to know everything about you." She sniffled. "Although I feel I know you well, there is a part of you that has been hidden all these years. I am hungry to know the depths of your hurts and your fond memories as well." She turned and looked at him in the moonlight. "I have also found out something about my own past that I want you to know."

"What is that, my love?" Philippe picked up a lock of her hair and smelled it. "I can smell the lavender." He smiled. "What was it you found out?"

"I was an orphan. My parents took me in when one of their servants, my true mother, died. So . . . our stations in life are not so far apart, after all."

"It really makes no difference anyway, does it? As long as we can be together, it really doesn't matter." He kissed her hand.

They sat huddled in each other's arms by the fireplace and talked as the room grew colder and the night edged into the morning hours.

"Did you have a sweetheart in France?"

"Of course not. I was only fifteen when we came to the New World. There has been no one but you."

"Not even when you were at Versailles?"

"No one. There was a young woman who helped me learn the court dances."

"Aha! I knew it."

Philippe put his finger on her mouth. "She was Pierre's former lover."

"Oh."

"She was very patient with my bumbling through the steps. It was part of my courtier training."

"What was her name?"

"Lisette."

"Was she beautiful?"

"Very. I felt sorry for her, because the fact that Pierre was in love with my mother had become obvious. She aided in Pierre's escape from the Bastille."

"Escape? From the Bastille? Tell me, tell me. You see? There is so much I do not know."

"Now is not the time to go into all this."

Charles began to talk in his sleep.

Philippe smiled and shook his head at Bridget. "*Shhh.* He must be dreaming." He gathered her in his arms, and they snuggled beneath a quilt. "Try to get some rest. We have the remainder of our lives to fall asleep in each other's arms."

BRIDGET WOKE UP TO PHILIPPE STANDING OVER HER, SHAKING her, then kissing her cheeks. She threw her arms around his neck and kissed him in return. "Is this a dream? Am I really waking up to the love of my life showering me with kisses?"

Philippe laughed softly and smiled at her. She ran her fingers over his face, his jawline, and through his thick, dark hair. "I fear I'm going to wake up and you will be gone—and I will be getting married to Edward."

"This is no dream. It is very real. God has made a way for us."

"He did, didn't he? I prayed last night for him to rescue me, and he sent you. Philippe, God sent you to rescue me." Bridget gathered the quilt around her and looked around the room. "Good morning, Charles. Did you sleep well?"

Charles ran his fingers through his hair and put on his hat. "As well as could be expected, considering the fact that some of us stayed up all night." He cuffed his brother's arm.

Bridget looked over toward the end of the bed. "Where is Sophie?"

"She went downstairs earlier. My love, you need to get ready." Philippe spoke urgently. "We'll leave at the first sign of daylight. And without anyone seeing us, if possible." He stood. "Charles and I will go saddle the horses. Hurry."

She loved his soft, mellow voice. It sounded almost melodious when he spoke. She clung to his arm. "I don't want you to leave me even for a minute."

He took her hand and kissed it. "I'll be back for you before you know it."

PHILIPPE STROKED LEGACY'S NECK AND PUT HIS BRIDLE ON. He felt his jaw tighten.

Lord, thank you for allowing us to rescue Bridget and for protecting us. But I don't understand why you allowed that . . . that awful thing to happen to Bridget. Where were you then? To have her innocence and purity ravaged by that brutal man? A tear trickling down the outside of one eye surprised him. He brushed it away. *Why could you have not protected her? I am offended that you did not protect her.*

—I sent you to protect her.

He recognized the voice. *I should not have rejected her, is that what you are saying, Lord?*

—You made the best decision you knew how to make at the time. Don't look back now. Trust me for the future.

Philippe hung his head. *I do trust you, Father. I just don't understand your ways. You have made a way for us . . . a way for us to be together, but did this path have to contain so much heartache? Did Bridget have to be the victim?*

He heard nothing else. He finished saddling his horse and tied him to the hitching rail.

Bridget looked around the room and spotted a blue-and-white pitcher on a painted table. She poured water into the basin and splashed it on her face. She piled her hair up underneath her riding hat.

Sophie came into the room with mugs of tea. "The cook was already up," she said.

"Oh, Sophie, how thoughtful." Bridget took a mug off the tray. "I hope you will consider coming with us . . . permanently, I mean." She began lacing up her riding boots. "Abigail has a new baby, and her husband works for my father, so they will want to stay at Whisper Wood. But I'm sure my father will find a place for you, and then when Philippe and I have our own house . . . would you consider coming with us to the valley?"

Sophie smiled, revealing surprisingly straight white teeth. Despite the fact that she had escaped with very few of her things, she still presented a picture of neatness, her brown hair braided into a twist and tucked into her cap. She looked down, her thick eyelashes brushing her cheeks. "I would be honored, Mistress Barrington. I have no place else to go."

"I don't believe I've ever seen you smile before. You are a very pretty woman, you know."

Sophie ducked her head. Bridget patted her hand, stood, and put on her jacket.

Philippe came back into the room. "Are you ready?" he asked.

"Yes. Sophie brought us tea."

"Thank you, Sophie." He drank his down quickly. "Come, then. Charles is waiting for us. Let's go home—to the Schuylkill Valley. Home."

Bridget smiled, then her smile disappeared. "Philippe?"

"Yes."

"Edward will come after me."

"We will deal with that when it occurs." He extended his hand. "Come, we need to hurry."

The three of them walked down the stairs together and scurried across the property to the horses.

Bridget tugged on Philippe's arm. "Could we stop at Whisper Wood? I'd like to get a few of my things. Edward won't even know I'm gone for a few more hours, and he doesn't know for sure where we are going. If we go straight to Whisper Wood—"

"Hold on, hold on." Philippe laughed. "I happen to agree with you. But we must get underway." Philippe mounted and pulled Bridget up behind him.

Charles did the same with Sophie, and they walked their horses through the alley beside the inn out onto the dark street. It was deserted. No business owners opening shops. No one going to work. It was Christmas Day.

"Stop! Philippe Clavell, wait up!"

Philippe and Bridget twisted around. Her heart started pounding. Mister Clark came running out of the inn waving a bag. "I had my good wife pack a knapsack for you."

"Thank you, sir. That is very kind."

"You are welcome . . . and Merry Christmas."

"Merry Christmas to you." Philippe tipped his hat.

Mister Clark turned and went back into the inn, waving at the Clavells. "Merry Christmas!"

BRIDGET SWIVELED AROUND AND CALLED TO CHARLES AND Sophie. "Only another ten minutes to Whisper Wood."

Philippe whipped Legacy into a canter and rode down the very familiar road to the estate where he had spent his adolescent years. Whisper Wood came into view, and Bridget giggled and squeezed Philippe around his waist. "We're home, Philippe."

He turned around and smiled. "Not yet, my love."

She laid her head on his shoulder. "I know, but it's a first stop on our journey home."

Contentment rushed through her like she had never experienced before. How astonishing that yesterday she was the most miserable woman on earth, and today she had to be the happiest! She closed her eyes and remembered the days when Philippe had saddled Kimi for her, and they'd ridden through the pastures and cornfields. She knew she'd fallen in love with him from the beginning and wondered when it was that he began to develop feelings for her. She would ask him that—soon.

And now they were to be married. She opened her eyes and looked at the back of his head with his thick hair tied with a leather strip, and his broad shoulders that tugged at the seams of his jacket. She ran her hand across his shoulders.

He turned around to peer at her—his dark brown eyes filled with love. "Yes?"

"Nothing. I am simply having trouble believing that this is happening. I want to touch you to make sure it is real, that it's not a dream."

"It is a dream, our dream, and we are living that dream." Philippe guided their party through the gate and around the side of the house to the stables. Bridget jumped off Legacy.

"Charles and I will get the wagon ready." He turned to Bridget. "Which horses do you want to take?"

Bridget smiled and reached out for his hand. "Kimi, of course, and then you choose the other. You know them as well as I do, or better. You know what we'll need. Do you think it would be smoother travel with the sleigh?"

Philippe nodded. "Very well. I'll put the cover on it, and we'll be ready shortly."

"Come with me, Sophie." Bridget got her pack and started up the path past the smokehouse to the house. The servant scurried after her.

Bridget threw open the back door. "Abigail! Abigail, I'm home!"

Abigail came into the keeping room from the pantry holding her baby wrapped in a quilt. Zachary followed close behind, holding their two-year-old. "Mistress Barrington! What are thee doing home already?" Both Zachary and Abigail turned to look at Sophie. "What about . . . the wedding?"

"This is Sophie, Mister Edward's former maid. The wedding . . . well, that's a long story."

Philippe and Charles came into the kitchen and hung their jackets on pegs inside the door.

"Philippe!"

Philippe grinned and took off his hat. "Good morning, Abigail." He motioned to Charles. "This is my brother, Charles."

Bridget gestured with her hands. "To give you the most concise explanation possible, Mister Moorehead has been found to be a man of questionable character and integrity. Philippe and I have . . . have cared for each other for many years, but neither of us had the courage to vocalize it." She moved to Philippe's side, and he put his arm around her shoulders. "By God's grace we found each other in time, and we made a bold decision to defy tradition and go with our hearts." She laughed and took Philippe's arm. "We are running away. Philippe and I are going to be married, have babies, like you and Zachary, and be happy. That's the glad news that we bring." She reached out and caressed the baby's cheek. "However, we must hurry. Edward will certainly come here looking for me."

Abigail nodded. "When will thee be getting married?"

"As soon as possible. The events of the last few hours have happened so quickly that we've hardly spoken of future plans. We much desire to be married right away." Bridget looked up at Philippe, suddenly realizing they had not thought about clergy or a priest or banns, or anything except that they wanted to be married. "I . . . I suppose we need some sort of officiate. Philippe?"

Philippe hugged her closer. "We will solve that small dilemma. Maman and Pierre were simply married at the home of a pastor in Switzerland. Surely . . ."

Abigail smiled and shifted her baby to the other arm. "In our Quaker faith, thee can simply say the wedding vows in front of witnesses, and it is done. Zachary and I would be honored to be witnesses to thy vows."

Philippe's eyes widened. "Of course." He turned to Bridget. "God has already made a way for us, before we even asked. Would that be acceptable to you—to say our vows here in front of Charles and Abigail and Zachary and Sophie?"

"Yes, but what about you? You would not want to wait until your family . . . ?"

Philippe shook his head. "I do not want to wait for anything. I want us married as soon as possible." He leaned down and kissed her on the cheek.

Bridget touched her cheek and blushed. "So do I."

What a gentle man Philippe is. So unlike . . . so unlike Edward.

A momentary flash of Edward dragging and shoving her onto the bed threatened to spoil her happiness, but she refused to allow it to do so. She would not ever have to deal with Edward Moorehead again. Once she and Philippe were married, Edward would be out of her life forever.

Philippe looked around the room at his brother, and Abigail and Zachary and their family, and Sophie lingering by the fireplace. "Can we do it right now?"

Bridget's hand flew to her chest. "Oh. Oh my." She looked at the circle of encouraging faces, nodded, and took a deep breath. "Very well, let us proceed. Shall we go into the parlor?"

The group moved quickly into the more formal room. The sunshine played through the casement windows and glistened on the dark furniture. Bridget took Philippe's handkerchief out of her jacket pocket and held it in her hands as they faced each other in front of the windows looking out on the snow-covered landscape.

Philippe looked at Zachary. "How do we begin?"

Zachary chuckled. "Simply say what thee would like to her, and promise to be a good husband."

Philippe cleared his throat and began, his voice low but confident. "Mistress Bridget Barrington, you are the love of my life. I have never loved another. I covenant to love you only better as my beloved wife. I will protect you, take care of you, and provide for you to the very best of my ability. I will be a good, faithful, and proper husband. I will allow no harm ever to come to you." He kissed her hand. "And as God as my witness, I will cherish you, my wife, as a most precious treasure."

Bridget gazed at her beloved's dark eyes. He blinked away tears as he spoke. She felt as if she were floating. Surely her feet were not touching the ground. All she could see was Philippe and his smiling face.

She did not know what she was going to say, but began to speak and all the thoughts and emotions of the years came to the surface. "Philippe, I fell in love with you on that very first miserable, rainy day on the docks. It pained me to see a family of such obvious quality and refinement being torn apart and sold into servitude. But it was more than that. Something touched my heart of hearts about you. It was more than fantasy and young love. True love awakens the soul, and my soul pulsated with life whenever I was with you. When I was away from you, I counted the minutes until I could arrange to be in your presence once more. I was, and am, hopelessly in love with you.

"My parents attempted to make the perfect match for me by arranging a marriage of means and property, but I knew all along my perfect match was you. I promise to be by your side always, through whatever may come. I promise to support you and provide a warm hearth and home. And as God as my witness, I promise to be a faithful, good wife and will love none other."

The two lovers stared at each other. Philippe looked at Abigail and Zachary. "Is that all we need to do? We're married now?"

The young couple nodded, smiling at the newlyweds.

Philippe bent down and kissed Bridget tenderly. "I love you, Mistress Clavell."

"And I love you more than I can say, *Monsieur* Clavell."

The bride and groom embraced, tears mingling with laughter.

Charles strode to the couple and enfolded his brother in his arms. "Well, I suppose congratulations are in order." He bowed to Bridget and took her hand. "Mistress, I am honored to have you as my brother's wife. But we had best not tarry. Let's get your things and depart as quickly as possible."

Philippe kissed Bridget once more on the cheek, and he, Charles, and Zachary went to the stables. Bridget, Abigail, and Sophie took the children and ran up the stairs.

At ten o'clock Ella knocked on Bridget's door. No one answered. She knocked again and tried the doorknob. She opened the door and peeked in. Lying on the bed was the wedding dress that had been Edward's mother's, with her diamond brooch pinned on the bodice. The box that the beaver cloak had come in was on the bed as well, with the hat and muff. She opened the wardrobe. All of the gowns were still there. Only Bridget's personal small case and her riding habit, hat, and boots were missing. Ella sighed and started out the door. She nearly ran into Sarah.

"Is the beautiful bride-to-be getting ready? The ceremony takes . . . place . . ." Sarah stepped into the room and looked at the wedding dress on the bed. "Wh-where is Bridget? She's going to be late. Ella?" Sarah turned around in a circle. "Where is my daughter? Where is Bridget?" Sarah's voice rose to a screech.

Ella came in behind her and closed the door. "Aunt Sarah, I don't know where Bridget is, but she left me a message to give to you. She wants you to know that she is safe, and that she will contact you in due time—as soon as she feels she can."

"B-but where did she go? Why? Who is she with?"

"We'd better let the others know. We may as well get ready for a tirade. All I can tell you is that when she told me the whole story, I agreed with her decision to leave."

"I don't understand." She began to cry. "Amos! Amos, come in here!"

Amos appeared at the door, his vest unbuttoned and without his cane. He hobbled to his wife. "Whatever is wrong? Where's Bridget?"

"Oh, Amos. She's gone! I don't know where or with whom. Our baby's gone." She sat on the edge of the bed. "Oh my. What shame. What disgraceful behavior." She broke down into wails that soon brought the other members of the household flocking to the bedroom.

Amos turned to Ella. "What do you know about this? Where did she go?"

Ella shook her head. "I can honestly say that I do not know where she has gone."

David came to the door holding Davey who, upon seeing Sarah

crying, began to cry too. Bradley and Penelope, who had already arrived for the wedding, stood on the fringes of the bystanders. Bradley picked William up, took Penelope by the hand, and walked over to David. "What's going on?"

David shrugged his shoulders. "I have not a clue."

Some of the Moorehead children crowded around the door, already dressed in their wedding finery, wide-eyed at the scene. Nervous laughter from the adolescent boys' changing voices and giggles and titters from the girls echoed in the hallway.

Jacob and Faith shooed their children away from the door as Edward bounded up the stairs two at a time.

"What is going on up here? Is Bridget . . . ?" He shouldered his way through the gathering in the doorway and burst into the room. He took one look at the wedding dress on the bed and began to bellow and roar. "Where is she? Where did my bride go? Where *is* she?" He stomped around the room. "She can't have simply disappeared."

He turned to Amos and Sarah, his face purple with rage. "Tell me where she is. You're her father. Do you have control of your household? Can you not maintain better control of your daughter?" He shook his finger in their faces. "She cannot escape from me. Not again, she won't." His behavior belied his impeccably powdered and coiffed hair. He had unbuttoned his ivory and gold jacket and stood with his fists on his hips.

Amos stared at the uncontrollable display of rage from the man who had been scheduled to become his son-in-law that very day. He straightened himself up and looked Edward directly in the eyes. "Young man, I understand that you are upset, but no one is allowed to speak to my wife nor myself in that manner. We are as shocked as you are, and have no idea where she has gone."

Edward stepped back and took a deep breath. "You are right. I'm sorry. Please forgive me." He looked at the circle of onlookers. "Does anybody know where she has gone?" His eyes rested on her cousin. "Ella? Do you know where she went?"

Ella shook her head. David looked at his wife. She evaded his eyes.

"Does no one know what has happened to my bride? Did no one see anything?"

Servants started to gather in the hallway.

Edward began to shout again. "I want everyone in the house questioned, including servants. Someone had to have seen something."

Children and servants scattered in the face of his anger.

He stormed toward the door, stopping in front of Faith and Jacob. "Our guests are already beginning to arrive. Take care of them."

"Where are you going?"

"To look for Bridget."

Jacob shook his head. "And where are you going to look? Don't you think you need to do some investigating before you take off like a wild stallion? She could be anywhere. Wait until we find out some more facts."

Edward swore and punched his fist into the wardrobe, splintering the wood of the door. "Everybody out!"

The rest of the spectators hurried out of the room. Ella took Davey from her husband. "Let's leave Edward to his misery . . . and his tantrums."

Edward glared at her as they left the room.

EDWARD WALKED TO THE STABLE, PULLING ON HIS GLOVES, his mouth grim. By questioning the servants and cooks, he'd been able to piece together bits of the story and had deduced what had happened. The Clavell brothers had come after Bridget. Why, he did not know for certain, but Edward had a hunch that Bridget fancied herself in love with one of them. And his Sophie had gone with them. That was a further jolt to him.

The Osbornes and senior Barringtons planned to leave after dinner, but Amos and Sarah would stay with their relatives a few days to recover from the shocking incident. Ella thought they might do some shopping. Perhaps it would be good for Sarah, to get her mind off the scandal of her daughter running away with another man on her wedding day. Bradley and Penelope had already gone home.

Edward didn't care what their plans were, just as long as they left his house. Sarah's crying and blubbering about the shame and disgrace annoyed him. He wanted nothing more than to get out of there and pursue those who had wronged him. Getting a late start going after them perturbed him. He still felt like Ella knew more than she was revealing. He was chagrined, mortified, and humiliated. He would make Bridget Barrington pay. She would *not* get away with this.

Jacob walked with him to the stable. "I wish I could go with you, but I need to get the family back to New York." He stopped Edward. "Listen, Edward, take some advice from your older brother." He smiled, but his eyes reflected his concern. "Let this go. I'm sorry it happened, and that your bride-to-be proved to be less than what you had hoped for, but she's gone. Even if you find her and force her to come back to you, what have you gained—a reluctant, bitter wife? I don't think that's what you want, is it?"

Edward snapped his gloves against his leg. "No one betrays me and gets away with it. They will pay the consequences."

"And what consequences might you have in mind?"

"I'm going after them. If I cannot have Bridget, then neither can anyone else."

"Edward, you are not thinking properly." Jacob caught his brother by the shoulder.

Edward pushed him aside. "Get out of my way."

"You are making a mistake."

"Maybe so, but I cannot let this pass without taking some action." Edward got on his horse and turned his horse's head north toward Whisper Wood. That's where they would be. That is where he would catch up with them. They would not escape their just due.

TWENTY-NINE

The tavern was dimly lit, smoky, and loud—exactly how Leo Zwicken liked it. He sat in a corner alone, drinking his third mug of ale. He watched the crowd come and go, some men hanging on the bar all day, probably dreading having to go home to nagging wives. He wondered why the tavern was so full on Christmas Day. The barmaids leaned over his table periodically and brought him more ale, but he didn't indulge himself. He needed to think.

What makes Moorehead think he can get away with implicating me in his smuggling operation? And then he has the gall to dismiss me. I've kept his foundry running and making a profit for years, and he cuts me off? Arrogant, pompous fraud. I'll expose him. I'll ruin him. He'll think again before tampering with Leo Zwicken. I have friends and influence. I don't need him.

A group of rowdy British soldiers came in, laughing and jesting. The crowd at the bar moved to make room for them. They paid no attention to Zwicken. He stared at them through his lowered, bushy eyebrows, his grim mouth turned downward in a sulk. He didn't recognize any of the soldiers, but that didn't halt his ire. How dare they invade his business? The British military had overstepped its bounds.

I worked hard and produced a good product and made a profit for my partner. Shouldn't I receive some credit? Don't I matter? I'll show Mister Edward Moorehead. I don't care if he did just get married. He's going to hear from me. And his innocent little bride. I'll tell her a thing or two about her new husband. Anyone associated with Moorehead is headed for trouble. It's simply a matter of time.

Zwicken pushed his chair back and tossed the last of his ale down. He swayed and caught hold of the back of his chair. He put on his hat and staggered out the door. It was only the middle of the afternoon, and he was already nearly drunk. He leaned against the building and watched men going in and out of the tavern. A horse and rider raced by, going much too fast and splashing mud and water in all directions. He wiped the splotches of mud off his face and cursed.

That's Moorehead! What was he doing racing through town? Wasn't he supposed to be married today?

Zwicken got on his horse and followed. Edward was headed out of town, and not slowing down. This was most strange but . . . he had nothing better to do. Zwicken spurred his horse to a gallop, keeping Edward in view on the road ahead. He patted his rifle. This might prove to be a most convenient coincidence.

BRIDGET HURRIED DOWN THE STAIRS WITH HER ARMS FULL. "Abigail!" She set her packages beside the front door and ran upstairs for more. She came down with a second load, followed by Sophie. Bridget held a letter in her hand.

Abigail appeared in the foyer as Bridget approached the bottom step.

"I would like you to give this letter to my parents when they return home. It explains everything." Bridget added another traveling case to the stack.

Abigail took the letter. "I will make certain they get it."

Philippe came in the front door, having pulled the sleigh around in front of the house. He looked at the luggage and then at Bridget, then at Abigail. He chuckled and rubbed the growth of new beard on his cheek. "A *few* things?"

Bridget cocked her head coyly at Philippe and smiled. "Well, I *am* leaving home, and a girl needs her things. I left most of my gowns at Edward's."

"You are not going to need gowns in the valley," Philippe said gently. "What you are going to need are plain skirts and dresses to work in and riding clothes. Sturdy shoes and boots. Aprons. Warm clothing—shawls and coats."

Her face fell. "You don't understand, I . . . I—"

"I do understand. Do you think that coming from the court of the king of France to being an indentured servant wasn't a shock for me? Believe me, your finery will simply be a burden. We will be living in one small room to begin with. It has very little storage." He gestured with his palms up. "When we build our own place, we can come back and get the rest of your belongings."

Bridget sighed. She started sifting through the garments. "May I take just one gown?"

"One."

"There might be a dance or a party sometime, mightn't there be?"

Philippe shook his head and laughed. "Perhaps." He turned to Abigail. "Would you help her separate out what she will need as a farmer's wife? And hurry, please. I feel an urgency to get out of here."

Abigail smiled and nodded her head. "Yes, Mister Philippe."

Philippe turned and looked at Abigail. "Simply Philippe is fine."

"No, sir. Thee are a gentleman now, no longer a servant. Thee are *Mister* Philippe."

THE STACK WAS WHITTLED NEARLY IN HALF BY THE TIME Abigail finished winnowing out the unnecessary items. Philippe and Charles were already loading the sleigh. They would switch off driving duties, but Philippe and Bridget were to start out, with Charles riding alongside, leading Legacy and Kimi.

Philippe looked up as he was loading the final chest. "Charles, get our rifles and ammunition. Now."

Charles turned in the direction Philippe was looking. A rider was galloping full speed down the long road toward the house, mud and slush splattering from the horse's hooves. Charles ran to their mounts behind the sleigh and pulled out both rifles. He got the powder, wad, and ball, and loaded one rifle and tossed it to Philippe.

"It's Edward."

Bridget and Sophie came out on the porch carrying sacks of supplies and flasks of ale. Sophie turned and ran back into the house. Bridget started to run to Philippe, but he turned to her, concern written in his knitted brow. "Stay in the house. Get a gun, but stay in the house."

"But—"

"Go, now!" He softened his voice. "Go, my love. I will not allow him to hurt you ever again."

BRIDGET RAN INTO THE HOUSE AND DROPPED HER PACKAGES on the stairs. Going to her father's gun cabinet in the parlor, she removed a pistol and a flintlock rifle that she had learned to shoot as a young girl. She handed the pistol to Sophie. "Do you know how to shoot this?"

Sophie nodded.

Bridget opened an ammunition box in the bottom of the cabinet. They loaded the weapons and stationed themselves at the windows.

"Mistress Barrington?"

Bridget whirled around with the rifle in her hands.

Abigail backed up. "What are thee doing with the rifle?"

"It's Edward. He's followed us. Take your children to the barn. And don't come back until someone comes for you."

"But, mistress—"

"We'll be fine, but there may be some shooting in the meantime. I don't want your children in harm's way. Go!"

Abigail turned, gathered her babies up in quilts, and ran out the back door.

Edward brought his horse to a stop directly in front of Philippe, who was standing in front of the sleigh with his rifle by his side. The horse reared and whinnied, foaming at the mouth. Edward glared at him. Charles stood on the front of the sleigh with his rifle in his hands.

"The two escapees. How convenient. We shall take care of both of you in one blow."

"We? I don't see anyone else."

"I don't need anyone else. I've come to get my bride. She is rightfully mine."

Philippe stepped toward him. "I don't believe she ever became your bride—no vows said, no wedding ceremony, no blessing of the priest."

"So it's the older brother she has taken a fancy to. I'm not surprised." He smirked at Philippe. "Perhaps no vows were said, but the most important joining took place one delicious night before the wedding. And I might add that Mistress Barrington was quite the willing participant. No screams or struggle. It really was quite nice." He smiled.

Philippe threw his rifle down and lunged for Edward. The man raised his whip, but Philippe pulled him from his saddle before he had a chance to lower it. Edward struck the younger man on the shoulder with the butt of the whip, but Philippe dragged him to the ground and hit him on the cheek with his fist. Edward's hat flew off as he staggered to his feet.

"That's not the story I got. You took her against her will! You're not fit to live." Philippe pulled back and punched Edward full in the mouth and nose. Blood spurted onto his fashionable jacket. "You will never claim Bridget as your wife. You are too late. We said our wedding vows just a short while ago."

Edward swung at Philippe and grazed the side of his face as Philippe ducked. Edward bent down and pulled something out of his boot.

"Watch out, Philippe! He has a knife!"

The horses skittered and pranced backward. Edward swung upward with the knife and caught Philippe in the thigh.

Charles rushed Edward and kicked the knife from his hand, and it spun across the cobblestone drive. Philippe pulled Edward up by the collar of his jacket and began to bang his head against the cobblestones. Blood splattered against Philippe's face as he raged. Again and again he pummeled the man's head against the stones.

Charles grabbed his hands. "Stop, Philippe. Stop it. You'll kill him."

An acrid memory triggered in Philippe's mind of the ambush on the dragoons in France. He'd been just a boy, but he had killed a man that day in the woods. Philippe let go, and Edward lay still in a bloody heap. The young man stepped back, breathing heavily. "I've already killed one man. I do not wish to take another life."

Edward looked up at him, crimson rivulets trickling down his face. He felt the back of his head and moaned.

"And you are not worth the agony of killing. I understand that now. Never attempt to contact Bridget. She is Mistress Bridget Clavell from now on. You will never be a part of her life again. What started in the cornfield that day when she observed your gun smuggling and saw you shoot that unfortunate man in the back is over. It's *over*, Moorehead. You are ruined. Not Bridget."

Philippe looked down at the blood on his pants.

Charles came to his side. "Are you injured badly?"

"I don't think so." He wiped his hand on his pant leg where blood had seeped through. "I think it's just a surface wound."

Philippe pointed at Edward. "It pains me to have to do this, but my faith demands it." He stopped and sighed. "I for—" He looked at Charles through eyes seared with anguish. "I cannot."

Charles nodded his head. "Yes, you can. You must. For your own good—and that of Bridget's, too, Philippe—you must."

Philippe towered over the man who had violated the dearest

treasure of his life. "You . . . you are forgiven. I release you and what you have done to God Almighty. It's not what I want to do. My preference would be to bang your head against those stones until you have to face God himself and account for what you have done. But that would accomplish nothing. God will have to deal with you. I cannot." He looked down at the wreck of a man. "May God have mercy on your soul."

Philippe turned and started hobbling toward the sleigh. Bridget had come out on the porch holding her rifle. "Put the rifle down, Bridget, and get in the sleigh. You too, Charles. We're leaving. Sophie and Abigail can take care of his wounds and send him back to Philadelphia. I don't think he will bother us anymore."

Bridget and Philippe got in the covered sleigh, with Charles riding behind on Legacy. Kimi followed alongside the sleigh as they bumped along the cobblestone drive and onto the snow-covered road that would lead them home.

LEO ZWICKEN WATCHED THE SLEIGH *WHOOSH* PAST. HE pulled his horse onto the road from the snow under the trees where he had delighted to watch Philippe best Edward Moorehead. He rode up the driveway, coming alongside his former partner, who was struggling in the bloody slush and mud to get to his feet.

Edward's fancy hat lay in the mire, along with his knife. As he reached for it, a shadow crossed his face. "Zwicken. What are you doing here?"

"I followed you. You nearly ran me down in front of the tavern, so I decided to see what the rush was about." He started laughing. "You don't look so high and mighty right now, my friend."

Edward struggled to his feet and attempted to wipe the mud off his hat. He snarled at Zwicken. "What do you want?"

Zwicken drew his rifle and pointed it at Edward. "Revenge. What is rightfully mine. You can't get rid of me by simply writing me a letter of dismissal. Who do you think you are?"

A shot rang out, and Edward flew backward. Zwicken ducked and whirled his head around. The shot had not come from his rifle—

Sophie stood in the snow at the bottom of the porch steps with the pistol in her hand, staring at Edward.

Zwicken backed up and looked down at his former partner. Edward's glazed eyes fixed on Leo, and he reached his hand toward him, then slowly exhaled. His hand fell by his side at an awkward angle, and his body grew still as death claimed him. Zwicken knelt beside him and touched his chest. He looked up at Sophie. "He ... he's gone. I was angry, but I didn't wish him dead."

"I did." She stared at the body. "I wished him dead every day I worked for him." She dropped the pistol and went into the house. "I'll get a blanket."

As the shadows began to lengthen into the evening of Christmas Day, Sophie stood on the front porch of Whisper Wood and watched as a lone horseman rode away from the house, leading a mount with a body draped over the saddle. Retrieving a bucket of water and a brush from the house, she set about scrubbing the blood from the cobblestones. Then she walked across the yard to the barn to hail Abigail's family. She spoke of the grisly deed to no one.

THIRTY

A muffled gunshot from the direction of the house echoed over the field. Charles twisted in his saddle and looked toward Whisper Wood. Philippe and Bridget were engrossed in conversation and seemed not to hear it. He prayed they truly had not heard and would not want to turn back.

PHILIPPE TURNED THE TEAM OF HORSES TO PULL THE SLEIGH alongside the cornfield, its stubble now covered with the residue of old snow.

"Where are you going?" Bridget touched his arm.

He smiled at her. "There's something we need to do." Philippe turned to Charles, riding beside them. "Bridget and I need to take care of something before we start home. Trade with me." He jumped out of the sleigh and took Legacy's reins. He helped Bridget exit the sleigh and motioned for her to mount Kimi. "Wait here for us, Charles. We won't be long."

Charles shrugged his shoulders. "Certainly. Don't mind me." He stole a glance toward the house, but saw nothing. "Don't tarry."

"We won't."

Whisper Wood faded from their view as they rode into the cornfield. Bridget started to turn to go around the cornfield, but Philippe caught hold of Kimi's bridle.

"No longer, my love. You never need avoid the cornfield again. We will go through it . . . together. It will never hold control over you again."

They walked the horses at first, then they began to trot. Philippe let go of the bridle as the horses started into an easy canter. Bridget looked at Philippe, then took the lead and began to gallop. As they galloped past the spot where the murder had taken place, the wind whipped around their faces and dried the tears that had begun to spill down Bridget's cheeks.

They raced across the meadow to the edge of the forest. They picked their way through the snow and down the embankment to the fallen log.

Philippe dismounted and helped Bridget off her horse. He took her hands, led her to the log, and they sat down. "I wanted to bring you here, where my love for you really began. I think I truly saw who you were that day when you first brought me here."

He pulled the blue ribbon out of his pocket. "After I left Whisper Wood, each time I took your hair ribbon out of my pocket, the fragrance of lavender reminded me of you. And I wanted to see you and hold you. It seems I was living my life in shades of gray until I acknowledged my feelings for you. Since then a rainbow of brightness and color has burst into my world. You brought layers of understanding to my heart. Every time I imagined having a wife and children, building a house, and working the land, it was always you I pictured by my side, you I pictured as the mother of my children, you I pictured standing at the door to welcome me home. I want to spend all of my days beside you."

Bridget looked down and began to cry, her tears spotting the ribbon. "I find it difficult to sincerely believe that any gentleman would still want me after . . . after . . ."

Philippe took her hands and knelt in the snow. "I want no other. I vow to spend the rest of my life making up to you what has been taken from you. Can you . . . will you ever be able to forgive me?"

Bridget stared at him. "Forgive you? Whatever for?"

"If I had told you how I felt that day at Whisper Wood, perhaps none of this would have happened." He removed her gloves, turned the palms of her hands up, and kissed them.

Bridget shook her head. "No, don't blame yourself. My parents would have gone ahead with their plans regardless."

"But if I'd only told you how I felt, you never would have agreed."

"How can we say what might have been and what it means? All I know now is that my heart overflows with love and joy at being loved by you and becoming your wife. There's no need for forgiveness. I love you with all that I am, and that's what that means." Bridget sniffled and blinked her eyes.

Philippe smothered her hands with kisses. "Thank you, my love. Thank you. I pledge to make it up to you."

She touched his bruising cheek and the wound in his thigh, which by now had stopped bleeding. "I think you've already started trying to make it up to me."

It had begun to snow. He gathered her in his arms and held her close. She swept an icy, lacy flake from her eyelashes as she looked into his eyes. He kissed her gently, searching her lips, softly brushing them with his own, as if he did not wish to offend her wounded sensibilities in any way. They both trembled as they surrendered to the warmth of each other's arms. She felt herself responding to his tenderness. She wanted more and more of him.

He stepped back and tilted her chin. "Mistress Philippe Clavell, I meant what I vowed to you. I promise you I will never let anything hurt you again. Let us leave the heartache and regrets of the past here—here in your special place where you always felt safe. I will always love you and take care of you. God will be your refuge, and your safe place is now here in my arms."

Tears flowed down Bridget's cheeks, and she reached up and touched his face. "Take me home, Philippe. Take me home to your valley."

AMOS AND SARAH BARRINGTON RETURNED TO WHISPER Wood the day after Christmas. Eb pulled in front of the house and assisted the Barringtons as they exited the carriage. No snow had fallen since they'd left for Philadelphia. Amos noticed a stain on the cobblestones, but said nothing.

Abigail greeted them as they moved up the steps. "Welcome home, Mister Barrington. Mistress Barrington."

Sarah began to cry immediately upon stepping into the house. "You're not going to believe what happened. It was absolutely the most humiliating ordeal I've ever lived through in my entire life." She took off her cloak and handed it to Abigail. "I've never been so ashamed."

Abigail handed Bridget's letter to Amos. "Mister Barrington, Bridget and Philippe were here. She left this for thee. I believe it will answer all of thy questions."

Amos tore open the letter and began to read. Sarah read over his shoulder and cried even harder.

> Father and Mother,
>
> I do not wish to cause you further pain. I love you. When you have read this letter, I believe you will understand why I had to take drastic action.

The letter continued and related the story, beginning with Bridget's witnessing the murder when she was a little girl and ending with the fact that the young couple had stated their vows and were already married. Bridget had signed the letter,

> I am confident I will be safe and happy with Philippe as we make our home in the Schuylkill Valley. Please give Sophie a secure place of employment until we can come after her in the spring. Until then, I remain,
>> Your loving daughter,
>> Bridget

Sarah sat on the edge of the settee and intermittently shook her head and blew her nose. Amos got up, lit his pipe, and paced.

The Barringtons looked at each other, and Amos patted Sarah's hand. He took a deep breath and puffed on his pipe for a few seconds. "Well." He nodded his head. "Well. That's quite a story. And it does put a different light on the situation. I need our daughter's forgiveness for not heeding her reservations about Edward Moorehead. If I had, this whole series of events could have been prevented. And I owe Philippe an apology. We could not hope for a finer young man for our daughter. I am indebted to him for protecting Bridget and treating her with respect."

Sarah nodded slightly and wiped her eyes. "But I had hoped for—"

Amos turned to his wife. His eyes glinted. "For what, Sarah? What more could we hope for than a man of character and integrity who loves our daughter with his whole being? I have no doubt that he will take care of her in a most honorable manner." Amos jabbed the floor with his cane and jutted his chin in the air. "They have our approval."

TWO DAYS LATER SOPHIE WATCHED FROM THE UPSTAIRS window as a black buggy pulled in front of the house. Only a remnant of the telltale brown stain remained on the cobblestones beneath the mud and slush of old snow. Two men emerged and tromped through the icy mix, unaware of the gruesome blot beneath their boots. Sophie recognized Jacob Moorehead, but the other man was a stranger. The clank of the pewter door-knocker rang through the house. She tiptoed to the landing and, her heart thumping against her chest, strained to hear as the men asked to speak to Amos.

Jacob's voice, so similar to Edward's, led the queries. "My brother has been missing since the day that was supposed to be his wedding day. Do you have any knowledge of his whereabouts?"

"I have not seen Edward since we were at his residence for the wedding, which . . . *a-hem* . . . as you well know, did not take place."

"Might I inquire as to the whereabouts of your daughter?"

"She has gone with her new husband, Philippe Clavell, to his family's home in the Schuylkill Valley."

Sophie could hear the shuffling of feet and nervous murmuring.

"She has already married? Obviously she did not truly care for my brother if she so quickly jumped into the arms of another man." Jacob hesitated. "Did she see Edward before she left?"

"I have not seen her myself. She left only a letter for us."

An unfamiliar voice spoke. "What about your servants? Could they possibly have seen Mister Moorehead?"

Sophie stepped back into the shadows.

The tapping of a cane indicated that Amos was walking to the door of the parlor. The servant's bell chimed. Sophie watched as Abigail, holding her infant, walked past the stairs to the parlor.

"Abigail. Would you come here, please? Have you seen Mister Moorehead?"

"No, Mister Barrington."

"Have you seen Bridget and Mister Philippe?"

"Yes, sir. They stopped by here on their way to . . ."

"All is well. You need have no fear of telling the truth."

"Mistress Bridget and Philippe and his brother, Charles, stopped by here to get a few of her things before they proceeded to Mister Philippe's family's place . . . north . . ."

"Yes, continue."

"They said their marriage vows before us as witnesses and did not tarry. They packed up the sleigh, and . . ." The servant paused. "I do not know what happened after that. My husband and I went to the barn before they left."

Jacob again. "So when you came in from the barn, they were gone?"

"Yes, sir."

"And you haven't seen my brother?"

"No, sir."

"What about Sophie? Where is Sophie?"

Amos' strong voice interjected. "She is here. I've employed her at Bridget's request until there is a place for her with my daughter." A chair scraped on the wooden floor. "Do you wish to speak to her?"

A tense moment crawled by as Sophie held her breath, gripping the banister.

Jacob spoke. "No, I don't suppose that is necessary."

The unfamiliar voice entered the conversation again. "You will notify our offices if you hear anything, will you not?"

"Yes, of course."

They moved toward the door. Jacob again. "Incidentally, Leo Zwicken has completely vanished. No one has seen nor heard from him. I'm convinced my brother's disappearance is connected with his."

The men said their good-byes and left. Sophie exhaled and sat on the top step with her head in her hands. Abigail emerged from the parlor and paused at the bottom of the stairs. She looked up at Sophie, then ducked her head and proceeded to the keeping room.

Sophie returned to the kitchen and sat down at the trestle table to quiet her trembling knees. Zwicken was gone. Even if Edward's body were to turn up, she didn't think it likely that anyone would look in the direction of the Barringtons or their servants. Still, she looked forward to the day when Bridget and Philippe would come for her and take her away to the hills of central Pennsylvania.

THE SLEIGH JOSTLED DOWN THE HILL, ROUNDED THE CURVE to cross Bushkill Creek, and then started up the road toward the houses. Twilight settled over the woods, and the lengthening shadows reached across the road, spilling over the sleigh. Charles had ridden ahead to alert the family.

Bridget snuggled next to Philippe, shivering in the cold. "Will we make it by nightfall?"

Philippe nodded and chucked the reins, urging the horses to pick up their pace. "It's just over the rise."

Bridget felt a knot in her stomach. Gripping Philippe's arm, she whispered, "I'm so frightened. Will your family . . . are you certain your mother will . . . accept me?"

As the horses climbed from the creek bottom up the hill, the houses came into view, silhouetted against the pink sunset sky. The sleigh bumped over the ruts in the road.

Philippe pointed toward the house. "Look, my love, look!"

From every window shone a lighted candle. A soft halo of light wrapped its luminescent arms around the picturesque scene. Philippe urged the horses to pick up the pace, and the snow began to fly beneath the runners. Approaching the house, they could see a woman with a shawl wrapped around her shoulders standing on the porch.

Madeleine Clavell Bovée slowly stepped off the porch, and then began to run. Her shawl fell into the snow as she stretched out her arms toward them.

Philippe turned and grabbed Bridget's hand as she began to cry. He laughed. "There's your answer. The invitation is extended. Welcome home, my love. Welcome to the family."

EPILOGUE

A LITTLE OVER A YEAR LATER

This way!" Philippe looked over his shoulder from astride Legacy as he guided the horse down the road that lead to the bridge over Bushkill Creek. Bridget, atop her beloved Kimi, followed close behind. The meadow was alive with dandelions, violets, and trillium. Bright green leaves on the trees opened their tight foliage to the sky. Bridget turned her face to the sun. The thin rays of the early season warmed her skin, although the air was still crisp.

She laughed. "Where are we going?" She rode up beside her husband.

"You shared your special place at Whisper Wood with me. I want to show you mine here."

They dismounted and walked the rest of the way down to the creek. The water gurgled over the rocks and raced downstream.

Bridget bent over and dipped her hand into the stream. "It's really cold."

Philippe nodded. "This is where I brought Maman when I told her that I was going after you. The creek was frozen on top, but the water still flowed beneath the ice." He enfolded Bridget in his arms. "I told her that it was like my love for you. It perhaps would freeze over for a season, but it would still be raging underneath the surface. And when spring came, it would bubble to the surface and flow again. I wasn't willing to live like that. I had to at least try to claim you." He looked down at her. "Are you cold?"

Bridget shook her head and cuddled close to him. "No, I just like for you to hold me." She looked up at him and touched his cheek. "Thank you for being courageous enough to rescue me."

Philippe smiled. "How could I not?" He helped her mount. "Let's go. We had best be getting back."

As the house came into view, Madeleine, holding a bundle in her arms, rose from the rocking chair on the porch. Vangie sat in a chair beside her. Adriaen worked the butter churn up and down, with Liberty and Freedom toddling up and down the steps. Sophie came around the corner from the barn with her apron full of eggs.

Bridget jumped off her horse and ran toward the house. She stepped up toward Madeleine and took the baby from her arms. "How's my little François Philippe?"

"He is wonderful, *ma fille*." Madeleine smiled and gave the baby a kiss as she handed the child over.

Bridget looked at her husband's mother. "I love it when you call me daughter."

"That's how I feel about you—you are truly my daughter. When I think how I almost—"

Bridget shook her head. "That's all in the past. I have learned so much from you. I am truly honored that God has allowed me to be a Clavell."

"It feels as if you have always been a part of our family."

Philippe tied the horses to the hitching rail and joined the women on the porch. He took little François from Bridget and held him in the air, then nuzzled the baby's neck.

Claudine appeared at the door. "Dinner is ready."

Pierre, Jean, and Charles walked onto the porch from the watering trough, wiping their hands dry on their pants.

"Look who's awake." Pierre took the baby from Philippe. "Come here to your *grandpère*." The baby cooed at the Frenchman. "See? He knows who loves him."

Philippe laughed and put one arm around his mother's shoulders and one around his wife, pulling them close. "I think there is ample love in this family for everyone."

Madeleine smiled and gazed at the idyllic scene. "Just look at us—to have come so far, from the dark days in France to this land of freedom." Tears shimmered in her eyes as they walked into the cabin. They sat down to a table, not lavish, but with adequate provision, together at last—bittersweet memories lingering in their spirits of those they had lost on the journey, but with hearts full of thanksgiving for the faithfulness of their God.

Dearest Reader,

"Welcome home. Welcome to the family." I feel as if every one of you, my readers, is part of the family. How can I ever thank you enough for going on this journey with me to visit my Clavell ancestors through these books?

One of the questions most frequently asked when I speak to book clubs or at writers' conferences is: How much of the story is fiction, and how much is fact? So I thought I would answer those questions for you at the conclusion of the first three books as we wrap up the story of these particular characters.

I knew nothing about my French Huguenot heritage until I inherited a published family genealogy several years ago and read the history of my mother's ancestors. Who would have guessed this humble little lady had such a rich heritage? I don't think she even knew the full story of her family.

The history of the persecution and plight of the French Huguenots in seventeenth-century France was as historically accurate as I could make it. My family were French Huguenots who lived in southern France around Grenoble in Dauphine Provence and experienced the horror of being persecuted for their faith. I softened many of the atrocities to which the Huguenots were subjected during that period, but one of my ancestors actually was sentenced to the galleys for his faith. The Clavells eventually fled to Geneva, Switzerland, then to Auerbach, Germany, and on to Pennsylvania.

Books One and Two, *In the Shadow of the Sun King* and *A Prisoner of Versailles*, were set about fifty years earlier than the time of my literal family in order to incorporate the very colorful character of Louis XIV. The other characters were combinations of people. Madeleine's "real" name was Louisa—however, one can readily see that "Louis" and "Louisa" would have been most cumbersome. Thus, the name change to Madeleine.

The germ of the story of a love affair between Madeleine and the king came from a true episode in the life of the young King Louis. The king's chief advisor, Cardinal Mazarin, had a niece with whom Louis fell in love. He was forbidden to marry her, but legend has it that she remained the true love of his life. This part of the story, as far as my family is concerned, was fictitious. Pierre and Vangie are completely fictitious characters.

My ancestor Louisa (Madeleine) actually landed in Philadelphia a penniless widow with two boys, Franz (Philippe) and George (Charles) in 1737. My story is set around 1686. Her husband had been washed overboard and had their money on him. She did have to sell her sons to the redemptioners to pay for their passage. That part of the story is true. I cannot imagine her agony. What a strong woman! Alone, she followed the ship's passengers into the Schuylkill Valley and remarried, and as soon as the boys gained their freedom, they joined her. They all settled on land in Bushkill County on adjoining land. Bridget is a fictional character.

They soon changed their name to Clewell—for what reason the family does not know.

I thank God for the rich heritage from which I have come. I praise him for allowing me the privilege of enjoying the freedom they fought for. May those who follow us be able to declare that our faith was strong as well.

—GOLDEN KEYES PARSONS

ACKNOWLEDGMENTS

The "great cloud of witnesses" continues to gather with each ensuing book that I write. Because of them, *Where Hearts Are Free* is a better book than I could ever have made it.

Where Hearts Are Free was a difficult book for me to write. During the time that I was working on it my husband experienced a drop-dead attack in the Albuquerque airport and was brought back to life by an amazing young Army Captain in the Medical Services Corps. The next month we moved to another state—back home to Texas from our pastorate in New Mexico—and my husband had quadruple by-pass surgery. Then we bought a home and moved again after living with our middle daughter and her family for six months. All during that time I was writing this book. It took three major rewrites to get the book into an acceptable format. The vision that I initially had for it is not where the book finally wound up, but I'm pleased with the final product. It's been an interesting and educational journey.

Although our children are grown and have families of their own, I still need to thank them for their encouragement and support. My daughters, Amber, Andra, and Amanda who go with me to events when I need a helping hand, give me ideas, provide me with illustrations, are a constant source of inspiration for me. Our granddaughter, Crysta, who traveled with me on several promotional trips and who helps me with office and computer support; and of course, my husband, who never doubts that each book will be better than the last.

My editor, Natalie Hanemann and the Fiction Team at Thomas Nelson, my outside editors, Jamie Chavez and LB Norton, who keep pulling me out of literary ditches and putting me back on the right path.

My research assistant, Jennifer Wilford, whom I have never met. She is the granddaughter of our dear friends, Ken and Victoria Skinner, and she simply loves doing research. Nothing is too large or too minute for her to ferret out of the dusty archives—or cyber archives as the case may be. I hope to meet her someday and be able to give her a big hug and thank her face to face.

My agent, Mary Beth Chappell, who is always there as a sounding board with wise and sensible advice . . . and who believed in this series in the first place.

My distant cousin, Rich Heckman, whom I met doing research on the Clavell family in Pennsylvania. His genealogical expertise on the family and his willingness to share that information was priceless.

READING GROUP GUIDE

1. In the beginning of *Where Hearts Are Free*, Bridget reveals to Philippe a secret which she has harbored for several years. Secrets hold a terrifying power over us—they erect walls between us and the people we love and with whom we are supposed to be in relationship. The revealing of the secret breaks that power. What power did Bridget's secret hold over her? How did it manifest itself in her life and personality?

2. What secret did Philippe harbor that he was unwilling to admit even to himself? What power did that secret hold over him?

3. What do you think would have happened to Philippe if he had not admitted his love for Bridget and gone after her? What would have happened to her?

4. Philippe risked it all for love. Have you ever done that? What happened?

5. Why do you think Madeleine found it so difficult to give her approval for Philippe to go after Bridget? Were her fears valid?

6. My ancestor literally had to leave her two sons in Philadelphia as indentured servants to pay back the money for their passage to America, after losing her husband on the voyage over. Try to imagine the anguish of that mother. Is Madeleine's desire to maintain control of her family a bit more understandable in light of those circumstances?

7. Who was your favorite character? Why?

8. Who was one of your favorite secondary characters? Why?

9. What was your favorite scene? Why?

10. Do you consider Sophie's murdering Edward an act of self-defense? Why or why not? Do you think she should have been prosecuted?

11. What did this book say to you about God and your faith?

AUTHOR TO AUTHOR

The Thomas Nelson Fiction team recently invited our authors to interview any other Thomas Nelson Fiction author in an unplugged Q&A session. They could ask any questions about any topic they wanted to know more about. What we love most about these conversations is that they reveal just as much about the ones asking the questions as they do the authors who are responding. So sit back and enjoy the discussion. Perhaps you'll even be intrigued enough to pick up one of their novels and discover a new favorite writer in the process.

Golden Keyes Parsons

Beth Wiseman

Golden Keyes Parsons: I know this is a question you are asked over and over, but I think our readers will be interested to know how you got started writing Amish fiction.

Beth Wiseman: I have a deep affection for the Amish and their simpler way of life, so when my agent asked me if I would like to try Amish fiction, the decision was easy.

GKP: It's my opinion that the simpler way of life is a major part of the appeal of the Amish fiction genre. I believe there is something within all of us that yearns for that simplicity. Tell us how you go about researching your books.

BW: I have connections in Lancaster County, so I have lots of help as I go along, and I have an ex-Amish friend who reads the books prior to publication to verify authenticity. I also read a lot of books about the Amish (both fiction and nonfiction), scan newspaper articles relevant to Lancaster County, continue to educate myself about their ways, and visit my Amish friends in that beautiful part of the country as often as I can.

GKP: It is indeed a beautiful part of the country with the picturesque farms, colorful flowers, and rolling hills. This is the area where my French Huguenot ancestors settled. Do you foresee writing in a different arena eventually?

BW: The popularity of the subgenre suggests that I will be writing Amish fiction for a long time. I'm currently contracted through 2013, and those in the publishing industry believe this "trend" is establishing itself as a stand-alone genre.

GKP: Your books were bestsellers right off the bat. For an unknown author, that's quite a feat. To what do you attribute that fact?

BW: I think I was in the right spiritual place at the right time and able to hear God calling me to write stories that glorify him.

GKP: What is your favorite part about being an author? Your least favorite part?

BW: My favorite part is when the story writes itself and I can feel God spreading his word through me—that is an amazing feeling. Honestly, I don't have a least favorite part. The entire process is exciting for me, and I feel incredibly blessed.

GKP: I feel the same way, Beth. I even like the rewrites and edits. What is the faith message you hope your readers will come away with?

BW: That a one-on-one relationship with God is the only way to true peace and happiness. And it doesn't matter if you live in Lancaster County, Pennsylvania, among the Amish, or across the continent.

GKP: That's my prayer as well. I also hope that readers will catch a glimpse of the faithfulness of God, even in the difficult places in the lives of believers. What one thing would you like to incorporate in your own life that you have learned from the Amish lifestyle?

BW: To shed fear and worry. Sometimes it consumes me, and I'd like to be more like the Amish in that respect— to trust that all things are God's will, even when we can't possibly understand his plan for us.

GKP: You have mentioned to me how much you have enjoyed my series on the French Huguenots. Do you see any similarities between our two series?

BW: Yes, I've enjoyed reading the series. I think we both write strong protagonists who are also somewhat vulnerable at times, which gives the reader a three-dimensional look at our characters.

GKP: Yes, I love strong female protagonists. And I love the challenge of giving her a believable flaw or weakness, then following that thread to show how God is faithful and makes a way for her in spite of her faltering. What's next for you in your writing?

BW: Amish, Amish, Amish. And I have no complaints. I love writing about these wonderful people and plan to do so for as long as I can.

Thanks, Beth, for your time and your comments.

If you've not read Beth's books, do yourself a favor and pick one up soon. You will find yourself immersed in the story of a simpler life with plenty of plot tension that keeps the pages turning.

HIT LIT

HIT LIT

Cracking the Code of the

Twentieth Century's Biggest Bestsellers

James W. Hall

RANDOM HOUSE TRADE PAPERBACKS

NEW YORK

Published in the United States by Random House Trade Paperbacks,
an imprint of The Random House Publishing Group,
a division of Random House, Inc., New York.

RANDOM HOUSE TRADE PAPERBACKS and colophon are
registered trademarks of Random House, Inc.

LIBRARY OF CONGRESS CATALOGING-IN-PUBLICATION DATA
Hall, James W. (James Wilson).
Hit lit : cracking the code of the twentieth century's
biggest bestsellers / James W. Hall.
p. cm.
ISBN 978-0-8129-7095-1—eBook ISBN 978-0-679-60496-9
1. Best sellers—United States—History—20th century.
2. Popular literature—United States—History and criticism. 3. Books and
reading—United States—History—20th century. I. Title.
Z1033.B3H35 2012
381'.450020973—dc22   2011012619

Printed in the United States of America

www.atrandom.com

2 4 6 8 9 7 5 3 1

FIRST EDITION

Book design by Dana Leigh Blanchette
Frontispiece and part title photo: © iStockphoto

This one's for my students.

For four decades you've given me more than I've given you. Testing me, pushing me, opening my eyes, clarifying what I didn't understand, forcing me to consider and rethink comfortable ideas I'd clung to, all the while letting me pretend I was in charge when it was never true. You were always running the show. I couldn't have done it without you.

FOREWORD

My love affair with books began as most serious romances do, when I was least expecting to fall in love. I was ten years old, maybe eleven, and for years I had dutifully read the required books in school. But because they were required and because I was tested on my comprehension of them, I had decided that reading books ranked alongside long division and penmanship as simply one more bothersome educational duty.

Context is important here, for I was a young male in a southern town of the 1950s. In other words, that I would read a book just for fun was about as likely as my deciding spontaneously to knit a sweater for the football coach. It wasn't done. At least not by any of the male role models who shaped my thinking at the time.

So when my mother deposited me at the public library that

fall afternoon to get me out of her hair while she went about her downtown errands, she might as well have dropped me off in the middle of Death Valley. The gloomy building was one of those WPA structures built in the heavily ornate style of the Old South. That creaky battleship was piloted by a wispy, white-haired woman in a dark dress and thick glasses, a living cliché who floated noiselessly up and down the stacks, replacing volumes in their proper slots and leaving the dry dust of tedium in her wake. As a young boy who aspired only to muscular achievements on hash-marked fields or gymnasium floors, I was mortified. Frightened out of my skin that I would be spotted by one of my friends in such a place.

To make myself as invisible as possible, I moseyed down aisle after aisle, studying the titles of those musty tomes, bored to death by the prospect of spending an hour or two in that dismal room. When the passing librarian seemed to sense my discomfort and began to home in on me, a fit of panic spurred me to nab a random book from a shelf, pop it open to the first page, and feign deep interest.

As my eyes ran down the lines of print, I was suddenly breathless. Though my vocabulary was no larger than that of any average ten-year-old boy of my place and time, I did know the word *nude*. It was one of those special, cherished words, not quite a curse, but nonetheless a word loaded with magical potency. And lo and behold, that very word leapt out of the first page and seized my full attention. The fact that the word *nude* turned out to be an adjective modifying the word *woman* made my knees weak and put a wobble in my pulse.

I looked up, certain that the librarian was about to rip this smutty book from my hand, grab me by the collar, and toss me onto the street. By evening it would be all over town: "Little Jimmy Hall was caught reading that nude woman book in the library." But magically, the librarian melted back into the stacks and I was left alone with my first murder mystery novel.

For the nude woman was dead, and it was her corpse that had been found in a field by a man chasing butterflies. How did she get there? Who was she? Who would have done such a thing? I was mesmerized. Weak of breath and nearly fainting from a preadolescent tumult of emotions, I located a private corner near a window. I looked around and planned my getaway should my mother suddenly reappear and find me reading such filth. Then I sped through as many pages as I could manage before she returned and called me away.

So this was why people read! Books were about adult things. Strong emotions, extreme behaviors, the inside stuff of a world I had never imagined existed. In this, my first recreational book, I suddenly realized that novels could fill one with heart-pounding fear as well as lip-smacking lust. That they could, in fact, suddenly expand the boundaries of the hillbilly town where I had always lived and where I imagined I always would stay.

Tramping across the bogs of the English countryside in pursuit of the heinous killer of that nude woman, I was suddenly freed of my homebound life. I was set loose in the world and allowed to know every crucial thought of that droll British detective and was just as stumped as he, just as frustrated, and finally just as delighted when the logic of his deductions led him to the surprising culprit.

It took me several more surreptitious visits to the library to finish that novel. Surely my mother and father were deeply puzzled by this new enthusiasm, but they had the good grace not to ask where it was coming from. That might have quashed it all.

The day I finished that first novel, I looked up to find the amiable librarian staring down at me.

I gulped.

"You like mysteries?" she asked.

I gazed at the book in my hand as though it had just materialized there.

"Oh, this?"

"Yes, that. That book you've been reading these last few weeks."

"I guess so," I said.

"Well, so do I." She beamed. "I just love a good murder story." And she gave me a conspiratorial look that still floats into my mind whenever I am feeling isolated from the human race. For as I have come to understand, reading is at once a private and communal act. While books are savored alone, they grant you membership into the most fascinating club I know: fellow readers. Fellow voyagers into the vast uncharted waters of imaginative literature.

That afternoon, the librarian gave me a private tour of that big dusty room and she showed me the best mysteries in the house. Hard-boiled, cozies, Sherlock Holmes. She made a pile, got me a library card, helped me fill it out.

"Tell me what you think," she said.

"Okay," I said uncertainly.

"Oh, don't worry, this isn't school," she said. "There's no test when you bring them back. I won't take your library card away from you if you don't read one all the way through."

"I don't know," I said. "I don't know if I'm smart enough to read all these." I patted the stack of books.

"Oh, my," she said. "No one starts out smart. That's why we read."

Over the next few years, I gradually expanded my reading

list with Dickens and Hardy, and later I fell in love with Virginia Woolf, Lawrence Durrell, and John Fowles, Faulkner and Steinbeck, and the poets Sylvia Plath and Anne Sexton and Robert Frost. It came as a shock to learn that sports and reading were not mutually exclusive. In fact, when I discovered Hemingway and began reading about his intense competitive exploits, I started to picture the unspeakable—that I might someday learn the craft of writing well enough to create the very things I so dearly loved to consume.

Though that creaky library no longer exists in my small Kentucky hometown, and though I have fled her narrow streets and scrubby fields forever, the largest part of what I am today and what I know about the world and about the affairs of the human heart springs from that one autumn afternoon when I plucked a book from the shelf and encountered that nude woman lying in the grass and I began this long journey, year after year, filling myself beyond the brim with the great accumulated wealth of books.

School year led to school year until I'd accumulated all the degrees there were to be had in my chosen field, and in the process, the reading of books became not just my private passion, but my profession. As so often happens in any career, I began to specialize.

In graduate school, a certain kind of novel that was considered avant-garde caught my fancy and later became my area of concentration when I began to teach at the university level. Call them metafiction or postmodernist, these novels are experimental, fresh, and exciting, and best of all they require someone like me to help the uninitiated student fully comprehend and appreciate their esoteric beauty.

For the first ten years of my teaching life, I held up these challenging novels as the gold standard of literary achievement, and I touted them as superior in every regard to novels that still employed such old-fashioned techniques as plot and character development.

Then one afternoon I was exploring the reference stacks of the university library, trying to devise the course I would teach the following semester, when I happened on a collection of year-by-year lists of bestsellers from the past. I paged through the book with growing fascination as I came across novel after novel that I had read long ago, books that set off starbursts of nostalgia. And there were many more books on the lists that I'd always meant to read but had put off because of my academic studies.

Maybe it was time to take a break from my specialty. Oh, why not.

So I put together a course in popular fiction, and not just any popular fiction. For that initial class, I chose ten books that were the bestselling novels of their decade. These books were big. Bigger than big.

Though teaching such a course started out as little more than a whim, it proved to be the watershed moment in my intellectual and artistic life, and the truth is, I've had a lot more fun ever since.

We started with *Gone with the Wind*. I'd seen the film but never read the book, so I was unprepared for the full-bodied Scarlett O'Hara and how deeply she would move me. She was maddeningly silly, yet totally captivating. I was bowled over. Scarlett's tale engaged me emotionally in ways I hadn't experienced since my early days of reading. There was nothing to deconstruct, nothing to decode, nothing to distract the heart. Just fascinating people caught up in a rousing tale.

In the second week, we began to discuss *From Here to Eternity*. Same thing. Once again I was deeply stirred by the book. The novel's scope and primitive power and its fabulous characters swept me up and took me to an emotional land I'd almost forgotten existed after all those years of cerebral study. I was a kid again, encountering Dickens and Hardy and Austen for the first time, mesmerized by these robust characters who magically migrated from the page and took up residence inside me, who became as real and gut-wrenching as any humans I'd ever met.

Without intending it, I had rediscovered the excitement I'd felt in that creaky old library in a small town in Kentucky, when I couldn't turn the pages fast enough, when I disappeared into worlds more real than the one around me. I had returned to the wellspring of one of my great passions.

On that day over twenty years ago, I also began an odyssey to try to understand what makes a book "successful." What makes us connect with it, what makes us fall in love the way I had.

It suddenly seemed obvious to me that when millions of readers, whether they are formally educated or not, have expressed their separate opinions by buying and delighting in a particular novel, there is some larger wisdom at work. Thus, it seemed self-evident to ask one simple question: What is it about this or that enormously popular book that inspires such widespread fervor and devotion?

I began to wonder what my students and I would learn if we reverse-engineered these novels, breaking them down into their component parts. Would we find any common features lurking in the most popular books of all time? Was it possible to figure out what made these books so irresistible?

WHY THESE TWELVE?

The term "best seller" was coined and came into common use because it filled a need. A term was needed to describe what were not necessarily the best books but the books that people liked the best.

—FREDERIC MELCHER, 1946

Before we begin, it's important to understand that the twelve novels I've chosen to discuss aren't your run-of-the-mill best-sellers. To spend a week or two on the *New York Times* best-seller list, a hardback novel could sell a hundred thousand copies or half that many. Depending on the other books it's up against at any given moment, maybe a little more or a little less will be required of the average bestseller. Those are terrific numbers in the book business, but they fall well short of the sales figures for the bestsellers-on-steroids we'll be examining.

In fact, one of the quirky features of the bestseller list is that appearing on it depends more on velocity of sales than on total sales. If Book A managed to sell ten or fifteen thousand copies in the first two weeks after it was published, it would almost surely appear on national bestseller lists, even if its sales dropped off to zero in the weeks after that. While Book B could sell many times more copies in the course of a year than Book A, if its sales were slow and steady, without the initial surge that Book A had, Book B might never appear on any bestseller list at all.

In any case, the novels I'll be discussing in this book were spectacular megahits, selling in the multiple millions, and a few of them continue to show up on bestseller lists fifty years after their publication. To bend Mark Twain's famous analogy, the difference between these blockbusters and an average bestseller is like the difference between lightning and a lightning bug.

The common features I've identified recur with such frequency, it's almost as if these books have been spun out of identical genetic matter. I would go so far as to say that these twelve novels are permutations of one book, written again and again for each new generation of readers. True, these twelve novels have radically different settings, different characters, very different plots. But no matter which decade they were written in or what publishing vagaries brought them to the forefront, all have used strikingly similar techniques and themes to provide deep enjoyment to millions.

But it's not the ingredients alone that create the magic of highly popular stories. If it were that simple, this book would be only a few paragraphs long and I could end the semester on the first day of class. It is how those ingredients are combined and the unique ways they intermingle and resonate that set a megabestselling novel apart and make it appealing to such a vast audience.

In the following pages, we will analyze these particular elements in detail and examine the ways they are employed, and we will puzzle out the reasons for their enduring appeal to so many millions of American readers.

Along the way, I'll show how these recurring features in bestsellers spring from a single purpose: a desire to capture the uniqueness of the American story, its inspiring traditions and its bold idealism, its moral struggles, its violence, its contradictory values, and its extraordinary characters.

So without further ado, and before I say more about my methodology, here's our reading list, with a glimpse at the publishing history of each.

1. *GONE WITH THE WIND,* Margaret Mitchell, 1936

Scarlett O'Hara is in love with the vapid Ashley Wilkes, but he shuns her and instead marries his cousin—a tradition in the Wilkes family. However, Scarlett will not give him up that easily and schemes constantly to win his heart. As the Civil War presses closer around her, Scarlett uses any means she can to save her family's Georgia plantation, including entering into a series of increasingly lucrative but increasingly unhappy marriages, until she meets her match in the roguish Rhett Butler.

Number one bestseller for 1936. Six months after its release in December 1936, the novel had sold 1,000,000 copies. By fall of 1941, it had sold 2,868,200 copies. In 1946, authorized foreign sales of the book were estimated to be up to 1,250,000, and American sales had reached 3,713,272. In 1956, worldwide it reached the 8,000,000 mark; by 1962, it had grown to 10,000,000; by 1965, it was 12,000,000. In 1983, the number reached 16,000,000. During the 1980s, the novel continued to sell 100,000 hardbacks a year worldwide and 250,000 paperbacks a year in the United States. Estimates put the sales figures near 30,000,000 in the 1990s.

2. *PEYTON PLACE,* Grace Metalious, 1956

Conceived during an illicit love affair, Allison MacKenzie grows into an introverted and sensitive young girl who struggles to free herself from her overprotective single mother, Constance, as well as the narrow-mindedness of the quaint New England town of her birth. Just when it seems she has escaped and established a successful writing career in the city, she decides she must return to her hometown to cover the sensational trial of her old friend Selena Cross. While there, Allison finally comes to peace with the cruelty, kindness, and complexity of Peyton Place.

This was Grace Metalious's first and most successful novel. According to Alice Payne Hackett's *80 Years of Best Sellers, 1895–1975, Peyton Place* sold a total of 10,670,302 in hardcover and paperback combined.

3. *TO KILL A MOCKINGBIRD,* Harper Lee, 1960

Scout Finch is bursting with innocent mischief as she starts first grade in her sleepy Alabama town. Soon after, her father, Atticus, a lawyer, takes on the legal defense of Tom Robinson, a black man who has been accused of rape by a white woman. The trial rocks the town to its core and forces Scout and her older brother, Jem, to wrestle with grim racial and social wrongs.

Published in 1960, *To Kill a Mockingbird* remained on the bestseller list for eighty-eight weeks. (Rose as high as number three on the 1961 year-end list.)

The paperback edition has had 135 printings, with well over 14,000,000 copies sold.

4. *VALLEY OF THE DOLLS,* Jacqueline Susann, 1966

Full of confidence, Anne Welles arrives in New York City just after World War II. She takes an exciting job in the entertainment business and soon has two new roommates, Neely O'Hara and Jennifer North, and a dashing suitor, Lyon Burke. But when the lives of her beautiful and talented friends begin to unravel, they take Anne Welles down with them into a tragic, drug-fueled spiral.

Number one in 1966. Approximately 30,000,000 copies sold worldwide, which puts it roughly in the same category as *To Kill a Mockingbird* and *Gone with the Wind.*

5. *THE GODFATHER,* Mario Puzo, 1969

After the head of the Corleone crime family, Don Vito Corleone, is shot by a rival, the empire he has devoted his life to building is in danger of dissolving, until Michael, his favorite son, a war hero and upstanding citizen, takes charge. Michael is a natural leader and quickly learns to navigate the inner workings, crude politics, and secret rituals of the Mafia, and by employing a series of swift and brutal moves, he attempts to restore power and respect to the family.

In the first two years after its publication, 1969–1970, *The Godfather* sold more than 1,000,000 copies in hardcover and

8,000,000 copies in paperback. By 1975, over 12,000,000 copies had sold in both hardback and softcover.

6. *THE EXORCIST,* William Peter Blatty, 1971

Chris MacNeil, divorced single mother and successful actress, is living in Washington, D.C., with her twelve-year-old daughter, Regan, while shooting her latest film. Regan, once a curious and happy girl, grows moody and strange. After numerous doctors and psychiatrists fail to diagnose her, Chris reaches out to a young priest, Father Karras, who realizes Regan is possessed by a demon. The battle between Karras, a religious man with shaky faith, and the devil that inhabits Regan's body is a fierce and violent struggle that results in numerous deaths but ultimately in victory for the MacNeil family.

Four years after its publication, 11,702,097 hardback copies and 11,000,000 paperbacks had been sold.

7. *JAWS,* Peter Benchley, 1974

The resort town of Amity is preparing for the summer on-slaught of beachgoers from the city when a young woman taking a late-night swim is killed by a shark. It is Police Chief Martin Brody's task to decide whether to keep the beaches open for the big holiday weekend. Under pressure from town leaders, he lets them stay open, and as a result, a six-year-old local boy becomes the shark's next victim. Driven to set things right, Brody teams up with Quint, a salty shark hunter famil-

iar with local waters, and with Matt Hooper, an academically trained shark expert, and the three men head out to sea in Quint's boat to capture the murderous creature.

The novel stayed on some hardbound bestseller lists for forty-four weeks, making it 1974's longest-running fiction bestseller. More than 1,000,000 in sales in 1974.

By 1975, 9,275,000 copies of the Bantam paperback were sold.

8. *THE DEAD ZONE,* Stephen King, 1979

Johnny Smith is working as a high school teacher, an average guy in love with another teacher, Sarah Bracknell, when a serious head injury puts him in a coma. Years later when he wakes, Johnny discovers he has acquired the supernatural gift of foreseeing the future. He sets about finding ways to put his newfound ability to good use, solving crimes and helping individuals, until his path crosses that of Greg Stillson, a rising politician. After Johnny sees a vision of Stillson leading the nation to disaster, he decides he must do whatever is required to prevent Stillson from reaching his goal, even if it means risking his own life.

This was King's first novel to break into the year-end top ten. His earlier hardback novels, *Carrie* and *Salem's Lot,* had sold modestly. But when the film version of *Carrie* was released in 1976, King's career moved into a higher gear. It has continued to shift ever higher with a prolific output over the last twenty years. Throughout the 1980s and 1990s, it was a rare year when one of King's novels did not appear on the year-end top ten list, frequently landing at number one.

9. *THE HUNT FOR RED OCTOBER,* Tom Clancy, 1984

At the height of the cold war, submarine captain Marko Ramius, who is commanding the Soviet's newest top-secret nuclear sub, decides to defect to America. Ramius's intentions, however, are not clear to the Americans, who enlist the aid of Jack Ryan, a naval historian and part-time CIA analyst, to help the U.S. military plan an appropriate response. When Ryan discovers that the Soviets have apparently developed a new supersilent propulsion system that could shift the military balance of power between the nations, mild-mannered Ryan is thrust into the middle of an escalating confrontation that could very well result in World War III.

The hardcover edition of this first novel sold 365,000 copies, according to a 1987 article in the *Washington Post* "Book World." Five to six million copies have sold in hardback and paperback. One million copies were sold in Japan alone.

10. *THE FIRM,* John Grisham, 1991

Mitch McDeere, a top Harvard Law School grad, is snapped up by Bendini, Lambert & Locke, a prestigious firm in Memphis. Mitch and Abby, his bride, are thrilled by the perks: the new house, the flashy car, the big salary. But they quickly realize the firm is working on behalf of a Chicago crime family,

and members of the firm are perfectly willing to commit mur-
der to conceal this fact. After Mitch is secretly recruited by
the FBI to help with its investigation of the law firm, his
snooping endangers his life and the lives of others. So Mitch
devises a complex and risky scheme that is meant to satisfy
the FBI and free him and Abby from the sinister grip of the
firm.

The Firm spent forty-seven weeks on the *New York Times*
bestseller list. Grisham's publisher shipped over a million
copies of his next novel, *The Client,* and two and a half million copies of the following book, *The Chamber.*

11. *THE BRIDGES OF MADISON COUNTY,*
Robert James Waller, 1992

In the mid-1960s, Robert Kincaid has been assigned by Na-
tional Geographic *to photograph the covered bridges of Mad-*
ison County, Iowa. Shortly after arriving in Madison County,
he meets Francesca Johnson, a farmer's wife, who is home
alone while her husband, Richard, and her children are away
for a week's visit to the Illinois State Fair. A brief and passion-
ate affair between the seasoned traveler and the lonely woman
ensues. After days and nights of wild romance, the pair real-
ize they must decide their future before Richard and the chil-
dren return. Both Robert and Francesca are heartsick at the
prospect that they might have to part.

After selling poorly for a few months following its publication, the novel was rejuvenated when a section was published
in *Cosmopolitan,* which attracted a large audience of female

readers. Then word of mouth among independent booksellers began to spur more sales, until the book rose to become the number one bestseller in 1993, dropping to number nine the following year. Roughly 50,000,000 copies sold worldwide.

12. *THE DA VINCI CODE,* Dan Brown, 2003

When Jacques Saunière, head curator at the Louvre in Paris, is murdered, Robert Langdon, a highly regarded Harvard symbologist, is summoned to the scene and is immediately whisked away by Sophie Neveu, a French cop and cryptographer, who warns him that the police are trying to pin the murder on him. In trying to solve the murder of Saunière and absolve himself, Langdon embarks on a quest to expose a conspiracy that is centuries old and involves the Priory of Sion, the Holy Grail, intricate codes, and Jesus Christ.

The Da Vinci Code sold 81,000,000 copies worldwide, making it the top bestselling novel of all time.

(More detailed plot summaries of these novels can be found in the appendix.)

In choosing these twelve, I first consulted Alice Payne Hackett, the leading authority on which books sold the most throughout the twentieth century. Hers is the book I bumped into in the library stacks three decades ago that set me on this course to begin with. Although her *80 Years of Best Sellers* is a bit dry, it is indispensable for anyone interested in popular fiction. With the zeal of an IRS auditor, Ms. Hackett spent years analyzing sales figures compiled by her employer *Pub-*

lishers Weekly, a magazine geared for industry insiders, and put together a master list of the most commercially successful novels of previous decades.

While Ms. Hackett's work is the gold standard for book sales info, her commentary on popular novels is largely a recitation of publishing factoids, interspersed with a few dreary plot summaries. A far more lively account of bestsellers is Michael Korda's excellent survey *Making the List: A Cultural History of the American Bestseller 1900–1999.* Mr. Korda relied on lists from *The Bookman,* a periodical that first began to publish a monthly bestseller list in 1895. The modern lists Korda used appeared in *Publishers Weekly.* (*The New York Times* didn't begin to print its own list until 1942.)

Most of the pages of Mr. Korda's slender volume are taken up by the fiction and nonfiction lists themselves, but what text exists is richly spiced with tidbits. Did you know, for instance, that Mark Twain never made the bestseller list in part because he found it more profitable to sell his books himself through the earliest form of book clubs, as well as through house-to-house sales? Knock, knock. Who's there? Mark Twain with your new copy of *Adventures of Huckleberry Finn.*

Although Mr. Korda doesn't try to determine what constants bestsellers might possess, he does a solid job of sketching out the general contours of bestseller land. He's particularly good at presenting the history of publishing trends and demonstrating the book business's symbiotic connection with major world events, such as war, the Depression, and the flower power era of the 1960s. Though the connection between book sales and popular fashion is a slippery subject, Mr. Korda is masterful at making the case that a novel's success is often influenced by larger cultural forces in vogue at any given moment.

When it came time for me to formulate the basic structure of the reading list for this book, Ms. Hackett's "combined list" (which adds together paperback and hardback sales figures) was the obvious starting place.

Here are Hackett's bestselling novels between 1895 and 1975 (with the novels I've selected in bold).

1. **_The Godfather,_ 1969, Mario Puzo, 12,140,000 sold.**
2. **_The Exorcist,_ 1971, William Peter Blatty, 11,700,000 sold.**
3. **_To Kill a Mockingbird,_ 1960, Harper Lee, 11,120,000 sold.**
4. _Peyton Place,_ 1956, Grace Metalious, 10,670,000 sold.
5. _Love Story,_ 1970, Erich Segal, 9,905,000 sold.
6. **_Valley of the Dolls,_ 1966, Jacqueline Susann, 9,500,000 sold.**
7. _Jaws,_ 1974, Peter Benchley, 9,475,000 sold.
8. _Jonathan Livingston Seagull,_ 1970, Richard Bach, 9,055,000 sold.
9. **_Gone with the Wind,_ 1936, Margaret Mitchell, 8,630,000 sold.**
10. _God's Little Acre,_ 1933, Erskine Caldwell, 8,260,000 sold.

It's interesting to note that the decades of the 1960s and 1970s contain more than their share of the largest bestsellers of all times, while the 1940s is missing in action, as are the first two decades of the century. For those readers interested in such matters, Korda's _Making the List_ sketches out some of the historical, economic, and cultural factors that shaped these decade-by-decade differences in sales figures, but such considerations are not my focus here.

For the purposes of this book, I made some nips and tucks to Hackett's master list. I've jettisoned two mushy books, *Love Story* and *Jonathan Livingston Seagull*, replacing them with the more recent (though, let's admit it, equally mushy) *The Bridges of Madison County*. I've also dropped that ode to incest and small-town squalor *God's Little Acre*, because those same subjects are already well represented by *Peyton Place* and *To Kill a Mockingbird*.

To flesh out the total to an even dozen, I included four more novels. I'm confident the authors I've added would be on any modern reader's top ten list: John Grisham, Stephen King, Dan Brown, and Tom Clancy.

OUT OF PRINT

All the books on our reading list are still in print, but the same cannot be said for the great majority of bestsellers from the past century. Most of the smash hits of yesteryear can no longer be unearthed except by shopping at rare-book dealers. Such novelists as Warwick Deeping, Russell Janney, Ethel Vance, May Sinclair, and Harry Bellamann (whose *Kings Row* was made into a film starring Ronald Reagan) all had their fifteen minutes of literary fame, riding atop the bestseller lists of previous decades, but all are virtually unknown today. Which makes you wonder which of the huge bestsellers of our current age will still be around fifty years from now and beyond, and how and why one lives on and another doesn't.

For instance, how about *Lamb in His Bosom* by Caroline Miller? Still in print, though no longer widely read, Ms. Miller's 1934 novel, which is set in pre–Civil War Georgia and won the Pulitzer Prize, will always be a quirky footnote in American bestseller history. After witnessing the great commercial success of Caroline Miller's novel, Macmillan editor Harold S. Latham went shopping for other books with similar southern settings and in the process discovered Margaret Mitchell. Would *Gone with the Wind* have been published and heavily promoted without *Lamb in His Bosom* nudging open the door? It's one of those intriguing and unanswerable questions. But it's entirely possible that Caroline Miller is as responsible for our knowing and loving Rhett and Scarlett and Ashley Wilkes as Margaret Mitchell was.

FIRST NOVELS AND BREAKOUT BOOKS

Successful first novels are more likely to reveal popular tastes than bestsellers written by an established author. Because of the brand-name effect, a tenth or twentieth novel by Danielle Steel or John Grisham or Stephen King is virtually guaranteed a spot on the bestseller list and as such is less an indicator of public tastes than an indicator of public habits—and therefore is not particularly useful in demonstrating the recurring features that helped make it popular.

When an author's first novel does manage to overcome the incredible odds against it and turns into a commercial success, the student of popular culture needs to pay special attention. In such a case, readers and publishers had little reason to come to it beyond the appeal of the story itself. The combination of factors that sets apart that bestselling first novel from the hundreds of other first novels that remain in obscurity is exactly what my research was attempting to uncover.

After first novels, the next most instructive books are those that used to be known as a "breakout" novels—that is, the first book of an established author that cracks the bestseller list.

Back when publishers had the patience and the financial wherewithal to nurture a writer through the early, unprofitable stages of his or her career, it was not uncommon for a novelist to publish half a dozen books or more that didn't make a profit without being abandoned by the editor or publisher, usually because the editor was convinced the writer's work was solid and worthy and would one day find a larger audience. As a more tightfisted corporate model gradually replaced this charitable system, and publishers were buffeted by a succession of economic and industry upheavals, the patience required to wait for a "breakout book" all but disappeared. These days, if a writer does not succeed on the first or second try, his or her career is likely to flatline.

Of the twelve books on the list we'll be examining, a surprising seven were first novels: *To Kill a Mockingbird, Peyton Place, Valley of the Dolls, Gone with the Wind, Jaws, The Bridges of Madison County,* and *The Hunt for Red October.* The rest appeared early enough in the writers' careers to qualify as "breakout" novels. Grisham's *The Firm* was his second attempt, while *The Godfather* was Puzo's third book. William Peter Blatty wrote four comic novels before he circled in on *The Exorcist. The Da Vinci Code* was Dan Brown's third try. Stephen King had already cranked out eight books before *The Dead Zone* finished as the year-end number six bestseller.

The Dead Zone is unique among the others on my list. At roughly 175,000 hardbacks sold, its numbers fall far short of *The Godfather* or *Gone with the Wind* or the others we're considering. I included *The Dead Zone* because it was the first year-end bestselling hardback from one of the top commercial writers in history, a novelist who went on to publish dozens of number one bestsellers. How could any study of bestsellers omit Stephen King?

FEMALE SCRIBBLERS

Another factor I considered in fine-tuning my reading list was gender. Diversity is a tricky matter. As Leslie Fiedler wrote in "Literature and Lucre," "The struggle of High Art and low has, moreover, been perceived as a battle of the sexes. Referring to the writers who had preempted the paying audience before he ever entered the scene, Nathaniel Hawthorne called them a 'horde of female scribblers.' "

When more than three-quarters of the book-buying public are women, one would assume that female authors would populate the bestseller lists in greater proportion than men. But that's not the case. Based on a quick and totally unscientific sampling, using the results for the year-end bestselling totals for the opening year of each decade, I found quite the opposite to be true:

In 1900 two of ten were women.
In 1910 five of ten were women.
In 1920 three of ten were women.
In 1930 four of ten were women.
In 1940 one of ten were women.
In 1950 three of ten were women.
In 1960 two of ten were women.
In 1970 two of ten were women.
In 1980 two of ten were women.
In 1990 five of ten were women.

So in the twentieth century, the average is somewhere around two or three women on the year-end list. Far less than half and not at all what Nathaniel Hawthorne so chauvinistically imagined. John Bear, in his collection of intriguing facts about bestsellers (*The #1 New York Times Best Seller*), graphs the gradual increase in female authors who have achieved the number one slot on the *Times* list. From the forties through the eighties, the percentage of women reaching the pinnacle of the bestseller list hovered around 20 percent, while in the nineties the percentage climbed to 27.9 percent.

For the purposes of this book, I've bumped that figure up to 33 percent. One-third of the twelve novels we'll consider were written by women.

OPRAH, ADVERTISING, AND OTHER CONSIDERATIONS

Inevitably, any discussion of bestseller lists must take into consideration the impact of marketing and Oprah Winfrey. How valid is it to draw cultural conclusions from the bestseller list if a great many book buyers are motivated to buy a book not by the intrinsic elements in the book itself, but by slick ad campaigns or a television celebrity who caters to a unique demographic base?

Well, first, the hard reality is that clever marketing campaigns tend to work only a few times before they are copied by other marketers, thereby neutralizing the advantage. For instance, it was once rare for a writer to hit the road to promote his novel. Mark Twain is a colorful exception. With his trademark white suit and bushy mustache, his catchy nom de plume, and his stand-up comic routine, he established himself on the rough-and-tumble lecture circuit, selling his books by hand as he moved from one small-town venue to the next. In the modern era, Jacqueline Susann is often credited with breaking new ground in book promotion. Dressed in her Pucci outfits and carrying her poodle, Josephine, under her arm, the indefatigable Ms. Susann went so far as to visit truck stops, buttering up the drivers who used to select which books to stock on the spinning racks in drugstores and groceries. Twain and Susann were pioneers of what has become commonplace with modern authors, tireless and often flamboyant self-promotion.

Over the last few decades, however, the practice of book touring has become so widespread that on any given night in any given bookstore across the land, an author can be found pacing up and down the aisles, waiting and hoping for his or her audience to appear. The novelty of actually meeting a living, breathing author face-to-face has long ago worn off.

Then, more often than not, the latest advertising bright idea fails entirely to produce the intended results. Even lavishing hundreds of thousand of dollars on a promotional campaign is no guarantee of a book's success. Sometimes it works, sometimes it fails. Though they would wish it were otherwise, publishers are less in control of the destiny of individual books than the public (and most authors) often imagine.

My point is that knowing the historical details and the exact method a publisher used to promote a book to bestsellerdom would ultimately tell us very little, since the whole enterprise is fraught with unpredictability. Over the years, I've heard dozens of publishers or agents say some version of the following: "How the hell did that book make the List?"

"At least half the books on any given week's bestseller list are there to the immense surprise and puzzlement of their publishers," says Michael Korda, bestselling author and long-time editor. "That's why publishers find it so hard to repeat their successes—half the time they can't figure out how they happened in the first place."

As for Oprah, well, bless her amazing heart. Starting in 1996, her book club brought enormous numbers of new readers into the marketplace and conferred on dozens of otherwise obscure writers a measure of fame and fortune that, while ephemeral in many cases, was surely deserved.

However, for the decade that her book club operated at its peak, her chosen books tended to skew the bestseller list toward a type of novel that might not be so heavily represented otherwise, and thereby her selections squeezed off the list (and out of view) novels that many people might have chosen using guidance from more varied sources such as book reviews, booksellers, and word-of-mouth recommendations.

In any case, I didn't feel the need to include an Oprah pick on our reading list since at least two of the novels, *To Kill a Mockingbird* and *Peyton Place,* already stand squarely in her demographic promised land.

Finally, the five authors I've added to Hackett's all-time bestselling list are all from the last quarter of the twentieth century, with a strong tilt toward contemporary novels. I've done this bit of updating for the simple reason that I wanted to make this study of bestsellers more germane to a modern reader.

CONTENTS

RECAP

THE TWELVE FEATURES

FEATURE #1

An Offer You Can't Refuse

The most difficult thing in the world is to make things simple enough, and enticing enough, to cause readers to turn the page.

—HELEN GURLEY BROWN,
FORMER EDITOR OF *COSMOPOLITAN*

Some tricks of the trade that make our bestsellers unput-downable.

When Coleridge's Ancient Mariner intercepts an impatient guest who's rushing to a wedding, and grabs hold with his skinny hand and glittering eye, and proceeds to mesmerize the man with his haunting sea story, Coleridge has given us a nifty metaphor for the foremost mission of a bestseller writer. These books grip you and refuse to let you loose until they've finished their tale.

For the popular audience, first and foremost a novel must be entertaining. It's a fact so painfully obvious, I shudder to say it. For a novel to rise to the sales level of these twelve blockbusters, it must be a page-turner. A book you can't put down, that you want to read in a gulp. One that keeps you up all night. Gripping. Edge of your seat. Mesmerizing. Fast-paced. Spellbinding. A roller-coaster thrill ride. Unputdown-able.

Novelist and historian Les Standiford, a university colleague of mine, is fond of telling roomfuls of aspiring novelists, "The only place people read books they are not interested in is college."

The focus of this chapter is twofold. First I'll share what my students and I came to call the "mechanics of speed." Various ways in which writers initially engage readers, then keep them securely hooked while moving fast through a few hundred pages.

Then we'll look beyond narrative devices at the other key ingredients that helped these twelve novels seize the attention of so many readers.

MOVIE-FRIENDLY

Hollywood filmmakers can teach us a thing or two about speed, for moviemakers have turned storytelling into a science, using certain formulaic devices that consistently accelerate the forward movement of the narrative.

It's true that all twelve of the novels on our reading list were made into major motion pictures, and without a doubt some of their sales success as books was spurred by their filmic version. However, the common belief that a movie of a novel is the main factor in driving a book's commercial success is not supported by the facts. For instance, *Jaws* sold around a million copies before the film even came out.

In the cases of *Valley of the Dolls* and *The Da Vinci Code,* which are two of the biggest bestsellers of all time, so many copies had already been sold by the time the movie hit the theaters that it was unlikely any movie ticket buyers had not already bought the novel. Indeed, they seemed to be drawn to the film *because* they knew and loved the book.

That said, the effect of a successful film on the novel's long-term sales can be substantial. *Gone with the Wind* is the top-grossing domestic movie of all time, adjusted for ticket price inflation. Without a doubt, the film's ongoing popularity keeps the sales of the novel perking along. However, it's important to note that Margaret Mitchell's novel sold two million copies within a year of its publication, long before David O. Selznick got his hands on it. In this case, as in many others, the movie obviously helped the book's long-term sales, but the film was only one of many factors contributing to the book's overall success.

The permutations are endless: Bestsellers that flop at the box office (*The Lovely Bones*). Novels that have marginal sales but become spectacular hits as films (*Forrest Gump*). Novels that were moderate bestsellers but become movie legends. (Larry McMurtry has done it often.)

But such considerations are ultimately beside the point; at least, they're beside *my* point—which is that popular novelists have undeniably absorbed many lessons from the craft of filmmakers, and either intentionally or unintentionally, they have made their stories more "movie-friendly." These are the books that Hollywood folks *want* to make into movies. And moviemakers, in turn, have sharpened their storytelling craft by employing techniques of successful novelists. This cross-pollination of the two storytelling art forms is natural and mutually beneficial.

Steven Spielberg puts it this way: "I like ideas, especially movie ideas, that you can hold in your hand. If a person can tell me the idea in twenty-five words or less, it's going to make a pretty good movie."

Being able to compress a novel's complex plot into a single sentence is both a useful exercise for a novelist struggling to understand the dramatic forces driving his or her own work and a helpful marketing tool in the publishing industry and the film world. There are numerous commercial benefits to being able to frame a story in intriguing shorthand. For one thing, if a novel can't be summarized succinctly and engagingly, then word-of-mouth buzz isn't as easy to generate, and a marketing campaign is less likely to succeed; sales reps simply have a harder time selling the book to their bookstore accounts if they can't give a concise and appealing description. That's three strikes against any story so murky or complex that it can't be simplified to a tasty kernel.

For example:

When a rogue Russian sub commander who's piloting a vessel so technologically advanced that it could upset the balance of world power engages in a cat-and-mouse game with a brilliant CIA analyst who has the entire U.S. Navy at his disposal, World War III is only one small mistake away.

A resourceful young girl's innocent childhood is shattered and her family members threatened when she is thrust into the center of the racial turmoil that erupts in her small southern town.

Just for fun, check out this one-liner for *The Wizard of Oz* (often credited to Richard Polito, a journalist in California), which makes Dorothy's story sound like a hallucinatory episode from the life of Charlie Manson:

Transported to a surreal landscape, a young girl kills the first woman she meets, then teams up with three complete strangers to do it again.

The literary version of "high concept" is what's known as "the dramatic question," which is another way of capturing in a single catchy phrase the dramatic energy coiled within a novel.

Generally speaking, each genre has its own standard question. In mysteries: Will the detective catch the killer? Romance: Will the woman hook up with the man of her dreams? Horror: How will our hero manage to survive or defeat these terrifying events? Or in coming-of-age-novels: How will the character's adult life be shaped by the events of his or her youth?

Our twelve bestsellers are anything but coy about showing their hands from the beginning. Will the shark come back for a second bite? Will Scarlett ever marry Ashley? What will success do to Mitch and Abby McDeere? Will Anne Welles and her two girl pals find love and happiness in the big city? Will that faithless priest be able to save the little girl from the clutches of Satan?

Good questions, sure. Most readers' interest would be piqued. But are these questions sufficient to attract and compel large numbers of readers? No. More is required.

One way our twelve bestsellers stand apart is that each of them enhanced these dramatic questions by using unique and creative mash-ups of traditional genres. For instance, at its heart *The Hunt for Red October* is a detective story, and its dramatic question is straightforward. Will the detective, Jack Ryan, locate the rogue Russian sub commander and thwart his mission?

But if that were all this story was about, it's doubtful it would have risen above the other popular novels of its time. Its grip on so many readers springs in part from Clancy's mingling the dramatic structure of the detective story with the familiar tropes of the novel of international intrigue, then combining that with elements of the sea adventure, and finally tossing in one inventive new ingredient, a feature that has become a staple of the techno-thriller: the use of cutting-edge hardware and technology, which plays a role as central as the characters themselves (not unlike science fiction). So in *The Hunt for Red October,* the potency of the standard dramatic question that fuels the detective story is increased exponentially when these additional elements begin to slosh together.

An average reader may not observe any of this consciously, but even the most jaded among us can't help but be intrigued when we confront a never-seen-before species that somehow echoes other stories we've read and loved. We love the familiar and are excited by the new. A combination of both is irresistible.

While it may not seem as fresh and original to us now, in its day *The Hunt for Red October* was almost experimental in its novelty. A large part of its success as both fiction and film was due to this crafty mixing and matching of genres and its use of a movie-friendly principle called "high concept" that helps seize our attention from the very first pages.

THE SECOND ACT AND BEYOND

Once the reader has been snagged by a novel's high-concept premise, on one level we are drawn forward by the momentum of the unfolding story as one complication after another challenges the central character and the original dramatic question mutates into another question and another.

How will Scarlett ever manage to marry Ashley Wilkes now that he's engaged to Melanie? And how will she achieve her dream when she impulsively marries Frank? Then there's the big annoying complication of the Civil War. How will Scarlett ever seduce Ashley when he's off being gallant at the front lines? And when Rhett Butler makes a beeline for Scarlett's affections, will she be able to resist his obvious charms and remain available for Ashley? There are lots and lots of plot complications branching off the trunk of this main dramatic question, but everything in this sweeping novel stays firmly rooted in Scarlett's single-minded focus to win the one man she can't have. Ashley, Ashley, Ashley. What are the consequences of Scarlett's bullheaded and maddeningly foolish love for Captain Wilkes? It takes a thousand pages to answer that question.

In *The Firm*, Mitch McDeere's too-good-to-be-true first job also raises a dramatic question that takes a few hundred pages to resolve. Will this nice young couple grab the brass ring, or will the brass ring grab them? Once the reader begins to see the pickle Mitch and Abby are in, that question morphs into another even more lapel-grabbing question: How will Mitch and Abby ever extricate themselves from this perilous trap they've stumbled into?

The first question *The Godfather* asks seems harmless enough. How will Michael Corleone resist being drawn into the family business? Well, for starters, he'll keep his distance and marry a girl who is the exact opposite of a Mafia princess. But once his father is the target of an assassination attempt and the family is forced into a war that threatens their very existence, the question is no longer about how he will resist. Now the question is, How will this good boy, a war hero, not ready for prime-time Mafia work, meet the minimum job requirements? Then once he has taken command, the question changes again. How the hell is this all-American kid who seems to be in over his head going to live up to the Godfather's dark example?

When it becomes clear in the early pages of *The Dead Zone* that Johnny Smith has the gift of precognition, our first question is a natural one. How will this ordinary kid employ this extraordinary perception? Will he, like many in his place, use his new skills for fun or profit?

Sure, that could be a titillating story line, but we find out pretty quickly that's not where we're headed, because Johnny isn't greedy or self-indulgent. This psychic has a virtuous heart and wants to use his powers for some benefit to the world. So what saintly purpose will Johnny decide upon? That's the question that drives us through the heart of the book and right into the depraved mind of Frank Dodd, a murderous fiend whom Johnny brings to a just and bloody end.

Okay, good. But now what? Will Johnny simply keep assisting the police and solving crimes, bringing to justice one killer after another? How do you top a vicious serial murderer like Frank Dodd?

Greg Stillson is the answer. Turns out that Stillson has monstrous plans for the entire world. A killer to the thousandth power. We watch as Johnny's simple wish to use his talent for the greater good evolves into a dark obsession. Step by step, he reaches the horrific conclusion that he must kill Greg Stillson before this tyrant-in-the-making can rise to power and bring darkness to the entire world.

When good John Smith sets off on a lone-wolf mission to

assassinate Stillson, the reader is both jittery and fascinated. We can't help ourselves from asking a new and troubling question: Is John crazy or is he sane? Don't all lone gunmen have similar visions or voices commanding them to do the unthinkable?

It's these last dramatic questions that keep us riveted to the end.

MAGNETIC RESONANCE

What starts as a simple premise (Scarlett wants to marry Ashley) is made ever more engaging by the complications and difficulties that arise. The challenges that Scarlett must overcome, which force her to dig deep into her bag of tricks to keep her original dream alive, generate an emotional response in readers in direct proportion to the intensity of her determination.

All the heroes in these novels are men and women of deep conviction and fervent, stubborn resolve, capable of passions that rise well beyond the normal range of human experience. Even the seemingly laid-back and world-weary Robert Kincaid in *The Bridges of Madison County* is stirred to proclaim to his lover Francesca, "I have been falling from the rim of a great, high place, somewhere back in time. . . . And through all those years I have been falling toward you."

Even the waffling priest Father Damien Karras and the long-winded professor Robert Langdon find the strength within themselves to become men of action as the danger before them erupts. In the end, this clarity and intensity of purpose, and the decisive actions these men and women undertake, differentiates the main characters of bestsellers from those thoughtful, inward Hamlet types who often parse and debate and dither and vacillate before rising from the couch to take a swat at the problem.

We are told by the latest scientific research that readers respond empathetically to fictional characters. (This is news?) Cognitive scientists and literary scholars have been teaming up lately to try to unravel the chemistry and biology behind our attraction to folks like Scarlett and Mitch and Michael Corleone. One of their scientific methods consists of sliding novel readers into MRI machines to see what regions of their brains light up while they are reading texts of different levels of difficulty. (I'm not inventing this.) While preliminary results are a little sketchy, there seems to be a connection between activity levels in the brain and those novels that require the reader to decipher the secret thoughts and motives of their central characters.

Allow me to propose a simpler and less expensive testing method. Take a handful of fictional characters that have proven track records of stirring the emotions of millions of readers and ask what common threads run through them. One answer jumps out.

The most frequently recurring characteristic that Michael Corleone and Scout and Scarlett and our other protagonists share is a high level of emotional intensity that results in gutsy and surprising deeds. These actions may not always take the form of swashbuckling heroics, but rest assured, not one of these heroes or heroines sits idly on the sidelines pondering or strikes endless matches to watch them burn while stewing about the great issues of the universe. There's nary a navel that gets gazed upon. Our heroes and heroines act. They act decisively. They go out in creaky boats to hunt for enormous sharks. They devise plans to save their skins by outwitting both the FBI and the Mob. They are on the front lines, shoving and jostling and pushing forward against the barriers. They are all pushed to their emotional breaking point and beyond and forced to stay at the outer limits of what they can endure for page after page.

No magnetic resonance imaging required.

MATTERS OF THE HEART

The fierce loyalty readers feel for certain characters grows out of a shared connection with the character's emotional journey. A reader has to understand and sympathize with the driving force at work behind a hero's actions. Without that connection, a fictional character's emotional intensity can seem as senseless as a live wire spewing sparks.

From the first pages of *Gone with the Wind,* we suspect that Scarlett's father is right about Ashley. He's not the man for her. But Scarlett won't hear of it. Because her love for Ashley is based on a childish whim to win the heart of an unattainable man, we find ourselves pitying this naïve child, fearing she'll crash against the rocks of her foolishness. In other words, we start to care. Start to give this headstrong lass the benefit of the doubt. She'll figure it out, realize her mistake. We start to warm to her, start to anticipate the trouble she's inviting if she doesn't wise up.

At first her love for Ashley overshadows everything, even Tara.

"I don't want Tara or any old plantation. Plantations don't amount to anything when—"

Gerald cuts her off and roars that land is the only thing that truly matters.

It takes a while, but eventually Scarlett sees Gerald's point. Tara is worth fighting for. Tara is worth marrying a man you don't love or a man like Rhett Butler whom you actively hate.

Despite all its contradictions and its association with slavery, Tara has a value most readers can appreciate. It is home, the place where Scarlett was once happy. Its soil is fruitful, and there are poignant echoes of Scarlett's parents everywhere. What matters most to Scarlett is something that matters greatly to many of us. Whether she winds up in Rhett's arms or Ashley's or someone else's doesn't matter nearly so much as Tara. It is the worthiness of Scarlett's love for Tara that makes a reader's fierce loyalty to her possible.

In *The Dead Zone,* Johnny slips and falls and bumps his head while playing. He just wanted what we all want, a little joy, a little pleasure. He's not doing anything foolish or mean-spirited out on that pond. He's simply a kid the way all of us were, testing out this slippery world with a perfectly ordinary gusto.

His fall is everyone's fall. His suffering and confusion and the missing years that flow from that incident are horrors we can identify with.

Though Johnny's accident eventually leads him to an extreme state of mind, we tag along because we've come to care about this kid who was once perfectly normal, skating on a pond. And when Johnny begins to formulate a murder scheme, we may have our doubts, but we're still beside him. Pity and fear, Aristotle said, pity and fear are the great emotional engines for tragedy.

And sure enough, each of our novels is powered by those twin reactors.

In *Peyton Place,* Allison MacKenzie comes to visit Selena because Selena is her friend. She hadn't come to peep through the window. The curtains were open. The violence and sexual abuse she witnesses is the equivalent of her own fall on the ice, an accident that sends her off on her own long journey to an outlandish and scary place: Manhattan. We pity her naïveté and fear for her safety as she navigates that treacherous town.

All but the sociopaths among us have a natural tendency to empathize with those who suffer. Especially those who inadvertently bring suffering upon themselves, those who cause their own tragedies. We understand that, because most of us have made our own choices that turned out poorly, changed the course of our lives, and cost us something we cherished.

Anne Welles, the heroine of *Valley of the Dolls,* sets off on her journey to the big city looking for excitement, experience, and love. Who cannot admire her for turning away from a safe but suffocating future with a fiancé she has no feelings for? She's not some gold-digging hussy looking to snag a rich sugar daddy. She wants what we all want, nothing more, nothing less. Her tragic fall is all the more painful to watch because she seemed to be doing nearly everything right.

Scout is determined to hold on to the freedom and independence of childhood, and we can't help but root for her although we know her wish is doomed. Childhood's end is inevitable. We pity and fear her certain loss of innocence. But it's even worse than we could have imagined. She's yanked viciously from her youth and forced to confront the worst that human nature has to offer: racial hatred, incest, murder. Though she stands tough against it all, we know how much it's hurting her. And we can't help but feel her pain.

Michael Corleone also wants a future most can appreciate. He intended to marry a good girl, settle down, and enjoy the fruits of his legitimate labor. In so doing, he meant to keep his distance from the dark whirlpool of his family business.

It's most everybody's story. We may not come from a crime family, but most of us understand the wish to make a clean break from our nest.

So when he crosses the fateful line and commits his first act of violence, we cringe. Michael isn't going to be able to break free after all. Gradually we come to understand that Michael, like his father, has taken this step to protect his family's survival, a goal most of us would consider worthy, and as this becomes increasingly clear, our emotional bond with him solidifies again. We look on in horror and fascination as he grabs the reins his father has dropped. Fear and pity.

Like every hero and heroine in these twelve bestsellers, Michael seems for a while to be overmatched. The task before him appears so daunting as to be nearly impossible. We can't imagine what strengths of character he will summon to survive the savagery and duplicity of an all-out Mafia war. Like the sheriff on the shark boat, like Jack Ryan drafted to solve an international crisis, like young Mitch McDeere who takes a job beyond his wildest nightmares, like the doubting Father Karras who's sent into hand-to-hand combat with Satan, Michael seems out of his league.

Francesca Johnson also finds herself in over her head when she steps across the fateful line into adultery. Moral beliefs may keep some readers from full approval, but who cannot sympathize with a woman with a dispirited heart who seizes a chance at love? And when she chooses to forfeit the love of her life for the dull normalcy of her family, our old friends pity and fear are present at the moment of her decision.

The emotional dynamics of all these twelve bestsellers are similar. A character's intense commitment to his or her cause, while not always pure and selfless, is ultimately a goal most of us find worthy and important.

If what matters to Mitch McDeere doesn't matter in some important way to the rest of us, his story is not worth our time. If Robert Langdon's mission were simply an intellectual exercise in decoding ancient documents, most readers would not be emotionally aroused. But partly because the fate of a passionate young woman, Sophie Neveu, hangs in the balance, a reader finds a solid reason to engage with this tale about unraveling old secrets.

Bestsellers have a primal aim—to stir the reader's heart and to make us forge a powerful emotional bond with a fictional character that is, more often than not, composed of one part pity, one part fear.

MECHANICS OF SPEED

"The past is never dead. It's not even past." Faulkner may have been right, but one of the elements of speed my students and I identified in bestsellers is that references to the past are mostly pared down to essential information. By streamlining the narratives and minimizing the use of what Hollywood refers to as "backstory," these twelve novels keep the reader's eye fixed to the page much the way good Hollywood films keep us transfixed by the images on the screen. We don't want to miss what happens next, because something is always happening. No dead space, no long asides, hardly a moment to catch your breath.

This is not an easily measured factor, but over many years of classroom study, I was regularly struck by how little background information was provided about the previous lives of characters like Mitch McDeere or Jack Ryan or even Scarlett O'Hara. They seem to arrive fully formed on the stage before us, and we learn about them mainly through the things they do and say in the here and now.

A SERIOUS BUMP

Another device that grabs our lapels and accelerates the pace is the use of suspense, in particular the threat of danger. Without fail, some form of serious peril, be it physical or psychological, appears within the early pages of each novel and our pulse is given a serious bump; then, as the pages go by, this giddy arrhythmia gradually accelerates.

Although half of the biggest bestselling novels of all time are novels of suspense, the other half are not. However, when you examine all twelve books side by side, whether they are coming-of-age novels, love stories, or thrillers, the techniques of suspense they employ are remarkably similar.

The Dead Zone opens with Johnny Smith skating on an icy pond. He falls and bumps his head. His mind clears quickly, and he's back out on the ice in no time. But the foreboding is palpable. That minor accident has changed Johnny. We're not sure exactly how, but he's not the same cheerful kid he was before the fall. In the chapter immediately following, we meet Greg Stillson, who's selling Bibles door-to-door when he's confronted by a growling farm dog. Stillson brutally murders the dog without a second thought, and at that moment, less than ten pages into the novel, we realize these two men will eventually cross paths, and from that instant forward the reader's anxiety level is jacked up and continues to be jacked up, notch by notch by notch.

Atticus Finch takes on the rape case of Tom Robinson, a black man accused by a white woman of raping her, thus initiating a series of growing threats against the Finch family. When Atticus accepts the case we are one-quarter of the way into the story, at a structural point that a modern screenwriter would consider plot point one, that watershed moment when the story line takes an unexpected yet inevitable turn.

Scout's anxiety level follows a rising arc along with these increasing tensions, from racial taunts at school, to the facing down of a lynch mob, to the high drama of the courtroom scenes, then to the aftermath of the guilty verdict when Bob Ewell, who feels he's been humiliated by Atticus on the witness stand, first spits on Scout's father and then later threatens to kill him. Suspense builds as Ewell stalks the perimeter of the Finches' lives until these threats reach a climax when Ewell attacks Scout and Jem as they're walking home in the dark after a school play.

It would be difficult for all the other elevated issues of social justice and racial intolerance that give the novel its moral heft to capture our attention without the load-bearing underpinning of that suspense story.

Early on in chapter 3 of *The Firm,* we learn there are microphones planted within the walls of Mitch and Abby's home; the couple's conversations are being recorded, their views of the firm analyzed. And we also discover there were multiple mysterious deaths among Mitch's predecessors at the firm. These warning signals are in place early, and they spice the early chapters with an unmistakable creepiness, made more suspenseful because the reader is privy to facts that Mitch and Abby are not. This is what literary types call "dramatic irony," a private exchange between author and reader, a device that when it's working well can create increased sympathy in the reader's heart for the unsuspecting hero.

In *Jaws,* a great white shark sucks down a skinny-dipper before you've had time to draw your first breath. And without further ado, any reader knows the shark has fixed its sights on the juicy citizens of Amity. That primordial threat hovers over every scene thereafter, until the shark returns to eat again at this well-stocked human buffet.

The dangers of the small and outwardly charming town of Peyton Place are also established early. We discover right away that this town is "highly sexed" and has a volatile tension among the folks living on opposite sides of the tracks. We're less than a fifth of the way into the novel when Selena Cross, an adolescent girl, is sexually attacked by her shiftless, drunken stepfather, an act that her school friend Allison MacKenzie happens to witness. The seeds of danger have been planted, and the consequences of this violent act roll through the story, galvanizing the two main female characters and causing the central dramatic events of the novel to unfold, including a court trial much like the one in *To Kill a Mockingbird,* which does much to shape the destinies of the main characters.

We're barely a tenth of the way into *The Godfather* when that celebrated horse's head winds up on the pillow next to its owner. A classic cringeworthy moment. If somehow a reader has not already sensed the book's direction, this outlandish threat of violence makes it clear both to Jack Woltz, the owner of the horse, and to any reader that the Godfather is a man capable of extreme acts of brutality. Henceforth, we are on full alert.

Within the first few pages of *The Bridges of Madison County,* readers are forewarned that the story we are about to read might be considered "tawdry," but despite the danger that it could sully the reputations of a husband and wife, it is too "remarkable" and "worth telling" to ignore. Once Robert Kincaid has arrived at Francesca's front porch and finds this beautiful lady is temporarily absent her husband, the sexual tension kicks in, as does the inevitable anticipation that a nosy neighbor—or even worse, Francesca's husband—will walk in unexpectedly and catch the couple in flagrante delicto. Is this threat as physically dangerous or as primal as the ones posed by *The Exorcist* or *The Dead Zone*? Well, farmers have been known to be mighty protective of their spousal units. Shotguns, pitchforks, and all that.

The threat is established early in this slender romance, just as it is from the start of the tragic story of Anne, Jennifer, and Neely, the dauntless and doomed heroines of *Valley of the Dolls*. Each of these young ladies will face hazards that are as life-threatening as anything offered up in the other novels. Their heads will spin because they're drugged on love and out-of-control ambition and caught in a spiral of self-destructive chemical addiction. They will each be bitten in half by the razor-sharp teeth of exploitive men.

The character at the center of the novel, Anne Welles, has escaped the dangers of a loveless engagement to a fiancé she can't stand and fled a suffocating middle-class existence back in Lawrenceville for an adventure in the city; but before she makes her getaway, she is warned of an even greater danger awaiting her in the wider world. "There is no such thing as love," Anne's mother counsels before Anne sets off, a dire "beware the Ides of March" prophecy that Anne will verify in the cruelest of ways. Within hours of her arrival in Manhattan, Anne is cautioned a second time by her new employer about a certain aptly named scoundrel, Lyon Burke: "Lyon keeps blinding you with that smile and it fools you at first. You think he's friendly. But you can never get really close to him. No one could."

The red flags are rippling wildly. There's a shark out there, he's big and bad and circling closer, beware, beware his empty smile. But does any of this keep Anne Welles from paddling out into ever-deeper water? Oh, no.

Within a few pages of the opening of *The Exorcist,* Chris MacNeil hears something spooky rapping and tapping inside the walls of her sleeping daughter's bedroom. The sounds "were odd. Muffled. Profound. Rhythmically clustered. Alien code tapped out by a dead man."

Forget about calling a plumber, girl, get yourself a priest and quick.

The furniture mysteriously takes new positions, the clothes in Regan's closet are rearranged, the youngster herself is talking to an imaginary being. Nothing too extreme, but any vigilant reader knows something nasty is slithering our way.

The threat of danger that opens *The Exorcist* or *Valley of the Dolls* is not even close to the bloodcurdling predicament Jacques Saunière, curator of the Louvre, finds himself in in the opening pages of *The Da Vinci Code.* I'll skip a recounting of the early violence and threats of violence. Suffice it to say that on the structural level, the novel is a breathless series of high-speed chases and cliff-hanging feats of derring-do and ricocheting bullets, interlarded with hundreds of disquisitions on matters arcane and distressing, much like a meaty lecture tucked inside the warm bun of suspense.

THE BIG CLOCK

The power of the ticking clock to seize our attention and stress our hearts dates back to the Industrial Revolution, when men and women of the soil, who'd always earned their bread the old-fashioned seasonal way, migrated to the city, where their usefulness was thereafter measured by the merciless heartbeat of a machine. Modern man has come to react to the pressures of time in ways so reliable that writers of popular novels had to take notice. And did they ever.

The barbecue party at Twelve Oaks has hardly begun before the thunderclouds of war that were gathering all afternoon begin to rumble. We are roughly one-tenth of the way into Scarlett's story when the boys saddle up, and with a whoop and a holler they ride away to glory.

Events speed up accordingly once the Big Ben of the Civil War begins to gong the hours. Scarlett is married and becomes a widow in a single sentence at the beginning of chapter 7. Thereafter, the steady march of the Yankee army gives the novel its subliminal pulse. Like clockwork, the invaders inch toward Atlanta, and every new crisis in Scarlett's romantic journey seems timed to the next footfall of their approach.

The war brings deprivations and hardships to the good southern ladies; it forces them to spend their hours amusing other ladies like themselves (and therefore engage in their own version of an uncivil war); from time to time, the advancing war fills the dancing floors with dashing uniformed men on leave, then fills the hospitals with sweet young boys with missing limbs; then, as that giant clock ticks on, the war finally shows up in all its gruesome glory on the outskirts of the city.

Naturally, Scarlett waits till the last possible second before fleeing amid explosions and chaos, and the advancing front lines of the war race her back to Tara. Then comes the terrible aftermath of the war, with its scalawags and new racial order ticking off the final hours of the Old South.

Without this ever-moving second hand constantly raising

the anxiety level, all the romantic skirmishes in the novel might easily become tedious and harebrained. It's unlikely that even the escapades of a man-hunting genius like Scarlett, who was "constitutionally unable to endure any man being in love with any woman not herself," could keep us enthralled without the hypnotic beat of that dreadful drummer boy.

Each of the other books finds an ingenious way to up the ante by forcing its characters to beat the clock. Francesca and Robert, the adulterous lovers of *The Bridges of Madison County,* must time their affair to the fixed return of Francesca's husband. John Smith is watching the hours tick by until election day, which will likely mark the end of his chance to assassinate Greg Stillson. The clock is running out on Mitch and Abby, minutes flying by as fast as the Xerox machine spitting out incriminating documents that may or may not save their lives. The Soviet submarine heading to the shores of America is making damn good time as well, and before another day or two, Jack Ryan's last chance to intercept the ship at sea is gone. Regan MacNeil can't hold out much longer, as Satan has his way with her. It's a toss-up who will die first, the sweet, innocent girl or the exhausted priest who's trying to save her.

FEATURE #2

Hot Buttons

When a thing ceases to be a subject of controversy, it ceases to be a subject of interest.

—WILLIAM HAZLITT

One surefire way to rile up folks is to raise the controversy du jour. Whether it was a conscious strategy or not, the authors on our list raised one or more highly contentious topics of their day.

If ripping a story from the headlines were all there was to it, anyone could sit down with *The Washington Post* and construct a novel that sold a million copies. The formula would be simple. Select an issue that makes the blood boil in many normally levelheaded Americans. Old reliables like abortion, gay marriage, church and state, global warming, school prayer, gun control, race relations, immigration policy, or capital punishment are always handy. Then gather up the loaded language of that subject matter. Create a simple story line that idealizes one position and demonizes the other and you're ready to roll.

But there's a crucial second half to this hot-button equation that deepens and broadens the subject matter, an approach that all our bestsellers employ to one degree or another. For a hot-button issue to have real wallop, it also must express some larger, deep-seated, and unresolved conflict in the national consciousness.

Take the Civil War. Now there's a hot-button winner. Thousands of books about the Civil War, fiction and nonfiction, have mined the same vein but have failed to exhaust the supply of combustible material. Why is that?

Rarely does a month go by in our national discourse that we aren't treated again to a tooth-and-nail wrangle over the Confederate flag or the role that slavery played in the war between the blue and the gray or some other iteration of that long-ago conflict. The subject still raises hackles because all the sympathies and antipathies that divided us as a nation back then divide us still, though usually in more subtle and less violent forms.

HOT BUTTON #1
Hate Her and Love Her

It wasn't just the glorification of the Old South and its racial politics that made *Gone with the Wind* controversial. Scarlett's ruthless, money-grubbing resourcefulness during and after the war also gave the novel a hot-button hook.

Published in 1936, the novel reenacts a story that was painfully familiar and fresh in the minds of readers of that era who had just witnessed their own version of financial collapse. Scarlett's scrambling, hustling survival skills were vividly recognizable to a generation who'd so recently had to resort to every manner of improvisation simply to subsist.

Her calculating, survive-at-any-cost morality and slippery situational ethics were perfectly suited for the time this novel appeared. To many, Scarlett's cutthroat lust for cash and power and the freedom they brought was an embodiment of all that was wrong with capitalism, while to others she was a symbol of all that's right. To many it was both at once.

And for a woman to dominate her male counterparts in both the boardroom and the bedroom also made many bristle.

As the film critic Molly Haskell says about Scarlett, "You hate her and you love her, a heroine of ambiguous morality who is revolutionary . . . in that she refuses to be chastened, brought to heel. . . ."

These issues, of course, are still with us and still have the power to boil our blood.

HOT BUTTON #2
Gray Flannel Hot Pants

Peyton Place caused a lot more blood to boil. In particular, midcentury New Englanders were outraged and offended that their folksy cover had been blown and their steamy bedrooms laid bare. In the conservative age of Eisenhower and *The Man in the Gray Flannel Suit,* this gaudy novel of drunks and incest and sexually permissive single moms and Peeping Toms and masturbation and teenage petting and illegal abortions set hearts atremble.

"Everybody knew that the South was degenerate," Merle

Miller asserted in the *Ladies' Home Journal,* but they were unprepared for *Peyton Place,* which according to Merle presented the view "that Puritan New England has all the southern vices and a few others that not even William Faulkner had come across."

These days it's harder to profitably press the hot button of sex because that button has just about been worn out from overuse. But in 1956, Grace Metalious, who pressed it hard and often, managed to create an incendiary blend of several of America's favorite hot-button issues, sex and race and class and the emancipation of women.

HOT BUTTON #3

Whistling at a White Woman

Five years before *To Kill a Mockingbird* was published, in a state adjacent to the one where Scout grew up, a fourteen-year-old Chicagoan named Emmett Till was visiting his extended family when he made the fatal mistake of whistling at a white woman. He was beaten and murdered and his body thrown in a river. The trial that followed was a farce. An all-white jury acquitted the two white men charged with Till's murder. The case caused widespread and heated debate and helped fuel the fledgling civil rights movement.

At about the same time, in Montgomery, Alabama, where the fictional Atticus Finch went to study law, a very real black woman named Rosa Parks refused to give up her bus seat and move to the "colored section" at the rear. Martin Luther King was rising to prominence about the same time and played a significant role in leading the ensuing boycott of the Montgomery bus system.

To anyone living and breathing and reading novels in 1960, there was no doubt which headlines Harper Lee was ripping. Headlines much like those we still find in our newspapers a half century later.

HOT BUTTON #4
Sexploitation

The same could be said six years later, when *Valley of the Dolls,* Jacqueline Susann's roman à clef sexploitation novel, was published. Following in the tradition of Harold Robbins, whose *Carpetbaggers* was once described by a reviewer as "a collection of monotonous episodes about normal and abnormal sex," Susann's novel was groundbreaking, at least in gender terms. *Peyton Place* had paved the way for an American woman to write bluntly about sex, but no woman had yet graphically depicted the erotic lives of the rich and famous in fictional form.

Was Helen Lawson, the over-the-hill diva, actually based on Ethel Merman? Did Ethel Merman, the Hollywood star, have a hot and sweaty lesbian affair with Jackie Susann back in the day when Jackie was a wannabe actress? Was Neely O'Hara's fictional persona really Judy Garland, or maybe Betty Hutton, who did in fact have a contentious understudy relationship with Merman (as Neely did with Lawson)? Following this?

Well, they were certainly following it in 1966, when the novel was published. This was all salacious gossip column material. Toss in issues that were trendy at the time like alcoholism and pill popping, then hint at other big names like Marilyn Monroe and JFK and Frank Sinatra and Dean Martin, and you have a prescription for tabloid sensationalism.

If *Valley of the Dolls* seems more dated than the other novels on our list, it might be due to an overdependence on the topical issues of its day. After a few years passed, and those newspapers yellowed, and Ethel Merman was replaced and replaced again by new generations of divas, the elements that sustain a novel's long-term survival simply were not present in the same abundance as we find them in the other bestsellers. That's because Susann tilted the hot-button equation a bit too far toward the faddish, gossipy side and didn't fully take into consideration the long-term simmering cultural implications of her own material.

HOT BUTTON #5
New Vein

Frank Sinatra had a return engagement three years later in *The Godfather,* this time portrayed as the character Johnny Fontane. The Kennedy family also takes a turn. To many readers, it was obvious the Kennedy estate in Hyannis Port was Puzo's model for the Corleone compound, which helped further the suggestion that these two powerful families with shady backgrounds were echoes of each other. But the novel's notoriety didn't grow out of gossipmongering. It was a hit because it struck a new vein in a very old mine.

The exploration of the shadowy, illicit side of American moral life has been with us since Hawthorne outed Puritan hanky-panky. The new vein discovered in that old mine was, of course, the first appearance of the *famiglia mafiosa.*

These days when we are all so fully versed on folks like the Sopranos and their ilk, it's hard to imagine a time pre-*Godfather,* even though it existed for most of recorded history. What Puzo did was give us the photo negative of the American success story. The dark doppelgänger to the bootstraps myth.

By conjuring up long-standing legends about the Kennedy clan and other prominent American families, Puzo pressed another hot button that was then and still is a subject that spikes the blood pressure of many Americans: the story of an immigrant father so determined to see his family prosper in their adopted land that he resorts to any tactics necessary, including extortion, robbery, bootlegging, political bribery, and violence.

HOT BUTTON #6
Maharishi

The Exorcist tackles an altogether different cultural flashpoint of the late sixties, the clash between traditional religious faith and the rising tide of secular humanism and swamis and maharishis and all manner of religious kooks. Representing the new agers, we have Sharon Spencer, the pretty blonde in her twenties who tutors Regan and acts as Chris MacNeil's social secretary and who is experimenting with self-hypnosis, transcendental meditation, and Buddhist chanting, all the while filling the upstairs of the MacNeil house with the hippie-dippy reek of incense and the dronings of some Far Eastern mantra.

Chris is a proud atheist and single working mom and Hollywood star, a job that brings her into contact with the likes of Burke Dennings, a film director who was once studying to be a priest himself but has swung about as far the other way as one can swing. He's a drunk and disbeliever who calls the

priesthood a bunch of "fucking plunderers." Throw in a Jesuit priest who no longer believes in God's existence and you
have to ask yourself, Is it any wonder that Satan picked this
brownstone to make a house call? These are exactly the kinds
of nonbelievers Beelzebub prefers, folks whose religious laziness needs a ruthless test.

At a time when death-of-God theology was featured on
the cover of *Time* magazine, this novel, which challenged the
beliefs of nonbelievers, hit a cultural nerve that was already
raw.

HOT BUTTON #7
Evildoers

In the case of *Jaws,* there's a civic tension at the crux of the
story that is as old as our nation itself. Before he can close the
beaches and protect the citizens of his fair town, Sheriff Brody
must get the approval of an unsympathetic mayor and town
council. The politicians who run the island don't want to yell
"Shark!" at the town's most profitable time of the year. By
pitting government-supported greed against populist forces
and the general welfare of the common man, *Jaws* tapped
into both the long-term American mistrust of political authority and its contemporary manifestation, which at that
point in our history had reached hot-button proportions after
years of cultural clashes over the Vietnam War and the recent
resignation of Richard Nixon.

Given all that, it was no wonder that elected officials were
seen by many as the greatest evildoers, right up there with
sharks, men who had only the interests of the wealthy and
powerful in mind when deciding policy. At the same time,

almost as many readers were sympathetic to the opposite position, a belief that the conventional structures of power should hold firm against dangerous counterculture lawlessness.

The central conflict of the first third of *Jaws* fits that pattern perfectly by reenacting a moral sellout of its citizens by its political leaders, a conflict that split the nation back then and splits it still.

At the same time, from its very first scene the novel raised another topic that was about as hot-button as it got back in the dawning of the age of Aquarius, when one female member of a group of pot-smoking, orgy-loving Woodstock types has some liberated sex right out on a public beach, then goes swimming nude in the ocean, where that young lady gets exactly what she deserves. Eaten.

HOT BUTTON #8
News That Stays News

Ezra Pound, that modernist poet and literary kingmaker and political nut job, had a good one-liner for poetry that seems appropriate here. He called it "news that stays news."

By that he meant something similar to what I'm saying about hot-button issues that stay hot. Good writing passes the spoilage test. It doesn't smell after a year or two of being left out on the counter.

That's the sort of writing that characterizes *The Dead Zone,* in which Stephen King snagged the attention of many contemporary readers by providing a very hip up-to-the-minute social history of the four-year span when Johnny Smith was missing in action, hospitalized in a supernatural

coma. Poor Johnny missed a lot of stuff, but it was mostly the
kind of news that grows a little rank after a week or two.

> Nixon was reinaugurated. The American boys started
> coming home from Vietnam. . . . The second Arab-
> Israeli war came and went. The oil boycott came and
> went. Bruisingly high gasoline prices came and did
> not go.

A lot of this, King seems to suggest, is well worth sleeping
through. The ebb and flow, the rise and fall, the coming and
going of one political outrage after another. This news-crawl
vision of current events is the background against which the
monstrous rise of the Hitlerian Greg Stillson is set. Stillson is
the news that stays news, a hot button that will always be
hot. He's an election year archetype, the second coming of the
Antichrist, the rough beast whose hour has come round at
last.

HOT BUTTON #9
Hush-Hush

Becoming President Ronald Reagan's favorite book brought
The Hunt for Red October out of the depths of obscurity. But
for that missile of good fortune to lock on to its target and
blow sales records to smithereens, this novel had to deliver a
payload that folks beyond the D.C. Beltway cared about.

Clancy accomplished that by using such an abundance of
technical detail and by being so fluent in military protocol
and seafaring lingo that he created the illusion he might be
privy to national Defense Department secrets. He seemed to

know stuff that was so hush-hush, so explosive, so supersensitive, it was easy to believe the actual reason the POTUS summoned Clancy to the White House was to have him debriefed by the CIA.

Published in that Orwellian year of 1984, the novel rode the last crests of cold war paranoia. Perestroika and glasnost were just up ahead, but our periscopes couldn't yet make them out. So the country was armed and dangerous and nervous as hell, and a book like this submarine novel that reflected well on our native resourcefulness, our blue-collar ingenuity, our military hardware, and our grace under a hundred fathoms was the right story at the right time with the right ingredients that appealed to the right wing of the American reading public.

HOT BUTTON #10
Greed Is Good

Sellouts like Mitch McDeere were all the rage in the decade of greed known as the eighties, when he and his fellow yuppies made down payments on their luxury cars and minimansions from their first week's paychecks and started looking for a better class of cocaine dealer. With his fresh law degree and his glamorous young wife, he was a perfect model for the latest incarnation of the me generation.

Grisham takes both sides of the "greed is bad vs. greed is good" debate that seethed back then just as it has off and on for most of the nation's history. The novel starkly portrays the Reaganomics of the era. It was a time when supply-side trickle-down voodoo economic arguments could ignite furious passions. MBAs and law degrees were being minted as fast as new tax laws cut marginal rates. Corporate deregulation and union busting were in the air. Go to it, boys. Make a fortune. Wallow in a little luxury, don't be shy.

One of the key theoretical arguments supporting Reaganomics was something suitably named the Laffer curve, which supported the idea that cutting taxes led to a rise in total revenues. Enter Mitch McDeere, a highly educated lawyer whose specialty is tax cheating. He heads south to work for a WASPy firm whose clients turn out to be not some legitimate struggling small-business CEOs overburdened by taxes and regulations, but mobsters who want to launder their money and not let any of it trickle down to law-abiding citizens. The huge tectonic plates of dissension grinding beneath Mitch's story give the novel a shuddering larger significance. When Mitch and Abby sail away on their schooner as winners in this sweepstakes of greed, both sides of this American hot-button issue have further fuel for their arguments.

HOT BUTTON #11
Nuclear Family

In 1992, when Robert Kincaid came striding into bookstores across the land, "family values" was the hot-button issue on the lips of many, including Vice President Dan Quayle, who that same year notoriously derided the prime-time TV show *Murphy Brown* for its "poverty of values." Mr. Quayle's complaint, which was supported by a great many voters, was that the show positively portrayed a single professional woman who had decided to bear a child alone, and thus the show was helping to undermine the sanctity of the nuclear family.

The nuclear family and its sacredness was smack dab in

the foreground of *The Bridges of Madison County,* which opens with a don't-think-about-it-too-hard explanation of why the two Johnson siblings allowed their mother's private journal to be published for all to see.

Yet in a world where personal commitment in all of its forms seems to be shattering and love has become a matter of convenience, they both felt this remarkable tale was worth telling.

Bridges heated up the passions of a few million readers and divided them along party lines, stimulating fond memories and regrets over loves lost and paths not taken in one group while irritating the self-righteous sensibilities of others who'd held firm against such adulterous temptations.

HOT BUTTON #12
Holy Mother

There's a type of novel that courts controversy and scandal, like *The Da Vinci Code,* that might be categorized as speculative history. Such books try to imagine what might have gone on backstage at the scenes of celebrated events, then they tantalize us with half-truths and gradually weaken our resistance with allegations that are impossible to disprove and spread themselves virally among us with their provocative and outlandish claims.

When the target of such feverish accusations is a once omnipotent but now weakened entity, like the modern-day Catholic Church, whose followers make up a quarter of the population, a strong reaction is guaranteed.

The hullabaloo and polarizing debate that erupted after Dan Brown's novel was published set staunch defenders of the church in passionate opposition to legions of cynics and nonbelievers who were happy to finally see their own grievances, doubts, and prejudices portrayed so entertainingly. A killer monk. A two-thousand-year-old conspiracy. Sexual rituals. Yes, yes, I knew it must be happening!

In the face of this awesome display of provocative storytelling, we can do nothing but bow in awe and kiss the ring of the holy mother of all hot buttons.

WHAT WE'VE LEARNED AND WHAT'S COMING NEXT

So popular novels are fast and they appeal unapologetically to the baser emotions. Now we also know a few key devices and tricks of the trade that authors have used to hook us and keep us hooked. These stories grip us by using an intriguing high-concept premise, and their speed is enhanced by accessible prose, by pressures of time, by the use of unrelenting suspense, and by favoring action over interior monologues. Matters of the heart dominate. Our heroes and heroines are passionate in their devotion to some cause and act boldly to achieve their ends. Their passion grows hotter as the original premise grows more complex and their challenges become more difficult to overcome. And all of these stories explore some hot-button social issue of their day that is rooted in a long-term national dispute.

Next we will turn to considerations of substance. As we're flying through the pages of bestsellers, gulping down this comfort food, some might want to know: Is it possible that something that tastes this good and goes down so easily can actually be nourishing?

The chapters that follow take on this question, but I can provide the one-word answer now. Yes.

FEATURE #3

The Big Picture

The United States . . . has already reached the foremost rank among nations, and is destined soon to outdistance all others in the race. In population, in wealth, in annual savings, and in public credit; in freedom from debt, in agriculture, and in manufactures, America already leads the civilized world.

—ANDREW CARNEGIE,
TRIUMPHANT DEMOCRACY, 1886

Colossal characters doing magnificent things on a sweeping stage.

From its earliest days, the novel portrayed individuals struggling against the large and indifferent machinery of class and racial prejudice and social injustice. Over the last two centuries of the novel's existence, most of the successful literary characters have been more than simple individuals; they have been men and women who were embodiments of their age.

Most of the great American masterpieces like *Adventures*

of Huckleberry Finn, Moby-Dick, The Age of Innocence, My Ántonia, The Great Gatsby, The Grapes of Wrath, The Invisible Man, From Here to Eternity, and *Native Son* tend to have a sociological orientation—they are more likely to be stories about the ways in which men and women work out their destinies within large groups and communities rather than alone.

Again and again, American bestsellers depict the broad affairs and actions of men, their customs, their beliefs, placing their heroes and heroines on expansive historical or social stages, rather than focusing on the finer calibrations of their thoughts and the subtle renderings of their emotions and consciousness.

As a purely practical matter, just as there is a seesaw effect between action and characterization in most novels (as one goes up, the other inevitably goes down), there is a similar relationship between the creation of inner lives versus the creation of outer lives. As an author devotes more narrative energy to placing a character in historical context with attention to such matters as customs, behaviors, dress, and the artifacts of the age, there is simply less time left to devote to the specific density of the interior self.

Wide-angled scope has been a feature of many of the most popular and some of the most grudgingly respected novels of all time. Sinclair Lewis, Pearl S. Buck, James Jones, John Steinbeck, James Michener, and any number of American novelists adopted a panoramic view and set their characters against backdrops of enormous scale and consequence.

VITAL, EARTHY, AND COARSE

A small story told against a sweeping backdrop—that's the pattern repeating again and again in the most successful bestsellers.

Early on in *Gone with the Wind* Scarlett O'Hara gazes at her father, Gerald, and tries to explain why she finds him so comforting: "There was something vital and earthy and coarse about him that appealed to her. Being the least analytic of people, she did not realize that this was because she possessed in some degrees these same qualities. . . ."

Scarlett's lack of introspection is a common feature among the protagonists of these novels. What's true for Scarlett is also true for Allison MacKenzie and Jack Ryan and Mitch McDeere and Professor Robert Langdon. These characters are not self-absorbed or contemplative. Instead, they are shown primarily from external observations. We see their social interactions, their behavior, their dress, what they say and what they do in public and in private, but rarely do we go wading into the stream of their consciousness.

Readers are carried away by big stories, stories of import set on a large stage, ones that also feature a wide assortment of social classes. For scope applies not just to a wide-angle treatment of subject matter, but to demographics as well.

From the very beginning, novels have been the most democratic literary form, written in a raw, simple prose that gives free and easy access to all comers. It required little education beyond simple literacy to read the first English novels, and it requires little more today to consume a bestselling work of fiction. In fact, the democratic spirit that defined the first English novels is still the defining characteristic of the American bestseller.

The novel was born in the eighteenth century as the industrial age was making it easier for men and women at every class level to lift themselves up in rank. From the outset, those early English novelists considered it their primary duty to inform their readers about how this transformation might be achieved, using the most accessible language and style available to them and creating characters who originated from the vital, earthy, and coarser classes.

Today, the most commercially successful American novels continue to appeal to the same demographic and to focus on the same issues those first novels did two hundred years ago: social mobility; racial, gender, and class fairness; the struggles and triumphs of the poor set alongside similar conflicts of the powerful. In other words, they are stories about characters pitted against large forces, not characters in conflict with themselves.

Scarlett spends most of the novel struggling to return to the safe, predictable haven of the prewar Tara, where once she could bat her eyelashes and men would fall at her feet. Though her nostalgic wish to return to a prewar world is as hopeless as her fantasy of marrying Ashley Wilkes, that harsh fact never seems to dim her ambition.

The fact that Scarlett doesn't grasp the magnitude of the historical moment is part of her silly charm. She's simply annoyed at the inconvenience of the war, a little grumpy at all the nonsense she's required to do to survive, and she winds up whining more than whooping in protest. In that sense, she's almost a comic character, unaware of the gravity of her situation and therefore innocently undaunted by the overwhelming obstacles facing her. It simply never occurs to Scarlett that she's acting heroically.

For most of the novel, Scarlett's tribulations center around mundane matters of survival in the social realm, and most readers would surely understand how treacherous this realm can be. Scarlett has to master the complex minuet of manners and proper behavior of polite society at the very moment those things are in a state of radical transformation.

As she is coping with wartime realities and the new condition of being a widow and living in Atlanta's hothouse of decorum, Scarlett's personal story unfolds against the backdrop of the most tumultuous period in our history. Scarlett thrives, turning herself into a smashing business success, chiefly by marrying anyone who can help her achieve her ends. In this sense, the novel is as much a story about female empowerment and the redefining opportunities of the industrial age as it is a flirty romance. Big themes, sweeping issues, a very large stage for one of American fiction's biggest stars.

Later, in scenes with panoramic sweep, Scarlett O'Hara takes charge of her family and leads them home to Tara amid smoldering scenes of battle and death and destruction. She must tear up her petticoat to use as a halter for a cow. Later she must pick cotton to survive. She kills a Yankee soldier who invades her house. She loses a child and two husbands (a third, if you count Rhett), and she rises to every occasion, fueled by romantic longings as vast as the larger-than-life landscape she passes through.

Scarlett's focus is outward. She keeps her sights on the exterior realities of social politics, the finer points of corsets and ball gowns—the nitty-gritty sociology of her era. Without the giant wheels of history clattering behind her, her story might have collapsed into a froth of silliness. But with the enormity of change occurring before our eyes, the violent death of the Old South and the reinvention of American life, the cataclysmic changes in racial arrangements and class and gender values, Scarlett's struggles take on greater scale and more heft as well.

As is the case with most bestsellers, two stories are at work, one small, one large. And two Scarletts are required to merge these stories into one. The foreground narrative is about the emotional cravings of a petty, narcissistic ingenue—Scarlett's ceaseless pining for Ashley and her schemes to win his love—while the other story is a broad-canvased epic that features a tough-as-nails young woman who confronts Yankee soldiers, triumphs in a ruthless business world, and successfully adapts to the most wrenching social changes our country has ever known.

RACIAL POLITICS

An entirely different type of scope is found in *To Kill a Mockingbird*. On first blush, this portrait of secluded small-town life rendered through the eyes of a preadolescent girl would seem an improbable candidate for a novel of scale.

Many of us have a tendency to associate the large political and social convulsions of any particular era with urban centers, believing those upheavals to be muted to inconsequence by the time they filter out into the hinterlands of rural America. Al Zuckerman, in his guide to writing a "blockbuster," puts it bluntly: "Less than 1 percent of the population can afford to buy hardcover fiction with regularity, and that affluent group tends to be more interested in rich people than in poor ones, in city dwellers rather than in rural folk, in movers and shakers rather than in the downtrodden."

Well, that's not exactly accurate. *To Kill a Mockingbird* is one of the most commercially successful novels of all time, and its setting is as far removed from urban America as one can get. But because the novel sends its taproot deep into the loamy soil of vital American concerns, its appeal stretches far beyond its rural setting.

In the isolated backwoods of Maycomb, Alabama, the large moral and political issues of the Depression era sifted into the courtroom and the front parlor, the public schools and the church sanctuary. Like Scarlett, Scout Finch roams the social spectrum. She journeys to places no ordinary character could take us, from First Purchase African M.E. Church, to the living room of the pious upper-crust church ladies who are supporting missionaries in distant lands, and on to the angry streets where a lynch mob gathers to murder Atticus Finch's black client. Scout sees it all and takes us on a tour of the nooks and crannies of Maycomb. Luckily for us, she is an astute observer of the sociological structure of her hometown.

The Crawfords mind their own business, a third of the Merriweathers are morbid, the Delafields are all born liars, the entire Buford clan have that same strange walk. Scout can reel off every detail of the caste system in Maycomb effortlessly.

Scout truly scouts the entire social gamut from top to bottom and back again in this brief but expansive story. Though the city limits of Maycomb may be cramped and the population small, the sweep of Scout's gaze is unbounded, stretching outward toward the nation that resonates beyond the borders of her small town.

BIG, BIGGER, BIGGEST

The Da Vinci Code challenges the core values of institutions no less vast than the Catholic Church and Western art, to name only two, yet lest we forget the grandness of scale the novel is operating on, we are given repeated reminders in the form of superlatives of every kind. You want big? I'll give you big. Here are nine examples, but there's virtually one on every page.

1. "the world's most famous paintings . . ."
2. "the longest building in Europe . . ."
3. "the most famous mathematical progressions in history . . ."
4. "the most famous piece of art in the world . . ."
5. "one of the world's most documented inside jokes . . ."
6. "the most sought-after treasure in human history . . ."
7. "one of the most enduring mysteries of all time . . ."
8. "the most famous fresco of all time . . ."
9. "one of history's greatest secrets . . ."

Superlatives abound. Greatest this, biggest that. Most famous this, earthshaking that. Another elbow in the ribs and another. Get it? Get it? This is important! This is big! Really, really huge!

Surely most readers glide past these passages without a blink, so swept up in the constant puzzle solving and didactic passion for all things related to Catholicism, symbolism, goddesses, Western art, and Parisian and London travel guide info. In fact, in the case of *The Da Vinci Code,* such trumpet-blaring announcements of the importance of the story are unnecessary, because the scale of the story, the grandeur of its subject, and the momentous nature of its revelations would have easily carried the day.

SUPERPOWERS

Tom Clancy puts Jack Ryan on the largest geopolitical stage going: two superpowers using their highest-tech toys to play saber-rattling games somewhere in the vastness of the Atlantic Ocean. The Americans are trying desperately to locate a Russian nuclear submarine so quiet, so undetectable by conventional technology, it could shift the military balance of power once and for all.

Though we know little about Jack Ryan's inner life, he's smart and well schooled in military matters, and though he's reluctant to do so, he bravely answers his country's call and uses his good old American common sense and his military savvy to avert World War III. How can we not care about such a man? And why do we really need to know more about the mechanics of his state of mind to be fully engaged with his bold and enterprising deeds?

Mario Puzo gives us not just a story about a Mafia family, but a story about the Mafia. Like *Gone with the Wind, The Exorcist, Jaws,* and *The Hunt for Red October,* it's a war story. One Mafia family at war against other Mafia families and the Corleones at war with the civilized law-abiding world.

Part of the novel's appeal is that it provides us with an exhaustive diagram of the power structure of a vast and widespread criminal organization that reaches into nearly every corner of American society. That we learn little of Michael Corleone's psychodynamics or spend practically no time at all inside the Don's mind seems a small price to pay for such a thorough tour of this network of killers and thieves.

And what of *Jaws* and that great white shark that rises from the sea like . . . a supersilent, supersecret nuclear-powered submarine? It is not some puny fish, no, but the ultimate shark, the shark to beat all sharks, coming from earthshaking depths. It rattles the entire island town of Amity, from lowly fishermen to the haughty mayor, and the ripples of its passing spread well beyond the tiny town it's taken such an interest in. A shark with scope.

Then there is *The Exorcist*. Is it possible to find an antagonist of any greater scale than Satan himself? Not likely. It is Satan's voice and Satan's sickening smell and Satan's horrifying possession of a young girl-child that calls forth the full weight of Christianity to exorcise it. Good versus Evil with head-spinning terror.

Peyton Place is not simply a small New England town. It is *every* small American town with its secrets, its hypocrisies, its abortions, its incest, its teen sex, its pulsing, heaving, sweaty sexual violence. Peyton Place is America, the polite, mannered façade pulled back to reveal the squirming reality below. Like *To Kill a Mockingbird,* the book is a broad examination of the corrupt mores and class warfare that Americans would rather not admit to. In that sense, it is far more than a lurid exposé of the naughty private lives of the citizens of a small New England town. It attempts to chronicle the principal social issues of the postwar era—primarily the repression and exploitation of women and the impoverished—and seeks to record their brave attempts at emancipation.

In *The Firm,* John Grisham doesn't just take us on a ride through the inner workings of a small southern law firm. He sends a top Harvard Law School grad, Mitch McDeere, to work for a firm so shady, so murderous, so utterly corrupt, that a man no less grand than the director of the FBI shows up in an isolated public park to recruit Mitch to exorcise this malignant multinational business from American life. As one FBI agent puts it to Mitch:

"You can build a case from the inside that will collapse the firm and break up one of the largest crime families in the country."

Big, bigger, biggest.

When Jacqueline Susann creates an early incarnation of *Sex and the City,* she plops her three young working gals into two of the biggest American cities, New York and Los Angeles, sending them off to mingle with the most glamorous celebrities and showbiz personalities of all time. We are dazzled by movie stars, Broadway celebrities, the most influential entertainment power brokers, and debauchery on the grandest of scales.

In *The Dead Zone,* Stephen King sets John Smith's story against a backdrop of political upheaval, the sixties and early seventies. Woodstock, Watergate, Kent State. John misses four years of that tumultuous period while in a coma and wakes to find the Vietnam War ended and Nixon hounded from office. Putting the novel in political context is crucial to the foreground story, for after John wakes from his Rip van Winkle snooze, he must decide whether or not to put his precognitive abilities to use in a scheme to assassinate Greg Stillson, a megalomaniacal politician with his eyes on the White House. By this point in the novel, John's "second sight" has been widely publicized and his exploits have become the stuff of national news.

In the smaller foreground story, set against this sweeping backdrop, John Smith realizes with growing dread that he must execute Stillson, because John has seen in one of his precognitive visions of the future that Stillson plays a crucial role in promoting evil. Stillson is about to become a Hitler or bin Laden, and John Smith is the world's only hope to prevent a certain Armageddon.

The stakes are high. They couldn't be higher.

FROM SEA TO SHINING SEA

While Americans can stake no claim to the epic form, or to novels with panoramic sweep, we do have a national predisposition for expansiveness in general and a weakness for boastful, sprawling Whitmanesque stories. I am large, Whitman liked to say, referring to America. I contain multitudes.

It seems that when book buyers decide to spend the price of a restaurant meal for a work of fiction, most want their stories to be more than just a plate of tapas. They want to gorge on big, bustling, manifest destiny, shining city on a hill, sloppy Joe calories. We want our books to measure up to our own supersized sense of what matters most.

So it is that Scarlett and Mitch McDeere and Jack Ryan and Scout and their brethren are unmistakably American in the vastness of their aspirations and their outsized bravery in the face of enormous tasks and dangers. Though these characters are defined far more by their social class and their families and extended families and by their jobs than by the inner workings of their psyches, what they may lack in emotional dimensionality they make up for in scale.

Just as I expected before I read any of these novels, their pages are populated with apparent stereotypes—the self-absorbed, superficial southern belle, the young lawyer on the make, the stalwart, stuffy CIA analyst, the guileless small-town girl who loses her innocence. So how is it that each of these characters blindsided me with such force that they made me question my cocky assumptions that psychological complexity was the sine qua non of literary achievement?

My students and I came to believe that the answer lies partly in the wide scope of bestsellers. Because these characters perform against the vast backdrops of American politics and social upheaval, and because their personal destinies, their wishes, and their dreams are inextricably fused with the largest and most crucial concerns of the nation, Scarlett and Mitch and Jack and Scout and the others cannot help but stir us. They are ordinary American folks from humble roots who have answered some resounding call and risen beyond their limitations to impossible heights. If their battles had been smaller, less important, less connected to the national pulse, frankly, most of us wouldn't have given a damn.

FEATURE #4

The Golden Country

For a transitory enchanted moment man must have held his breath in the presence of this continent, compelled into an aesthetic contemplation he neither understood nor desired, face to face for the last time in history with something commensurate [with] his capacity for wonder.

—F. SCOTT FITZGERALD,
THE GREAT GATSBY

America-as-paradise, an idea that so powerfully shapes our national identity, is one of the key motifs in all our twelve bestsellers.

It's hard to top Fitzgerald when it comes to rhapsodizing about the New World, but here's Thomas Morton in 1622, a more or less typical colonial settler, enthusing about the lush wilderness of America: "I do not thinke that in all the knowne world it could be parallel'd . . . so many goodly groves of trees; dainty fine round rising hillucks . . . sweet crystal fountains, and cleare running streams."

Nearly four hundred years after Morton stepped ashore, fictional portrayals of the natural world still have immense power to stir our American hearts. And it seems that bestselling authors have absorbed this lesson well.

As my students and I were beginning to compare bestsellers from past eras, this feature was one of the first we spotted—images of a lost Eden. We came to refer to this recurring phenomenon as the Golden Country, a phrase we lifted from George Orwell's bestseller *Nineteen Eighty-four.*

> The landscape that he was looking at recurred so often in his dreams that he was never fully certain whether or not he had seen it in the real world. In his waking thoughts he called it the Golden Country.

In a time of perpetual war, with the thought police and Big Brother constantly spying, Winston Smith, the protagonist of the novel, escapes frequently to this wistful, sexy fantasyland to reestablish his connection to a lost natural world he only vaguely recalls. It is a place of languid streams and verdant fields and swaying elm trees with leaves stirring "in dense masses like women's hair."

What relief Winston feels from the pressures of his robotic routines is fleeting. Yet for the reader, the lyrical glow of these fragments stands out sharply against the no-frills prose Orwell uses throughout the novel to portray the drab and oppressive futuristic society.

American writers typically portray Eden with a bit more ambivalence than the Englishman Orwell. Take the famous portrait of American paradise in *Walden,* Thoreau's celebrated treatise on living in the wild. Utopian, yes. Edenic, yes. But *Walden* is at least as much a pragmatic how-to manual as it is an inspirational document. Thoreau was an American writer through and through, as interested in the utilitarian methods of surviving in the wilderness as he was in the rhapsodic descriptions of natural beauty. And so it is with the presentation of nature in American bestsellers, where we find Edens that for all their restorative beauty are both ephemeral and dangerous landscapes that must be mastered.

AMERICA, THE OLD WORLD AND THE NEW

American readers have a powerful hankering for stories grounded in the earth itself. Surely part of this hunger is connected to one of our central national myths—America as the new Eden. A land of second chances, fresh beginnings in the virginal wilderness.

By and large, our Puritan forebears were rapturous about the abundance and beauty of God's handiwork that greeted them in the New World. They saw in the pristine forests an earthly paradise with all its pleasures and temptations. Later generations of Americans, both religious and secular, have seen our awe-inspiring mountain ranges and woodlands and great canyons as national monuments, roughly equivalent to the great cathedrals of Europe. Sure, we may not have Notre Dame or Chartres, but just look at those Rockies.

The American wilderness forged our pioneer spirit and helped stamp us with an enduring rough-and-tumble sensibility that distinguishes us from our fussy cousins across the Atlantic. For Americans, nature is not just some sublime and misty mountain peak awash in a romantic glow, it is also the bronco that needs breaking, the rocky, stump-filled pasture that must be cleared if we are to plant our crops and survive, or that mountain range that must be conquered so our westward progress can continue. It is the dense forest where savages hide, where grizzlies, rattlesnakes, and other decidedly unfriendly creatures lurk.

Such is the dangerous Eden that Michael Corleone stumbles into in *The Godfather*. After murdering an American police captain, the Godfather's youngest son, Michael, flees to Sicily to lie low until the legal fuss blows over back home. It is a decidedly utilitarian and unromantic man who arrives in Sicily, an American pragmatist through and through.

But during his idyllic interlude he encounters a primal young woman named Apollonia, and Michael is immediately struck by an emotional thunderbolt: "This was an overwhelming desire for possession, this was an unerasable printing of the girl's face on the brain. . . ."

After a brief courtship, the two are married and Michael spends a few blissful pages under the spell of Apollonia's sensual aura as well as the lush primitivism of Sicily. One morning, Michael awakes and in a passage exceedingly unique in *The Godfather* for its poetic imagery, he seems more mellow, more vulnerable, and more stripped down to his essentials than he is at any other moment in the novel. "The Sicilian sun, early-morning, lemon-colored, filled Michael's bedroom. He awoke and, feeling Apollonia's satiny body against his own sleep-warm skin, made her come awake with love. When they were done, even the months of complete possession could not stop him from marveling at her beauty and her passion.

"She left the bedroom to wash and dress in the bathroom down the hall. Michael, still naked, the morning sun refreshing his body, lit a cigarette and relaxed on the bed."

A page or two later, Apollonia is murdered, and Michael is badly injured in the bomb blast. Eden didn't last long for Corleone, but in his short-lived stay in the sunny meadows and groves of Sicily, Michael's character was redefined in a fundamental way. After his sojourn we see him as a man whose destiny is rooted in his ancestors' native soil—a simple, primeval land that lingers in his memory and ours through the rest of the novel.

Without this interlude in the Golden Country, a crucial facet of Michael Corleone's character would go unexpressed and his complexity would be seriously diminished. The innocent yet powerful love he finds in the Golden Country establishes Michael as a man of tenderness and passion. From that moment on, Sicily stands as a crucial reference point, as though a tuning fork has been struck and for the remainder of the novel it hums its quiet note in the background of Michael's consciousness.

Michael Corleone is expelled from Eden and in the process is forced to confront a deeper awareness of man's brutality. His loss of innocence transforms him into a man of resolve, a harder, more cynical hero who is unlikely to know again the depth of love he found in Apollonia's arms. He's become a warrior, and as he marches forth from Sicily, the shield and spear he carries have been forged in the fiery explosion that brings his peaceful idyll in the Golden Country to an end.

His loss of Apollonia gives his future acts the feel of justifiable vengeance and subtly brings us into his sympathetic orbit. No crime he later commits, no thuggery he's involved in, seems as sinful as it would have if Michael had not been baptized in the ancient waters of the Golden Country.

TARA BEFORE THE WAR

Again and again in twentieth-century bestsellers, the Golden Country is used as a baseline, the true homeland that our hero or heroine is tragically alienated from and in some way is struggling to return to.

Part of what makes Scarlett appealing beyond all her faults, and what makes *Gone with the Wind* rise beyond its literary limitations, is its primitive insistence on the importance of the emotional over the intellectual, the simple and raw over the cerebral and refined. For Scarlett is no fragile southern belle who haunts only the parlor and ballroom. Like her outdoorsman father, she is equally at home roaming the grounds of Tara, her stately house surrounded by cotton fields and lush primeval forests.

But her love of the land is severely tested when Scarlett returns to Tara and must bring the fields back to life if she and her family are to survive. Despite the wearying labor, her spirits rise as the cotton grows and eventually is harvested. Cotton reassures her, steadies her, just as Gerald had forecast a few hundred pages earlier.

The land and its bounty lift her spirits. Scarlett becomes aware of the power of the natural world to humble as well as elevate. Both aristocrat and common man are rendered equal before the crucial, life-sustaining soil.

In class terms, an intimate knowledge of nature favors the sons of toil over the lord and lady, for it is the common man who regularly gets his hands dirty and it is the common man who lives more closely and more respectfully with the natural world and is able to make it bear fruit.

Cultivated, that word we've appropriated to describe the highly evolved aristocrat, at its root has as much to do with agriculture as with high culture. In a literary form that since its beginning sought an audience of ordinary folks, an emphasis on earthy matters is no coincidence. The novel's roots reach deep into our shared agrarian past.

Of course, the Golden Country's clearest expression in *Gone with the Wind* is the plantation life at Tara before the outbreak of the Civil War, an antebellum paradise of mindless parties and summery ease. Without those early chapters that give us vivid portrayals of a land both bountiful and uncomplicated, Scarlett's desperate passion to return to her childhood home and rebuild it would be meaningless.

Just as Michael Corleone never fully recovered from his stay in the Golden Country of Sicily, Scarlett O'Hara is forever marked by those years of lazy, eye-batting coquetry in the Edenic plantations of the prewar South.

She too is exiled from her land, sent packing to the muddy streets of Atlanta, where she will test herself against another set of obstacles entirely. But what strength she has, what resources she is able to muster, are all rooted in her connection with the Georgia dirt, a landscape as luxuriant as it is treacherous.

For Michael Corleone, there is murder lurking just behind the olive groves and rocky hillsides of Sicily. Eden always has a snake. In Scarlett's case, "the little negro boy . . . is part of the picture of Tara." What rips apart the utopian antebellum dream is the harsh hiss of slavery. No Eden can last. Eventually the original sins of our fathers, or our godfathers, implicate us and we are all expelled from the garden, and the only way we can return to our version of Tara is to travel there as Winston did in *Nineteen Eighty-four,* in our imagination.

After Scarlett is expelled from Tara, she spends the rest of the novel pining to return. Michael Corleone is expelled from Apollonia's Sicily and for the remainder of the novel devotes himself to getting even for the loss.

A BITE FROM THE APPLE

In *To Kill a Mockingbird,* the eviction is just as violent and sudden, but Scout is exiled not from a sheltering natural place, but from a more general state of innocence.

The Golden Country in *To Kill a Mockingbird* is evoked by the lazy days spent lolling in the grass, those scenes of summery indolence that open the novel when Scout and Jem are joined by Dill and are swept up in his "eccentric plans, strange longings, and quaint fancies."

For Scout, that Golden Country also holds a form of gender equality that she is to lose as soon as Jem grows into adolescence and becomes embarrassed by his kid sister. But for those few perfect summer months, Scout enjoys full membership in the gang of three, and their "routine contentment was: improving our tree house that rested between giant twin chinaberry trees in the backyard" and acting out roles in dramas they'd read or invented. It is a time of creativity, gender neutrality, naïveté.

This stage of childhood innocence can't last, and the trial of Tom Robinson, a black man accused of raping a white woman, brings Scout's brief stay in the Golden Country to a premature and ugly end. With Atticus Finch defending the black man in the face of boiling racial hatred and even an attempted lynching, Scout must confront a heap of harsh lessons, and in the process her innocence dissolves and her childhood is effectively brought to a close.

What she discovers during the course of the trial about bigotry and decency, cowardice and bravery, and the limits of justice to transform the hearts of men forces her to mature more quickly than she would have otherwise. But once again, it is the lingering memory of the Golden Country from which she is banished that defines her character thereafter.

The trial that rocks Maycomb County, Alabama, might as well have been the Civil War refought a century later. The courtroom scenes serve the same function as the war in *Gone with the Wind* or Apollonia's murder. It is the violent eruption, the watershed moment that divides innocence from grim awareness, childhood games from the burdens of adulthood.

In novel after novel, the Golden Country is a blend of place and time: either some splendid natural location, some wild or secret place that forms the backdrop for an innocent, frequently sensuous idyll, or else a time before it all got so damn complicated, before the turmoil and the heartbreak and the deadened senses. It's a nostalgic, wistful zone, a faraway Shangri-la that pulses at the core of bestsellers—appealing perhaps to some sense of regret and longing in many of us, a vague awareness that something crucial slipped away when we weren't looking, our childhood, our purity, our dreams, our sexual innocence, our national idealism.

THE SNAKE OF GREED

At the opening of John Grisham's *The Firm,* we are given a snapshot of Mitch and Abby McDeere's life in law school. Abby comes home from work, opens the apartment door, and is greeted by Mitch in a state of arousal that's part sexual and part celebratory. He's been offered a fantastic job. He yanks her into the apartment and pulls her onto the couch, and they kiss and grope and fondle and moan like teenage lovers.

The young couple goes on to celebrate the new job offer with a feast of chicken chow mein and egg foo yung and a cheap bottle of Chablis and some more romance on the couch. Ah, yes, the sweet, simple innocence of law school.

As the novel clips along, Mitch McDeere is tempted by the snake of greed and winds up selling his soul to the highest bidder. Unfortunately, the law firm doing the bidding happens to be controlled by a relative of Michael Corleone's. The bliss Mitch and Abby initially embrace is one defined by a shiny new BMW, a low-interest mortgage, and other material perks of the self-indulgent 1980s. As his delight begins to unravel along with his marriage and his own moral principles, in a rare moment of self-awareness, Mitch thinks longingly of that more authentic Golden Country that he has left behind, telling Abby, "I think we were happier living in the two-room student apartment in Cambridge."

Grisham devotes only a paragraph or two to their innocent law school life and only that single sentence to invoke the nostalgic regret for the lost Golden Country. However, without those key passages, Mitch McDeere's ambition would seem like little more than unbridled avarice, and the novel would stand as simply one long ode to self-indulgence that went badly off course.

Instead, by invoking the Golden Country even so briefly, Grisham hints at a man whose youthful idealism and purity were corrupted by the tempting fruits of financial achievement, a man who realizes his mistake and is able to return to the lost paradise with a deeper appreciation for its natural beauty.

The scrappy kid who made it to Harvard Law and became

a hotshot recruit at a big-time law firm is the guy we glimpse again at the end of the novel after he is expelled from the false Eden of BMWs and McMansions and finds a way to start afresh in a new Golden Country, a better one than any he'd imagined. An unpretentious white-painted wood house on Little Cayman, where Mitch and Abby celebrate a new and improved simple life with plenty of rum and some quality sex on the beach.

CONTAMINATED GARDEN

In *Peyton Place,* the Golden Country is once again rendered as a natural landscape that is both beautiful and redemptive, or so it seems at first.

Allison walks through the woods and arrives at an open field of goldenrod. The clearing is lush with yellow blooms, and as Allison wades into their goldenness she's swept away in a "feeling of pure ecstasy" and opens her arms wide to the world that envelops her.

This is Allison MacKenzie's secret place. She's thirteen and has discovered her very own Golden Country—an unspoiled bit of woods at Road's End, one of the last surviving forests in New England that was never harvested. It's as close to pure, unadulterated Eden as one can find in the area around Peyton Place. Allison goes there to commune with nature and to bask in its calming effects. However, only twenty-five pages after this moment when we first see her bathing in the golden ecstatic glow of her secret garden, Allison leads her tough-minded friend, Selena, to her spot, and at that moment everything changes.

Selena refuses to walk out into the woods with Allison.

And Allison calls her mean and hateful for rejecting her "secret place." Taking a perverse pleasure in deflating her innocence, Selena reveals to Allison that this is where boys bring girls at night to make out. It's been happening forever at this exact spot.

Naïve Allison has unwittingly chosen lovers' lane as her Golden Country. And not just any lovers' lane, but lovers' lane in Peyton Place, a town of sexual extravagance and all manner of smutty behavior. The poor girl has chosen for her personal holiest of holies the most profane spot in a profane town.

In its irony and dark realism, this scene is a paradigm for the entire novel. Sooner or later, nearly every character will go through a shift of awareness similar to Allison's. In the course of the story, whatever illusions they once held are eventually stripped away.

In fact, Allison returns to her secret place later in the novel and shares a first kiss with a boy named Norman Page. Norman discusses what he's learned about sex from reading a book on the subject. His bookishness, however, doesn't stir Allison's blood, and his gentle kisses fail to arouse her. Their foreplay in the heart of Allison's Golden Country comes to nothing.

The payoff for this unfulfilled sexual moment is decisive, however, and reshapes the trajectory of Allison's life. She decides she wants a man whose passion isn't book-learned but springs from some natural sensuality that is as wild and unrestrained as the wilderness that backdrops her first kiss. Much of what she becomes as an adult can be traced to a few crucial scenes that take place here.

In the final pages of the novel, after being cruelly deceived by a lover and learning of her own illegitimate birth, after coming to grips with Peyton Place's sordid history of suicides and abortions and incestuous rapes, Allison returns to her Golden Place for solace. It doesn't have all the magic it once had, but it has enough. She sits and reflects for a long time, fondling a flower, rediscovering a portion of the profound comfort she felt as a child.

GOLDEN OPPORTUNITY

For the islanders in *Jaws,* paradise is an isolated sanctuary that they rent out to interlopers for part of each year. Their economy depends on the annual migration of tourists. But before the throngs arrive, we get a glimpse of the island in its natural state.

Soft winds ripple the sea, a crispness fills the air at night, after long sunny days that warm the sandy beach. It's all so calm and beautiful.

Shortly thereafter, a skinny-dipper's mutilated body washes ashore, and that's the end of paradise. The good sheriff Martin Brody wants to go public with the truth, that a killer shark is on the prowl. But the mayor fears economic catastrophe if the vacationers who are the lifeblood of the community are scared away. In effect, the mayor wants to perpetrate a hoax—to make believe that Eden is still Eden, that the finned snake has not appeared.

For those like Brody, the natural world of Amity, the beach, the ocean, the sunny summer days, and the shark itself have religious heft. On the other hand, the mayor and his allies view nature as a commodity whose only purpose is to be merchandised. As is so often the case in America, one man's Golden Country is another man's Golden Opportunity.

Just as commerce contaminates Mitch and Abby's Shangri-la and lustful teenagers invade Allison MacKenzie's secret place, tourists from the city will intrude on this sanctuary and put the islanders' Eden under siege.

It becomes Sheriff Brody's mission to help kill the shark and return the town to some semblance of normalcy. Given the short attention span of the summer people, maybe one day soon Amity can sell itself again as the beach lover's Golden Country. But for most locals, after the ravages of the shark, that idyllic view is gone. What's been lost is the innocent belief that what is beautiful and natural is also benign. This year when the tourists finally leave, it's doubtful there will be a restoration of the Golden Country. The shark has put an end to the town's comfortable seaside fantasy. All that will remain is the ghostly yearning for some bygone innocence.

THIN ICE

Again with *The Dead Zone,* an image of something close to paradise appears within the first few pages just before John Smith, our hero, takes his crucial spill while "skating on a cleared patch of Runaround Pond in Durham." The kids were playing hockey with beat-up sticks and potato baskets as goals. The younger children played around on the edges of the pond, and in another corner a bonfire of rubber tires burned. A few parents hovered close by, keeping watch on their kids, giving the scene a Norman Rockwell sense of glowy security.

In only a page or two, John Smith will fall on this idyllic ice and the bump on his head will endow him with a mildly psychic ability thereafter, a kind of stage one in his banishment from Eden. His stay in the Golden Country is not exactly over by the end of the prologue, but that bump on his head lays the groundwork for the creepy precognitive skills that will be induced by a second, more serious thump.

In Stephen King's world, we are all skating on slippery ice. Fate or accident can launch us out of the ordinary world we all inhabit in a millisecond and send us spinning out into the stratosphere of altered consciousness and terror. It is true in *The Dead Zone,* and it has been true in his big bestsellers since. The St. Bernard in *Cujo,* for instance, chases a rabbit into a hole and accidentally becomes stuck. He is attacked by rabid bats, and it is this cascade of random events that precipitates much of the rest of the novel.

It is true that in King's novels, other factors besides bad luck can occasionally expel a youngster from the Golden Country of childhood. For instance, religious zealots are often the cause of the expulsion. Indeed, in *The Dead Zone,* as in *Carrie,* there are vivid examples of a domineering Christian extremism that banishes characters from their innocent condition.

But over and over again it is pure chance, the slipperiness of the ground beneath our feet, that is the real danger. There is no way to protect ourselves from the threat of misfortune. That's one of the ways King torques up the fear factor in his novels. In KingWorld, no amount of tiptoeing caution will save us from the existential horrors that lie just beyond the borders of the Golden Country. The only hope we have is to do as John Smith does in *The Dead Zone* and find some way to use our own cursed condition for some greater good.

VALLEY OF THE PEACH TREES

In *Valley of the Dolls,* a novel of sex and drugs and more drugs and more sex, wilderness and nature play a limited but crucial role in the narrative. Although the young women whose lives we follow have sworn allegiance to city life with all its concrete and honking horns, nightclubs and cramped apartments, there is one small moment that poignantly evokes the Golden Country.

Anne Welles, the novel's leading lady, is alone with Lyon Burke, a cosmopolitan young man who "dwarfed anyone she'd ever known." Lyon recounts a war story to Anne, a story whose implications he clearly does not fully grasp. Lyon and a young soldier were spending the night in the ruins of a barn. The young corporal kept sifting some dirt from one hand to the other. "This is great earth," he kept repeating. Turns out the corporal owned a peach farm back in Pennsylvania, and during those long dark hours in the wartime barn, before heading back into a crucial battle, the corporal described to Lyon Burke the agricultural challenges he faced with the soil of his land back home that was not as fertile as he wanted it to be. He wanted the farm to prosper and for it to sustain his children when they came of age.

The next day, Lyon tells Anne, the soldiers went their separate ways, but Lyon soon came to discover that the young corporal/farmer had been shot down in the hours after they parted. He held the young man's dog tag in his hand and mused:

> "Last night it had been a man—a man who wasted his last night on earth worrying about fertilizer and

soil. And now his blood would fertilize some foreign soil."

He looked at her and suddenly smiled. "And here I am, wasting your time talking about it."

Since nearly everyone in this novel is busily seducing nearly everyone else most of the time, it seems natural to assume that Lyon Burke is trying to use his war story to soften Anne's resistance. A great pickup line: "Had we but world enough, and time,/This coyness, Lady, were no crime." Nothing like a little carpe diem to get the evening turning in the right direction.

Lyon Burke would like Ann to interpret the story for its existential meaning: Our lives are so short, our deaths so random and unpredictable, we must not waste time on trivial worries like protecting our virtue.

But for the corporal, the opposite interpretation holds true. What concerned him in his final moments was something more enduring, more profound, more fundamentally American, than simple existential turmoil.

In those desperate hours on the edge of the battlefield, the corporal was returning to his own Golden Country, the literal terra firma he loved. He was a man of the soil, a man for whom peach trees were as important as bags of gold. Indeed, the dirt he sifts through his hand gives him a level of reality and integrity that hardly any other single character in this novel possesses.

The natural world he recollects and returns to briefly in his mind is like Winston's from *Nineteen Eighty-four,* an escape from war and death and oppression to his own Edenic memory. Lyon Burke had it all wrong. Rather than wasting his last hours, the corporal was invoking his Golden Country with all the solemnity of a final prayer.

In a novel glutted with the cheap stimulants of cash, fame, drugs, and an endless whirlwind of sexual partners, this single passage stands apart. This corporal occupies only a paragraph or two, yet his brief appearance in the novel resonates like the chime of a well-struck bell through the rest of its pages.

TWO PARADISES

In *The Hunt for Red October,* the Golden Country is an imaginary far-off destination. Locked away inside a submarine thousands of feet beneath the surface of the sea, Marko Ramius, the Russian commander of the *Red October,* summons a striking image of Eden when he announces to his crew that they are headed for the tropical paradise of Cuba. If they manage to go undetected by the imperialist American dogs, they will soon be lying on the white beaches beneath palm trees and enjoying the comradeship of the local ladies.

Secretly, Ramius intends to defect to his own version of the Golden Country, the United States of America, but to mislead and motivate his crew, he intentionally invokes the Communist Party's version of heaven on earth, that exotic island in the Gulf Stream.

Eventually, Jack Ryan guesses correctly that Ramius's motivation for defecting is the compelling allure of the United States: "America, Ryan smiled, could be pretty seductive to someone used to the gray life in the Soviet Union."

There is little subtlety in Clancy's novels, but this is an instance of a fundamental irony around which much of the novel's action and its patriotic stance is built. Simply put, the "gray life" of Soviet society can make even a shabby paradise like Cuba seem appealing, while the true Golden Country, as anyone with any smarts understands, is the Eden of America.

For Sophie Neveu in *The Da Vinci Code,* paradise is her grandfather's country home, a natural world far removed from Parisian urban life, where most of the novel is set. The country home is a place that's central to Sophie's formative experiences.

In an early scene at the country home, Jacques Saunière indulges his granddaughter's instinctive love for riddles by sending Sophie on a circuit of the house in search of her Christmas gift. Following his complex clues, she is eventually led to a bright, shiny bicycle. It's a moment of unadulterated joy that stamps itself permanently in her memory.

But later on, Sophie's Eden is spoiled when she returns to the same country house unexpectedly from college and stumbles into a scene that appears to be an orgy in which her grandfather is a major participant. From that moment on, Sophie is alienated from her grandpa and refuses to return to the Golden Country of her youth.

As with Michael Corleone, Ramius, Allison MacKenzie, Scarlett O'Hara, and most of our other protagonists, Sophie Neveu's Golden Country is a natural setting that churns with erotic energy, and when the innocence is lost, it is never quite regained. Late in the novel, when Sophie learns the true nature of the strange rite her grandfather was participating in, an exercise that's religious rather than sexual, she can't let go of her revulsion.

Even Robert Langdon, who tries to set her straight, realizes it's not so easy to explain away the scene she witnessed: "Admittedly, the concept of sex as a pathway to God was mind-boggling at first." Well, yeah. Once an apple that juicy is bitten into, there's just no cleaning the taste from one's mouth.

It would be false to claim that images of the Golden Country or lost Edens are unique to bestsellers. But what I can say for sure is that without exception, every single novel in this sampling prominently features a lost Eden, and that image plays a pivotal role, changing the dynamics of characterization, as in Mitch McDeere's and Michael Corleone's cases. Or as we see in *Peyton Place* and *Gone with the Wind* and *Jaws*, the portrayal of an idyllic natural setting is a cornerstone of the thematic power of the entire novel.

FEATURE #5

Nothing but the Facts, Ma'am

Franklin himself . . . was practical, industrious, inquiring, convivial, and middle-brow philosophical. [He] celebrated civic virtue, mutual benefits, the improvement of self and society.

—WALTER ISAACSON,
BENJAMIN FRANKLIN: AN AMERICAN LIFE

An abundance of facts and information, including everything from etiquette to the nuts-and-bolts layout of a submarine, fills these twelve books. The didactic function is as old as the novel form itself and continues to be a chief attraction in bestselling novels.

Ben Franklin, that uncommonly ingenious common man—kite flier, printer, bookseller, inventor of the bifocal lens and the flexible urinary catheter, namer of the Gulf Stream, and creator of the first American subscription library—will stand forever as a representative of at least two fundamental virtues of the American character: practicality and self-improvement.

At the age of twenty, Franklin made a to-do list, much like the one Jay Gatsby devised, an inventory of personal goals that captured the spirit of his countrymen at that time and for the centuries thereafter. Number six on his list was this promise to himself:

"INDUSTRY. Lose no time; be always employ'd in something useful; cut off all unnecessary actions."

Franklin was a busy reader and a student of the early English novel. Though he claimed the book that influenced him most was *Bonifacius: Essays to Do Good* by the Puritan preacher Cotton Mather, historians claim Franklin was also well instructed by a book that Mather would have considered hard-core porn. Lustful Ben managed to be one of the first Americans to own a copy of John Cleland's scandalous novel *Fanny Hill; or, Memoirs of a Woman of Pleasure,* a book that contained explicit erotic descriptions and that might well be regarded as an eighteenth-century sex manual. The man just wanted to learn.

Novel readers always have.

Indeed, part of the wide appeal of the earliest novels was based on their function as instruction manuals. Of course, it's also true that the first novel readers in eighteenth-century England were attracted to *Pamela* and *Moll Flanders* in some part to satisfy their voyeuristic yearnings. They were titillated by being privy to the secret lives of these two common women, one a young country girl who is hired as a servant in the manor house and the other a London prostitute, both of whom are placed in dire distress.

Certainly part of the appeal of these first novels is that early readers were able to identify with literary characters of their own social class portrayed in realistic detail. A kind of raunchy tabloid sensibility pervaded many of those early narratives that were stuffed to overflowing with carnal escapades. Low-tech reality TV.

But at least as important to most early novel readers was their desire to be informed. To learn about the larger world, particularly the secrets to social advancement. How was a farm girl who'd been hired as a maidservant in the manor house supposed to behave? How was she to fend off the master's lewd advances and still maintain her virtue without losing her job?

Samuel Richardson's English novel *Pamela* was in fact an early road map to the successful management of sexual harassment. Pamela's defense of her virtue was eventually rewarded when she married the master whom she'd formerly had to shove away. But the "virtue rewarded" moral was no doubt of minor importance to most readers compared with the thrill of witnessing the shocking realities that occurred behind the heavy locked doors of the upper class.

(The desire that a great many Americans have to master the rules of polite society propelled Emily Post's *Etiquette* onto the bestseller list in 1922, where it remained for a year and a half. It is now in its seventeenth edition.)

Learning the codes of behavior, the appropriate dress and salutations, the standard markers that determined one's class, and the ritualistic intricacies of courtship was to be Jane Austen's focus nearly a century after *Pamela*. Because her "novels of manners" were often seen as "husband-hunting stories," they were disparaged as an inferior literary subgenre. Such scorn finds new targets in our supposedly more enlightened era, when labels like "romance novel," "women's fiction," or "chick lit" are considered by many to be vicious put-downs.

But the fact is, the terrain that Jane Austen was working is not much different from that of Mario Puzo or Tom Clancy or John Grisham. The social arrangements, class distinctions, and codes of behavior aboard a nuclear-powered submarine or within the ranks of the Cosa Nostra or within a top-tier law firm are the central topics of these male-dominated novels. Just as the group dynamics within the town of Peyton Place or Maycomb, Alabama, are of critical importance in Grace Metalious's novel and Harper Lee's.

NUTS AND BOLTS

The other form of information that bestsellers frequently contain is the sort of factualism that today we associate with nonfiction—the kinds of nuts-and-bolts data like Clancy's detailed renderings of submarines or Dan Brown's encyclopedic cataloging of architectural, religious, and cultural factoids. We readers have come to expect two or three large scoops of factual information even in our detective stories, our thrillers, our adventure novels, and our science fiction. Few (if any) bestsellers fail to supply this service.

Telling a rousing story is in the job description, and making it seem real, seducing the reader into suspending disbelief: All of these were the novelist's tradecraft from day one.

There's no absolute way to prove the causal connection between high dosages of information and high sales, but in the years my classes combed through bestsellers, this feature was by far the most widespread and consistent.

THE DISH

Inside information, the scoop, the dish, gossip, the lowdown, the straight dope: This is the juicy side of information. Readers love to be taken somewhere they've never been before by an authority on that unexplored alien subculture.

One of the appeals of Grisham's *The Firm* was that it gave the reader the unvarnished story of the inner workings of high-powered law firms seeking glamorous Harvard Law School grads, complete with snapshots of the interview process and the bidding wars. We even learn the dollar amounts for billing hours, spicy details of an entire profession that until then had been the exclusive domain of writers such as Erle Stanley Gardner, whose interest was courtroom drama, not the down-and-dirty dollar figures that hotshot lawyers command or detailed descriptions of the flashy houses and cars that are paid for by crushing hours of work. Clearly, part of the fascination that drew many readers to *The Firm* came from this tell-all aspect. Slide the curtain aside, show us the play-by-play details of what's going on back there.

In *Valley of the Dolls,* Jacqueline Susann's raison d'être is to expose the behind-the-scenes double-dealing of showbiz. Do you want to know some practical strategies for how to succeed as a young ambitious babe in Manhattan or hear stories about the couches you'll have to stretch out on to break into the movie business? You want to know about the pitfalls, the payoffs, the seductions, the heartbreaks, the Lotharios, the Demerol, the Seconal? Hey, girlie, you want to know how to fend off the lord of the manor house and still keep your job? Well, read this book.

It's not a big step from *Pamela* to *Valley of the Dolls*. Virtue is rewarded (by marriage to the boss) and licentiousness is punished. Jennifer, the resident bimbette in *Valley of the Dolls*, puts her worldview into this shameless axiom: "She stroked the beaver coat—one night with Robby. That's what a great body was for, to get things you wanted."

A few chapters later, poor beaver-coated Jennifer is punished for her lack of virtue when she OD's on "dolls." True to narcissistic form, she leaves behind a narcissistic suicide note to Anne, the good girl of the novel:

> Anne—No embalmer could make me up as well as I do myself. Thank God for the dolls. Sorry I couldn't stick around for your wedding. I love you. Jen

The three young women of *Valley of the Dolls* give us a backstage pass to the petty and soulless world of American show business. The trio of innocents either die, become hopelessly addicted to downers, or turn terminally cynical toward the possibilities of love. It's a tragic tale, cautionary in tone. But as with *Pamela* or *Moll Flanders*, the moralizing aspects of the novel are no doubt of less interest to most readers than the roller-coaster ride through stardom and addiction, drying out in sanitariums, and back to the bright lights of the stage. Local color, facts, education.

STUFFED WITH FACTS

When you open the covers of *The Da Vinci Code,* an avalanche of Post-it notes spills out, as well as file cards and a clutter of short essays. Jottings about the Louvre, riffs on goddesses and feminism and the male and female symbols, the Hebrew alphabet, Mary Magdalene, Opus Dei, the Priory of Sion, the Depository Bank of Zurich, lambskin velum, and cryptics of every sort.

That a dozen books seeking to rebut some of Mr. Brown's claims have appeared in the years since *The Da Vinci Code* was first published suggests that it is the information as much as the characters or the plot that drove the success of this novel. Whether it is fact or hokum that "the Church burned at the stake five million women" or that Jesus was married and had a child is irrelevant to the immense popularity of the novel. These assertions are only a couple of the hundreds that critics seize on to try to overturn Mr. Brown's credibility. But fact is one thing, truth quite another. Readers everywhere have found the novel's compelling and entertaining premise to be sufficiently convincing to waive their rights to disbelief.

And Clancy? What is true for Dan Brown's astonishingly jam-packed novel is even more true for *The Hunt for Red October*—more than anyone ever wanted to know about submarines and the alphabet soup of governmental agencies and this protocol and that procedure and this bolt and that nut. I'd wager that there is more pure data on a single page of *The Hunt for Red October* than in many entire novels by Faulkner or Hemingway.

PURPOSEFUL PLEASURE

Fact-based fiction has broad appeal because it is simple, hearty fare. No highly refined palate required. Anyone can buy a ticket. Information is the red meat that sticks to the ribs. It satisfies a craving in nearly anyone who turns to a book in search of purposeful pleasure. By giving the story amplitude, a sense of nutritional value, information satisfies a basic need in most readers. All of which suggests that in large measure, people read to improve themselves or further their education. And like the early fans of Defoe and Richardson, they read in order to peer inside secret places not open to them otherwise—the daunting and mysterious manor house where innocent young Pamela goes to work.

Whether his or her taste is refined or not, the mass reader has always yearned to see beyond the shut door, be it the top floor of the Vatican or twenty leagues beneath the sea.

Margaret Mitchell's exhaustive rendering of the details of an antebellum household and the social intricacies of party planning for an evening ball rivals in its comprehensive detail Tom Clancy's blueprint walk-through of a nuclear sub and his loving descriptions of an array of military hardware.

When an interviewer from *Contemporary Authors* questioned Clancy about the amount of research labor his books display, he dismissed the notion offhandedly: "The most time I have spent researching any of my books was three weeks and that was for *Patriot Games*."

That must have been one hell of a speed-reading cram session.

A GOOD BOOK VERSUS THE GOOD BOOK

Surely the American tendency to honor the collection of facts and information is due in part to the ingrained pragmatism of our culture—a desire to improve ourselves in Gatsbyesque fashion by accumulating ever more practical knowledge in case we ever want to practice a little Yankee ingenuity.

And don't discount the importance of the Protestant work ethic in shaping our ideas about what a book should be. From the time of the Pilgrims until today, for many Americans the only good book is the Good Book. For a large segment of the reading public, any book without a heaping of useful information would be considered even more suspect.

It is clear that readers of our most popular novels hunger for more than vivid characters, a rousing story, realism of detail, or psychological subtleties. They want to be instructed and informed, to emerge from the novel with a wider understanding of some grand or esoteric subject matter. It is clear that bestselling novelists understand the hunger in their audience and are willing and able to supply heavy doses of information in highly entertaining packages.

FEATURE #6

Secret Societies

As opposite as George Bush and John Kerry may seem to be, they do share a common secret—one they've shared for decades, and one they will not share with the electorate. The secret: details of their membership in Skull and Bones, the elite Yale University society whose members include some of the most powerful men of the twentieth century.

—*60 MINUTES*, CBS NEWS

All twelve of these bestsellers expose the inner workings of at least one secret society.

Readers of popular fiction can be forgiven for thinking that Dan Brown discovered the subject of secret societies. But while he's certainly mined the topic exhaustively, he's not the first American bestseller writer to use a secret society as a cornerstone of his narrative, nor is he alone in tapping into the paranoid sensibility that seems a staple of American culture.

In that immensely popular TV show of the fifties *The*

Honeymooners, Ralph Kramden (Jackie Gleason) and his best buddy, the inestimable sewer worker Ed Norton (Art Carney), were active members of the International Order of Friendly Sons of the Raccoons, whose lodge members employed code words and hailed fellow members by flipping the tails on their coonskin caps and greeting one another as "brothers under the pelt."

Getting laughs in the fifties was as easy as flicking a furry extremity in the face of those snooty Rotarians or Freemasons or DeMolay or whoever was the object of their satire. Audiences got the message. Secret societies were uppity and goofy, and whatever power was conferred by membership in such groups was self-delusional.

However, during the same years that *The Honeymooners* was mocking secret societies, Joe McCarthy, senator from Wisconsin, rose to national prominence by exploiting Americans' anxieties about them, by claiming to have the names of Communists and Soviet spies and sympathizers who had infiltrated the innermost levels of the federal government. For years, McCarthy held public hearings in which he grilled citizens from every walk of life about their loyalty to their country. And while McCarthy was giving anticommunism a bad reputation, Mickey Spillane was selling millions of books like *I, the Jury,* which tapped into that same streak of paranoia that seems to run deep in our national sensibility. Killing fictional Commies made Spillane very rich.

Conspiracy theorists have been alive and well in America since at least 1798, when a group of New England reverends alerted their congregations to a plot by Illuminists (a gaggle of European intellectuals), who were said to be hell-bent on extinguishing the Christian religion and bringing down government control.

Pitting Them against Us seems to be one of the surefire strategies to incite an audience. From Father Charles Coughlin to the John Birch Society to the KKK to the radio and television shock jocks of today, we have seen the muscle-flexing power of groups that feed on hatred and prejudice and flourish by identifying other groups as a threat to our way of life.

Perhaps because we are a nation of immigrants, where there's always a reliable and steady stream of Others to stoke our tendencies toward suspicion and mistrust, it is inevitable that secret societies would play a prominent role in our popular culture.

PRIVILEGED GLIMPSES

In a celebrated passage from the opening of *The Great Gatsby,* Nick Carraway claims he's emotionally exhausted after being immersed in the melodrama of his friends' lives, and he's decided he wants "no more riotous excursions with privileged glimpses into the human heart." After months of exposure to the confessions and excruciating tragedies of Jay Gatsby and Tom and Daisy Buchanan, he's fatally fatigued and desires nothing more than to resign his membership in their elite circle.

For many readers, this demurral only whets the appetite for the story to come. Most of us yearn for a few of those "privileged glimpses" into the guarded fortresses, the inner sanctum of the holiest of holies, the penthouse, the boardroom, the Oval Office. Bestselling novels mine this craving by regularly sliding aside the curtains and exposing the secrets of a wide assortment of secret societies.

The Mafia, Opus Dei, elite nuclear submariners, law partners fronting for the Mob, Broadway superstars, shark fisher-men, exorcists, small-town cliques, and the southern aris-tocracy: Each of our twelve novels has at least one secret society at its nucleus.

For definition's sake, let's call a secret society any group that for one reason or another has isolated itself from the rest of the world by creating a collection of rules, rites, sacra-ments, or covert behaviors that reinforces its separation from the larger population. The group is exclusive, usually power-ful in some domain, with its own initiation rituals and its own sense of justice and duty, sometimes its own language, and even its own criminal code.

In the innermost circle of any social group, we expect to find an elite few who have been inducted into the private cer-emonies, have mastered the conventions, dress, and behavior that mark them as elite members of their particular secret society, or else have paid some exorbitant membership dues that mere mortals could never manage. Gated communities within gated communities, with security guards and grim-faced sentinels at every stage.

Behind layers of sentries are characters like Don Corleone, or the pope's henchmen, or a powerful law firm's senior part-ners, or perhaps the elite commander of a nuclear submarine, or maybe even a master angler whose knowledge of the sea and the frightful creatures swimming in its depths gives him an unequaled authority, something close to the status of a savior.

While social class might overlap with these descriptors in certain ways, the kind of exclusivity we find portrayed in bestsellers is rarely a function of class status alone but is rather an earned seniority. Neither wealth, social standing, nor a privileged background is an important ingredient in

Don Corleone's power. Indeed, his rise from poverty to a position of great influence is typical in bestsellers. The poor or the lower middle classes far outnumber their economic betters as the heroes in the megahits under review.

SECRETS OF THE SEAS

Although he doesn't wear a coonskin hat, Quint, the veteran shark hunter in *Jaws,* is Grand High Exalted Mystic Ruler of the seas, complete with arcane techniques, specialized jargon, and inviolable shipboard rules.

His authority and mastery of his element are unquestionable. Quint's the man you call when the biggest, baddest great white shark shows up on your shores over the Fourth of July holiday and threatens not only to eat your citizens, but to destroy the well-being of your entire tourist economy.

Because Quint has lost his first mate recently, a rare chance exists for an outsider to come aboard the *Orca* and audition for a spot as Quint's acolyte. That task falls to Sheriff Martin Brody as agent for the community, and it is Brody who over the course of the novel is slowly inducted into the privileged secret society of shark hunters.

"Lost your mate?" Brody says. "What, overboard?"

"No, he quit. He got nerves. Happens to most people after a while in this work. They get to thinking too much."

So Brody finds himself aboard the *Orca,* trying very hard not to think. He works shoulder to shoulder with Quint and is forced to learn the ropes quickly or risk expulsion—which in practical terms means being pitched overboard into sharky waters.

Though the captain is a reluctant mentor, Brody never stops asking questions, determined to learn as much as he can, as fast as he can. At one point when Brody pushes Quint for a more detailed explanation, Quint brushes off his question with the finality of a master to his dunderheaded apprentice:

"Those are the rules."

After the puny blue shark is brought alongside, Quint gives Brody an instructive demonstration, disemboweling the fish, letting its entrails spill into the water, then cutting the shark loose. In a spasm of instinct, the shark swims beside the boat, slurping up its own guts, and is promptly attacked by a school of smaller sharks.

One lesson after another. One question after another. The first day of the hunt melts into a second, with Quint softening under Brody's respectful curiosity about the tradecraft of fishing. The two men don't exactly bond, but Quint's brusque insults lessen, at least those directed at Brody. However, there is little doubt that Hooper, the wealthy, intellectual marine biologist, is not going to win his membership card in Quint's secret society anytime soon. He lacks the right stuff, the proper obeisance, and the down-home authenticity. His scholarly, book-acquired knowledge entitles him to absolutely nothing in Quint's view. Experience is all that matters, and grinding it out day after day on the blood-soaked decks of the *Orca* is the only schooling that counts.

When the great white shark first explodes into view and opens its mighty jaws an arm's length away, Brody is dumbstruck. While Hooper blathers on about its beauty and gigantic proportions, Quint goes quietly about his business, and

Brody, the fumbling amateur, remains paralyzed with fear. After the shark disappears into the depths, Quint mocks Brody's shocked reaction:

"Gave you a bit of a start."

"More'n a bit," said Brody. He shook his head, as if to reassemble his thoughts and sort out his visions. "I'm still not sure I believe it."

The master prods his apprentice, and the novice admits his ignorance. In the secret society of the *Orca,* this is proper behavior and will be rewarded.

Some secret societies, like the ones we find in *The Da Vinci Code, The Godfather, The Hunt for Red October,* or *The Exorcist,* are so obviously central to their novels' purpose that they don't require a lot of elaboration. Opus Dei, the Mafia, nuclear submariners, and Catholic exorcists each indulge in a hefty dose of hocus-pocus and abracadabras to give an aura of mystery to their activities. Exotic chants, rites, and prayers, a specialized lexicon, rules of authority and hierarchy, incense-drenched ancient ceremonies of worship, and formal acts of obedience all play roles.

Such is the case in the scene at the outset of *The Godfather* when Don Corleone, following traditional custom, opens his inner sanctum to a string of petitioners on the occasion of his daughter's wedding. When one is stepping before the Don, there is a right way to ask for a favor and a wrong way. There is ring kissing and bowing and circumlocutions that require the supplicant to master his part of the script before he recites his request to the Godfather. Flunk the test and you're history.

On board the *Orca* it works the same way, although Quint practices the plain vanilla version of induction ceremonies. There's no mystique to shark fishing, no pomp and circumstance. In fact, he harshly deromanticizes his own profession. Fishing for the largest and most dangerous fish anyone has ever seen is nothing but unpretentious work, on a par with the lowest forms of menial labor.

When Brody asks if the captain considers the fish his personal enemy, Quint scoffs:

"No. No more 'n a plumber who's trying to unstick a drain."

This blue-collar ethos repeats with regularity in bestsellers, as we're seeing. We're all just plumbers, these authors seem to say, just ordinary folks. Storytelling is nothing more or less worthy than clearing sludge from the pipes.

On what will be their final day of sharking, before boarding the *Orca*, Brody asks if Quint has found a replacement for Hooper, who was killed by the shark the day before. Quint's solemn response has the tone of a sacred confirmation:

"You know this fish as well as any man, and more hands won't make no difference now. Besides, it's nobody else's business. . . ."

Permission to come aboard is granted, and as Brody steps onto the *Orca*'s deck for the final fateful voyage, the local chapter of world-class shark hunters has increased its membership by one. In fact, Brody learns his lessons so well that it is he, not Quint, who survives the ordeal of the great white.

Quint makes a fatal error and steps inside a coil of rope lying on the deck, the other end of which is attached to the shark. Overboard he goes. The sheriff, who has dutifully paid his dues, lunges to save his mentor, but Quint is "pulled slowly down into the dark water" like a modern Ahab. Brody, in Ishmael's role, can only watch in horror, then start his slow journey back to shore. You can almost hear the echo of Ishmael's famous last line: "And I only am escaped alone to tell thee."

BEDROOM SECRETS

In *The Bridges of Madison County*, Kincaid and Francesca form an adulterous secret society that stays hidden until both of them have passed away. The frame story that has Francesca Johnson's children, Michael and Carolyn, discovering their mother's notebooks after her death seems a trifle less clumsy when you consider it as the planned dissolution of a secret society—a time capsule meant to give Francesca's children a glimpse into the private world their mother once experienced.

The two lovers took a vow of silence that was meant to protect the living, yet Francesca felt the need to pass the knowledge of her romantic swoon to her children, presumably hoping they would be inspired by her dalliance—inspired to recast their memory of Francesca as a noble soul who sacrificed her one true love to return to the duties of motherhood.

Taking the measure of what lessons the grown-up children absorbed is hard to do, since the novel ends with them just beginning to grasp the revelation. But clearly it's not infidelity but faithfulness that's at the heart of *Bridges*. A secret society of two made a painful pact and for decades devotedly maintained their pledge, an act of mutual self-sacrifice in which both parties abandoned the love of their lives so an ordinary American family could be preserved.

Sappy, perhaps, but for me and a few million others who consumed this sugary confection, there's something quaintly poignant and even a little complicated about the secret society Francesca and Robert formed.

For one thing, it took a huge dose of old-fashioned will-power and self-discipline to make that decision, then to keep their love affair concealed and spend their remaining years in a state of emotional frugality, without ever abandoning their rapturous memories.

Then there's Francesca's decision to let her children in on the secret, an act that seems to be her way of releasing them from the lie that was her life and her marriage. This final act of revealing leaves us with a riddle that gives the novel a smoky aftertaste. Did Francesca and Robert do the right thing by giving up their love? Or did they deny themselves a greater joy, bullied into accepting the mundane and empty obligations of a conventional life? Was their sacrifice an emotional tragedy or a triumph?

In an age brimming with irony, the earnestness these two characters demonstrate can seem sentimental, but to fully appreciate these bestsellers a reader must accept that subtlety, intricacy, and ambiguity are not often the ingredients of popular novels. For the most part, these novels are thoroughly sincere and heartfelt. There's no attempt to cast furtive signals to the reader, no evidence the language is trying to say anything more than exactly what it says. It is that simplicity of tone, that artlessness, that wins the hearts of so many readers, and it does so for the very reason that it is not exclusive. There is no attempt in the style or the storytelling method to favor readers in the know over normal folks. Anyone and everyone is freely admitted and on equal footing. No segregation allowed. No secret handshakes permitted.

PENETRATING THE CLAN

For so small a town as Maycomb, Alabama (the setting of *To Kill a Mockingbird*), there are a surprising number of secret societies flourishing in its midst. When Dill and Jem and Scout get mobbed up, creating their own summertime drama club, the rules are clear—anyone lacking an imagination and a taste for danger and a willingness to test authority need not apply. Nor should any adults even consider membership. These kids are picky. They target the stiff and phony neighbors as objects of their derision and reenact lampoons of everyone up and down the street.

Little by little, with Atticus's help, the kids learn a modicum of respect for some of the grown-ups who are the objects of their parodies, and each time another lesson is absorbed, the secret society must slightly alter its rules of engagement. The one person who stays within their sights, however, is Boo Radley, the mysterious recluse ostracized by the community and transformed into a bogeyman by the children.

Although he's the focus of their heckling, Boo isn't daunted but works in the shadows to win favor the same way Brody earned his place aboard the *Orca,* by keeping his distance while he observed the society's rules and behaviors, adjusting his own actions accordingly. Or the way that Mitch McDeere worked his ass off to qualify for a spot at the holiest of holies conference table.

"You reckon he's crazy?" Scout asks the trustworthy Miss Maudie about Boo.

Miss Maudie shook her head. "If he's not he should

be by now. The things that happen to people we never really know. What happens in houses behind closed doors, what secrets—"

It is the nature of secrecy, Miss Maudie seems to say, the nature of insulated systems, to stunt those who are imprisoned within them. The Radley household has isolated itself and become some kind of terrible echo chamber, and whatever was wrong with Boo before has probably metastasized into something far worse after all these years of being shut in.

Boo studies the children's comings and goings with the same focus Sheriff Brody employs on Quint. He places sly offerings in the hollow of a tree. He repairs Jem's torn and mislaid trousers and surreptitiously returns them to the youngster. Staying out of sight, he courts the children while observing from a safe distance the workings of their closed circle.

For Boo knows very well what everyone in Maycomb knows, that mixing one clan with another, one race with another, even one brand of Christianity with another, is forbidden. Secret societies abound in this small town. Everyone is segregated from everyone else, by race, by gender, by religious practice, by family lineage, and by narrow definitions of class. Scout is astonished when Atticus describes the trashiest family in town as having a snobbish aspect. "He said that the Ewells were a member of an exclusive society made up of Ewells."

Add to the list those missionary ladies who meet in the Finches' front parlor. Those good ladies are as exclusive and rigid in their costumes and ceremonial customs as the Mrunas, the African tribes these silly old women fantasize about saving. But it's not just the good Christian white ladies who are exclusionary. Many in the black congregation of the First

Purchase African M.E. Church murmur uneasily when Scout sits in their midst. "I wants to know why you bringin' white chillun to nigger church," one of them wants to know. Their society has its regulations as well.

Groups like Opus Dei or its elite squads of killers, or the New York Mob, all employ a highly organized structure. Like the partners of Bendini, Lambert & Locke, they are a caricature of a tight-knit family, a family that operates under strict guidelines. For one thing, in Don Corleone's secret society, as in Bendini, Lambert's, you do not resign your membership without risking death. Those who have tried to bail have not been heard from since.

The secret societies operating within *To Kill a Mockingbird* are as treacherous as those in *The Godfather* and *The Firm*. Though it would seem on first look that the ground rules for the play group that Scout, Jem, and Dill are members of are relaxed and easygoing. After all, Dill is readily admitted into their club when he proves himself to be at least as imaginative and devoted to playacting and daredevil stunts as they are. These are kids just being kids, right?

Not really. For their merciless targeting and demonizing of Boo Radley uncomfortably echoes the lynch mob that puts Tom Robinson in its lethal sights. Sure, they're kids, but this threesome is also a closed system that feeds on suspicion, prejudice, and fearmongering. They have copied—innocently, of course—the group dynamics of the KKK.

As the story concludes, Boo is close by when Scout and Jem are attacked on their way home from a school play. In a protective fury, Boo Radley murders their attacker, and this act of violence turns out to be the price of admission into the Finches' world.

Once Boo is on equal footing with the Finch children, their

clique disbands. Just as Bendini, Lambert & Locke cannot absorb one truly honest man like Mitch McDeere and just as Robert Langdon single-handedly penetrates and dissolves the centuries-old, murderous wing of Opus Dei, Boo Radley brings an end to the Finch kids' gang of three.

In an event that would have seemed unthinkable a few chapters earlier, Boo is welcomed into the inner sanctum of the Finches' home. At the end of that traumatic evening, with Jem laid out from his injuries, Boo is escorted home by Scout. Carefully protected perimeters are broken, secrets are revealed, and there is even a physical touch between Boo and Scout.

Standing on Boo Radley's front porch and seeing the world from his vantage point, Scout grasps how their summer threesome was organized around an exclusionary principle. They've persecuted this guy, ganged up on him in a childish reenactment of the lynch mob coming to string up Tom Robinson. It is the moral of the story. A simplistic one, that's true, but a message with profound resonance. Walk in another man's shoes, Atticus says. Empathize. "You never really understand a person until you consider things from his point of view."

Whether it's the KKK, the Ewell clan or the Cunninghams, the First Purchase Church, the missionary ladies, or Jem, Scout, and Dill acting out childish games, secret societies, no matter how harmless they may appear, can be training camps for intolerance and bigotry and thus inimical to a fair and open society.

The novel stands forcefully against the destructive nature of secret groups, while demonstrating how they can be altered by the least among us, by children whose sense of equality is our hope for social progress. Among other things, it is this dreamy, hazy, hopeful stew of idealism and wishful thinking, leavened with just enough hard-edged skepticism, that helped make *To Kill a Mockingbird* a much-loved and perennial bestseller.

CONSPIRACY OF SECRETS

What *The Hunt for Red October* is to submarines, *The Da Vinci Code* is to secret societies. The Priory of Sion, Opus Dei, Freemasons, Knights of Templar . . . oh, the list is long. The novel is bubbling over with highly secretive brotherhoods that have been around for centuries, working behind the scenes to rig world affairs. Turns out they are even engaged in an ongoing battle with other secret societies and occasional lone crusaders like Robert Langdon whose goal is to rip aside the veil that conceals their nefarious deeds.

The Da Vinci Code takes its place at the head of a long list of popular novels that capitalize on the widespread suspicion that deceitful and universal powers are conspiring against them, a list that includes such diverse works as Ayn Rand's *The Fountainhead* and *Atlas Shrugged* to *Dr. Strangelove* and Umberto Eco's *Foucault's Pendulum*.

Using a favorite target of conspiracy novels of the past, *The Da Vinci Code* marches deep into a minefield of politically incorrect and highly charged views about Roman Catholics. Though the folks who run Opus Dei's website would have you believe that they are a "Catholic institution founded by Saint Josemaría Escrivá . . . [whose mission] is to spread the message that work and circumstances of everyday life are occasions for growing closer to God, for serving others, and for improving society," Dan Brown paints a starkly different fictional portrait.

Employing what sound like facts copied and pasted from newspaper accounts, in one short paragraph alone he associates Opus Dei with doping its new members so they will believe they've experienced religious ecstasy, then describes another new recruit who gives himself an almost fatal infection by beating himself with his *cilice* belt, and then provides a third example of the depravity of the organization, which conned the life savings from a young man, a scam that drove him to attempt suicide.

Suddenly Corleone's Mob seems warm and cuddly in comparison.

Every inch of forward movement in the plot of *The Da Vinci Code* is propelled by one attempt after another to expose one shadowy secret society after the next. To break the code, to solve the puzzle, to penetrate the layers of high-tech security of the Depository Bank of Zurich, to use the key that fits the lock to open the safe that hides some titillating secret, to locate the keystone that explains the sign of the Rose, to interpret the "flash card catechism" of the Tarot, to follow the labyrinthine trail of clues to the wooden box that holds the . . .

Oh well, it's easy to see the narrative structure. A series of Chinese boxes. Open one, there's another; open that one, it sends you running for your life in a new direction, chasing one permutation after another of the greatest secret of all time, forever pursued by an albino monk who is determined to keep the secrets hidden. This single device drives the story forward at breakneck speed and is the source of nearly every thrill and chill, all of it driven by a single dramatic goal: to expose the secret, the awesome fact that "the Holy Grail is Mary Magdalene . . . the mother of the royal bloodline of Jesus Christ."

Apparently there must be a bit of the conspiracy theorist in all of us, or at least in the eighty million readers of *The Da Vinci Code*. To some critics of the novel, this plot device grows quickly tiresome, a kind of one-trick narrative pony in which paranoia has run amok. After a few hundred pages of this, they argue, we could easily find ourselves questioning the Girl Scouts and the Brownies and all those other institutions we so foolishly thought we could trust. They're all devious and sinister, no doubt playing some part in the grand cabal that has infiltrated every corner of Western art and culture.

Though in the end Langdon's efforts manage to save his own skin and Sophie's, we discover that the Holy Grail is more slippery than Robert led us to believe. Marie Chauvel, a minor character who appears near the end of the novel, puts it bluntly. Robert Langdon's quest has been little more than an elaborate wild-goose chase: "The Holy Grail is simply a grand idea . . . a glorious unattainable treasure that somehow, even in today's world of chaos, inspires us."

Well, okay, so the Holy Grail was not a golden chalice or some other fabulous artifact but merely an abstraction. Still, few would deny this was a pulse-quickening ride. A little like the roller coaster: Once you're done, your stomach is hinky, your hair is mussed, but otherwise you're back exactly where you began—in a world where elaborate confederacies continue their knavish skullduggery. A world where our last best hope rests on the broad shoulders of a dauntless interpreter of symbols, the ultimate defender of the proletariat, a man who has made it his mission to penetrate and expose secret societies.

SMOKE-FILLED ROOMS

American readers are drawn to novels that expose the inner workings of secret societies for a simple reason. They want to comprehend the silent forces that shape their destinies, to have a few "privileged glimpses" into the hidden boiler rooms that power our world. Furthermore, as a resolutely democratic people, we have a natural suspicion of institutions, public or private, that might in some way undermine our personal liberties. We're distrustful of organizations that lack transparency, that perform their rituals behind closed doors.

On a regular basis, bestsellers like these enforce our rights under the Freedom of Information Act—they kick open the door to the smoke-filled room and expose the scheming rascals and neutralize their power. Those novels that allow all comers access into exclusive and esoteric worlds get extra credit in the popular culture. Even more credit is given to those books like the ones on our list, which portray the triumph of a righteous individual over the often dehumanizing prejudices of a secret group.

FEATURE #7

Bumpkins Versus Slickers

Whither goest thou, America, in thy shiny car in the night?
—JACK KEROUAC,
ON THE ROAD

In most bestsellers, there's a central character who sets off on a journey that takes her from rustic America into turbulent urban landscapes, where her agrarian values either help her succeed or doom her to failure. Almost as often, the heroes of bestsellers make an exodus in the opposite direction, from the pressures of cities to the bucolic countryside.

Journeys of this type have mythic echoes as old as the *Epic of Gilgamesh* (one of the earliest-known narrative tales), a story in which the hero left the safety of the walled city to trek off to the edges of the world. This narrative structure, the hero's journey, as it is sometimes called, was the basis of Joseph Campbell's landmark work *The Hero with a Thousand*

Faces. In our contemporary era, the same structural under-pinnings are at work in popular films from *Star Wars* to *The Wizard of Oz,* as Christopher Vogler so thoroughly describes in his practical guide for aspiring Hollywood screen writers, *The Writer's Journey.*

A character is called to adventure. After initially refusing the call, he is galvanized into action by some event and leaves the safety of his ordinary world, crossing the threshold into a foreign land. Relying on mentors, some of them with supernatural abilities, and tested by various enemies, he eventually reaches a perilous place that Vogler calls "the inmost cave." There he faces some terrible ordeal but is finally able to summon sufficient inner resources to conquer his adversary. Afterward he begins the long trek back, which usually involves confronting a second ordeal before he can return home with the grail he has wrested from his antagonist. Think Dorothy, her three mentoring friends, the Wicked Witch's dreadful prison cell, and those magical red shoes.

That same mythic paradigm forms the bone structure underlying most popular fiction. Master storytellers have mastered its elements, either consciously or instinctively, and have found ways to create fresh permutations of an old, old story.

The journey motifs we find in the bestselling novels under review here have strikingly similar plot elements, but in particular they share a common tendency to send their traveling heroes back and forth between the countryside and the city. A rube goes to Manhattan, or a city slicker finds himself on the farm. These "fish out of water" story lines recur in every book on our list.

FISH OUT OF WATER

Once the Civil War begins, Scarlett is forever out of her element, relying on her quick wits and nimble values and sex appeal to make constant adjustments to each new environment. Each of the other protagonists is equally dislocated. Sheriff Brody, who hates the water, must go far out into it. Same with Jack Ryan, the naval historian, who must take a chopper ride out to sea to hop aboard a submarine, growing more seasick all the way. John Smith wakes from his coma to find he's missed his youth and is having one long out-of-body experience, a man who will be forever alienated from even the most conventional reality. Then there is Michael Corleone, comfortably at peace in the sunny clover of Sicily but exiled back to the gritty city streets of New York.

Each of these novels in some way explores the clash between city values and rural ones. Characters journey from teeming urban landscapes to the peaceful countryside, or vice versa, in what might be described as a restless yearning to find their true American home.

COUNTRY GIRLS IN THE CITY

We see this migratory pattern enacted in *Peyton Place* when Allison sets off from her provincial New England home to take on the challenges of New York just as her mother, Constance, did before her. Constance Standish, not exactly a feminist, had very clear goals for her long-ago journey.

Because she was beautiful and stubborn and full of pride, at nineteen she decided to ditch the confines of Peyton Place, and against her mother's loud protests she headed off to the Big Apple to find a job and marry a rich man. In no time she went to work for a gentleman named Allison MacKenzie, who was good-looking and ran a very successful fabric store. In less than a month they were sleeping together. Badda bing, badda boom.

But when Constance learns that her lover, Allison, is a two-timer who is married and has two children living upstate, she flees back home to Peyton Place, pregnant with a daughter whom she names after the man who deceived her (for reasons that defy explanation).

Published ten years later, *Valley of the Dolls* records a strikingly similar journey for Anne Wells, who rejects a stifling existence in Lawrenceville, Massachusetts, and sets off in search of love and success (that is, a husband) in that hotbed of deceit and double-dealing, New York City—the same den of iniquity that treated Constance Standish so cruelly.

In an early episode, Anne Wells declares her independence from small-town life with the same fervor a "Go west, young man" might have used a century earlier when departing the suffocating eastern seaboard to set off for unexplored territories.

She escapes the orderly life her mother and her mother's mother had embraced. She dumps her fiancé, a solid boy she doesn't love, and she absolutely refuses to live in the family's New England home that was passed down for generations. Most of all, she says no to the smothering conventions of good behavior as they are defined by the small-town arbiters of propriety and decorum. She wants to be free, damn it.

CITY BOYS IN THE COUNTRY

Mitch McDeere makes the other half of this journey in *The Firm* when he rejects job offers from law firms in various American urban centers and abandons the highly competitive universe of Boston, which he has conquered handily, so he can test himself against the perils of the relatively slow-paced southern town of Memphis. Mitch has already completed the first half of this yin and yang cycle by departing from his rural roots to head off to Boston in the first place. If he hadn't worked hard and won his way to Harvard, who knows what would have become of him? He might have wound up in prison like his brother or working in the Waffle House in Panama City Beach like his mother.

The conflict between urban and rural American values informs *The Bridges of Madison County* as well when the man-of-the-world, Yeats-quoting Robert Kincaid shows up in the provincial backcountry of rural Iowa. The luster of his urban ennui is part of what makes him seem so glamorous to the isolated and vulnerable farmer's wife he romances.

Francesca is susceptible to his charms in some measure because she was once somewhat worldly herself, a free spirit with lofty expectations when she set off on that youthful journey from her birthplace in Naples, Italy, to join Richard Johnson on his farm in Iowa.

For Francesca, the sweet promise of America turns into the aching dullness of Iowa. So when worldly Robert Kincaid sweeps into town while her dreary husband is off at the state fair, Francesca is primed and ready to lower her moral guard.

But Robert Kincaid is no simple city slicker. He's way

slicker than that. He's so damn sophisticated and worldly wise, poor Francesca doesn't have a prayer.

Here was a guy who exited military service in 1945 and put his job with *National Geographic* on hold while he went tooling down the coast of California on his motorcycle, running it to Big Sur, where he made love on a beach with a musician from Carmel. Hitting all the hippie stations of the cross.

By the age of fifty-two, our boy has done a couple of tours around the world and visited all the exotic places whose photos he'd once hung on his boyhood walls. The Raffles Bar in Singapore, a riverboat trip up the Amazon, and a camel ride in the desert of Rajasthan.

Robert Kincaid's rootlessness is a manifestation of a familiar type, the peripatetic American. As we are often reminded, our westward-ho pioneer ancestors were the sons and daughters of the hardy souls who braved the Atlantic to find a new home. It's as though we've been bioengineering our culture for the last three centuries, selecting for a wandering gene.

But for every incurable rover, there seems to be another American who decided, by golly, he'd had enough rambling and unsaddled his team of oxen and staked his claim to a piece of soil and just stayed put. The clash between these two prototypes is a recurring theme in our popular fiction as well as a favorite topic in nonfiction examinations of American culture.

In the 1970s, an era of mass migration to the suburbs and job relocations and general social waywardness, Vance Packard's *A Nation of Strangers* became a nonfiction bestseller by warning that the growing American rootlessness was resulting in "a society coming apart at the seams." The anomie that Packard described, of disintegrating communities and a growing sense of personal anonymity, is part of the backdrop against which Robert and Francesca play out their fairy-tale romance.

After the two lovers have shared a final kiss and said their good-byes, they bump into each other again one last time, where else but on the road. Francesca's husband is back from his trip, and he's driving Francesca from the isolated farm into town, and who should randomly appear in his pickup truck but wandering Robert. For a moment as they wait in traffic, separated by only thirty feet, Francesca imagines throwing open the door and running to Robert's truck and driving away with him. But no, she stays put, "frozen by her responsibilities."

And so Robert James Waller has given us one of our favorite cakes and let us eat it, too. We've vicariously enjoyed a hot and heavy fling between a wandering man and a housebound wife, then we've been purified of any guilt by Francesca's virtuous self-denial.

THE FALSE LABELS WE BELIEVE IN

At times, we Americans glamorize city life and demonize the heartland. But when it suits our purposes, we're happy to flip those labels to the complete opposite. There seems to be no middle way for us.

During every national election cycle, the heartland takes on a familiar mythic identity in the media. The clichés and stereotypes begin to roll out with a predictable drumbeat: Rural America is suddenly populated with "hardworking," "blue-collar," "real" people who value decency and honesty and "kitchen table" issues a whole lot more than city dwellers do, especially those urbanites living near the coasts, who are derided as self-involved elitists out of touch with mainstream values. City life is hopelessly fast-paced and materialistic and shallow, a frenetic, never-ending worship of Mammon, while country living is unhurried and more in touch with the godly virtues of neighborliness and generosity and family devotion, a wide-open space where firearms are proudly hung above the mantel and Old Glory waves in every yard.

Red state vs. blue state. Working-class vs. corporate elite. Virtuous vs. decadent. The Bible-trusting ordinary folks who still believe in the pioneer spirit and refuse to be tamed or corrupted by all those godless messages being broadcast from within the corrupt citadels of metropolitan culture.

In *The American Myth of Success*, Richard Weiss gives Horatio Alger a good deal of credit for popularizing these stereotypical views:

> Alger's settings are most often in the New York of the latter half of the nineteenth century, and his accurate descriptions of its streets, hotels, boarding houses, and restaurants made his books valuable as guides to those unfamiliar with the city. But his attitude toward the city he described so well was one of hostility. While the city was a place of opportunity, it also was a place of unspeakable corruption and moral turpitude. Virtue resided in the country. If the country boy could survive the city swindlers ready to prey on his innocence, his chances of success were greater than those of his city-bred peers. This was because he was usually stronger morally and had "been brought up to work, and work more earnestly than city boys." Country boys might come to the city to gain wealth, but city boys could well go to the country for moral regeneration.

While we all know these labels are bogus, they are so ingrained in our sense of national identity that we reflexively embrace them even as we discount their accuracy. This ambivalence toward rural and city values recurs in American bestsellers with such frequency, it's clear that vast numbers of readers are also fascinated by these competing views of national identity.

ALL OVER THE MAP

Despite all its apparent dangers and vices, again and again urban life is portrayed as the mythic proving ground for popular fiction characters, a place that challenges the likes of Anne Welles and Allison MacKenzie and Mitch McDeere and Scarlett O'Hara. Some survive, some flourish, some (like Atticus Finch) are enlightened by the experience and take that enlightenment home to the country.

When you add it up, our bestseller writers are all over the map when it comes to their use of urban or rural settings. Here's the rundown:

Gone with the Wind splits its time equally between Atlanta and Tara. While *Peyton Place* gives us short and crucial glimpses of life in Manhattan, the great percentage of the novel takes place in the semirural town of the title. *To Kill a Mockingbird* takes us on a long wallow in backwater America, with only a brief reference or two to the great cities that lie beyond its limits, while *Valley of the Dolls* takes us on a roller-coaster thrill ride through the exhilarating uppers and dismal downers of metropolitan life.

Except for Michael Corleone's jaunt to the countryside of the old country, most of *The Godfather* focuses on survival skills on the main stage of New York. Although Las Vegas and Los Angeles do have short walk-ons in the spotlight, there is no doubt where the lifeblood of those western cities originates: back east.

Our nation's capital, the home of American military power, is fittingly the backdrop for two of the war novels. Jack Ryan arrives in D.C. on the red-eye from London and works his military magic out of an office right down the street from where two priests are battling Satan for a young girl's soul.

In *Jaws*, the carefree island of Amity is only a half day's drive from the avenues of Manhattan, so it becomes a tranquil getaway for harried city people—at least until that damn shark shows up.

John Smith embraces the very New England small-town life that Allison MacKenzie and Anne Welles have so heartily rejected. Mitch McDeere leaves the relative safety of Boston to take his chances in the Deep South.

Robert Kincaid and Francesca Johnson are our only characters with their hearts and souls rooted firmly in the American West, though neither of them is completely at home in those wide-open spaces. Our other Robert, Professor Langdon, jets from Boston to Paris to London, an itinerary that qualifies him as an überurbanite.

SCARLETT'S TWO ROUND-TRIP JOURNEYS

Not to be outdone, Scarlett makes the round-trip journey from country to city not once but twice. The first time she journeys from Tara to Atlanta it is her mother's idea, a way to distract the poor child from the loss of her goofball first husband, Charles.

And, exactly as her mother had expected, Scarlett is energized and converted to a city girl. Crowded Atlanta exhilarates her far more than the isolated plantation of Tara, no matter how dear Tara is to her. There's a hum of excitement in the city that even Charleston with its gardens hidden by high walls is lacking. Scarlett is pumped and becomes a whirlwind of restless energy.

If virtue resided in the country, as Horatio Alger believed, you couldn't convince the highborn women of Atlanta of that, for by their lights, Scarlett O'Hara's country ways are about as unvirtuous as they come. Indeed, her wayward nature seems to have more effect on Atlanta than Atlanta has on her.

She's not about to be bullied into upholding the fussy rules of a bunch of citified old maids. She'll dance with whom she pleases even if she is a freshly minted widow. Like Scarlett's later incarnations, Allison MacKenzie and Anne Welles, the heroines of *Peyton Place* and *Valley of the Dolls*, Scarlett may be a small-town girl, but she has big-city ambitions and is not the least bit shy about fighting or flirting or flailing for what and whom she wants.

During the siege of Atlanta, Scarlett's courage eventually fails her. She decides she needs a shot of renewal and makes a desperate run back to the safety of Tara. But war has turned the world upside down, and now the countryside is not the regenerating paradise it once was. It's full of gruesome hardships and challenges beyond anything she's known. Back at home, Scarlett digs into the fertile soil of Tara, determined to revive the old ways of plantation life that originally made her who she is. A country girl first and foremost, a city girl as a last resort.

City-born scalawags and carpetbaggers are determined to uproot her, levying taxes on Tara that make staying there impossible unless she can deliver an exorbitant sum to these folks from the urban North. So it's back to Atlanta a second time, only now her mission is not consolation, as it was on that original trip. This time Scarlett is intent on marrying any man she can find who can pay her property taxes and allow her to reclaim Tara.

Again, the paradigm holds, for this most American of American heroines will brave the perils of city life only long enough to acquire the cash and the husband(s) that eventually allow her to return to her rightful place, the heartland.

For a novel that portrays the Civil War as a clash between the values of urban and agrarian cultures, it is fitting that Scarlett's personal battle would mirror these very elements.

SUMMER AT THE SHORE

In *Jaws* they are known as "summer folk" and "winter folk," but if you substituted the adjectives *city* and *country,* you wouldn't be far off. When the city people begin their annual migration to the tip of Long Island every summer, Ellen Brody, the sheriff's youngish wife, finds herself remembering the sophisticated city life she's abandoned to live out on the island in cultural deprivation. Her father was an adman whose agency had transferred the family from Los Angeles to New York, so Ellen had her urbanity passport stamped twice before she trudged off to Mayberry. After marrying Brody and moving to small-town Amity, she tries a few times to reconnect with her city friends, without success.

Ellen talked gaily about the community, about local politics, about her job as a volunteer at the Southampton Hospital—all subjects about which her old friends, many of whom had been coming to Amity every summer for more than thirty years, knew little and cared less. They talked about New York politics, about art galleries and painters and writers they knew.

Like it or not, Amity is economically dependent on the annual influx of New Yorkers. As Scarlett so well knows, when you're desperate for money, you either pack up your ball gowns and eye shadow, take a fortifying breath, and head for the city, or you find a way to lure the free-spending city folks to you. Money is in the city. Values are in the country.

That's how Amity works. Every June the summer people trickle back, drawn by the beach, the warm waves sloshing on the shore, boozy days in the sun. This is a town that goes to great lengths to stifle any news reflecting poorly on the community. If there are rapes, you won't read about them in the local paper. Though the vandalism of summer houses by winter teenagers is on the rise, the newspaper is loath to report on it.

Winter people depend so desperately on their summer cousins showing up and spending freely that Brody is overruled in his attempt to close the beaches after the first attack. The mayor and the board of selectmen will have none of it. One shark-eaten skinny-dipper more or less is not enough reason to sacrifice the local economy.

But when the great white shark returns for a second course and gulps down a local boy, Brody, full of guilt, shuts the beach and lets the whole world know there's trouble right here in Amity.

Some of the summer people flee. The spineless ones. To make matters worse, as word of the shark attacks spreads, the regular summer folks are replaced by a ghoulish lot, a lower class of city dweller, tightfisted types who tow campers behind their cars. These are tabloid readers making the long journey out to the country in search of a cheap thrill.

Sheriff Brody encounters such a family from Queens, who are deeply disappointed that the shark attack they just witnessed wasn't fatal and the fins of the shark were so unimpressively small. The father of this trashy tribe sneers contemptuously and suggests to the sheriff that this whole shark attack thing has been some kind of publicity hoax meant to draw people like him to Amity under false pretenses.

Brody explodes and calls the guy a jerk, then orders him to leave.

In a parting shot that underscores the cultural clash at work in this confrontation, the sleazy gawker calls Brody an uppity "snot-nose."

It is a favorite dictum of writing teachers that stories are often set in motion when a stranger arrives in town, throwing all the well-regulated routines out of whack. Well, the great white shark of *Jaws* certainly qualifies as that stranger. But in this novel there's a second outsider as predatory as the shark. Matt Hooper is his name—an expert on sharky things summoned from his lab at Woods Hole to provide expertise.

It just so happens that he hails originally from the same city as Ellen. He went to Yale, then after grad school he chased sharks around the globe. By golly, that sounds a lot like Rhett Butler, or Robert Kincaid, or even Robert Langdon, that famous Harvard symbologist. Dashing, a bit of a dandy, and just a little dastardly. A cosmopolitan, globalized kind of guy who's at home anywhere. Quick, lock up your women.

He swims past Ellen Brody's defenses and gulps her down

in a single swallow. They have a romantic lunch, followed by a motel room tumble. Though their romance tails away into narrative inconsequence by novel's end, and never flickers to life at all in the film version, Hooper's conquest of the sheriff's wife is in its own way as damaging as the great white shark.

But Ellen is not going to follow the city man back to the metropolis. She realizes her mistake and rationalizes that she was "driven to it by boredom, like so many of the women who spent their weeks in Amity while their husbands were in New York." Though Ellen has tried to adapt to the rural ways of Amity, the long shadows of the city still have a corrupting influence.

TIRED OLD TOWN

Although the action in *To Kill a Mockingbird* is confined to small-town life, the sophistication and broad-minded values of the urban world play a crucial role in the outcome of the story.

We are informed at the outset that Atticus has broken with Finch tradition by not staying at Finch's Landing, the family homestead, and making his living by raising and selling cotton. Finch's Landing was a humble farm compared with the ostentatious plantations around it. It would be a self-sustaining life, with all the luxuries like ice and store-bought clothes supplied by boats from the big cities upriver.

Before settling in that "tired old town" of Maycomb, Atticus studied law in the state capital of Montgomery. In a state where rural folks outnumbered the urban population by nearly three to one, choosing to abandon the familiar comforts of country existence for city life even for a short duration was a bold act.

Had Atticus abided by family tradition and assumed his duties as plantation master, the world would have lost an eloquent defender of the poor and unjustly accused. We can't be sure, of course, but it's likely that Atticus's sense of justice was broadened by his exposure to the more broad-minded views in Montgomery, which would mean that his strength to resist the racist tsunami in Maycomb was in a pivotal way dependent on his urban education.

RURAL REGENERATION

There's not much farmland or countryside or rural landscape described in *The Exorcist*. The novel takes place in Washington, D.C., and though the cityscape itself is not a major player in this novel of satanic possession, at a key moment when Father Lankester Merrin is summoned to join Father Karras in a final showdown with the devil who has inhabited the body of Regan MacNeil, Merrin is relaxing in a monastery in the countryside. He's out walking in the woods he loves, listening to a robin's song, watching a butterfly flitter onto a branch, when he receives the fateful telegram.

His journey from this pastoral setting to America's capital city will end in a victory over the devil, though Merrin's life will be lost in that effort. Although it would be a mistake to overstress the thematic role that rural versus city plays in *The Exorcist,* it's worth noting that in the final showdown between good and evil, it requires the combined efforts of a priest from the country and a priest from the city to purge Satan from this child.

RURAL EVIL

Robert Langdon in *The Da Vinci Code* casts his vote solidly for city values, in part because country people just can't be trusted. As he explains to Sophie, the very term *pagan* has its roots in the Latin *paganus,* a word that meant "country dwellers." The church was so threatened by rural folks that gradually, by the magic of etymology, "villagers" became "villains," and the very language turned against those wicked agrarian types who place nature before the church.

So by the lights of *The Da Vinci Code,* the word *rural* carries with it the dark fairy dust of its evil history. No way around it. Country people are suspicious, possibly dangerous, ergo city people are our only hope.

Indeed, *The Da Vinci Code* spends nearly all of its story-telling energies describing cities, rhapsodizing about the architecture and the cathedrals and the gritty backstreets and the hidden treasures thereof.

The longest visit Langdon makes to the countryside is his extended stopover in the "castle district," where Leigh Teabing's estate is located. Langdon and Sophie are on the run from some serious tribulations in the city, and Robert thinks Teabing's place will be an "ideal safe harbor." This guy Langdon might be a great symbologist, but hey, come on, he's not the shrewdest judge of character. For Teabing will turn out to be the novel's premier villain.

In one of literally hundreds of similar sweeping proclamations, Langdon reassures Sophie that Teabing "knows more about the Priory of Sion and the Holy Grail than anyone on earth," and he whisks her off into the pagan villages of the countryside.

Like everything in *The Da Vinci Code,* Teabing's crib is humongous. Like a replica of Versailles. And as the couple in peril arrive at this "modest castle," Sophie experiences the quiet calm of the countryside affecting her central nervous system in the same way that Tara always affected Scarlett. She feels her muscles relaxing and a swell of relief to be away from the city.

In the course of the evening spent in Teabing's remote country place, Sophie and Robert are treated to a lecture on the Holy Grail and its connection to the painting of the Last Supper and Mary Magdalene's surprisingly intimate role in Jesus's private life—that Mary carried the blood of Jesus Christ.

Sophie barely has time to absorb the implications of Teabing's revelations when pistols begin to appear.

With gunfire blapping behind them, Teabing, Sophie, and Robert Langdon flee their rural sanctuary with Silas, the evil albino monk, tied up in their backseat. Safe in their Range Rover, they plow through the forest branches until they are back to a highway, a short hop from civilization. Clearly Robert should have taken his etymology of the word *rural* more seriously and been a trifle more vigilant around those wicked country folks.

THE NORTHEASTERN CORRIDOR

If these twelve novels were all we had to go on, it would seem that the few American bestsellers not set in the Washington–

Boston–New York corridor will be set in the Deep South. A megabestseller set in the American West is rare, and one set entirely in Europe is a downright aberration.

This seems to suggest that the large population centers of the Northeast have greater appeal to the book buyer's imagination than those of the West. Such a geographic tilt might also reveal a partiality that reflects in some measure the demographics of publishing interests and book buying itself. The literary agents who filter books, the editors who select them, and the publishers who promote and distribute them are based mostly in the populous northeastern corridor. That they would give preference to books set in the world they're most familiar with is not surprising. And from this sampling of twelve gigantic bestsellers, it would also seem that a great many Americans, no matter in what far-flung provinces they reside, are fascinated by the mighty hum of the city.

A quick look at the electoral map of any recent election will help complete the political dimension of this thematic tension. City folks tend to vote in one direction while rural folks vote in the other. The rift is there and has been from the first days of our nation. Healing the political estrangement between the farmer and the office worker is certainly not in the job description of popular fiction writers, but it's clear that in these twelve bestsellers the tremors along the fault lines between one America and the other America resonate at the core of each story.

IMMIGRANTS AND PIONEERS

For all its political and financial power, the city world is still lacking half of what America requires for its complete entertainment. We are a nation that has made such a habit of glorifying our westward expansion and those forebears who trekked into the wilderness to escape the civilizing pressures of the eastern cities that one of our highest national accolades is to call someone a "pioneer."

With nearly equal pride, we honor our immigrant past. All those travelers arriving at Plymouth Rock or Ellis Island have shaped America's psyche and its mythology and its metaphors.

It's no surprise that American novelists have tapped again and again into this core of national identity. What might surprise some, however, is how often and how boldly bestsellers defy conventional expectations in this regard.

Popular art is often thought of as the social glue that holds society together, focused on reinforcing the presumed values of the reader. But when you look at the way these twelve novelists dealt with one of America's most enduring tensions—the conflict between urban and agrarian values—the exact opposite is the case. Collectively, the books argue both sides of the issue and every position in between. Scarlett challenges head-on the stuffy repression of city values, while the young protofeminists in *Peyton Place* and *Valley of the Dolls* are thrilled to bask in the metropolitan way of life, though as any reader can see, the corrosive effects of city living play a major role in causing their personal tragedies. In Dan Brown's world, the cityscapes of Paris and London are rich depositories of culture and art, while the rural side, sad to say, is wicked and villainous.

Of all the books, *The Da Vinci Code* is distinctive in being set entirely outside the borders of the United States. How fitting that in this world-is-flat era, Robert Langdon emerges as a new globe-trotting version of the American pioneer, marching into a wilderness of universal symbols as dense and danger filled as any old-growth forest.

FEATURE #8

God Is Great, or Is He?

Man is a Religious Animal. He is the only Religious Animal. He is the only animal that has the True Religion—several of them. He is the only animal that loves his neighbor as himself and cuts his throat if his theology isn't straight.

—MARK TWAIN

Our twelve bestsellers all feature religion in prominent ways, consistently critiquing orthodox religious practice and the dangers of zealotry.

According to conventional wisdom, the bestseller of all bestsellers is the Holy Bible—though in fact the book appears only a few times on the annual bestseller lists. Once, in 1952, the revised standard version sold over two million copies and came in at number one. *Tallulah,* by Tallulah Bankhead (an actress known for her sexual exploits), was nipping at the Bible's heels at number five. In 1953, the Holy Bible again finished in the number one position on the nonfiction list, followed closely by *The Power of Positive Thinking*, Norman Vincent Peale's classic how-to book, and coming in at number three was *Sexual Behavior in the Human Female*, by Alfred C. Kinsey and others.

And again in 1954, the Bible was the largest seller, while *Better Homes and Gardens New Cook Book* came in third, and fourth was *Betty Crocker's Good and Easy Cook Book*.

Religion, sex, and homemaking skills. It would be hard to find a more revealing American trifecta than that. More on sex and homemaking in a few pages, but for the moment our focus will be on God, religion, and belief.

GOD SELLS

Religious-themed novels have traditionally sold so well in the United States that most bestseller lists shunt them off into a separate category so the mainstream nonreligious books will have some slim chance of survival.

Even with that rigging of the game, on any given week the fiction bestseller list includes one or two books with a prominent religious orientation. Obviously, the enormous success of books like *The Da Vinci Code*, or the Left Behind series, or books from long ago like *Ben Hur, The Power and the Glory*, or Lloyd Cassel Douglas's *The Robe* (a number one bestseller in 1953), J. R. R. Tolkien's Lord of the Rings trilogy, or James Redfield's *The Celestine Prophecy*, is based in large measure on their spiritual themes.

Then there are a host of other "inspirational" novels with quasi-religious overtones, such as William Paul Young's hugely successful bestseller, *The Shack*, or Richard Bach's novel *Jonathan Livingston Seagull*, which rode atop the bestseller list for two years straight, in 1972 and 1973. Bach claimed the novel was dictated to him by a voice that came from somewhere "behind and to the right." Okay.

The novel used flight as a metaphor and was variously interpreted to be a celebration of getting high or an ode to man's miraculous engineering skills. Some saw it merely as a fictional reframing of Norman Vincent Peale's *The Power of Positive Thinking*, the American Bible of optimism and self-advancement.

Just as Mel Gibson's 2004 film, *The Passion of the Christ*, made a huge splash by luring to the movie theaters millions of conservative Christians who were not frequent filmgoers, novels that place a heavy emphasis on religious themes certainly attract readers who might otherwise avoid novels altogether. Attracting this part of the reading population is crucial to the making of a megabestseller. For even if every habitual book buyer were to purchase the same individual title, the sales figures would still fall far short of the multimillion level. To swell the ranks of consumers and break into these rarefied zones, a novel needs to catch the attention of large numbers of *infrequent* book buyers, and the religiously inclined are a common target audience.

SECULARISM

It should come as no surprise that of the dozen books on my list, almost all of them share one ingredient, a strong religious content.

What is surprising, however, is how heretical they are in interpreting what might be considered mainstream religious perspectives. For most of the bestseller authors under review here, skepticism is the shared religious stance. To one degree or another, each of the novels portrays characters afflicted with spiritual doubt. It would seem that the bestselling authors of all time are a collection of freethinkers and agnostics who share a tendency to ridicule religious hypocrisy and aggressively challenge standard orthodoxy.

That's not to say that the most popular books of all time are hostile to faith and organized religion. Rather, they seem to focus on the worldly consequences of religious practice rather than the spiritual aspects. In a word, the morality of bestsellers is rooted in a vision of culture that we know as *secular.*

Part of this secularism derives from the history of the novel form itself. As Ian Watt described in *The Rise of the Novel:* "The relative impotence of religion in Defoe's novels, then, suggests not insincerity but the profound secularization of his outlook, a secularization which was a marked feature of his age—the word itself in its modern sense dates from the first decades of the eighteenth century."

In addition to the tendency inherent in the earliest English novels to take a stand against orthodoxy, there is the particular American inclination to raise doubts about religious doctrine. Our forefathers, for all their religiosity, were the first great doubters. Take, for example, Thomas Jefferson in a letter to John Adams concerning the Bible's literary value:

The whole history of these books [the Gospels] is so defective and doubtful that it seems vain to attempt minute enquiry into it: and such tricks have been played with their text, and with the texts of other books relating to them, that we have a right, from that cause, to entertain much doubt what parts of them are genuine.

In the New Testament there is internal evidence that parts of it have proceeded from an extraordinary man; and that other parts are of the fabric of very inferior minds. It is as easy to separate those parts, as to pick out diamonds from dunghills.

OUTING HYPOCRISY

In *American Gospel*, Jon Meacham's fine work on the role religion played in our nation's development, he describes the unique American tension between the secular and the religious:

> A tolerant, pluralistic democracy in which religious and secular forces continually contend against one another may not be ideal, but it has proven to be the most practical and enduring arrangement of human affairs—and we must guard that arrangement well.

Examples of this secular skepticism can be found in all the bestsellers on our list, but let's start with an episode in *To Kill a Mockingbird*, in which Scout is sent to Aunt Alexandra's missionary circle to further her moral education. The missionary ladies are financially supporting Reverend J. Grimes Everett in his attempts to bring Christianity to the Mrunas, a jungle tribe.

Mrs. Merriweather, who was known as "the most devout lady in Maycomb," gets all weepy when she describes to Scout the terrible plight of the Mrunas and the saintly heroism of J. Grimes Everett, who is the only "white person'll go near 'em."

A page later, when Mrs. Merriweather has recovered herself and moved on to other topics, she complains to Mrs. Farrow about some "sulky darky" in her employ, then describes chastising the petulant household worker for not being more like Jesus Christ, who never went around moaning and griping about his plight. This reprimand puts the servant in her place, and Mrs. Merriweather takes satisfaction in having "witnessed for the Lord" in this small moment of racial humiliation.

The juxtaposition of the pious moment with the bigoted remark is no accident. Clearly, Harper Lee has a view of religious authenticity that's based on core humanistic values rather than hypocritical lip service. Scout is highly sensitive to these contradictions and in her quiet way scorns them.

Even when Scout visits the First Purchase African M.E. Church in the black quarter, she finds the preacher's message to be sadly flawed. After denouncing sin, he goes on to rail against the "impurity of women," which Scout observes is a preoccupation of all the preachers she's encountered.

Despite the misogynist message, Scout is impressed by other aspects of this passionate congregation. Without the means to buy hymnals, they still manage to sing the old songs from memory. They know every word by heart.

Digging deep into their pockets and handbags, this destitute group manages to scratch together ten dollars in dimes and pennies to contribute to the defense fund of the falsely accused Tom Robinson. The sacrifice involved in this tithing is in stark contrast with the sanctimonious blather of Mrs. Merriweather and her missionary ladies. While Harper Lee's method is indirect, it is nonetheless absolutely clear. Bigotry and false piety often march hand in hand under the banner of Christianity. But mouthing platitudes doesn't cut it. Even a young girl can spot that old con.

FAITH AND DOUBT

Grace Metalious was every bit as intent on calling out hypo-
crites as Harper Lee. While *Peyton Place* is one long castiga-
tion of pretenses and false pieties of every sort, religion comes
in for more than its share of scolding.

When one of the town's fine citizens, Marion Partridge,
marries into Peyton Place money, she promptly bails out of
one church to join another, but not for reasons one might
consider religious. Marion abandoned the Baptists for the
Congregational Church because the Congregationalists were
considered an upscale denomination. The church's only flaw,
as far as Marion was concerned, was that it sometimes admitted "undesirables" into the fold and therefore diminished its
snob appeal.

The heroine of the novel, Allison MacKenzie, sounds a
highly skeptical note when considering the religious explanations of her pastor, who claims that the Lord hears every
word of every prayer. She wants to know, if that's true, then
why does He so rarely answer? Well, the preacher responds,
sometimes God just has to turn down our pleas for our own
good. Okay, then, Allison wonders, why bother praying at
all?

And a few lines later, she takes the same religious stance
that in one way or another all these bestsellers do—falling
somewhere in a narrow range between doubter and agnostic.

When Allison was younger, she'd prayed day after day for
her father to return to the family, but he never showed. Which
makes her confront a terrible realization. How could a God
capable of miracles not do something so easy? How could He

allow a little girl to suffer so? It was this seeming injustice that destroyed Allison's faith.

SUPERNATURAL CALCULUS

After hearing a plot summary of *The Exorcist* (a priest exorcises a sadistic satanic force from the soul of a tormented child), most book buyers might reasonably assume they are in for a rip-roaring tale in which religious belief wins out over devilry. But it's not that simple.

In *The Exorcist,* Father Damien Karras, a Jesuit priest, is experiencing an agonizing loss of religious faith not unlike Allison MacKenzie's. He cannot confide in any of his colleagues, for he fears that they'll consider his reasons for doubt to be signs of insanity. And in various interior monologues, the priest does sound as though he's teetering on the existential edge. He's driven to the brink by considering such quotidian horrors as thalidomide babies and young altar boys attacked without provocation and set ablaze. How could a just God allow such vile suffering?

And to make matters worse, God's silence is driving him even more nuts. Why won't He reveal Himself? Why won't God speak to this man of faith, who has pledged his life to God and now is crying out in the most orthodox ways? His faith is in tatters. He's lost all hope in God's power.

The fact that Chris MacNeil is an avowed atheist doesn't keep her from summoning Father Karras to minister to her daughter, Regan, whom she believes is possessed by Satan. Karras, by now a skeptic to the core, tries for most of the novel to find a reasonable, secular explanation for Regan's behavior. He engages in an ongoing verbal joust with the being inhabiting Regan's body, a tête-à-tête that is part psychoanalysis and part Jesuit debate. However skillful Father Karras is at explaining away Regan's extreme behaviors, finally his psychological rationalizations crumble until he is left with only one conclusion: The devil has taken control of the girl.

Well into the novel, the bishop of the diocese consents to an exorcism. The great bulk of the story, however, is devoted to dramatizing Damien's attempts to use nonreligious explanations to come to grips with what is plainly a satanic possession. When all the scientific, logical approaches fail to help the poor child, Father Karras is forced to fall back on his wavering belief. While the head-spinning horrors and the guttural obscenities coming from the mouth of the girl might be the spice that accelerates the pulse of an average reader, the thematic backbone of the novel is the story of a priest who rediscovers God when he is forced to confront the devil.

It is Merrin, the elderly exorcist, who speaks the lines that are the takeaway religious stance the novel promotes:

> Yet I think that the demon's target is not the possessed; it is us . . . the observers . . . every person in this house. And I think—I think the point is to make us despair; to reject our own humanity . . . to see ourselves as ultimately bestial; as ultimately vile and putrescent. . . . For I think belief in God is not a matter of reason at all; I think it is finally a matter of love; of accepting the possibility that God could love *us*. . . .

Merrin dies before the exorcism is complete, and Father Karras must step in to battle on. In a scene that is withheld from us, Karras is ultimately victorious, the devil is purged, and the girl is saved, though Karras sacrifices his own life to the cause. As he lies dying on the sidewalk outside the Mac-Neil house, Karras receives final absolution. Since he is unable to speak to the priest administering the last rites, it is debatable whether Karras accepts this formal blessing willingly or not.

In any case, it is Chris MacNeil who has the last words on faith and religion in this novel that has been fixated on both. She says to Karras that despite everything she's witnessed, she's still a nonbeliever. But on the other hand, she has come to believe that the devil is very real. Very, very real.

Is it Karras's final acceptance of God's mercy and power or Chris's rejection of the same that stands as the novel's coda? Whichever view appears overriding in a reader's mind probably depends on the predispositions that reader brought to the novel. The remarkable fact is, however, that the secular position is given the last word, and in the supernatural bookkeeping of *The Exorcist,* it costs two priests to take down a single manifestation of the devil. That is what is known these days as an unsustainable economy.

UNCOMMON SENSE

When Kay Adams Corleone at last learns the true nature of her husband's criminal enterprise, her first reaction is to seek out a priest for instruction to become a Catholic. In the final lines of this bloody novel full of brutal revenge killings and murderous power plays, Kay goes to church.

She kneels in supplication, bows her head, folds her hands

over the rail, and "with a profound and deeply willed desire to believe," she says prayers for the eternal soul of Michael Corleone.

That her deeply willed desire to believe is actual belief is dubious. Certainly Mario Puzo's muted skepticism pervades this moment. After Michael Corleone has piled up four hundred pages of mortal sins, it seems unlikely that his soul can be saved by his wife, a new and wavering convert. Michael is, after all, the Godfather—a secular God if there ever was one.

In *Jaws,* the shark is considered by many in the town to be "an act of God," and its eventual destruction requires the deaths of several sacrificial lambs. Hooper, the shark expert called in to aid the seaside community, is awestruck by the fish, while Quint, the old salt who has been hired to kill it, begs to differ. Hooper believes the shark is a thing of beauty that shows the awesome power of nature and therefore confirms the existence of God.

Horseshit, is Quint's reply.

Later, Quint and Sheriff Brody discuss the religious implications of the shark's appearance, Brody mentioning the woman back in town who believes the shark is some kind of divine retribution.

But Quint, who puts no stock in religion, replies that the shark's appearance is simply "bad luck."

In the last lines of the novel, Brody survives the great white's final assault and watches as Quint is yanked overboard and drawn down into the sea in a posture that evokes the crucifixion, "arms out to the sides, head thrown back. . . ." A secular version of Jesus Christ, dying for the secular sins of others.

If the shark is truly God's way of reminding the townsfolk of His awesome power, then it damn well worked. But for

Quint, who stands as the larger-than-life voice of the common man, the alternative vision is one of randomness and accident—an existential universe in which God's will plays no part whatsoever. It is Quint, like Scout and Chris MacNeil, who voices the commonsense skepticism that undergirds the moral position of each of these books.

A COMMONER'S COMMON SENSE

Common sense, not religious conviction, is also a major tenet of Scarlett O'Hara's worldview. At the graveside ceremony when her father, Gerald, is laid to rest, the religiously formal Ashley Wilkes intones a few solemn clichés, then is followed by Will, a simple farmer who speaks off-the-cuff about the death of Mr. O'Hara.

> Scarlett . . . did feel comforted. Will was talking common sense instead of a lot of tootle about reunions in another and better world and submitting her will to God's.

Throughout the novel, Scarlett's religious beliefs are childish and shallow, characterized less by faith and devotion than by a ruthless pragmatism. For Scarlett, religion is nothing more than a bargaining chip. She has always made promises to God in exchange for some return on her investment. Since God had been such an unreliable business partner, "to her way of thinking, she felt that she owed Him nothing at all. . . ."

Indeed, for a character so deeply loved by so many readers, Scarlett O'Hara is surprisingly blasphemous. Like Allison

MacKenzie and Father Karras, she's lost faith. Scarlett refuses to believe in a God who won't respond to the million other prayers sent to Him daily on behalf of the Confederacy.

She's forsaken church and no longer prays. Her spiritual outlook is secularist, pure and simple. A humanistic view that is rooted in a commoner's common sense rather than in the rituals and liturgical ceremonies of the ecumenical elite.

Scarlett's skeptical views are echoed by those of John Smith in *The Dead Zone*. Johnny's paranormal abilities have given him a vision of a disastrous future if Greg Stillson is elected president of the United States. Oh, and by the way, remember, Greg Stillson got his start as a con man selling, of all things, Bibles.

Debating whether to go ahead with his plans to assassinate Stillson, John anguishes over God's failure to do the job first. He wonders why God would allow such an evil man as Greg Stillson to flourish. Why has God left it to Johnny to do His dirty work?

Even Jack Ryan, an otherwise play-it-by-the-book hero, squirms uncomfortably when asked by a Russian sub captain if he believes in God. Ryan fumbles a bit, then says sure, yeah, he believes in God, "because if you don't, what's the point of life? That would mean Sartre and Camus and all those characters were right—all is chaos, life has no meaning. I refuse to believe that."

Not exactly a ringing endorsement of religious faith. Ryan believes in God only because to do otherwise would be to support Camus "and all those characters." Meaning, I suppose, the French.

THE POWER OF BLASPHEMY

Could there be a more secular novel about religion than *The Da Vinci Code*?

> Sophie was skeptical. "You think the *Church* killed my grandfather?"
>
> Teabing replied, "It would not be the first time in history the Church has killed to protect itself. The documents that accompany the Holy Grail are explosive, and the Church has wanted to destroy them for years."

Secularism is one thing, but seeming to charge the Catholic Church with serial murder is a whole different animal. Is it any wonder that Vatican officials were outraged over the novel's assertions or that dozens of books sprang up to challenge fictional anti-Catholic claims that were taken seriously by many readers?

The narrative dynamics of *The Da Vinci Code* are clear. The protagonist, Robert Langdon, is a man of science, while his antagonists are men of the cloth. The conflict at the crux of the novel is a clash between science and faith, between academics and clerics, between reason and mysticism. Or between secularism and religion.

Consider the way Robert Langdon, the high priest of rationality, explains away religious belief to his love interest/student Sophie. He feels sure that he could provide hard evidence that contradicted the holy stories of every religious belief system, from Islam to Buddhism. He suggests that he could even demonstrate that Christ's virgin birth was just a metaphor, not a literal fact as so many devout believers assume. But Langdon has decided to let the poor fools stay deluded, for he believes that religious allegory (the lies that religion tells, like Christ actually walking on actual water) is a useful coping mechanism for millions of religious folks. Why spoil their fun?

As spokesman for puzzle solvers everywhere, Robert Langdon is the ultimate secularist. Everything can be explained. All mysteries, all supernatural phenomena, all religious faith, can be dissected and reduced to their component parts. For Robert, there is no rapture beyond logic and reason.

It's striking that millions of readers, many of them presumably devout believers in one religion or another, could be so swept up by a novel whose central character devotes so much of his time not only debunking Christian symbolism but challenging the very idea of religious belief.

No doubt part of the extraordinary appeal of this work of fiction derives from its handling of religious matters in so direct a fashion. Whether those readers share Langdon's view that "every faith in the world is based on fabrication" or not, they were clearly energized and possibly even flattered by seeing organized religion take center stage and its iconography and art elucidated in fresh and surprising ways.

FEATURE #9

American Dream/American Nightmare

I've not only pursued the American dream, I've achieved it. I suppose we could say the last few years, I've also achieved the American nightmare.

—KENNETH LAY, CEO, ENRON

Americans delight in reenactments of our national myths. The rise from humble roots to become rich and powerful. A character struggling against injustice and, finally, triumphing over oppression. And we are also grimly fascinated by the flip side of these stories.

Although Horatio Alger's novels, published in the late nineteenth and early twentieth centuries, didn't invent the "rags to riches" story line (folkloric versions like "Cinderella" were around for centuries), Alger's stories certainly helped to crystallize the vocabulary of a central part of what we've come to call "the American Dream."

Writing what today might be termed "young adult novels"

such as *Ragged Dick* and *Adrift in the City; or, Oliver Conrad's Plucky Fight,* Alger introduced into the national consciousness an image of down-and-out ragamuffins who, through sweat and labor, determination, and a hard-nosed sense of justice, pulled themselves up by their bootstraps and achieved some measure of wealth and social success. The heroes of these tales were most often orphaned boys with abundant street smarts who weren't afraid of a fistfight as a last resort against the advances of a bully.

There is the air of the fairy tale about Alger's novels. But the foremost achievement of Alger's work was to develop a clear and vivid narrative that dramatized one of our most treasured national myths: that even the poorest and most disenfranchised among us can achieve prosperity, material wealth, and personal freedom.

THE NIGHTMARE STORIES

While we yearn to believe in these optimistic principles, at the same time Americans seem to take a grim satisfaction in watching the opposite pattern unfold. We love with equal fervor to watch our national myths foiled, to see their limits, their frailty, sometimes even their emptiness.

These are the nightmare stories: a pious, God-fearing community that is racked by hypocrisy and double-dealing and crimes against morality (*Peyton Place*); the smart, talented, attractive young women who journey off to the big city seeking fame and fortune (and husbands), only to find the tragic hollowness and unimaginable perils of that dream (*Valley of the Dolls*); the ordinary all-American young man who lives by a Boy Scout's modest and hardworking creed but falls victim to unthinkable horrors (*The Dead Zone*).

What about John Smith's doppelgänger, the sharp, obsessively studious boy from the shabby trailer park who makes his way to Harvard Law School, then lands his dream job in America's heartland (*The Firm*)? Ah, yes. Mitch McDeere will meet the dark side of the American Dream as well and make a fatal Faustian bargain, taking a low-interest loan and shiny new BMW in exchange for his own soul, his marriage, and possibly his life.

In Mitch's case, his belief in the American Dream remains unshakable even after his discovering that very dream has betrayed him and put everything he loves at risk. He takes a breath, summons his courage, and gives it one more college try, proceeding to outwit the Mob, the FBI, and his lethal legal brethren, then sailing off into the sunset of everlasting retirement.

AMERICA HAS BEEN GOOD TO ME

And there's Bonasera, an outraged father who at the outset of *The Godfather* pleads for Don Corleone's help in getting revenge on the boys who beat and tried to rape his daughter. The boys were released by the courts, and now Bonasera comes to the Godfather for the justice he had trusted the legal system of his adopted country to deliver. "America has been good to me. I wanted to be a good citizen. I wanted my child to be American."

Don Corleone dismisses poor Bonasera for making the mistake of putting his faith in America, not in the Godfather.

Later, during a meeting of all the Mafia heads from around the country, Don Corleone makes a statesmanlike speech about what he feels is a belief that binds these criminals together, a belief in the American Dream.

By refusing to be puppets manipulated by the power elite, Don Corleone and his fellow Mafia leaders have laid the foundation for future generations of Corleones. Their children have found better lives. They are scientists and musicians and professors, and no doubt the next generation will "become the new *pezzonovanti*" (the new big shots, or ruling class). And who knows about the Don's grandchildren. Maybe there is a future governor among them, even a president. For "nothing's impossible here in America."

When the Don's son Michael reveals the true nature of the "family business" to Kay Adams, his white bread Protestant fiancée, he echoes nearly word for word his father's views on the American Dream.

He wants his kids to be raised under Kay Adams's influence, for them to grow up all-American kids. And he too holds out hope that one of them, or maybe someone in the next generation of his family, will become president of the United States. Why not? Michael learned in a history course at Dartmouth that some of our most revered presidents were raised by fathers "who were lucky they didn't get hanged."

THE IMMIGRANT NARRATIVE

If any single creed serves as the foundation for our national sense of self, it's the promise of social mobility. That hard work and fair play will be rewarded. Anyone can become a star, and conversely, it's all too possible for stardom to turn into a hellish fall from grace (*Valley of the Dolls*).

Even an eight-year-old girl in a tiny racist town can change the course of human events, as Scout does when she thwarts a lynching. Even a small-town cop who is deathly afraid of the water can go out to sea and help destroy a great white shark that is terrorizing his precinct. And even Scarlett O'Hara, a spoiled girl-child with few worldly skills beyond coquetry, uses those skills to full advantage, managing with ruthless determination to flourish as an entrepreneur, then save Tara from the Yankee invaders and the carpetbaggers.

Rhett Butler warns Scarlett that a woman has only two choices: She can either make money and be unladylike and be ostracized by polite society, or she can be poor and well mannered and have lots of friends. Fiddle-dee-dee, Scarlett says about all that ladylike reputation stuff. She goes on to make her Atlanta lumber mill into a cash machine that supports the rebuilding of her first and only true love, Tara. She's a capitalist wizard, using her heaving bosom and come-hither eyes to win husband after husband, each one lifting her to a higher income bracket.

That's not to say Scarlett doesn't get her hands dirty in a salute to the American virtue of hard work. After the war, back at Tara, she picks cotton, raises vegetables, and masters every skill the "darkies" used to handle. She replicates her own father's immigrant narrative, starting with nothing, forced to stoop and scratch and eventually rebuild her lost empire through the sweat of her brow and a crafty use of her feminine charms.

At one point, so desperate to raise three hundred dollars to pay the Yankee taxes that threaten to steal Tara away from her, she decides she must attempt to seduce Rhett Butler, who is being held in an Atlanta prison. Without a gown or fitting frock to wear on this crucial mission of enticement, she pulls down the velvet drapes in Tara's dining room and fashions a fetching dress that she just knows will assist her scheme. Rhett is fooled for a moment or two, until he takes her hands in his and sees how roughened they are from the manual labor she's been doing back at Tara. He scoffs at her silly attempts to actually toil her way to prosperity. She's better than that, Rhett believes, more shrewd. He counsels her simply to use her feminine wiles as he uses his masculine ones to gain what advantage she can.

Rhett's rejection doesn't thwart her. Moments after leaving the jail, Scarlett is still wearing the drapery dress when she bumps into Frank Kennedy, a successful store owner. Ah-ha. A quick pivot, and she's got a new potential husband within her sights. The one minor inconvenience with lassoing Kennedy is that he's the fiancé of her own sister Sue Ellen. But Scarlett brushes that aside and goes neatly from one man to the next, stealing her sister's beau, latching on to yet another man who can write a check on her behalf.

Scarlett is a whirlwind of cunning and free enterprise craftiness. Maybe her old way of life has been destroyed and the Confederacy defeated, but Scarlett is destined to turn America's greatest nightmare into her own version of the American Dream.

THE BOOTSTRAP MYTH

The power of individuals to change their own destiny, to rise or fall on the basis of their skills, their smarts, their craftiness, is at the core of each of these novels. No matter how insuperable the problem may be (finding a tiny needle like the *Red October* in the huge haystack of the Atlantic Ocean), a modest, unassuming, straight-talking, down-to-earth ordinary man with a little ingenuity and determination can save the day—or in Jack Ryan's case, the world.

As I've noted, the novel from its very beginning has been unabashedly democratic. Any reader, no matter his or her race, creed, social class, or previous educational training, is invited to enter freely. And the writers of bestsellers seem abundantly aware of their duty to keep all comers entertained with stories of success, the triumph of social mobility, or its evil twin, the cautionary tale of disaster.

For it's clear that in these bestsellers there is a right way and a wrong way to attain the American Dream. Take Hollywood mogul Jack Woltz, a man Don Corleone wants a small favor from. Woltz is a self-made man just like Vito Corleone, but there's something un-American about his makeover.

When he turned fifty, Woltz began to take speech lessons, hired an English valet to teach him how to dress, and employed an English butler to instruct him on social rules. He became a collector of paintings and sculpture and a patron of the arts. All this would be enough to put Woltz on the Don's blacklist, but what really seals his fate is turning down the Don's business deal, an act of disrespect that leads to Woltz waking up in bed next to the decapitated head of his prized horse Khartoum.

By comparing Woltz's hoity-toity vision of the American Dream with Don Corleone's rise from poverty, we get a vivid contrast between the false version of the dream and the authentic one.

To escape Mafia violence in his homeland, young Vito Corleone was sent off to America at the age of twelve to live with friends. As a youngster in his adopted land, he labors in a grocery store and after a few years marries a sixteen-year-old Sicilian girl and settles down in a Tenth Avenue tenement.

But Vito Corleone is destined for greater things. He will lift himself up from destitution and hardship through the use of intelligence and icy courage. After murdering a neighborhood tyrant named Fanucci, who was reputed to be a member of an offshoot of the Mafia, Vito settles into the olive oil business. Largely because of the respect (and fear) he's earned through removing Fanucci's ruthless rule in the neighborhood, his business flourishes, and Vito begins to employ a certain leverage to make it flourish faster. His business plan sounds like a dark parody of a Wharton School MBA course.

Vito Corleone spent years building up his business until Genco Pura was the bestselling imported oil in the whole country. He undercut his business rivals in price, he strong-armed store owners to buy less of his competitors' brands, and once his rivals were in a weakened position, he tried to buy them out. Since his olive oil was not in any way superior to the others on the market, it was the Don's own reputation as a "man of respect" that gave him a stranglehold on the imported olive oil industry. The fact that he had a reputation as a cold-blooded murderer certainly didn't hurt his rise.

Part of *The Godfather*'s immense popularity is no doubt due to its sly straddling of these two positions. On the one hand, the novel portrays a group of cutthroat criminals who use whatever bloody means necessary to succeed; on the other hand, the book could as easily be described as a tribute to the prototypical immigrant family, whose traditional American moral virtues (the Don refuses to deal drugs, for instance) and loyalty to friends and family allow them to overcome great obstacles and escape a life of poverty.

AMERICAN CYNICISM

The dark side of the American Dream is an equal and opposite force in nearly all of these megabestsellers. In *To Kill a Mockingbird,* Tom Robinson, the black man who is falsely accused of rape, is found guilty of the crime, though it is clear to everyone in the courtroom down to the youngest child (our girl Scout) that he is innocent. Justice is not even close to being just. While Atticus might take some solace in the fact that the jury took an especially long time to hash out their guilty verdict, that small step toward judicial fairness is small indeed and might seem more like a sad rationalization of bigotry than a hopeful view of social progress.

Similarly, cynicism toward the American Dream of success drips off every page of *Peyton Place.* Like the story of Roberta and Harmon Carter, a married couple with one son who live on a street that was considered the "second best" in Peyton Place. They could easily afford to live on the best street or even build a twenty-room castle if they weren't concerned about appearing ostentatious. Drawing attention to themselves is a little dangerous because these two conned their way to their improved social class status.

When they were young, Harmon Carter and Roberta Welch were an item. But it was clear to Harmon that his job as an accountant at the local mill was not exactly the fast track to the American Dream. So he planted a sinister seed in Roberta's mind by giving her constant reminders of the likely trajectory of their economic life together.

It'll be paycheck to paycheck, he tells her, the grim life of an office worker. She deserves more than that, he assures her. Roberta should have furs and diamonds and the most fashionable clothes. But none of those wonderful material possessions will ever come her way with him stuck in a dead-end job.

Though Roberta claims she loves Harmon and always will, whether they are rich or poor, clever Harmon will have none of that, and he turns her argument around, saying if she loves him that much, then that deep love will not desert her while she's married to Old Doc Quimby, the rich man whose house she cleans.

Roberta caves, and the scheming devils put their plan in motion. Of course, poor Old Doc falls for Roberta's seduction, and all of Peyton Place has a good long snicker. The Doc gradually realizes what a fool he's been, and a couple of weeks before the first anniversary of his marriage to Roberta Welch, Doc Quimby presses his revolver to his temple and kills himself.

Roberta inherits the Doc's loot and promptly marries Harmon. Bingo, they've just won the American Dream grand prize. Before long they produce a son, Ted, and they buy a far nicer house than they could have afforded on Harmon's accountant salary. But wait—the last laugh may be on them.

Ted, their pride and joy, falls hard for Selena Cross. Unfortunately, Selena is the town slut who lives in one of those tar-paper shacks over on the wrong side of the tracks. She's damaged goods, the stepdaughter of a drunk. Selena is never, ever going to have a sniff of the American Dream. And it is Selena who becomes an unpleasant reminder to Roberta and Harmon Carter of their own shabby social backgrounds and their scamming of Doc Quimby.

Ted graduates from the university, planning to return to Peyton Place and marry Selena and build a house on a hill, with lots of windows. He's going to be a lawyer and save Selena from her hard-luck destiny. The two of them will rewrite the perverted script Ted's parents read from. They'll act out a true Horatio Alger narrative.

In the end, young Ted Carter decides that love is not all it's cracked up to be, as so often is the case in this harsh rendering of American family values. The night before he's to take Selena's hand, he begins to hear his parents' hard-eyed practicality whispering in his head. After a sentence or two of debating the subject with himself, Ted decides it would be best if he dumped his fiancée. And in a blink, she's gone from his heart.

There must be something in the water in Peyton Place, some potent truth serum that forces characters to admit that the glittery promise of America is a damnable lie. Maybe the town was cursed from the beginning. After all, the place was named for Samuel Peyton, a black slave who escaped his master and ran off to France, married a white French lady, and returned to America during the Civil War to flaunt the wealth and refinement he'd scored abroad.

The folks around those backwoods where Samuel and his white wife settled didn't take kindly to that biracial union or the general uppitiness of Peyton. Even though Samuel had fulfilled the American Dream by making a fortune in Europe, enough money to buy a medieval castle and import it stone for stone to be rebuilt along the river in this valley that became known as Peyton Place.

Ostracized by the locals, he and his wife eventually retreated inside their castle walls and became the Mr. and Mrs. Boo Radley of New England. What was that black man thinking? That this was America, land of the free? Did he really fall for that old claptrap that if a man simply worked hard and made good, he could overcome the darkness of his skin? Well, we showed him!

Samuel Peyton's warped fairy tale is the inspiration for the novel Allison MacKenzie is trying to write. By the last few chapters, Allison has freed herself from the small-town pettiness and gone to the big city to live out her dreams of fame and fortune. She's broken into the book business, finding a job with a literary agent, and she's happily banging out her novel. She's not the least bit shy about staking her claim to the low road of bestsellerdom.

In fact, the novel she's working on sounds an awful lot like *Peyton Place*. Her agent, Brad Holmes, loves the book, though he may be a little biased since he's sleeping with the author. When Allison pitches her novel to David Noyes, a young up-and-comer who writes big books of "social significance," David lets his snobbery out of the closet and mocks Allison for wanting to write for such shallow motivations as fame and money. But she stands firm. Not everyone can be a brilliant boy genius, the next big thing in literature. She's content to stay on the low road of commercial fiction, writing the best book she can, even if there are those like David who consider the results trashy. The scene between them comes as close as any in these twelve novels to making a case for the inherent integrity of bestsellers.

THE YIN AND YANG OF THE AMERICAN DREAM

Allison MacKenzie should have held out for a writer-boyfriend like Stephen King. Now there's a man who knows a thing or two about fame and money and more than a little about the American Dream and its twisted fun-house mirror image.

The Dead Zone gives us a story of two converging characters who represent the yin and yang of the American Dream. One is the all-American, hardworking, though otherwise unexceptional John Smith, whose accidental fall on an ice-covered pond sets off a serious attack of paranormal powers. Johnny never wanted anything more than to marry Sarah, his sweetheart, teach school, raise a family, and enjoy the modest fruits of his very conventional labor. Now look at what he's got to deal with. The power to change the world.

On a collision course with John Smith is Greg Stillson, who begins his career as a door-to-door Bible salesman working the rural circuit. The first time we meet him he's knocking on a farmhouse door when a guard dog advances on him with its ears back. Stillson makes short work of the dog, shooting it, then finishing it off with a series of savage kicks.

After he's dispatched the poor beast and is sitting comfortably in his car, he coldly dismisses the incident and the dog blood on his shoes, musing instead on his dreams for the future.

It won't be long before Greg Stillson has left Bible selling far behind and is using his con man's skills to work his way up the political ladder.

Along the way, Stillson's ascent to power in the political circles of New Hampshire catches John Smith's notice. By late in the novel, John has become something of an amateur political scientist and is fond of attending rallies so he can shake the hands of candidates, because making this skin-to-skin contact allows him to use his precognitive skills to see which of them will make good leaders.

Before John can confirm anything definite about Stillson

by meeting the man flesh to flesh, he's decided he doesn't like Stillson's policies one bit. In fact, some of them seem downright scary to Johnny. Under Stillson's leadership, the library budget has been cut (a major sin in any book lover's world). During the same period of Stillson's reign, the police have gotten a 40 percent increase in their budget, which includes new cruisers and riot gear and military weapons. Stillson shuts the teen rec center, imposes a curfew for kids under sixteen, and cuts welfare by a third.

Gradually, a dreadful question takes root in John Smith's mind: "*If you could jump into a time machine and go back to 1932, would you kill Hitler?*"

Whether Stillson, this dog-killing, neocon crackpot, is actually as dangerous and evil as Hitler is beside the point. John Smith thinks he is, and his prescience has been proved right enough times to virtually guarantee the truth of his suspicions. If Johnny can't find a way to foil Stillson's steady rise, chances are good Greg Stillson will become the next president of the United States, and Johnny sees Apocalypse written all over that.

The linked destinies of these two men is a fitting metaphor for the way the American Dream and the American Nightmare intertwine in most of the bestsellers under review. John Smith sacrifices his own life to spare the world the cataclysm of Stillson's presidency. The good boy neutralizes the bad.

It's worth noting that had the story been rendered from a political angle slightly different from Stephen King's, Stillson's version could easily sound like a tragic telling of the American Dream: Stillson, a fatherless youth who rose from poverty through hard work and devotion to public service, was on the verge of staking claim to the highest office in the land when he was brought down by an underachieving kook who believed he was a psychic.

That these two versions of the American Dream story are so easily interchangeable is testament to the ambivalence that bestseller writers and readers of bestsellers seem to feel toward the subject.

On the one hand, this American belief in the "rags to riches" possibilities of our nation is an honorable and compelling pillar of our national identity. On the other hand, there are those who regularly exploit these worthy dreams of the people of America with false rhetoric and thereby manage to swindle their way to a higher station than they truly deserve. From Mark Twain to Steinbeck and Sinclair Lewis and Stephen King, bestseller writers have served a dual purpose in this regard: to tap into the wellspring of belief that so many Americans share, reinvigorate the righteous optimism and promise of their nation, while at the same time issuing a bitter "Humbug!" against the shysters and frauds who prey on this very sincerity.

THE GOLDEN PROMISE OF AMERICA

The last word on the American Dream must go to Tom Clancy, whose hero, Jack Ryan, in *The Hunt for Red October* rescues the world from certain thermonuclear war by using the golden promise of America to close the deal with a Soviet defector.

Were it not for Clancy's novel, we'd not have a single representative on the list of bestsellers that actually makes a wholehearted case for Horatio Alger's version of the American story. With Reaganesque audacity, Clancy paints the Soviet Union as a drab and evil empire, one whose bankrupt socialism, so full of fraud and incompetence, almost leads to World War III.

Marko Ramius, a heralded submarine commander, loses his wife, Natalia, in a series of bungled medical procedures that are described in Clancy's usual painstaking detail. Thanks to a widespread shortage of the French pharmaceutical-grade antibiotic ordinarily distributed to Soviet clinics, a batch of vials filled with distilled water had been surreptitiously substituted and administered, which put Natalia into a coma and eventually caused her death.

Faithless, bereaved, and enraged, Ramius puts together an audacious plan to abscond to the United States, where presumably such medical errors do not occur and where one's faith can be restored.

What propels Ramius across the cold and gloomy depths of the Atlantic is partly revulsion toward a failed political system and partly the overpowering allure of the American Dream.

By the time Jack Ryan has managed to bond with Ramius, the American continent, glowing with bright promise, is only a few hours distant. With nervous excitement, Lieutenant Kamarov, one of Ramius's fellow defectors, wants to know if the Soviet crewmen will be subjected to "political education" when they come ashore. Ryan laughs and explains to the lieutenant that someone will eventually take a couple of hours to explain how America works. Afterward he'll be free to criticize the nation like every other citizen. Then Ryan admits he's never lived in a country that wasn't free, so maybe he doesn't appreciate his homeland as much as he should.

Surely the implication of Ryan's admission is that many of

Clancy's readers might also be guilty of taking for granted the freedoms they enjoy. In that sense, *The Hunt for Red October* is offered as an entertaining political education, a reminder to the mass reader that such freedoms are safeguarded by the likes of stalwarts like Jack Ryan. No wonder it was one of President Reagan's favorite stories.

As the submarine full of Soviet traitors cruises ever closer to the promised land of America, they are treated to a video of Spielberg's *ET*. When the movie is finished, the assembled Communists have been brought to tears, proclaiming that the film is magnificent. One of them wants to know if all American children are so brave and free.

Ryan, honest to a fault, explains that the movie was shot in California, where parents are a bit permissive and kids a little more liberated than they are in other parts of the country. But still, he points out, on the whole American kids are a lot more independent than Soviet kids.

The Clancy version of political education continues as the defectors reach dry land. Since diplomatic conventions require these arriving Soviet sailors to be returned to their motherland unless they make a last-minute decision to defect, their military escorts give the sailors a little capitalistic brainwashing: the American Dream guided tour.

The men are welcomed aboard a VIP transport plane, given cigarettes and liquor, taken up to twenty thousand feet, and wooed by a running commentary on all the glorious abundance below. Their guide points out the vast middle-class neighborhoods where ordinary folks with ordinary jobs live.

Welcome to the shining city on the hill. Welcome to our vast and jam-packed cornucopias of materialism. Give 'em a look at Wal-Mart and Costco and they'll defect every time.

When Ryan happens to mention American supermarkets,

one of the Soviet officers demands he explain what such a thing is. It's a building as big as a soccer field, Ryan tells them, full of fresh fruit and vegetables and every kind of food imaginable.

Fresh fruit in winter? The Soviets can't believe it. Oh, yes, Ryan tells them. Hell, America even pays their farmers *not* to grow things. That's how lush, abundant, and overflowing with goodies our country is. And the sales pitch goes on:

> If you have money, you can buy nearly anything you want. The average family in America makes something like twenty thousand dollars a year, I guess.

Twenty thousand a year in 1985, when this novel was published, must have seemed an amazing sum to a Soviet defector. It might still. But surely the American Dream is something more than this, something more noble and slightly less tacky than the dollar figure of an average worker's yearly income.

By the final pages of the novel, Captain Ramius is on the last leg of his seafaring journey, riding aboard a tug toward the American shore, still questioning whether he made the right choice in abandoning his Soviet homeland. And Jack Ryan, flag-waver to the end, starts in again with his mantra, the hymn that all of us sing to ourselves from time to time when we are trying to remind ourselves what makes our American citizenship so unique and so dear.

As they approach the harbor entrance, their tug slows to a crawl. Ramius wants to know why they've cut back their engines, and Commander Bart Mancuso replies that the pilot has to be careful of civilian traffic, like some guy in a sailboat with the same rights as the big vessels steaming into port. A sailboat so small that it wouldn't even show up on radar.

"It's a free country, Captain," Ryan said softly. "It will take you some time to understand what free really means."

Sometimes the dream of social mobility that so inspired and energized Horatio Alger, and is such a cornerstone of American bestsellers, has little to do with the movement to a higher income level. At times it can simply refer to the freedom to move from one place to another unhindered by the almighty ships of state.

FEATURE #10

A Dozen Mavericks

The new habits to be engendered on the new American scene were suggested by the image of a radically new personality, the hero of the new adventure: an individual emancipated from history, happily bereft of ancestry, untouched and undefiled by the usual inheritances of family and race; an individual standing alone, self-reliant and self-propelling, ready to confront whatever awaited him with the aid of his own unique and inherent resources.

—R. W. B. LEWIS,
THE AMERICAN ADAM

The heroes and heroines of our twelve bestsellers are all rebels, loners, misfits, or mavericks. They don't fit in worth a damn, and that's one of the reasons we love them so much.

At the close of the novel that bears his name, Huck Finn realizes, dadgum it, he can't let himself get tangled up in the apron strings of the spinster aunt who wants to be his guardian. During his rafting journey down the Mississippi, he's learned too much about the conformity, hypocrisy, and double-dealing of respectable folks like Aunt Sally to ever feel comfortable living among them again, and in the final lines of that American classic, Huck makes his declaration of independence:

"But I reckon I got to light out for the Territory ahead of the rest, because Aunt Sally she's going to adopt me and sivilize me, and I can't stand it. I been there before."

As literary critic Northrop Frye once noted, the recurring hero of many American novels is "placed outside the structure of civilization and therefore represents the force of physical nature, amoral or ruthless, yet with a sense of power, and often leadership, that society has impoverished itself by rejecting."

In other words, he's a maverick.

James Garner played this familiar role in a 1960s television series set in the Old West. He was a gambler and reluctant gunslinger and a tumbling tumbleweed without destination or much sense of loyalty. In *Top Gun,* Tom Cruise, playing a fighter jet pilot, uses the same handle as his nickname. Or take our recent national election in which both the presidential candidate and his running mate, *each* of them citizens of the New West, adopted *maverick* as their brand.

In our popular culture and folklore, this term has a venerated status. Indeed, the word itself owns a colorful American pedigree. It derives from the surname of one Samuel Maverick (1803–1870), a Texas lawyer and ranch owner whose name entered our lexicon because he refused to brand his cattle. He took this radical position not in defiance of the customs of the time, but because he found the labors of ranching to be too damn much trouble.

So there you go. The word we've come to identify with rebels, bohemians, trailblazers, dissenters, loners, nonconformists, extremists, malcontents, independents, insurgents, eccentrics, oddballs, free spirits, outsiders, hermits, recluses, strangers, outcasts, pariahs, and exiles originates from a lawyer who was so indifferent toward his ranching duties that he couldn't be bothered to burn his insignia into the hides of his herd. An act of laziness as much as rebellion.

Surely even after all these years, a molecule or two of Samuel's indolence lingers in the word *maverick,* reminding us that there can sometimes be a razor-thin difference between a maverick and a slacker.

Our old friend Henry David Thoreau will do for one quintessentially American example. Thoreau turned his back on civilization and experimented with a Spartan existence for a couple of years beside Walden Pond in what he claimed was an act of mutiny against the puritanical dogmas of his time. Yet all that journal writing and introspection in the drowsy Concord forest certainly has a tinge of indolence.

Thoreau's pragmatic, law-abiding neighbors were no doubt unmoved when their freeloading neighbor, the dreamy transcendentalist, was hauled away to jail for tax evasion. Rebellion is one thing, doing your fair share for the public good is another.

A similar tension between mavericks and conventionalists operates at the core of the biggest bestsellers of all time. Scarlett O'Hara, Allison MacKenzie, Scout Finch, Anne Welles, Michael Corleone, Chris MacNeil, Sheriff Martin Brody, John Smith, Jack Ryan, Mitch McDeere, Robert Kincaid, and Robert Langdon each in his or her own way does righteous battle against the forces of conformity and repression.

Every one of them is a maverick of one denomination or

another. Most are teetering on the brink of flat-out rejection of conventional society and are ready to embrace an individualist isolation from the customs of the mass culture.

THE EBB AND FLOW OF ORTHODOXY

Social scientists who chart such things have long been fascinated with the American tendency to tout individualism in one decade, then urge conformity in the next—reliable mood swings that seem to occur every ten years or so. In the postwar 1920s, for instance, there was something known as the "hometown mind," a form of groupthink that acted as a restraining pressure on the new, young individualists with "subtle compulsions" not to speak out frankly or act out sexually. The flappers vs. the moralists.

During the decade of the twenties, the flappers mostly won the day, and mavericks of every kind flourished and could be found spouting their views in literary journals and over shots of absinthe in Parisian Left Bank cafés.

During the Great Depression, calls for more personal and sexual freedom subsided, and the conformity pendulum lurched back the other way for a good long stay. In her sociological study *In Conflict No Longer,* Irene Thomson found that in the 1930s (a period during which *Gone with the Wind* was written and *To Kill a Mockingbird* was set), the heroes and heroines in mass magazine fiction no longer favored "self-realization over and above group definitions." Instead, the most widely read stories of that decade depicted individuals making adjustments to fit into the larger social context.

While the ebb and flow of gray flannel conformity and tie-dyed counterculture rebellion clearly exists in the national culture at large, these twelve bestsellers are consistent in the stands they take regarding these issues. Scarlett and Scout and Mitch McDeere and Allison MacKenzie and Johnny Smith don't blithely accept the prevailing views or social pressures exerted by their families or the citizens of their towns, even if it means public disapproval or risking their lives to act in ways they believe are right.

Over the last century, the heroes and heroines who consistently strike the deepest chord for American novel readers have remained those who reject the pressures and deadening effects of conformity and strike out for new territory.

SCARLETT AND RHETT, A COUPLE OF MAVERICKS

From early on, Scarlett thinks of herself as a clashing mixture of her parents' unique bloodlines, her mother's "soft-voiced, overbred Coast aristocrat mingled with the shrewd, earthy blood of an Irish peasant. . . . It was the same conflicting emotion that made her desire to appear a delicate and high-bred lady with boys and to be, as well, a hoyden who was not above a few kisses." "Hoyden," meaning part heathen, part tomboy, and all maverick.

With self-conscious contempt for conventional good manners, Rhett Butler sets himself apart the first moment we meet him at the Wilkeses' barbecue, where he sneers at the assembly of gentlemen who are salivating at the prospect of war. He takes the floor, exuding his special blend of contempt and faux courtesy.

Rhett knows his lecture will be badly received by these

airy-fairy cavaliers, but he forges on anyway, telling them what they least want to hear. How many cannon factories are there south of the Mason-Dixon Line? How many iron foundries? What about woolen mills or tanneries or cotton factories? And what about our lack of a navy? Yankee ships could easily blockade southern harbors, and then how would we sell our cotton? All the rebels have is a bunch of arrogance and slaves. We'll be licked in a month.

As becomes increasingly clear to both of them, Rhett and Scarlett are maverick soul mates. Defying the thought police of Atlanta high society at every turn, Scarlett quickly earns a reputation for defiance. So it comes as no surprise that when Rhett Butler asks the recently widowed Scarlett to dance at a charity ball, even though the rules of propriety strictly forbid such a thing, Scarlett is irrepressible. She leaps up, her heart beating wildly, completely undeterred by the disapproving looks on the chaperones' faces.

Later, while helping Scarlett flee Atlanta along the road to Tara, Rhett decides abruptly to join the doomed Confederacy, leaving Scarlett to finish the dangerous journey on her own. He's confident she'll survive just fine without him. She wails for him to stay, but he's adamant. Then he tags Scarlett perfectly:

> "I love you, Scarlett, because we are so much alike, renegades, both of us, dear, and selfish rascals. Neither of us cares a rap if the whole world goes to pot, so long as we are safe and comfortable."

A renegade. A maverick. What's the difference? Not to quibble too much about the nuances of etymology, still, it's interesting to note that a renegade is one who abandons one belief for another; or else he's a turncoat, a person who has acted with disloyalty to a cause.

To be a maverick is more extreme, for a maverick rejects the general status quo and will not be branded by its white-hot iron of normalcy. A maverick is a dropout, a nonconformist, a misfit. In short, a maverick is fully independent of the herd, an individual who acts without regard to others' opinions or rules.

Though the word *maverick* wasn't in use at the historical moment when Rhett was making his proclamation, it seems the more appropriate description of the characteristics Mr. Butler believed he and Scarlett shared. Renegades abandon causes, but neither Rhett nor Scarlett ever had a cause worth fighting for other than self-interest.

AMERICAN TOMBOY

Jean Louise Finch, otherwise known as Scout, has her own thought police to outwit. Near the head of the list is Miss Caroline, her first-grade teacher, who is displeased by Scout in general but in particular doesn't like that the girl has arrived at school already knowing how to read. Scout's learned it on her own somehow, and this proves to Miss Caroline that the girl-child has an unruly spirit that must be reined in immediately. Scout's solution to this assault on her freedom is much like Scarlett's "tomorrow is another day" avoidance. She begins a pattern of staring out the classroom window till the school day is done, at which time she's free to resume her education.

A more worthy adversary for Scout is her father's sister,

Aunt Alexandra. Like Huck Finn's aunt Sally, Scout's aunt means to "sivilize" her niece, with special attention to the young lady's fashion sense.

Aunt Alexandra is obsessed with Scout's clothes and tries in vain to convert her from breeches to dresses. She is just as fanatic about the manner in which Scout spends her playtime, urging her niece to use the tea sets and small stoves and to play with the Add-A-Pearl necklace Alexandra had given her as a newborn. Naturally, Scout will have none of this and would rather consort with her brother and her brother's friend Dill than stay inside and learn the feminizing tea ceremonies.

To stand against the entire community's racist views as Atticus does when he defends the innocent black man Tom Robinson is the ultimate act of individualism. Both Scout and Jem are swept into the turmoil, rebuked and isolated and threatened by nearly the whole town of Maycomb. What follows is something resembling a maverick boot camp, with Atticus as drill sergeant.

Atticus is eloquent in explaining to Jem and Scout that the discomfort they feel being ostracized by their friends and the townsfolk of Maycomb will pass. Such maverick behavior, he goes on to explain, is based on compassion and conscience, two Christian virtues that Atticus cannot disregard, although doing so would be so much easier. Giving in to the social norms, the racial intolerance, and the small-minded views of Maycomb is simply not an option for him, even if it means endangering himself and his family.

On the surface, you couldn't find two more dissimilar mavericks than Scarlett and Scout. One is defiant out of selfishness and romantic delusion, chasing the mirage of Ashley Wilkes or trying to re-create the antebellum fantasy of Tara.

The other is a natural-born questioner of authority, an innocent seeker of the dadgum honest truth.

Yet the reality is that Scout is similar to Scarlett on many counts. She's as self-sufficient and every bit as brave as young Miss O'Hara—all of which becomes clear when Scout faces down a lynch mob, a group of men as grim as a gaggle of zombies and as dangerous as any Yankee soldiers Scarlett ever dealt with. The gang wear denim shirts buttoned to their throats, and most are in overalls, with hats pulled over their ears—sullen and sleepy-looking, as though they're not used to being up so late. Scout is not cowed and wakes them from their mindless daze by singling out one man and speaking to him disarmingly. The mob tension dissolves, and the men drift off.

As much of a maverick as Scarlett is on matters of social propriety, she hews close to the conventions of her era on racial matters. Numerous passages that most charitably might be considered instructional can sometimes sound an awful lot like rants of racial intolerance. She scornfully describes former field hand slaves as acting like "lords of creation" and "trashy free issue niggers," while the "better class" of slaves stayed with their white masters.

Though only twenty-five years separate the publication of these two books, their views on race couldn't be more different. By Scout's estimation, being black or poor or both is a hard lot, but the worst predicament of all is being ostracized.

It came to me that Mayella Ewell must have been the loneliest person in the world. She was even lonelier than Boo Radley, who had not been out of the house in twenty-five years. . . . She was as sad, I thought, as what Jem called a mixed child: white people wouldn't have anything to do with her because she lived among pigs. Negroes wouldn't have anything to do with her because she was white. . . .

Both these female mavericks win our respect by remaining unbranded, using every means at their limited disposal to butt heads against the pressures of convention. The fact that both are female southerners and therefore subject to an additional set of persnickety social demands and relentless pressures to conform only makes their independence that much more triumphant.

WANTING TO BE NORMAL

"All I want is a normal life," John Smith moans. Not that Stephen King is about to let that happen.

Not a natural maverick like Scout or Scarlett, Johnny sets his feet firmly on the path of normalcy, working as a public schoolteacher. The kids like him, though they spot him as something of an oddball, nicknaming him Frankenstein for his geeky appearance. He's also a little off center in his laid-back approach to teaching and a bit inept with Sarah, the more experienced lover whom he courts.

For all his desire to fit in and live a normal life, Johnny is cursed by his condition, just as Rhett and Scarlett are cursed by theirs. He's bumped his head twice, and those accidents have reconfigured his hard-wiring.

When he wakes from his coma after four years, all hope of normalcy is gone. Sarah has deserted him and married another and has produced a child. Johnny's mother, Vera, has become a religious kook and is eagerly waiting for the End of

Days. Ironically, Vera might have it right, if Greg Stillson comes to power. Unless Johnny can summon the ultimate maverick's courage and shoot down the psychopath before he's put in higher office, the End of Days may very well be here.

So there it is. Greg Stillson runs on a platform as an outsider, a man with fresh ideas, in what seems like a winning strategy. He's billed himself as a political maverick, and much of his appeal is based on the "straight talk," "straight shooter" attraction. He successfully charms the voters, but not the reader, who knows this man has kicked a dog to death and that he honed his persuasive skills as an unsavory con man selling Bibles door-to-door. And we also come to understand that Greg is cynical about his own maverick image. He's nothing but a manipulator running the biggest con of all.

The only one who can save us is a genuine maverick, a man willing to take the most extreme act of individualism one can imagine, sacrificing his own life to save millions of others.

DRAGGED BACK

The normal life that Johnny Smith wanted was a lot like the one Michael Corleone had in mind before he was dragged into the family business. Normalcy was all Mitch McDeere sought, to marry Abby, have some kids, make a decent wage. It's the sum total of what Jack Ryan has in mind. Come to America, do a little weekend CIA business, and scoot back to London with a stateside Christmas gift for his daughter.

But all four of these male protagonists who are conformists by nature bump their heads in one kind of traffic accident or another. Michael's car explodes with Apollonia inside it, sending him storming back home with a vengeance. Mitch discovers his car is wired with microphones, as is his bedroom, and he crashes head-on into a plot to launder the Mob's money. Jack Ryan has no aspirations to be James Bond, but he's dragooned into service because his brainpower is unsurpassed. He's a scholar and knows a lot of esoteric stuff that might just save the world.

All four of these men become mavericks, but not by choice. Maverickhood is thrust upon them. They are forced almost against their will to act beyond the conventional patterns of behavior they've always embraced.

They are forced to be heroic and must summon their special skills, from second sight in Johnny's case, to the grim combat skills Michael Corleone mastered while fighting for his country's survival, to the cunning legal expertise Mitch employs to incriminate those who seek to destroy him. Jack Ryan's knowledge base also comes in handy, and he's recruited to handle negotiations that are far beyond his comfort zone of military duties.

Each man simply wanted the ordinary satisfactions of the culture. They had intended to fit in. But circumstances forced their hand and gave them a test they dared not fail.

As a Dartmouth grad and war hero, Michael Corleone doesn't have the street cred of his brothers, Sonny and Fredo, or even the orphan the Don adopted, Tom Hagen, all of whom stayed home in the Mafia trenches and made their bones in the usual ways. Michael's desire to fit into conventional American life makes him a bit of a maverick as far as Mafia men are concerned.

When the Don gets whacked and is almost killed, Michael struggles to retain his outsider status. However, his Corleone genes ignite when a punch in the jaw from a cop seems to wake him from his civilian daze. He gives up his conscientious objector status and joins the fray.

In time, Michael will learn more about the roots of this organization he's taken over. He'll discover its own maverick history. How when his Sicilian ancestors were repressed by cruel rulers ("landowning barons and the princes of the Catholic Church"), the common folks had learned that "society was their enemy, so when they sought redress for their wrongs they went to the rebel underground."

Michael, the war hero, the Ivy League boy, who will always be something of an outsider, takes control of a band of antisocial types who have lawlessness at their marrow. A maverick leading mavericks.

ORANGE SUSPENDERS

As Robert Kincaid comes rumbling across the bridges of Madison County in his pleasantly dented pickup truck, he's wearing the all-American maverick costume of "faded Levi's, well-used Red Wing field boots, a khaki shirt, and orange suspenders. On his wide leather belt was fastened a Swiss Army knife in its own case."

In case his individualism isn't nailed down firmly enough by those orange suspenders, Robert provides further evidence in this recollection from his younger days. "When other kids were singing 'Row, Row, Row Your Boat,' he was learning the melody and English words to a French cabaret song."

Though his IQ was off the charts, Robert rejected all that intellectual crap and spent his time reading "all the adventure and travel books in the local library and kept to himself otherwise, spending days along the river that ran through the edge of town, ignoring proms and football games and other things that bored him. He fished and swam and walked and lay in long grass listening to distant voices he fancied only he could hear. 'There are wizards out there,' he used to say to himself. 'If you're quiet and open enough to hear them, they're out there.' "

Oh, they're out there all right. Huck heard them long ago. And John Smith hears them, too.

For Robert, being a maverick is conveniently conflated with being a seducer of married women. Though he experiences a moment of hesitation, considering "the propriety drummed in by centuries of culture, the hard rules of civilized man," those conventional restraints dissolve when he starts to wonder how her hair would feel and how her body would fit beneath his.

Later on, after Robert and Francesca have spent a few ecstatic hours between the sheets, Robert lets her know just what kind of maverick she's gotten mixed up with. He refers to himself "as one of the last cowboys" and goes on to explain how society's normal conventions don't apply to him. All its rules and regulations and social conventions and laws are way too "organized" for Robert. Hierarchies of authority? Fie on them. Long-range budgets? Pooh. A world of "wrinkled suits and stick-on name tags"? No thanks, not for this cowboy.

At moments such as these, when he claims he's exempt from morality and has an inalienable right to sleep with married women, Robert Kincaid seems like such a smugly narcissistic blowhard, my bet is the Honorable Samuel Maverick would be tempted to rise from his lethargy, fire up his branding iron, and put his mark on this guy just to show him what being a real cowboy is all about.

HARRISON FORD IN HARRIS TWEED

And what of Professor Robert Langdon? Well, considering he's on nearly every page of *The Da Vinci Code*, it's a bit surprising how little we know about his personal life, or even his appearance. In *The Da Vinci Code*, the most detailed physical description of him is that he resembles "Harrison Ford in Harris tweed."

This kind of shorthand, relying on the Hollywood parallel, has the virtue of suggesting that Robert Langdon's fictional character is modeled on a confection that's one part Jack Ryan (played by Harrison Ford) and one part Indiana Jones (also played by Harrison Ford).

That is, Langdon fits the Harrison Ford action figure stereotype, the scholar-hero who, when the situation requires, peels off his corduroy jacket with the leather elbow patches, snuffs out his pipe, and pops into action. He's the bookish guy dumped into the snake pit of an adventure novel; his only real skill, aside from his dexterity with a bullwhip, is an unsettling tendency to recite long quotations from source material he apparently memorized in grad school. Oh, the curse of an eidetic memory.

Like Clark Kent, mild-mannered reporter for a great metropolitan daily newspaper, our professor lives a dual life. First, he long ago made a maverick career choice, deciding to be permanently out of step with society by isolating himself in the ivory tower. Which means he's geeky and stiff and in that sense is a first cousin to Jack Ryan, Jack being the author of naval histories. Spending way too much time with his nose in a book has made Robert Langdon a bit of a bumbler, always slightly flustered when someone produces a pistol and aims it his way.

When he's forced to assume this action figure identity, again he plays the maverick role, for he's lacking in physical prowess. He has no karate skills, isn't a kung fu master or an ex–Navy SEAL, doesn't even know how to field-strip an AK-47. As an action hero he just barely gets by, and that's part of the charm of this hero subcategory. Part of its American aura. Not every American fictional hero is a gunslinger. Americans like to view themselves as humble and self-effacing, able to make do with what they have, using Yankee ingenuity and an occasional nuclear-powered submarine to compensate for what they lack in physical prowess. In fact, most of the heroes in our twelve novels are anything but tough customers.

Of the twelve protagonists, only three take another human life. Scarlett O'Hara shoots to death a Yankee soldier who's invaded Tara, an act of self-defense. Jack Ryan is almost too nervous to fire back at the Soviet secret agent who is shooting at him and then apologizes to the dying man as he passes away. It's only Michael Corleone who kills without remorse, shooting two men at point-blank range in retribution for an attempt on his father's life. Johnny Smith tries to murder the evil Greg Stillson but muffs it. Still, he manages to push Stillson into an act of cowardice so public that it destroys his future political prospects. Even though extreme violence is commonplace in these twelve novels and the body count runs into the double digits (not counting the millions dead in the Civil War), our heroes and heroines are averse to using extreme force and are anything but adept at gunplay.

BOOKS AND MAVERICKS

Bookish types, both writers and readers, appear with such frequency in bestsellers that it is tempting to give them a chapter all their own. As any bookish person knows, authors and book readers are by nature oddballs, flaky loners who like to go off somewhere quiet and sit in a corner turning pages or swiping their finger across an e-book screen. In short, they're a bit on the mavericky side.

In these twelve novels, Scarlett is atypical in this regard, for she is openly hostile to books, mocking some of her Atlanta lady friends as "subdued, churchgoing, Shakespeare-reading." She came by this aversion to books naturally. Her father, Gerald, not only mocks Ashley Wilkes for his bookish, effeminate ways, but belittles the whole Wilkes clan for buying crates of books in German and French from the Yankee scoundrels. Then those crazy Wilkeses laze around reading when they should be out hunting and gambling like real men.

Scarlett O'Hara notwithstanding, almost every other novel on this list is filled with characters for whom books are of crucial importance.

In *Peyton Place,* for instance, Allison MacKenzie won't quit reading. Books are her lifeblood, both a way to temporarily escape from her complicated life and a method for reimagining it. She is rebuked by her mother for caring too much about literature. Constance didn't understand how a twelve-year-old girl could bury herself in books all the time while other girls her age were fixated on pretty frocks and lacy underwear.

Underwear versus books? Well, for most of us mavericks,

the choice is clear. We'll go commando before we'll give up our books.

For all its overheated sexual display and attacks on social hypocrisy, *Peyton Place* is actually an old-fashioned *Künstlerroman,* a portrait of the artist as a young girl. A novel that takes us almost step by step through the literary education of Allison MacKenzie.

Speaking with an early boyfriend, Allison proudly stakes claim to the low road of literary aspirations. She wants to write a famous book like *Anthony Adverse,* a book that will make her a celebrity.

Allison won't be denied and grows into a full-fledged journalist with the dream of one day becoming a writer of novels. She goes to New York to fulfill that dream and sets about the hard work of breaking in. As a generous gesture to all the would-be writers in her audience, Grace Metalious even diagrams a primitive form of literary networking.

After a series of crushing rejections from numerous literary agents, Allison marches off to the New York Public Library, where she studies current bestsellers. It is there she discovers on the dedication page of one of the commercial hits a declaration of thanks to the author's agent, Bradley Holmes. Bingo.

Allison tracks down the agent, makes her case, and soon is sleeping with the guy, though eventually he doesn't think he can sell her book.

Books, books, books. They're everywhere in these bestsellers, a reminder of the strange and fanciful power of narrative and of the shared love that writers and readers have, the symbiotic relationship they enjoy.

Books and reading play a large role in Scout Finch's world. She doesn't remember learning to read, just as she doesn't remember learning to breathe. Since Atticus is a lawyer and a devoted reader of books and newspapers, it was probably osmosis.

At one point, Atticus punishes Jem by requiring him to read *Ivanhoe* to the odious neighbor Mrs. Dubose. Scout and Jem do their duty, and though the old lady dozes off now and then, she never seems to lose track of their place in the story.

The punch line of this episode is that Mrs. Dubose was addicted to morphine, a habit she was determined to kick before she died. It was Jem's reading of *Ivanhoe* that diverted her sufficiently from the withdrawal pains and made her last wish possible. Ah, the stimulating power of books.

In *Valley of the Dolls,* when Anne Welles briefly rejects the romantic heartthrob Lyon Burke, there's only one way he can console himself. He flies off to London to write a book. And of course it becomes a smash hit.

Books are also of crucial importance to John Smith in *The Dead Zone.* He's a reading teacher, after all, and when he wakes from his coma and learns he's been fired from his teaching job, he soon finds work tutoring poor Chuck Chatsworth in reading. Chuck is a successful jock and "the apotheosis of the BMOC," but his illiteracy reduces him to bending "grimly over his book like a machine gunner at a lonely outpost, shooting the words down one by one as they came at him."

Since pedagogy is Johnny's real gift, not that second sight stuff, in no time Chuck is reading *Jude the Obscure.* It's an educational triumph and a reminder of what nearly mystical power some teachers can have.

Teachers and writers and professors and scholars and priests and lawyers march through nearly every one of these bestsellers. Men and women whose life's work revolves around reading and interpreting books. Books, books, everywhere books.

The most famous and fabulous and fussy professor of them all, Robert Langdon, is a scholarly wordsmith, though you wouldn't know it from his cultural allusions. A lot more book titles appear in the pages of *The Bridges of Madison County* or *Peyton Place* or *Jaws* or *The Exorcist* than issue from Robert Langdon's lips. Although Langdon seems to have read and memorized every volume ever shelved in the Library of Congress, he's more likely to drop Tom Cruise's name or refer to a Disney film than mention *Jude the Obscure* or *Anthony Adverse*.

At one point when Langdon enters a library, King's College Research Institute, to solve the next step in his puzzle, he doesn't blow the dust off some ancient tome and turn its desiccated pages but sits at a computer terminal and does some kind of Google search. That's not to say that Langdon doesn't love books. He does, he does. He writes them, after all. He just doesn't refer to them much.

Robert Kincaid, on the other hand, quotes Yeats and Robert Penn Warren and is currently reading *Green Hills of Africa*, Hemingway's safari journal that is full of literary commentary on Flaubert, Stendhal, Tolstoy, and Dostoyevsky. Robert's own true love, Francesca the farmer's wife, "usually read in the kitchen—books from Winterset library and the book club she belonged to. . . . The television bored her."

In *The Godfather*, Mario Puzo has some fun with writers, those "shmucks with an Underwood," as they used to be called in Hollywood. The singer Johnny Fontane tells an anecdote about a novelist who became a celebrity in the literary world and arrived in Hollywood expecting to be treated with fanfare. The author was set up with a well-endowed starlet and was eating dinner with her at the Brown Derby when the girl spotted some second-rate movie comic who wiggled a finger at her across the dining room. Without a word, she dumped the hotshot writer, leaving him with a new understanding of the Hollywood pecking order.

So busy shooting up the place, most of the characters in this novel don't have much spare time to read. But there's one man, Dr. Taza, Michael Corleone's landlord during his stay in the old country, who knows the value of a book.

> Though in his seventies, [Dr. Taza] went every week to Palermo to pay his respects to the younger prostitutes of that city, the younger the better. Dr. Taza's other vice was reading. He read everything and talked about what he read to his fellow townsmen, patients who were illiterate peasants, the estate shepherds, and this gave him a local reputation for foolishness. What did books have to do with them?

Hookers and books keep the old guy young. With vices like that, Dr. Taza could become an honorary maverick.

FEATURE #11

Fractured Families

> [Literature] is undertaken as equipment for living, as a ritualistic way of arming us to confront perplexities and risks.
>
> —KENNETH BURKE,
> *PHILOSOPHY OF LITERARY FORM*

In each of our twelve novels, a member of a broken family finds an ingenious way to transcend his or her crazy stress.

If you Google "every family is dysfunctional," you'll get around 144,000 results in .2 second. Compare that with Googling "every family is healthy," where a meager 8 hits appear. And in 5 of those 8 cases, the word *not* precedes *every*.

Okay, so that isn't exactly what you'd call scientific proof. Still, it supports the conventional wisdom that a lot of us have a lot of experience with fractured families.

Families under economic stress, families at emotional war, families splitting apart, families with a missing parent, families dealing with disease, death, infidelity, job stress, or outright life-threatening danger. You name it. Badly destabilized families are featured in each of our twelve bestsellers.

1. Scarlett O'Hara loses a daughter, three husbands, and both parents. Fails to win the heart of the man she thinks she loves while losing the man she realizes belatedly she might have loved.

2. Scout and Jem Finch have no mother, nor does Mayella Ewell, whose phony rape claim sets off a tragic cascade of events. Boo Radley lost his mother before he was imprisoned by his father in his own house.

3. Allison MacKenzie, the star of *Peyton Place*, is illegitimate and fatherless, while her best friend, Selena Cross, is also fatherless as well as a victim of sexual abuse from her stepfather.

4. Anne Wells in *Valley of the Dolls* is also missing a father, and her mother is a suffocating bore. Neely has no parents. Jennifer has no father, and her mother goads her to exploit her body for cash.

5. Michael Corleone loses the love of his life in a bomb blast, but otherwise his family stays relatively intact until the Don is badly injured in an assassination attempt; then Michael's brothers begin to die until the family threatens to implode.

6. Regan MacNeil, who is possessed by the devil, is first dispossessed by her own father, who divorces her mother and forgets to call on Regan's birthday. Two fathers (priests) are required to save her.

7. While Police Chief Brody defends the beaches of Amity from a terrorizing shark, his wife is straying

into the tricky currents of an affair with a visiting shark expert.

8. After four years in a coma, John Smith wakes to find his mother has become a hopeless religious lunatic; shortly thereafter, the zealous lady has a stroke and dies. The young woman John intended to wed marries another man instead but has a brief fling with Johnny anyway. Greg Stillson, Johnny's antagonist, is also fatherless.

9. Ramius deceives his shipboard family and hijacks the *Red October* and heads off to America because his wife died needlessly, a victim of the incompetent Soviet medical system.

10. Mitch McDeere is also fatherless and estranged from his mother, while the new law firm that adopts him as a son turns out to be lethally dysfunctional.

11. Robert Kincaid is divorced and has a hankering for vulnerable married women. Francesca Johnson is unfaithful to her husband and never fully recovers from her love affair with Robert.

12. Sophie Neveu's parents are both dead, and she's estranged from her only relative, her grandfather, who dies in the first scene. She may be a distant relative of Jesus Christ, a family connection that nearly costs her her life.

So there you go. Twelve of the most successful novels in American publishing history and not a traditional, fully functioning family among them, yet all our heroes and heroines find ways to make peace with their extreme losses.

FAMILY THERAPY

While entertainment is one of popular fiction's obvious jobs, its other enduring function has been to educate readers, to provide, in Kenneth Burke's phrase, "equipment for living." As we've seen, this responsibility takes many forms, from presenting factual information to critiquing religious practice. As important as any other educational function that the popular novel provides is its emphasis on the emotional struggles characters experience within the family structure.

Long before Dr. Phil and Oprah and a host of media therapists invited TV viewers into daily family therapy sessions, mass culture looked to popular novels for good counsel and insight into affairs of the heart.

Increasingly in the last few decades that good counsel has been sorely needed. From 1936, when *Gone with the Wind* was published, to 2003, when *The Da Vinci Code* appeared, stresses on the American family skyrocketed. Sociologists, our dependable cultural explainers, see many reasons for this: the ever-increasing divorce rate, unrealistic marital expectations, a rapid expansion of women entering the workforce, shifting gender roles, and the appearance of no-fault divorce, to name a few.

Then for the fun of it, add to the list such large external forces as the Great Depression, two world wars, and two regional wars that killed thousands, maimed thousands more, and psychologically damaged many who served, while keeping married partners separated for long periods of time. All further strained family bonds. Throw in a rising tolerance of promiscuity and the growing sense that multiple marriages was the new normal, and what you have is a family structure that is redefining itself at warp speed.

In the last thirty years of the twentieth century, the number of unmarried couples cohabitating grew by a factor of seven to a figure that today reaches more than five million couples. Forty percent of babies born in 2007 came from unmarried parents. Such statistics send shivers through conservative pundits and political theorists like William Bennett, a staunch defender of the familial status quo, who no doubt speaks for millions of Americans when he claims (in *The Broken Hearth*) that "the nuclear family, defined as a monogamous married couple living with their children, is vital to civilization's success." Bennett goes on to claim that the "dissolution of the family is the fundamental crisis of our time."

"Dissolution" is a somewhat dire description of what some would say is simply a modernization of the family structure or a set of changes that reflect other transformations in modern culture.

Nevertheless, few would argue with the assertion that the traditional family model is in a state of flux. With such rapid transformations, where do individuals go for perspective? Aside from the low-cost alternatives like Oprah and her fellow empathizers, some go where they've always gone, to their closest friends. But we all know what that advice is worth. Many go to church and speak to the wise men there. For others who can afford it and overcome the stigma, there's always psychiatry.

But it's safe to say that many Americans looking for a vicarious connection with another troubled soul could do worse than snuggle up with Scarlett O'Hara or Francesca Johnson, Mitch McDeere or John Smith.

LIFE TRAUMAS

In 1967, psychiatrists Thomas Holmes and Richard Rahe studied the medical records of more than five thousand patients in an attempt to determine if stressful events caused illnesses. Eventually the good doctors listed forty-three life traumas, each with a "stress score." The study came to be known as the Holmes and Rahe stress scale.

While the focus of this chapter is on the stresses and conflicts within families, the Holmes and Rahe stress scale makes a handy checklist of dramatic situations that might find their way into the narrative of almost any novel and certainly would keep the familial pot boiling:

LIFE EVENT	LIFE CHANGE UNITS
Death of a spouse	100
Divorce	73
Marital separation	65
Imprisonment	63
Death of a close family member	63
Personal injury or illness	53
Marriage	50
Dismissal from work	47
Marital reconciliation	45
Retirement	45
Change in health of family member	44
Pregnancy	40
Sexual difficulties	39
Gain a new family member	39

Business readjustment	39
Change in financial state	38
Death of a close friend	37
Change to different line of work	36
Change in frequency of arguments	35
Major mortgage	32
Foreclosure of mortgage or loan	30
Change in responsibilities at work	29
Child leaving home	29
Trouble with in-laws	29
Outstanding personal achievement	28
Spouse starts or stops work	26
Begin or end school	26
Change in living conditions	25
Revision of personal habits	24
Trouble with boss	23
Change in working hours or conditions	20
Change in residence	20
Change in schools	20
Change in recreation	19
Change in church activities	19
Change in social activities	18
Minor mortgage or loan	17
Change in sleeping habits	16
Change in number of family reunions	15
Change in eating habits	15
Vacation	13
Christmas	12
Minor violation of law	11

Subject: Ms. Scarlett O'Hara

Death of a spouse: check, check

Death of a close family member: check, check, check

Pregnancy: check

Sexual difficulties: check

Change in residence: check, check, check, check

No doubt about it, Scarlett tops the list for stress events. And a few stressors not even on the list surely rank high on her inventory. The nuisance of the Civil War, for one, all those cannonballs exploding in the Atlanta streets. And there's that dashing young man Ashley Wilkes, who doesn't fancy her as much as she fancies him.

What are Scarlett's psychological coping strategies? How does our heroine manage the ever-mounting pressures thrown at her for nearly a thousand pages? What psychological lessons does she have to pass on to the mass audience hungry for insight? Well, fiddle-dee-dee, Scarlett suggests y'all should just think about all that tomorrow.

Actually, for much of the novel Scarlett is shielded from the harsher realities by her caring mother, her willful but indulgent father, her protective mammy, and her selfless sister-in-law, Melanie. This portrait of a successfully functioning family might have been Scarlett's model if the war hadn't interrupted things so abruptly and brought an end to her childhood before she'd fully matured.

After losing her mother's emotional counsel, then her father's blunt and accurate appraisals of human nature, Scarlett is basically on her own. Still a girl, but suddenly a wife, then just as suddenly a widow. Nothing to guide her but her adolescent fantasies and her will to survive at any cost.

Those survival instincts lead Scarlett to consider any husband besides Ashley as nothing but a necessary bother—strictly a means to an end. That end is not the nurturing warmth of family or any kind of domestic bliss. Husbands are not for love or even sexual satisfaction, and, oh my, they certainly aren't for having babies. For Scarlett, husbands are all about money and the physical security they bring. Tenderness and affection are merely weapons in her arsenal used to bring down her man.

Scarlett's notion of family relationships is just as cynical, a fact made clear when we witness her stealing her sister's fiancé because he can provide the goods and services she wants. And how does Scarlett respond to her sister's outrage and pain? She blows it off with a fiddle-dee-dee.

However, she continues to maintain one emotional soft spot: Scarlett's cynical view of marriage alternates with a delusional romantic vision of her ideal mate, Ashley Wilkes. This same vacillation between romanticism and cynicism is also a defining characteristic of the heroines of *Valley of the Dolls* and *Peyton Place*. Despite all evidence to the contrary, the heroines of those novels hold out hope that a fairy-tale version of true love awaits them and marriage to the right man will one day heal all their wounds and disappointments.

Anne Welles of *Valley of the Dolls* snags her right man, Lyon Burke, but the guy is as much a downer as the pills Anne is increasingly dependent on. Ducking out of her own party at the conclusion of the novel, Anne lies down on her bed, happy to have escaped the din of actors and actresses and entertainment types who are jamming her apartment.

Then who slips into the darkened room but the former man of her dreams and now her husband, Lyon Burke. Except he's not alone. He's brought along his latest hottie, a young actress type named Margie. Unaware of her lying nearby, they smooch and whisper in the dark while Anne lies listening. When they've gone, Anne rises from the bed, brushes her hair and freshens her makeup, and runs through the list of things she should be grateful for: "She looked fine. She had Lyon, the beautiful apartment, the beautiful child, the nice career of her own, New York—everything she'd ever wanted."

And though she understands Lyon will be unfaithful to her forever, she's reconciled to that. Her solace now comes in pill form, her own chemical fiddle-dee-dee. The way she'll get through the lonely nights ahead is by gulping down "the beautiful dolls." In fact, she decides to pop a couple tonight. Hey, why not? It's New Year's Eve.

Readers looking to these novels for psychological insight ("equipment for living") would see that Scarlett and the young ladies from *Valley of the Dolls* are tragically doomed and have sabotaged their chances for authentic love and familial happiness. Part romance novel, part critique of romance novel, these two stories strip bare the hopeless, swooning fantasies of their heroines.

SACRED FAMILY

To Don Corleone, family is sacred. He's willing to fight and die for his kinfolk and demands the same loyalty in return. Indeed, as part of his role as everybody's Godfather, he will occasionally agree to act as guidance counselor as well. When his godson Johnny Fontane, a Sinatra-like singer, comes to the Don in desperate need, the Godfather gives him some tough love, a chewing out the likes of which Scarlett never heard but probably should have.

Johnny is confined to a one-month sentence with the Don as his warden. Johnny must eat well, sleep, and rest. No booze, no girls, not even singing.

But Don Corleone's kids are a harder challenge. Even a man with the Don's menacing demeanor has a hard time keeping them in line. Sonny, his eldest, is just too reckless and self-destructive for anybody's good. When the boy is involved in a stupid armed robbery that nets next to nothing, the Don is livid. He rages at his son until Sonny has had enough and cuts his father off at the knees, telling him he saw Don Corleone kill a man.

The Don is dumbstruck. He hadn't known that as a child Sonny witnessed the Don's murder of the neighborhood tyrant. That life lesson, a stressor that Holmes and Rahe forget to add to their list, will overshadow every other good lesson the Don has to teach his boy. Sonny is lost to him, and all he can say at that moment is, "Every man has one destiny."

In effect, from that moment on, he washes his hands of parental responsibility for Sonny. It's the Don's own fiddle-dee-dee.

As for the women, well, they don't wield much power in this powerful family. In the superpaternalistic structure of the Corleone clan, Mama Corleone virtually disappears into insignificance. The same is true for Kay Adams, who marries Michael without knowing the real nature of his family business or fully understanding that she is brought aboard to fulfill the appearance of an all-American marriage. Her own romantic dreams about marriage evaporate as well.

Female empowerment, it would seem, is a fantasy that drives these women into relationships, but that fantasy is quickly shattered by the realization that the male-dominated

world each of these women enters is more rigid and perma-
nent than any of them bargained for.

FEMALE-FREE ZONE

Again and again, despite the vastly different subject matter in
these bestsellers, family tensions and parental legacies under-
pin critical events in the stories.

Even in *The Hunt for Red October,* a nearly female-free
zone, family issues crop up at odd and crucial moments. Not
surprisingly, it turns out that the families that get the most
face time in *The Hunt for Red October* are the crews of the
submarines. In fact, the American submariners seem to be a
happier family unit than any we see in Scarlett's world or the
Don's.

> The crew of the *Dallas* was like one big family . . . the
> captain was the father. The executive officer, everyone
> would readily agree, was the mother. The officers were
> the older kids, and the enlisted men were the younger
> kids.

Family is even at the root of the tensions between the two
superpowers. None of these world-endangering events would
have happened had Ramius, the Soviet sub commander, had
a normal childhood. The kid never knew his mother and was
deeply alienated from his old man, and thus was starved for
human love.

Compared with Ramius, Jack Ryan has a solid family life,
though he's a little sketchy on the details. A wife, two kids.

There might have been any number of reasons for Ra-

mius's defection, money, power, influence, ego. But it's none
of those. Family, pure and simple, is at the root of his rejection of the Soviet way of life. Without the foundation of a
nurturing childhood, Ramius pours all his love into his marriage. So when his wife, Natalia, dies from Soviet medical
negligence, Ramius descends into utter despair.

> Natalia . . . had been his only happiness . . . he was
> tormented by her memory; a certain hairstyle, a certain
> walk, a certain laugh encountered on the streets or in
> the shops of Murmansk was all it took to thrust Nata-
> lia back to the forefront of his consciousness. . . .

Of course, the rivalry between superpowers that nearly
leads to all-out war is the major narrative thread, the one that
grabs the reader's attention and makes the pages fly by. An
emotionally charged passage like the one above easily gets
lost amid the detailing of hardware and naval maneuvering.
But to Clancy's credit, flesh-and-blood creatures bound by
ties of love and affection and driven by haunting memories
form a human counterweight to this story of nuclear engines
and the supersecret technology that threatens the world.

Though maybe it's a little hokey, Clancy is determined to
give Jack and Ramius, his two adversaries, clear and certain
family lives that reflect the nations that spawned them. America is painted as the land of stability, where, by golly, a decent
man has a wife and two kids and is happily married. On the
other hand, his counterpart's Soviet family is shown to be
destabilized by the ravages of an ancient war and by the
strains of the gray bureaucracy that suffocates even its heroes.

After the two men play cat and mouse for a couple of hundred pages, Ramius and Jack Ryan finally meet face-to-face.

They shake hands, and the first words Ramius speaks are oddly personal.

"You have a family, Commander Ryan?" Ramius asked.

"Yes, sir. A wife, a son, and a daughter. You, sir?"

"No, no family."

Ramius turns away abruptly and addresses a junior officer in Russian. But the point is clear. To Ramius, family is of primary importance. It's where everything begins.

In this regard, Clancy is more subtle than he's usually given credit for. Despite all the political bluster and the machinery, the endless nuts and bolts of warfare that seem, at first glance, to overshadow all else in his work, lurking just below the surface, barely making a ripple on the thin skin of the sea, are his deep concerns with the relationships between his people, be they submariners or hapless CIA information analysts. It seems that Clancy's vision is as familial as it is political. For Clancy, both the dirty Commies and the freedom-loving Americans have the same urgent human need for domestic relationships. And it is the destruction of that, the shredding of the fabric of family life, that in Clancy's view is our greatest peril.

FAMILIES STAYING TOGETHER

For readers in search of families more dysfunctional than their own, *Peyton Place* would be an excellent choice.

Allison MacKenzie, writer-in-training, is doing fieldwork one day at her friend Selena Cross's tar-paper shack. She's interviewing Selena's mother, trying to grasp how a family manages to stay together in the face of the kind of sexual and physical abuse that Allison witnessed earlier, and Nellie Cross is giving her the lowdown, a glimpse into the cruel machinery of connubial relations.

"Why, honey, beatin's don't mean nothin'." Nellie cackled again, and this time her eyes did turn vague. "It's everythin' else. The booze and the wimmin. Even the booze ain't so bad, if he'd just leave the wimmin alone. I could tell you some stories, honey—" Nellie folded her arms together, and her voice took on a sing-song quality—"I could tell you some stories, honey, that ain't nothing like the stories you tell me."

Allison pokes around in other people's lives with a voyeuristic fascination, all in the name of learning her craft as a writer. The likelihood is that she will succeed in that tough literary field, for she's got the one great advantage of high-achieving people. She's missing a parent.

Her mother, Constance, says as much when musing about her daughter. She wonders if it's true that bastards are often successful in their chosen fields because they are driven to compensate for not having had a father.

MISSING PARENTS

Missing fathers, or missing mothers, or missing wives, propel most of these characters to greater attainments. Scout Finch's mother died of a heart attack when Scout was only two years old. Jem is still troubled by her loss. Sometimes in the middle of play, he will suddenly sigh and walk off to be alone. Scout understands and keeps her distance. Though she pretends she's unaffected by her absent mom, we can see through her bluff. The very fact that she's so aware of the source of her brother's pain is proof enough.

This missing-parent paradigm shows up as frequently in bestsellers as it does in traditional fairy tales. As Bruno Bettelheim noted in *The Uses of Enchantment,* his landmark work on the psychological function of fairy tales, the recurrence of missing-parent imagery serves a fundamental purpose in the education of a child. For one thing, it prepares a youngster for the wrenching passage to adulthood. At some stage in the process of growing up, the protective and kindhearted mother seems to vanish, replaced by a stern disciplinarian who sets rigid boundaries and rules. Fairy tales lay the groundwork for the jarring change of adolescence.

In the absence of a nurturing birth mother, Scout Finch has three surrogates: Calpurnia, the African American housekeeper, who monitors Scout's comings and goings; her aunt Alexandra, who endlessly disapproves of Scout's tomboyish ways; and Miss Maudie, a neighbor who plays the comforting, pampering fairy godmother role, though, as is true in fairy tales, her influence can't last forever. Like Scout's real mother, she drifts away symbolically, which leaves Scout to fend for herself and thus to learn how to break the ties of reliance on parental protection and become fully independent. These are the lessons that Cinderella had to learn, just like Scarlett and Allison MacKenzie.

That big bestsellers and fairy tales both use this pattern with such regularity is not surprising, because both storytelling forms serve a similar broad social purpose, to remind us of the archetypal journey we all share, a mythic passage from the safe, cozy nest where we spent our early days, shielded from the dangers of the world, to a challenging and often menacing larger world where we must rely on our own inner resources to survive.

MIRROR IMAGES

The families are so much alike in *Peyton Place* and *To Kill a Mockingbird,* it's hard to shake the idea that a little harmless cribbing was at work in Harper Lee's effort. Both books feature young female narrators who explore their small towns from stem to stern. The Ewell family who live beside the dump are a perfect mirror of the earlier Cross family in their shantytown, right down to a nearly identical incestuous relationship between father and daughter. A threatened lynching and a big explosive trial full of seamy revelations is a centerpiece of both books. Justice is served in Peyton Place, while justice fails in Maycomb. There's even a precursor to Boo Radley living down the street from Allison MacKenzie. Her name is Miss Hester, and she has the same creepy reputation and reclusive habits as Boo. And there's also a kid who accepts a dare to go up to her house and sit on her porch and see what she sees. But there the similarity ends. From Boo's porch, Scout has her major revelation and discovers empathy, finally viewing the world from Boo's point of view.

Norman Page's interaction with the bogeyman of Peyton Place results in a very similar outcome. He was "terrified of Miss Hester, and Allison had laughed at him and tried to frighten him even more by saying that Miss Hester was a witch." Determined to overcome that terror, Norman seizes an opportunity when Miss Hester makes a rare departure from her house.

He hangs around till she's gone, then runs across the street and through the scary lady's gate. It's the first time he's stepped onto her property.

He wades through the tall, unkept grass to the back porch and looks around the neighborhood from this new vantage point. What Norman Page sees through a split in the hedge is Mr. and Mrs. Card, the next-door neighbors, fondling each other, and Mr. Card unbuttoning Mrs. Card's dress and stroking her pregnant belly.

Norman gets a hot and heavy peek into the world of passion, while Scout gazes out with growing sympathy as she absorbs the neighborhood from Boo Radley's vantage point. At first these sharply dissimilar views seen from very similar porches suggest these two novels have little in common. One raunchy, one chaste. A missing father for Allison. A missing mother for Scout. But though their methods are radically different, their intentions are exactly the same.

Allison's mother, Constance, has never fully recovered from her affair with Allison's father and has sublimated her sexual energy, redirecting it toward raising her daughter and running her dress shop. But she will eventually find release in the arms of the new high school principal, Tomas Makris. Overcoming her sexual inhibitions brings Constance to a moment of discovery that could stand as the final psychological offering of this novel.

Makris and Constance are in bed together, engaging in some spirited back-and-forth. Constance first:

"Do it to me then."

He raised his head and smiled down into her face. "Do what?" he teased. "Tell me."

"You know."

"No, tell me. What do you want me to do to you?"

She looked up at him appealingly.

"Say it," he said. "Say it."

She whispered the words in his ear and his fingers dug into her shoulders.

"Like this?"

"Please," she said. "Please." And then, "Yes! Yes, yes, yes."

Later she lay with her head on his shoulder and one hand flat against his chest.

"For the first time in my life I'm not ashamed afterward," she said.

What Constance accomplishes in this scene is echoed throughout. Conquering sexual repression. Breaking taboos. Speaking the forbidden words. Shrugging free of puritanical prohibitions. The aspirations of this novel are as American as Hawthorne, as warm and gooey as apple pie. (Her maiden name, after all, is Standish, an echo of Longfellow's poem about an independent-minded woman being courted by an uncertain fellow named Miles.)

This novel that shocked the nation and was banned in Boston and railed against from pulpits has a simple and pure-at-heart intention. To heal by revealing, to cure by exposing, to alleviate the pressure we all feel by unzipping the tight girdle of false piety and showing us how families truly operate.

So from the porch of *Peyton Place* we peep on our neighbors' shameful acts and are given a glimpse of the unashamed reality of love. While from the front porch of the Radley house, we look through the eyes of a damaged young man and glimpse his longing and isolation. Two different paths for reaching the same destination: discovering the shared bonds of the human family.

LEGAL FAMILY

A solid family life is a requirement for employment at the legal firm of Bendini, Lambert & Locke. It's even part of the job interview, one of the first questions Mitch McDeere is tossed.

"Tell us about your family."

"Why is that important?"

"It's very important to us, Mitch," Royce McKnight said warmly.

They all say that, thought McDeere. "Okay, my father was killed in the coal mines when I was seven years old. My mother remarried and lives in Florida. I had two brothers. Rusty was killed in Vietnam. I have a brother named Ray McDeere."

Subject: Mitch McDeere

Death of a close family member: check, check (and a half check—brother Ray is in prison)

That criminal brother, Ray, meets with Mitch in the prison visiting room, and how do they use this precious time together? The two of them try to recall better days of their family's past. Once again we are reminded of the profound effects of fractured families—in this case fractured by madness.

They paused and studied their fingers. They thought of their mother. Painful thoughts for the most part. There had been happier times, when they were small and their father was alive. She never recovered from his death, and after Rusty was killed the aunts and uncles put her in an institution.

From the Don to Ramius to Scout to Allison and Mitch, the characters in these stories are struggling, first and foremost, with family issues. And no matter whether the novel is populated by submarines or sharks or mobsters or southern belles, the real focus is on healing the fractures, overcoming the loss, finding a way forward through family tragedies.

These bestsellers don't offer one pat answer to this recurring struggle. In some cases, as with Scout and Allison, healing means discovering empathy, or it can involve simply toughing it out in manly silence, as Jack Ryan, Robert Kincaid, and Mitch McDeere choose. Sometimes, for those like the Don and Scarlett and Anne Welles, it means simply saying fiddle-dee-dee and moving ahead ruthlessly into tomorrow.

FEATURE #12

The Juicy Parts

When I'm good I'm very, very good, but when I'm bad I'm better.

—MAE WEST

In every novel on our list, one key sexual encounter plays a decisive role in the outcome of the plot and in the transformation of the protagonist.

Sex sells, they say, and of course they're right.

Those in the business of quantifying such things have even nailed down the numbers, at least in a general sort of way. In their academic study on those bestselling novels that were published in the period between 1965 and 1985, Karen Hinckley and Barbara Hinckley tabulated that "books about sex are second in frequency [of sales] only to historical novels and are about as frequent as tales of spies and intrigue" (*American Bestsellers: A Reader's Guide to Popular Fiction*).

For the purposes of their study, they defined "books about sex" this way: "The topic—whether an activity, a preoccupation, or a problem—forms a major theme or is described frequently enough to be important to the book . . . one scene of battle does not make a war novel, and one scene of sex sufficient for an R movie rating does not make a book about sex."

Using their classification, only two of the books on our list of twelve megasellers are "about sex." *Peyton Place* and *Valley of the Dolls* feature numerous sexual encounters from masturbation to oral sex to lesbian encounters to incest and rape.

But numbering sexual acts tells us nothing about the role that sex actually plays in shaping the meaning of the novel. As my students and I discovered, in every novel we examined there was a striking repeating pattern: One key sexual encounter, no matter how slight it might have seemed or how euphemistically it was rendered, inevitably played a decisive role in the outcome of the plot and in the transformation of the main character.

What we also came to see was that sex scenes in bestsellers seem to be at the red-hot center of gender relations. The sweaty realities played out on fictional couches and beds and in the backseats of automobiles more often than not reenact one of America's most dramatic social movements in the twentieth century, the struggle of women for empowerment, equality, and independence.

GLORIED IN IT

After nine hundred pages of enduring Scarlett's childish fixation on the vapid Ashley Wilkes, Rhett Butler, the dark prince of *Gone with the Wind,* has had all he can take. Furious after witnessing an intimate encounter between his wife and Ashley, Rhett proceeds to get drunk and sweep Scarlett roughly into his arms. He hauls her up the stairs, and on the landing he kisses her savagely, and as she is about to faint away from his overwhelming passion, she realizes that Rhett is the first man she's ever met who is stronger than she is, someone she cannot intimidate or control, someone who in fact is intimidating and controlling her.

During the violent sex that follows, Rhett Butler "humbled her, hurt her, used her brutally through a wild mad night and she had gloried in it."

Gloried in it?

Well, yes. Because to Scarlett the quasi rape is evidence that she now has the one thing she craves most of all, control. Decades before the sexual revolution and the gender wars began to consume the American mass media's attention, Scarlett was experimenting with a feminist vocabulary by casting the sexual dynamics between a man and a woman in the political lingo of power and exploitation.

Scarlett glories in the thought that now Rhett is at her mercy. She knows the chinks in his armor. She has him exactly where she wants him and now "could make him jump through any hoops she cared to hold."

Oddly, the identical phrase appears in a crucial passage in *Peyton Place,* a postcoital moment after Allison MacKenzie has lost her virginity to Bradley Holmes, an experienced older man. Allison also glories in the mistaken belief that she has gained power over her sexual partner. After a weekend of sex, Allison is a changed woman. She is able to strut naked in front of Brad, feeling his eyes on her body, without experiencing a trace of shame or a flicker of fear, because she "had arched her back, and lifted her heavy hair off her neck, and pressed her breasts against his face, and gloried in his swift reaction to her."

Allison and Scarlett will soon discover their celebration of control and power over their lover was premature. For Rhett and Brad, the sexual events that meant so much to Scarlett and Allison were far from life-altering.

But these sexual episodes are watershed moments for the female characters. In the final pages of these two novels, after the heroines are rejected by the men they thought they controlled, each woman goes on to discover that true empowerment is far harder to achieve than the fleeting dominance they wielded in the bedroom.

Shortly after her rejection by Rhett, in a rare moment of candid self-appraisal, Scarlett succinctly describes the limitations and immaturities that have characterized her for the thousand preceding pages. Scarlett admits to herself that she never fully understood the two men she'd loved. If she'd truly known Ashley, she wouldn't have loved him. And if she'd truly understood Rhett, she'd never have lost him. For a moment, she wonders if she's ever really known anyone.

With almost any other literary character, this epiphany would stand as the climactic moment in an arc of development—a revelation about self that would propel that character to a new understanding in the final pages. But Scarlett O'Hara is so mired in her habits of mind, this moment of recognition is quickly shunted aside with her standard psychological dodge. Oh, fiddle-dee-dee. She'll worry about all that tomorrow.

In *Frankly, My Dear*, an analysis of both the film and the novel of *Gone with the Wind*, Molly Haskell argues that beneath her hoop skirts and petticoats, Scarlett is actually a revolutionary character for her era, a woman with some of the features of a modern feminist, "a predator who marries three men she doesn't love," "a rotten mother," and "a successful business woman."

Ordinarily, Haskell observes, a female literary character behaving in these "inappropriate" ways would be made to suffer "one or more of the following: sexual and psychological humiliation, a barrage of self-satisfied diatribes and blandishments from the people she's wounded; death, or, in its stead, an eleventh-hour reversal whereby she repents her wicked ways, is brought back to heel, and is transformed by love into a submissive female."

I beg to differ. While it's true that Scarlett transformed herself in some fashion into a modern woman by becoming an independent business owner who is every bit as savvy, hard-nosed, and cynically aggressive in her financial dealings as any man, at her core she failed to evolve, and we leave her in the last scene pretty much as we found her at the opening, just as silly and man-dependent.

In this respect, Scarlett is unique among the major female characters on our list of bestsellers. Most of the heroines break with gender stereotypes in a way that's more in line with modern feminism—they become stronger, more independent, more rigorously self-aware, and less deluded by the fantasies and fairy tales they believed in earlier. In terms of my study, what's truly striking about these gender transformations is that almost always the radical change of perspective is triggered by a single intense sexual encounter.

Allison MacKenzie's first sexual fling ends with the discovery that Brad Holmes, her lover, is married. He deceived her and exploited her innocence. When Allison "gloried in his swift reaction to her," she was clearly mistaking the rush of blood for something more lasting and real.

Like her mother before her, Allison flees the arms of her deceitful lover and returns home to Peyton Place. But Allison is from a new, more liberal generation. Unlike Constance, Allison does not allow her disillusionment with one man to fester into suspicion and bitterness toward them all. Instead, her own erotic discoveries help Allison come to peace with the crude sexuality that's always galled her in the affairs of Peyton Place.

In a final scene, Allison stands on a hillside with the toy-like town spread before her, and in language she might use to address her ex-lover, Brad, she expresses sympathy and forgiveness for Peyton Place. Accepting its meanness, its generosity, its cruelty. Now that she truly knows the town, truly understands the complex emotions at work in its narrow streets, Peyton Place no longer frightens her.

Her encounter with Brad Holmes makes this final reconciliation with her hometown possible. Wiser in the ways of sex, Allison now sees the behavior she'd once taken as lewd and sordid to be a natural and vital part of the human story. This discovery is crucial in her growth as an independent woman, and it's essential to her evolution as a fiction writer. For we know Allison MacKenzie now will be able to revise her manuscript with a greater understanding of her subject and create a full and mature portrait of Peyton Place. The tangible result of her journey of sexual discovery is a novel very much like the one we've been reading.

RUTTING

Sex is certainly not the first thing that comes to mind when considering *To Kill a Mockingbird*. Most readers would probably label the book as a young adult novel about racial tensions in a small southern town. But the fact is, the novel's plot as well as Scout's personal transformation are driven chiefly by a single sexual event.

Though the encounter between Mayella Ewell and Tom Robinson is a total fabrication devised by the Ewells, their lie radically changes numerous lives, spawning a lynching attempt, an explosive rape trial, the death of an innocent man, the attempted murder of two children, and the violent death of Robert Ewell. And on the psychological level, that same sexual accusation fuels Scout Finch's change from an innocent child to a young woman with a more mature understanding of the intimate relations between men and women.

If eight-year-old Scout at first doesn't understand what rape is, the courtroom testimony by Bob Ewell and Mayella removes any doubt. Speaking before an overflow crowd that includes the Finch children, Robert Ewell recounts his version of events of a recent November evening when he was bringing a load of firewood home and heard his daughter, Mayella, screaming. He dropped his load and ran to the window of his house and saw Tom Robinson "ruttin' on my Mayella."

As the trial continues, Atticus Finch questions Mayella about the details of the night in question, and Scout is exposed to two additional facts of life most girls her age and class would be shielded from—that daughters can sometimes be the victims of sexual and physical abuse from their fathers and that sexual desire can be driven by needs far more perverse than love.

Though Scout and the reader can only guess what really happened in the Ewells' shack that November evening, the novel strongly suggests Mayella made a pass at Tom, a provocative come-on that he was in the process of rejecting when Mayella's father arrived on the scene.

Tom ran. And Mayella was beaten by her father for her crime of interracial lust. To cover his shame and vent his anger, Bob Ewell summoned the sheriff and claimed Tom raped his daughter. All this Scout manages to infer from the Ewells' evasive court testimony.

Scout's training in gender politics actually begins long before the trial starts when Miss Maudie, who has been the target of religious zealots, explains to Scout that these "foot-washers think women are a sin by definition." Scout hears the same sexist message again in a sermon given at a black church when the preacher inveighs against the whole female race as impure and the root of all temptation.

Like Scarlett O'Hara, Scout is bombarded with messages about proper female behavior. Calpurnia chides her constantly about her tomboy antics. Her own brother, Jem, is increasingly uncomfortable with her gender.

As much as Scout would like to avoid the whole subject of sex and gender, she can't. By the end of the novel, the carnal desire Mayella felt for Tom warps into violence that overtakes Scout and her brother in the form of a knife-wielding Bob Ewell.

In the scene that follows, Scout meets Boo Radley face-to-face for the first time in a bedroom at the Finches' house.

At the moment when Scout and Boo touch, there is something electric, even sensuous, in their exploratory give-and-take and the gentle coaching that passes between them, as if this scene might be the innocent mirror image of the coarse encounter between Mayella and Tom Robinson.

In a reversal of traditional male and female roles, Scout leads Boo back to his house and drops him at his door. They part wordlessly, like lovers who've exhausted the possibilities between them. After this moment Scout will never see Boo again, but she is changed by the encounter, just as Allison is forever altered by her first intimate contact with a man. Both young women are stronger and more independent at the conclusions of their stories, budding feminists who are seemingly on their way to escaping the gender stereotypes that trap the other female characters in these novels.

WATERSHED SEX

In *The Dead Zone*, John Smith and Sarah Bracknell are about to have sex for the first time when fate intervenes. A violent car crash sends Johnny into a coma for four and a half years, and when he wakes, Sarah has moved on. She's married Walt Hazlett, and the couple has a child. But Sarah's not over Johnny, and he's definitely not over her.

For starters, Sarah can't help comparing her cynical husband with the good-hearted Johnny, a comparison that undermines her fidelity to Walt.

> In that moment she hated [Walt], loathed him, this good man she had married. There was really nothing so terrible on the reverse side of his goodness, his steadiness, his mild good humor—just the belief, apparently grounded in the bedrock of his soul, that everybody

was looking out for number one, each with his or her own little racket.

Johnny wasn't that way. He had a heart of gold before the coma, and when he wakes, Sarah decides she must get back in touch. She finds him unchanged by his ordeal, and the pent-up, unresolved sexual tension between them erupts. What follows is a sensuous fulfillment of all that was long deferred. For the two young people, sex is not an opening of a door to the future, but a closing of the door to the past.

Sinking into her was like sinking into an old dream that had never been quite forgotten.

"Oh, Johnny, my dear . . ." Her voice in rising excitement. Her hips moving in a quickening tempo. Her voice was far away. The touch of her hair was like fire on his shoulder and chest. He plunged his face deeply into it, losing himself in the dark-blonde darkness.

This sexual moment cauterizes their wounded hearts and allows each of them to let go of their romantic past. Sarah returns to Walt, and when we see her again at the end of the novel, she's had another child and seems reconciled to her marriage. Johnny goes on to use his energies and his psychic powers to help capture a sexual predator, the Castle Rock Strangler, and then moves on to his great act of world-saving self-sacrifice.

For both characters, the sexual moment between them was a watershed event, reminding them of what they'd lost and what they might have had if fate had been kinder. Johnny says as much in a letter to Sarah that she reads after his death: "But I wanted you to know that I think of you, Sarah. For me there really hasn't been anyone else, and that night was the best night for us. . . ."

Here, as with the other bestsellers on my list, this single sex scene is decisive, and without it events and characters would have moved in markedly different directions.

Jaws repeats the pattern with raunchy zest. In the novelistic version, the story opens with a sex scene between a nameless woman and a drunken man. He falls backward onto the beach and pulls her onto him, and they claw at each other's clothes. When they've satisfied themselves, the woman is still ready for a swim, but her date has already drifted off to sleep.

She walks naked into the Atlantic and paddles offshore, where the great white "smells her" and proceeds to take her apart limb by limb.

Given the novel's focus on the shark's highly developed sense of smell, one might reasonably ask if the shark would have located that swimmer had she not just had sex on the beach. The suggestion is unavoidable: The shark becomes an avenging angel, punishing the dissolute behavior happening back on shore. A kind of nasty Puritan backlash against counterculture types with their dope-smoking, self-indulgent lack of moral discipline. It's entirely possible that shark would've passed right by Amity if there hadn't been such a strong scent of decadence in the water.

The opening scene of the movie version avoids that question but raises another. A drunken college kid picks up a willing girl at a beach bonfire where dope is smoked, guitars are strummed, and necking is widespread. In the film, the drunken guy simply falls into a heap at the shoreline still clothed, while his would-be lover strips naked and walks into the waves, then swims out into the ocean as if flaunting her sexual freedom. In this case, one could ask if the self-sufficient woman who abandons her man in a drunken daze is being punished for the sin of independence.

Presumably Steven Spielberg made this alteration, having his shark target a liberated woman rather than a decadent one, because a feminist victim might arouse trendier emotions than a woman who was simply licentious.

Either way, it's a hell of a sexy way to open. Coupling the shark's violent rampage with the naked fumblings of two lovers puts into motion an erotic undercurrent that moves through the entire novel.

The only other true sex scene in *Jaws* involves a tête-à-tête between Brody's wife, Ellen, and Hooper, the visiting shark expert. Ellen's motivation for straying has more to do with a need to affirm her sexuality and her upper-class background than with a romantic attraction to Hooper.

Ellen gets her wish and spends a few steamy hours engaged in a hotel romp with Hooper. The experience redefines her in ways she hadn't expected. Hooper, it turns out, is about as sexy as an android on autopilot.

> His teeth were still clenched, his eyes still fixed on the wall, and he continued to pump madly. . . . After a while, she had tapped him on the back and said softly, "Hey, I'm here too."

Hooper must've learned his mating habits from the fish he studies—so spasmodic, so inhuman, so violent.

It would be a stretch to claim that Sarah and Ellen are "liberated" by their adulterous affairs. But both women do return to their marriages with a gratitude and calm that is noticeably similar. One could make the case that such a pattern might be simply a wishful fantasy that male bestseller authors promote about infidelity—that strong and wayward women will eventually see the light and return to the marriage bed with new commitment. Wishful fantasy or not, these two twentieth-century married women wind up sharing a similar toughness and resolve to renew their commitment to a traditional marriage.

CHEATING

John Grisham puts a tempting island girl in Mitch McDeere's path while he's off on a business trip to the Cayman Islands. On the deserted beach in the tropical darkness, this dark-haired beauty shucks off her bikini top and hands it to Mitch and wades into the sea. (Doesn't she know there are sharks out there?)

Mitch debates it for a sentence or two, then strips and wades out after her. They consummate their encounter back on the sand, with Mitch chanting to himself that no one will ever know.

Not so quick. The woman was a setup, part of the firm's master plan to keep their legal associates in line. Pictures were taken of Mitch and the island beauty, and the firm's enforcer shows them to Mitch with a threat. Play along, buy your new, flashier car, your bigger house, just like the other lawyers at the firm. But don't try to be heroic. Or these pictures will destroy your marriage.

Although it's an errant husband this time instead of a straying wife, the formula holds, for Mitch's infidelity eventually helps to renew the marriage. His relationship with Abby is under serious strain from Mitch's workaholic schedule. Abby chafes in the role of model wife and homemaker. She's increasingly lonely and frustrated, a young wife who has made one too many candlelit dinners that her husband failed to attend. For a marriage under so much stress, Mitch's one-night stand could be the final straw.

Like Sarah Bracknell's infidelity in *The Dead Zone* and Ellen Brody's motel fling in *Jaws,* Mitch's beach shenanigans become a watershed moment in his marriage. He never actually confesses, but he certainly sweats bullets when one evening he comes home to find Abby with a mailing envelope marked "Photographs" lying at the foot of the bed. It takes a few moments before Mitch realizes the mailer was empty—just a sadistic reminder from his adversaries that they have the power to expose his unfaithfulness.

After this crisis, the marriage takes a turn. Though we never see Mitch acknowledging his deceit, his guilt seems to tip the balance of power between him and Abby and gives him a new appreciation for his marriage. And though Abby is unaware of the cause of this change, she energetically embraces her new role as Mitch's co-conspirator. If they're not exactly equal partners, it's awfully close.

Holed up in a shabby apartment, copying incriminating evidence on Bendini, Lambert & Locke, Abby sheds her passivity and blossoms into a strong, decisive woman. One evening when Mitch arrives at the door of the rented apartment where Abby's working, it's like old times back in that law school flat—this time with Abby as the initiator of sex and behaving every bit like Mitch's coequal. Abby pulls open the door and throws herself on Mitch. The sex scene that follows is more heated and more satisfying than any before or after. It's a watershed moment between these two. Sex that seals the deal and establishes the terms of their new, more equal partnership.

The couple eventually pull off their scheme and escape to a safe Caribbean sanctuary, well beyond the reach of the Mob or the FBI or financial worries. However, the aftereffects of Mitch's hanky-panky linger.

In the novel's final scene, alone on their island paradise, Abby fills their cocktail glasses with another hit of rum punch and declares that as long as the two of them are together she can endure anything, even this Spartan isolation. As things warm up between them, she asks innocently if Mitch has ever had sex on the beach.

He fumbles for a moment, then lies and says no, he hasn't.

One could certainly argue that Mitch's dishonesty might eventually undermine the authenticity of the McDeeres' more balanced relations. But even with that caveat, it's clear that the Abby we see in the final scene is a stronger woman than we've seen before. With a new assertiveness in full flower, she is given the novel's last words. Calling the shots in a way that would have been unthinkable a hundred pages earlier. A newly independent woman determined to have her own version of a traditional family.

"Then drink up, sailor. Let's get drunk and make a baby."

SEXUAL AWAKENING

At the head of the class of adultery bestsellers is *The Bridges of Madison County*. Though Francesca's marriage to her boring farmer husband is not rejuvenated or strengthened in any way that we can see by the long hours of extramarital sex with Robert Kincaid, she certainly stores away sufficient memories of erotic satisfaction to console her for the rest of her days. And without a doubt, she's changed as radically by the brief affair as Allison or Scarlett or Abby or Sarah or Ellen Brody.

Indeed, the language of the one long and detailed sex scene suggests that Robert Kincaid's transformative powers are virtually supernatural. He takes "possession of her, in all of her dimensions." He seems "shamanlike" as he whispers in her ear . . . kissing her between his words. The man's a talker all right, almost hypnotic in his seductive powers.

This erotic possession could be seen as a much kinder, gentler version of the one described in *The Exorcist* when prepubescent Regan MacNeil, invaded by Satan, masturbates with a crucifix and spews vile sexual come-ons to the celibate Father Karras.

Though Francesca describes in flattering terms the otherworldly power Robert exerts over her, one can't help but question whose point of view is being stated when he "ran his tongue along her neck, licking her as some fine leopard might do in long grass out on the veldt."

The guy's an animal, the graceful kind who dominates with soft power.

The love affair transfigures Francesca. Her womanliness is awakened, her life is given a meaning and dimensionality it was lacking before. In a parting letter to her children, Francesca sums it up succinctly:

"In four days, he gave me a lifetime, a universe, and made the separate parts of me into a whole."

Of course, some would argue that Francesca's epiphany is nothing more than the sexist fantasy of a self-indulgent male author—behold what magical powers a man can bestow on a woman if she would just peel off that dress and lie back.

If *Bridges* were the only novel on our list of bestsellers that depicted the transformative power of sex, such a critique might carry more weight. But the pattern recurs with such regularity in bestsellers, whether written by men or women, that we must ask the larger question: Why does a single sexual episode play such a pivotal role in so many hugely successful American novels?

Well, it might have something to do with our intense and deeply rooted national ambivalence about sex and adultery. Our libraries are filled with works that many consider classics in which two opposing moral forces are at war: America's prudishness vs. its rebellious and rule-breaking spirit.

At the dawn of American literary history, we find a well-known precursor to the moral story line of so many bestsellers. Remember Arthur Dimmesdale and Roger Chillingworth and Hester Prynne and her out-of-wedlock daughter, Pearl, from Hawthorne's *Scarlet Letter*? In her Puritan settlement, Hester's promiscuity, which is made apparent by the birth of Pearl, is punished by a prison term. Upon Hester's release from jail, with Pearl in her arms, she is required to wear a red letter *A* emblazoned on her chest. Shunned by her God-fearing neighbors, Hester is the target of universal contempt, but somehow through it all she manages to retain a humble and forgiving demeanor.

Dimmesdale, the young, eloquent "cheating minister" who is Hester's secret lover, is the one who is truly tormented by guilt. As the story unfolds, little by little Hester wins back the respect of the townsfolk through acts of charity and kindness until finally this profligate woman is on the verge of being readmitted into mainstream society. But wait, there's a complication. Hester and Dimmesdale want more than forgiveness— they want to live together as man and wife.

Despite the danger, the lovers can't be kept apart. In a forest meeting, the two decide to flee to Europe, where they will be free to live openly with their child. Transformed by this decision, Dimmesdale gives a passionate sermon before his congregation that makes the identical case Atticus Finch will make again almost two centuries later. A paean to empathy in which Dimmesdale extols those "sympathies so intimate with the sinful brotherhood of mankind . . . that his chest vibrate[s] in unison with theirs."

In 1850 when Hawthorne's novel was published, reactions ranged from deep suspicion to outright scorn. Many believed Hester's promiscuity was treated far too sympathetically by the author. And, of course, those self-righteous critics were absolutely correct. Hawthorne's moral outrage was clearly leveled at the repressive society that ostracized Hester rather than at her adulterous misbehavior.

So it was from the beginning in American letters that sin and religious beliefs and moral righteousness were a central part of the discussion when it came to literary criticism. To many American readers, if not most, novels that were not morally uplifting were considered devious and corrupt.

However, Hawthorne saw it otherwise, and in that way he had written a novel that greatly resembles the twelve we're examining. From Hawthorne's time forward, the notion that a single sexual act, even if it's an act of adultery, can have a redemptive power has been a central pattern in American fiction.

At the very least, we can say that Americans are deeply conflicted about sex, and that powerful ambivalence is what we're seeing in these highly successful books.

RELIGIOUS SEX

In the beginning, Dan Brown created *The Da Vinci Code,* and it was good, and everybody liked it because it was about sex. No, scratch that. It was about religion. Well, no, make that religion and sex. Oh, okay, it was about religion, sex, and feminine power, and the long and sordid history of male suppression of women.

Here's a spoiler, so those two or three people who've not yet read *The Da Vinci Code* should skip the following paragraph.

Jesus had sex with Mary Magdalene. And lo, she became heavy with child, and the celibate priests, fearing the loss of their power, declared women to be unclean and hid Mary's pregnancy. A few righteous insurgents spirited away her child to some secret place, and forever after, the sinister wing of the Catholic Church went to great lengths in their pursuit of Christ's heirs and used every resource at their disposal, including murder, to keep Christ's sexiness hidden from humanity for a couple of millennia until Robert Langdon yanked back the curtains and exposed the truth.

So there's the capper—the big secret. Two thousand years ago, Jesus had sex. Women are not unclean after all. They're actually goddesses. Especially Sophie Neveu, who apparently is a direct descendant of Jesus Christ himself.

It should be clear by now that Mr. Brown was making use of a narrative pattern we've seen a few times before: one sex scene that changes everything.

In fact, this particular sex scene between Jesus and Mary Magdalene, a moment that of course is never actually presented dramatically but which readers are invited to imagine for themselves, is the driving force in this novel, the cornerstone on which is built the elaborate structure of a worldwide, multicentury conspiracy. It's the event that sets in motion the murder spree of an albino monk, and it's the cause of all the deadly machinations of Opus Dei that send our sturdy hero, Robert, and his plucky sidekick, Sophie, running for their lives through one long, treacherous maze.

That long-ago sexual incident is the equivalent of the love affair and marriage that fuel Ramius's desertion to America (*The Hunt for Red October*). It's the terrible sexual hypocrisy and double-dealing that are at the core of *Peyton Place* and *Mockingbird*. It's the dance of sexual exploitation that drives *Gone with the Wind* and *Valley of the Dolls*. It's the shark that punishes women who have sexually liberated themselves in *Jaws*. It's the devil that impregnates the blossoming young daughter of a proudly independent woman (*The Exorcist*). Again and again we see permutations of this pattern in our twelve megahits, as though bestselling novelists were channeling the biblical story of Eden: Once the snake has done its sneaky job, a new world dawns.

AMERICAN SEX

Five centuries after Boccaccio's *Decameron* first appeared, featuring sweaty sexcapades between Italian nuns and monks in convents, the book was seized and destroyed by American authorities. James Joyce's *Ulysses* suffered a similar fate, as did Henry Miller's *Tropic of Cancer*, which was not available from a U.S. publisher until almost thirty years after it first appeared in a French edition. And numerous literary luminaries including Theodore Dreiser, F. Scott Fitzgerald, Gertrude Stein, Djuna Barnes, and William Faulkner wrote novels deemed by many to be grossly improper, if not downright degenerate. While those novels were not banned outright, they were certainly the object of strong moral disapproval from many quarters.

Which is to say that it's important to remind ourselves that puritanism is alive and well in mainstream America and that many of us, despite a private devotion to the multibillion-dollar business of pornography, are still just a short distance removed from our book-burning ancestors.

It was in 1873 that Anthony Comstock created the New York Society for the Suppression of Vice, an organization determined to regulate the morality of the public. So successful was Comstock in making his case, he eventually engineered the passage of the Comstock Act in the United States Congress, making it illegal to deliver or transport "obscene, lewd, or lascivious" material. Or for that matter any information relating to birth control.

Though Comstock died in 1915, his priggish disciples live on today, targeting books like the Harry Potter series and even poor old Huck Finn as corrupting influences, trying to expel them from public libraries or high school lit classes or to publish new editions with all the offensive parts purged.

Despite what Comstock would have had us believe, naughty narratives have been heating things up since the Song of Solomon in the Old Testament and the Roman *Satyricon*. The Far East has its *Kama Sutra*, Europe has its bawdy Chaucerian tales, and there's that dirty old man Shakespeare and the whip-wielding Marquis de Sade, to name just a few. Even the earliest English novels were juicy: Indecent sexual romps like *Tom Jones, Fanny Hill,* and *Tristram Shandy* delighted in bawdily mocking the pomposity of the upper classes, a tendency that still lingers in the form today.

America, however, is a different story. Even in the supposedly enlightened twentieth century, a large portion of the straitlaced populace howled in protest over that dry account of sexuality, Masters and Johnson's 1966 tome, *Human Sexual Response*. Suffice it to say, those wails naturally had the effect of turning it into a notorious sensation and bestseller, all for the terrible sin of debunking some misconceptions about matters like female orgasm and lubrication.

Americans didn't invent censorship, but we've certainly worked long and hard on its behalf. There's a lengthy list of books that were once condemned as morally objectionable but which have now become literary standards. *Adventures of Huckleberry Finn*, *Native Son*, *The Grapes of Wrath*, and *The Catcher in the Rye*, for instance, have all made that journey from notorious to respectable, though there remains a small ongoing effort to ban even some of those books in certain pockets of America.

In the swinging sixties, sexuality swaggered across the national literary stage and confirmed forever, in the minds of many, a connection between elite cultural values and depravity. Back when college kids were growing their hair long, burning their bras and draft cards, and making real and literary forays into prurience, dirty books were everywhere. Nearly all of us of a certain age can make a list of books we privately feasted on during those wanton years: Terry Southern's *Candy*, Sylvia Plath's *The Bell Jar*, Erica Jong's *Fear of Flying*, Gore Vidal's *Myra Breckinridge*, Philip Roth's *Portnoy's Complaint*, John Updike's *Rabbit, Run*.

Published a decade prior to Woodstock and the sexual revolution, *Peyton Place* certainly helped pave the way for more sexual candor in fiction. In its day the novel was considered so raunchy, so luridly extreme, that it was banned outright in a few districts here and there and lambasted from pulpits across the country, though it was largely available in the depraved urban centers. To some, *Peyton Place*'s acceptance into the mainstream signaled that the pornification of American literature was under way.

These days, of course, what writer wouldn't want his or her book banned? Notoriety would be at the top of any publicist's wish list. However, of the twelve books we've been considering, only *Peyton Place* had that rare distinction. Famously disreputable, the novel became a guilty pleasure for millions of Americans who no doubt stashed it away in underwear drawers and on closet shelves and confirmed their worst suspicions about what their neighbors were doing behind closed doors.

Though *To Kill a Mockingbird* has now and then raised the hackles of a few moral arbiters and book-banning nutcases, it's never drawn much serious fire from hard-core moralists. Which is also true for the other books on our list of twelve. In fact, what's unique about the way sexuality is handled in these blockbusters is that the descriptive language is relatively euphemistic and chaste, PG-rated and for the most part less explicit than many modern Disney films.

The sexual language may be toned down to broaden the books' mainstream appeal, but copulation, both violent and extreme, still plays a crucial role in the outcomes of all these stories. So while Americans may give lip service, as it were, to a more virtuous sensibility, somewhere in our national consciousness we know that one good roll in the hay can change everything.

Hey, Adam. Come on, just have a little taste of this juicy morsel.

RECAP

Once Again, Quickly

These twelve very different bestsellers share a great many common features. They're fast, emotionally charged. They're full of familiar character types. They're fun to read—the opposite of work. Irresistible, unputdownable, brimming with schmaltz.

Written in earthy, simple, earnest, transparent prose with plots that are driven by a "high concept" and a minimum of backstory or psychological introspection, they are peopled by characters whose burning emotions drive them to commit bold and decisive actions. The various motives that drive the characters to such passion are clear and precise and easy to sympathize with. Early on in each narrative, the hero seems to be in well over his (or her) head, which helps to stir the reader's sense of pity and dread.

Within the first quarter of the story, though usually sooner, some threat of danger inevitably occurs, and that danger grows in intensity as the story progresses, while simultaneously the relentless pressure of time increases the stress on the characters.

Each of these novels explores some controversial or divisive issue of its day, an issue that is rooted in some larger national clash that has existed for a long time and still continues to trouble the heart of American culture.

Bestsellers are novels of scope, which means the stakes are large, the cast of characters represents a broad demographic spectrum, and the small story told in the foreground is set against a sweeping backdrop of epic consequence.

Images of nature or wilderness that might be described as Edenic occur with regularity. Usually these wild places are sexually charged or they glow with an idealized sense of innocence and purity before they are violently transformed.

Bestsellers assume a didactic role and are full of facts and information. They teach the reader while they entertain. The facts might be as mundane as descriptions of the nuts and bolts of a submarine or the more subtle rituals and manners governing the social interactions of a small southern town or a pre–Civil War plantation. These novels all plunge us into exotic worlds and give us the road maps for how one would survive or flourish within them.

Each novel features some form of secret society. In true American fashion, the heroes of these novels penetrate and expose the workings of these clandestine groups and battle to neutralize their corrosive effects.

The heroes and heroines often move between rural landscapes and urban centers, a journey that dramatizes a clash between agrarian values and the cultural norms of the city.

Conventional religious beliefs and practices are often the

object of criticism in these novels. Commonsense or secular viewpoints are offered up as better alternatives.

These novels either celebrate or harshly critique some of America's most cherished myths. For instance, the notion that the poorest and most disenfranchised among us can achieve prosperity, material wealth, and personal freedom is frequently glorified and just as frequently mocked as false.

Rebels and loners and mavericks play the leading parts in all of these novels. These outcasts struggle mightily against the pressures of conformity and conventionality, often risking their lives to do so.

Broken families are spotlighted in all the books, and their faults and eccentricities and neurotic group dynamics threaten the well-being of the heroes and heroines and force them to find remedies or methods of escape.

In all the novels, sexual incidents play pivotal roles. The story's outcome is frequently dependent on the hero or heroine coping successfully with the result of some extreme sexual act.

A Bonus Chapter:

No Tears for the Writer

Back when I first had the bright idea to teach a course in popular novels, I was also trying to publish a novel of my own. In fact, I'd written four of them by the time I taught that first bestseller class. Modeled on the experimental fiction I was teaching, my novels were populated by flamboyantly absurd characters and were rendered in surreal and disjointed narratives and lavish prose, and the narrators were all smug and self-conscious critics of many aspects of modern culture, including the novel form.

By the time I first taught *Gone with the Wind,* those four experimental novels had collected some fabulous rejection letters, but no publisher had seen fit to put any of them into print.

After that first eye-opening semester, while I was flush with newfound admiration for bestsellers, I decided to make a radical course correction in my creative life. Instead of imitating those hip, high-culture novels I'd been teaching, I drew a deep breath and decided to take a crack at a crime thriller like the ones I'd been sinfully snacking on in private for years.

My semester of reading these popular books had been so liberating, the decision seemed inescapable. Two years after I completed that original bestseller class, my first crime thriller, *Under Cover of Daylight,* was published. It got some great reviews and sold several times what the average first novel sells, winding up on a number of bestseller lists. My metafiction days were officially over. I was now a crime novelist, and a bestselling one at that.

Of course, I give a lot of credit for this success to the techniques I absorbed in that first bestseller class. But there was something else I discovered in the long hours that I labored over that first thriller. Simply using the recurring features as a paint-by-numbers template wasn't good enough. The early drafts of that novel were flat and dull—not exactly the characteristics you want in a thriller. It took a while, but I finally saw that by depending too heavily on the recurring features, using them as a formula, I had allowed my writing to become little more than a mechanical process.

"No tears for the writer," said Robert Frost, "no tears for the reader." From the beginning of my writing career, this had been an article of faith. All writing was personal. Without something emotionally at stake, the writing process is a sham, and the resulting work is likely to be nothing but a sterile exercise. It had to matter to me before it could matter to anyone else. This was the value I'd temporarily lost sight of as I struggled to employ the bestseller techniques.

So before I turned back to that early draft of *Under Cover of Daylight,* I spent a while trying to discover how these elements might be linked to my personal concerns and passions. How did the story I was trying to tell dovetail with the elements at the core of so many commercially successful novels, and how were my own passions connected to the themes and approaches my class and I had spotted in those bestsellers of the past?

HERE'S A SAMPLING OF WHAT I DISCOVERED

In my teens, when I started reading for pleasure, I found that books could teach me secrets about the real world that I could discover nowhere else. Over the years, as my study of literature became more academic and sophisticated, the objective of reading turned into an intellectual exercise that emphasized literary dissection and careful analysis of the storytelling process. In short, I lost my connection with one of the simple joys of reading—experiencing some new corner of our common world.

After that first bestseller class, I decided I needed to do more than just write beautiful sentences. I needed to know a few things that were worthy of communicating. This shift in my goals as a writer changed my creative process in a fundamental way. I began to place a greater value on the nonfiction aspects of fiction writing.

Today, each of my sixteen novels is invested with a high dose of factual information, which means I spend a month or two before starting each novel doing research in some area the novel will feature. My research has led me to some exotic places, from Borneo, where I investigated international animal smuggling, to the Gulf Stream, where I got firsthand knowledge of big-game marlin fishing, and to police departments and newspaper offices and rape clinics in big-city hospitals.

That month or two of fact-finding, of acquainting myself with my chosen subject, is now one of the most fruitful periods in my writing cycle. It's the time when I accumulate characters and settings as well as facts and start to test my enthusiasm for the dynamics of my chosen subject. It's also the time when, much to my dismay, I sometimes realize I've taken up the wrong subject entirely and have to start fresh.

Since it takes me around a year to research and write a book, the nonfiction subject I choose has to meet a rigorous standard. It cannot be simply a subject that might have topical or popular interest to others. My chosen field of study must be sufficiently rich to sustain my interest for a long stretch—a year to explore, refine, and dig deep into one of my passions.

Another result of my bestseller studies is that Edenic imagery has become a mainstay of my work. Nothing gets me churning like watching the desecration of paradise. Of course, living in Florida makes such research easy. As a lover and student of the natural world, an outdoorsman since my youth, I've had an intimate education in the subject. For forty years this feature has been in my blood. Depicting the strangely beautiful flora and fauna, birds and fish, weather and light, and fragile landscapes of my adopted homeland also allows me to keep my poetic muscles toned. Describing the loss of the unspoiled landscape inevitably suggests other forms of innocence lost, a theme that the best crime novels regularly explore.

When my students and I spotted the recurring tensions between rural and urban values in those first bestsellers, it struck a chord with me. I was born and raised in a small town in Kentucky but have lived all my adult life in America's urban centers. The conflicts between those two Americas is very real to me, and as I came to discover, it's fertile creative ground.

Most of my novels are set in Key Largo, where I lived for years—a small island community fifty miles south of Miami. The clash between the city life of Miami and the island life of Key Largo has come to play an organic role in most of my novels and expresses a deep-seated tension in my own heart. I am a country boy who has relocated to the city, and though I move about freely in both environments, I also regularly experience twinges of that modern malaise known as cognitive dissonance. That feeling of being a half step removed from the place I call home.

Many of the families in my novels are royally dysfunctional, another subject I come by naturally. I'll spare you the particulars, but as Flannery O'Connor liked to say, I believe that anyone who has survived childhood has enough material to write for the rest of his life.

All my novels explore the complicated dynamics of fathers and sons and daughters and mothers and brothers and sisters. Those endless permutations of conflicts among loved ones continue to fuel my imagination. Even after using families as a centerpiece of the plots in seventeen novels, I'm still fascinated by the subject, all the varied ways that blood relations can turn deadly and the many heroic means that families use to heal even the deepest wounds.

Perhaps because I was raised in a religious home, my earliest career goal was to be a preacher. Though I must admit the attraction was based largely on my misperception that a preacher worked only one day a week. Seemed like a pretty good gig. The college I attended was Presbyterian in name only, for as I came to discover, its curriculum was devoted largely to a questioning of conventional faith. My faith didn't hold up long to such close inspection, and gradually I decided to swap a religious career for an academic one. The perks weren't quite as good—three days a week of teaching instead of one day preaching—but it still looked better than five days slaving in an office. In any case, my formative years were marked by religious considerations. And in my fiction, the conflicts between secular and religious views of justice and the ways in which men of different moral orientations face down evil have become two of my most productive themes.

I could go on, but surely you get it. The missing ingredient, the magic elixir that breathed life into my first novel, was personal passion. Knowing the twelve elements was not enough. I had to figure out how each expressed a deeply rooted emotion of my own.

Without this one last ingredient, a novel might easily contain all the recurring features but still remain a lifeless pile of mush. So call it the yeast or call it the magic powder that catalyzes these inert ingredients—this last recurring feature is key.

It is the author's honest passion that breathes life into Scarlett and Scout and Mitch and dear old Professor Langdon. It's an earnest, wholehearted devotion to the material at hand. As sentimental as the story of Robert Kincaid and Francesca may be, it's honest sentimentality. And sure, the girls of *Valley of the Dolls* are a dopey bunch, but they are as genuine as the three young women sharing the apartment down the hall. No amount of fakery would have produced the desired results.

While it may sound self-evident that writers should choose subjects that honestly stir their own hearts, I've been repeat-

edly surprised to find in my best writing students a tendency
to select story lines and characters they have little interest in
themselves, solely because they think these ingredients will
stir the passions of their teachers or potential editors.

The writers of these twelve bestsellers, however, did not
make that mistake. They all tapped some wellspring of feeling
in themselves. They believed deeply in Scout and Francesca
and Michael Corleone and Sheriff Brody, and they felt pity
and fear for their predicaments. And in so doing, they managed to stir the hearts of millions of readers.

ACKNOWLEDGMENTS

There were several early readers of this book who provided invaluable, though often daunting, criticisms and guidance. Chief among them was my wife, Evelyn Crovo-Hall, whose suggestions were crucial in correcting some early wrong turns. At every stage Les Standiford, my colleague and friend, gave sage and practical advice about the focus of this book, helping to rescue it from academic stuffiness. I must give special thanks to John Unsworth, dean and professor of library and information science at the University of Illinois, who kindly posted his extensive website describing his bestseller class at the University of Virginia. This site proved to be an invaluable tool for my own teaching and research over the years. Chuck Elkins, professor emeritus at Florida International University, read an early draft of the manuscript and provided critical and incisive suggestions that greatly improved the final product. David Gonzalez, who wrote the plot summaries at the end of this book, was also a helpful sounding board as the book was taking shape. Without the inspired editing and excellent judgment of Millicent Bennett and Kate Medina, I would never have found the real book hiding inside the early drafts.

And I must thank that long-ago librarian who got me hooked on books and steered me to a larger, more interesting world than I would have known otherwise. Librarians like her exist today, as well as many valiant English teachers, who against great odds are still guiding readers, young and old, to books they would otherwise not discover—making countless lives richer in the process and instilling a lifelong passion for reading in generations to come.

TOASTING A FEW OF MY STUDENTS

At the time Barbara Parker entered one of my bestseller classes, she was writing romance paperback originals. After that semester, she changed direction and turned her attention to legal thrillers. Her novels, such as *Suspicion of Deceit,* eventually became *New York Times* bestsellers.

To my surprise, she kept attending seminars and classes that I was teaching in bestsellers. Though by then she was something of a star, her enthusiasm for the material was undiminished. For Barbara, there was always something to learn from these commercially successful novels. Discoveries that delighted her and fueled her own work for years.

Barbara Parker passed away in 2009, at the age of sixty-two. At the time of her death, she had published twelve mystery novels. One of her books was a finalist for the Edgar

Award and was subsequently made into a CBS television movie of the week entitled *Sisters and Other Strangers*.

Dennis Lehane was writing literary short fiction when he arrived in graduate school, though his knowledge of popular culture, both films and commercial novels, ran deep. I remember arguing with him in the bestseller class about a novel we were studying by Dean Koontz. Dennis believed the plot was too familiar, and he ticked off several other novels that had employed a similar structure. I didn't argue on behalf of Koontz's originality but made the case that narrative structures could be similar and still the stories could be vastly different, just as the underlying structure of the skull doesn't limit a wide variety of facial appearances. The point Dennis was making demonstrated his ability to see the larger form and shape of a story, a skill that most of his fellow grad students lacked. Lehane's success as a novelist (*Mystic River, Shutter Island, The Given Day,* all *New York Times* bestsellers) is due in some measure to this talent for seeing the global structure of his stories so clearly, which frees him to manage its many moving parts with great dexterity.

Dennis was in the same class with Barbara Parker and a couple of other students who have gone on to publish successful novels. When I asked him what, if anything, he recalled from the class, this was his answer:

What I most remember from the class was the concept of bestsellers imparting new or specialized information and/or distilling complex theories into more user-friendly forms, as Crichton did with chaos theory in *Jurassic Park*. It's something I still see at play, most often in good television, where we are brought into the specifics of a world that we didn't know as much about as we thought we did—N.Y. advertising in *Mad Men* or the crank trade in *Breaking Bad,* for example.

Lynn Kiele Bonasia took the same graduate class in bestsellers as Dennis and Barbara, but in a different semester. She was an aspiring novelist who hadn't yet broken into print. Since then she has gone on to publish two novels, *Summer Shift* (2010) and *Some Assembly Required* (2008), both published by Touchstone/Simon & Schuster. The booklist of bestsellers that Lynn studied was different from Dennis Lehane's or Barbara Parker's, but the same elements in bestsellers emerged. What she remembers about the class touches on the last ingredient I listed here, the catalyzing power of the writer's emotional commitment to the materials:

It was really fascinating to take a look at a very diverse group of bestselling novels such as *The Exorcist, From Here to Eternity, The Virginian*, and *Valley of the Dolls*— books that many would feel have little in common—and be able to isolate characteristics that they all shared: a secret code to successful fiction. To this day, I find myself measuring bestselling books against these components.

The challenge becomes how to use this information, because I believe a good novel has to grow organically and can't be based in contrivance. You can't just throw the ingredients into the pot; you need to literally inhabit the soup for a while. Every now and then, when we write, we step away from our work and assess what we've got. Perhaps this is the time to reflect on what

Jim's book teaches us. It was a surprise to me how many of these elements my first novel contained, perhaps unintentionally, or because I had learned these components and subliminally wove them in.

Sandra Rodriguez Barron was a student in the bestseller course while she was working on her first novel. That book eventually was titled *The Heiress of Water* and was published by HarperCollins. Her second novel, *Stay with Me,* was published in 2010, also by HarperCollins.

Interestingly, Sandra was already employing one of the twelve recurring features in that first novel, but the class helped her see that depending on this feature too heavily might actually be counterproductive.

This course gave me the confidence to lean more deeply into the emotional aspect of story writing. When I started writing fiction, my comfort zone involved weaving in a lot of facts about nature, science, and medicine. (I think the graduate workshop environment triggered this.) But taking the course made me realize that although facts can provide a fascinating intellectual backbone to a plot, readers want to see these elements used to heighten emotion.

After all, they can go research any subject themselves. What readers want the writer to do is to breathe life into it; take it to a new level. If the writer's ego and desire to sound "smart" creeps into the writing, it drains it. The books with the broadest appeal are the ones that can strike a balance between making the reader think and feel.

Christine Kling also was starting her first novel when she took one of my early classes in the bestseller. That first manuscript turned into the novel *Surface Tension*, a fine thriller published by Ballantine and followed by numerous excellent suspense novels, including *Cross Current* and *Wreckers' Key*.

Like many of my students over the years, Christine felt guilty about the kinds of books she secretly loved. Part of the importance of the class for her was to liberate her from this uneasiness and give her permission to write the books she truly wanted to write.

Throughout my days as an undergraduate English major and then in the MFA program, I kept quiet about the books I really loved—the guilty-pleasure books by Stephen King, John D. MacDonald, Hammond Innes, and the like. They were books to be gobbled up, not savored. I recognized that the books I loved transported me to other worlds in ways that good literature often did not. In the "good reads," the proscenium of the physical book disappeared and "I" ceased to exist. Losing myself in the story like that was pure incomprehensible magic to me. Your class, then, was like going to a magic show where the magician shows you how he does the tricks, and surprisingly, it doesn't ruin the magic—quite the contrary, because you come to appreciate the magician's skill at creating his illusions. You started me down this long road of trying to figure out what makes a story you can lose yourself in—to understand that story is where the magic is, and it is not merely a sum of its literary parts.

APPENDIX

Plot Summaries

To refresh the memories of those who haven't reread these novels lately, and to inform those who haven't yet gotten around to them, here are plot summaries of each. The summaries were written by a graduate student of mine, David Gonzalez. David is in his early thirties, born and raised in Miami, and though he's a passionate reader and a highly accomplished fiction writer, believe it or not, he had not read any of the novels on this list prior to taking on the job of summarizing these books.

In that way, David was like most of the students who took this course from me over the years. Like many of my former students, David Gonzalez has been immersed in the works of Ray Carver, Flannery O'Connor, Gabriel García Márquez, Virginia Woolf, Junot Díaz, Charles Baxter, and Herman Melville. Quite an eclectic mix.

What limited exposure David had to these popular best-sellers came through their film versions. So I was pleased, though not surprised, that he greatly enjoyed reading these hits of the past. His favorite was *Gone with the Wind,* and his least favorite was *Peyton Place,* which he found rambling and poorly plotted, its narrator (Allison MacKenzie) "aimlessly floating around town." He also found the sappy and egocentric voice of Robert Kincaid, the narrator of *The Bridges of Madison County,* hard to take seriously.

David says that when he originally read *Valley of the Dolls,* he was "turned off by the daytime soaps vibe to it." But months later, upon reflection, his opinion changed: "I'm glad that I read it. I can appreciate it for the standard it set, albeit a relatively trashy one."

I've tried not to tamper too much with David's voice in these plot summaries to give a feel for the views of one fervent reader of Generation X.

GONE WITH THE WIND, Margaret Mitchell, 1936

Scarlett O'Hara is young, brash, seductive, and stubborn. Not exactly the usual traits synonymous with young debutantes of the pre–Civil War South. But she can't help it. She takes too much after her father, Gerald O'Hara, a hard-drinking Irish immigrant with the proverbial heart of gold, who wiggled his way into society using the power of money and a gritty determination.

The novel begins when Scarlett learns that Ashley Wilkes will propose to Melanie Hamilton at a party at the Wilkeses' family plantation. When Scarlett professes her love to him,

Ashley admits that he does care for her but that "like must marry like," and he likes Melanie. After Ashley leaves, Rhett Butler, a handsome and devilish rogue, admits to overhearing the entire conversation. Scarlett is doubly humiliated and, in a fit of anger and jealousy, accepts the marriage proposal of Charles Hamilton, the shy, awkward, somewhat pitiable brother of Melanie.

Only weeks after their marriage, Charles suffers an ignoble death in a sick tent on the Civil War battlefield, and Scarlett is forced to "grieve" publicly over the loss of a husband she's secretly glad to be free of. In an attempt to assuage Scarlett's melancholy, her mother, Ellen, decides to ship her off to Atlanta, where Scarlett finds work at a hospital, caring for the wounded. It's not quite Scarlett's ideal job, since most of the available men are either missing limbs or dying.

At a charity ball for the hospital Scarlett again encounters Rhett, and the two quickly become Atlanta's most popular bit of gossip.

News arrives that Ashley has been captured. At the same time, Melanie is desperately ill with her pregnancy, and every day the sounds of battle inch closer, until finally cannonballs start landing in Atlanta's streets. Scarlett assists at the birth of Melanie's child, then leads a group of family, friends, and slaves on a dangerous escape back to Tara, the O'Haras' plantation. When she arrives, she finds her home has been ransacked, her mother has passed away, both her sisters are sick, and her father is going nuts.

This is it. Scarlett's had it. Never again will she allow her family to suffer or to starve. The person she used to be, shallow, self-involved, is gone, and left in her place is a single-minded woman full of determination who will stop at nothing to safeguard her future. Even murder. Scarlett doesn't even hesitate when she shoots and kills a Yankee who has invaded their home.

When the war ends, Ashley returns to Tara, but after he and Scarlett share a passionate encounter, he tells her that he cannot, in good conscience, stay at Tara with his wife and child, under the thumb of Scarlett's charity. But Scarlett needs manpower and, more important, money, if she is to keep Tara from the grubby carpetbaggers who have gained power and raised the taxes on her property. She begs Ashley to stay, and she leaves to talk to the only man with money at a time like this: Rhett Butler. Unfortunately, he is where all the good rogues wound up after the war, in a Yankee prison.

Rhett learns of her scheme and promises to leave all the money in his will for her after he is hanged. Scarlett wishes the Yankees would hurry up, then.

In a fit of panic over the fate of Tara, Scarlett convinces Frank Kennedy, a former Confederate, to marry her. When Frank falls ill, Scarlett takes over his business and becomes a ruthless entrepreneur, so desperate to make money that she even consorts with the Yankees and carpetbaggers in town, an act deemed unforgivable in the eyes of the Old Southern society.

Scarlett's reckless independence leads to her being attacked one day by some squatters living in the woods. Avenging her honor, Ashley and her husband, Frank, raid the camp of squatters. Ashley is severely injured, and Frank is killed. For the first time, we see Scarlett suffer a flutter of grief and remorse. If only she hadn't been so stubborn and willful, Frank, her meal ticket, would still be alive.

No sooner is Frank buried than Rhett (now freed from prison) proposes marriage. If the members of the Old Southern society were in a tizzy when Rhett and Scarlett danced at a charity event, their marriage so soon after Frank's death is downright revolting. Neither of them cares much for their reputation, but when Scarlett gives birth to Bonnie Blue Butler, Rhett sets about repairing their family image, if only for his daughter's sake.

Much to everyone's surprise, Rhett becomes a different man now that he's a father. But when Bonnie Blue dies, all that made Rhett a decent man dies with her.

Everything Scarlett has treasured is gone. Rhett has become an angry drunk. Her children are terrified of her. Her parents have passed away, and the people of the Old South shun her. Melanie, the only friend who loved her unconditionally, is dead, and Ashley, who was always a little frail and dreamy, is a shell of his former self. At the close of the novel, after Rhett tells Scarlett he doesn't give a damn about her anymore, our heroine, in denial to the bitter end, begins to scheme for a way to lure Rhett back.

PEYTON PLACE, Grace Metalious, 1956

When Samuel Peyton, a freed slave, returned from Europe a very rich man and engaged to a white woman, he quickly realized that he would not be welcomed by society. In a fit of anger and hurt, he imported a medieval castle, rebuilt it brick by brick, shut its doors, and lived the remainder of his life locked within those walls—an inauspicious beginning for the town that eventually would bear his name.

When it comes to Peyton Place, a fictional New England community in the 1930s, few things are as highly valued as image, status, and reputation. And practically everyone in

Peyton Place carries with them some secret, some dark, sordid mishap in their past, that they try to hide at all costs.

Take Constance MacKenzie. Her daughter, Allison, was conceived in a love affair with a married man, and although this man passed away when Allison was three years old, Constance lives in fear that the truth about her daughter's illegitimate birth will one day be discovered.

Constance is a beautiful woman, but her guilt and remorse have kept her from remarrying; she prefers the role of the hardworking and sympathetic widow. As a result, Constance is cold, stern, and single-minded in her withdrawal from romance and its repercussions. Allison, on the other hand, is sensitive and thoughtful, full of aspirations, and doesn't see the world through her mother's grim eyes. At least not yet, anyway.

Allison's closest friend is Selena Cross, a sensuous young girl from the "tar-paper shacks" who lives with her mother and her stepfather. Allison has no idea of the skeletons that lurk inside the closets of Peyton Place, until one day when she peers through the window into the Crosses' kitchen and sees Selena's stepfather, Lucas, tearing drunkenly at Selena's blouse.

Soon after, Lucas is carted off to a hospital because of his alcoholism, and Selena finds romance and comfort with Ted Carter, a handsome and generous young man from an affluent family. Constance then hires Selena to work at her apparel store and hires Nellie, Selena's mother, to clean her house.

When the principal of the local high school passes away, Leslie Harrington, the wealthiest, most powerful man in Peyton Place—and chairman of the school board—hires Tomas Makris to replace him. Makris is a handsome Greek man, Ivy

League educated, from New York. Constance immediately fears that he may have some connection to her past and dreads the presence of the new stranger in town. The moment he sees her, however, Makris falls in love and sets about wooing the unwilling Constance MacKenzie.

Two years later, Allison, who dreams of being a writer, lands a job at the local newspaper writing human-interest stories about the people and events that shape Peyton Place. By this time, Makris has made headway in his romancing of Constance. They're secretly engaged, a fact that Makris keeps insisting Constance reveal to her daughter.

Meanwhile, Selena Cross visits Doc Swain because she's discovered she is pregnant and knows that her stepfather, Lucas, is responsible. Abortions are illegal, but Doc Swain performs one anyway, believing himself to be saving Selena from a terrible situation. The procedure is a success, and soon afterward Doc Swain forces Lucas to leave town.

Bereft over her miserable existence, Nellie Cross hangs herself in Allison's closet. Allison, having lashed out at Nellie for her harsh view of the people in Peyton Place, blames herself for Nellie's death, but Doc Swain lies and says that Nellie Cross was seriously ill and committed suicide as a result.

Under cover of night, Lucas slinks back into town and attempts to rape Selena yet again. This time Selena murders him, and together she and her younger brother bury him in the sheep pen in their yard. Selena's crime is soon discovered, and she is taken to jail.

Allison, now working as a reporter for a New York magazine, returns on assignment to cover the sensational trial of her old friend. During the testimony, Doc Swain, at the risk of destroying his career and possibly being sent to jail, reveals the truth about Selena's abortion. The jury acquits Selena. And Doc Swain, so admired for his brave actions, is excused for his behavior by the citizens of Peyton Place.

When Allison returns to Peyton Place, she, like her mother before her, is having an affair with a married man. Realizing she is on the verge of making the same mistakes her mother did, Allison sees that the only way to avoid the same fate is to break free of the love affair and finally come to peace with the cruelty, the kindness, and the ugliness of her hometown, Peyton Place.

TO KILL A MOCKINGBIRD, Harper Lee, 1960

Atticus Finch is a widowed lawyer in Maycomb, Alabama, in the 1930s. His daughter, Scout, her brother, Jem, and their friend Dill spend their summers relishing all the mischief their childhood can provide. They work on their tree house, play-act some of their favorite stories, and, in a fit of boredom, decide to lure Boo Radley, the town bogeyman, out of his home.

As the school year nears its end, Scout and Jem discover that someone is leaving them treats and toys inside the knot-hole of the tree in front of the Radley place. They find chewing gum, Indian Head pennies, soap sculptures, and a broken watch. But as soon as the children begin leaving things themselves, the knothole is filled with cement. The children are saddened at losing the connection to Boo but gradually realize he is still reaching out to them in other understated ways.

One day at school, Scout is teased about her father's defending the black man Tom Robinson. The town begins to ostracize the children, and Atticus pleads with Jem and Scout not to argue or fight back. Tom Robinson is being accused of raping a white woman, Mayella Ewell, and Atticus, who believes the man is innocent, knows Robinson doesn't stand a chance of getting a fair trial. Even his sister, Alexandra, thinks Atticus is shaming their family by taking on this case.

When the trial begins, Jem, Scout, and Dill all watch from the upstairs balcony, the only place blacks are allowed. Sure enough, even after Atticus does a convincing job of establishing Tom's innocence, the jury finds Tom guilty. Atticus soon goes to work on an appeal, but Tom, sensing the unfairness of the system he's up against, attempts to escape from prison, only to be shot and killed. Atticus tries to console Jem and Scout by suggesting that because the jury had taken a long time to reach their verdict, some "progress" on racial issues is being made.

Later that fall, Scout plays the role of a ham in a school pageant. Scout wears her costume home, and Jem walks along with her. The children are soon attacked by Bob Ewell, the man accused by Atticus of beating his daughter and lying about Tom Robinson's rape. In the struggle, Jem's arm is broken and he falls unconscious. Scout, because of her costume, can't rightly tell what happens. When she arrives home, a strange man is carrying Jem inside the house, and Scout realizes the man is Boo and that he was the one who saved them from Bob Ewell.

In fact, Ewell had a knife and tried to stab Scout; only her costume protected her from injury. During the scuffle with Boo, Bob Ewell "fell" onto his knife and died almost instantly.

Tom Robison is dead, and so is Bob Ewell. It wasn't pretty, but the children are wiser to the strange sort of justice alive in Maycomb, Alabama. In a final moment, when Scout walks Boo back to his house, she gets a glimpse of the view their strange neighbor has always had and understands what Atticus has been harping on for so long, that we can understand others only by standing in their shoes.

VALLEY OF THE DOLLS, Jacqueline Susann, 1966

It's New York, 1945. The war is over and the world is brimming with optimism. When she arrives in the Big Apple, so is Anne Welles. Anne is beautiful, resourceful, and sincere, thrilled by even the simplest pleasures of living in the big city. She's beautiful enough to be a model, but Anne Welles just wants to work in an office and soon lands a secretarial job at Bellamy and Bellows, one of the top theatrical firms in town.

Anne befriends Neely O'Hara (Scarlett's granddaughter?), a talented young ingenue who stars in a two-bit vaudeville act and lives in Anne's building, and Jennifer North, a buxom blonde with all the talent of a tin can.

Before you know it, Anne is enamored of Lyon Burke but is engaged to Allen Cooper, a dopey insurance salesman who turns out to be a multimillionaire; Jennifer has just dumped her Arabian prince boyfriend and has now set her sights on Tony Polar, the debonair lounge lizard; and Neely, soon to become a star in her own right, is engaged to her boyfriend, Mel Harris.

Neely becomes a huge star in Los Angeles and completely neglects Mel. She drinks and does drugs. He grows bored, and they divorce.

Jennifer learns that Tony has a form of mental retardation. His sister controls his image, his decisions, and his life, and she tells Jennifer that whatever Tony has, he's likely to pass on to his children. Jennifer aborts their child, and they too divorce.

Anne never wanted to marry Allen but was engaged regardless. She calls it off and professes her love for Lyon Burke. Burke claims to love her, too, but won't marry her until his career as a writer can support the two of them. When Anne's mother passes away and leaves her the house in Lawrenceville, Burke offers Anne a compromise. He'll marry her right away if they can live in this house. But Anne so desperately wants to stay away from her hometown that she denies Burke's offer, and, brokenhearted, he leaves for England.

Jennifer visits Neely in Los Angeles and learns that she's going to marry her fashion designer. Neely also fills Jennifer in on which "dolls" can help her sleep at night and which can help take the weight off after a pregnancy. If Jennifer is going to star in French art-house films (which she is), she's going to have to look her best. It's topless, at least.

With Lyon Burke out of the picture, Anne marries Kevin Gillmore, the owner of Gillmore Cosmetics. Anne finally attempts a career at modeling and becomes an overnight sensation. Her union with Gillmore is passionless and unsatisfying, and he reintroduces Anne to Burke as a test of her love—a test she fails miserably as she and Burke renew their romance.

Neely, on the other hand, is drinking heavily, addicted to the "dolls," and losing money for the film studios; she has witnessed her husband kissing another man, missed her children's birthdays and attempted suicide once.

In a fit of desperation, she begs Anne to let her come to New York and stay with her. Just as she's poised to make her comeback, she loses her voice. Fearful and anxious, Neely slits her wrists. She survives, barely, and is committed to a sanitarium.

Jennifer then returns to the United States from her art-film sojourn and becomes engaged to Senator Winston Adams. She thinks she's finally found the right man, but when she's diagnosed with breast cancer, she realizes he loves only her body. Jennifer opts to take her own life rather than lose a breast.

Anne concocts a scheme to help Burke buy out the agency and take on Neely, fresh from her stint in rehab, as their first major signing. The setup works for a while until Neely and Burke begin to have an affair. Anne is already pregnant, so instead of losing the marriage, she ignores the betrayal.

Neely demands that Burke divorce Anne, but he refuses to leave her because it might mean losing his daughter. The agency then signs a newer, younger sensation, Margie Parks, and Neely attempts suicide a third time when she realizes that Burke is having an affair with this younger actress.

During a New Year's Eve party at their house, Anne witnesses Burke's infidelity with Margie. Realizing that there will always be a line of Neely O'Haras and Margie Parkses, and steadied by her dependence on the "dolls," Anne returns to the party understanding that in some strange and unfortunate way, she got everything she wanted.

And they all live unhappily ever after.

THE GODFATHER, Mario Puzo, 1969

According to Sicilian tradition, no father can deny a request for a favor on the day of his daughter's wedding, and so it is that Don Vito Corleone is meeting privately with guests who hope to receive the help and support of their Godfather. All the Don asks in return is their undying loyalty and friendship. One favor he won't grant, however, is supporting Virgil "the Turk"

Sollozzo's foray into drug trafficking. The Don's denial of Sollozzo is what ultimately sets off "the five families war of 1945."

Angry at the rejection of his business plan, Sollozzo arranges a hit on the Don. The Godfather is badly injured, and Sonny, the eldest son, rages out of control with bloodlust. Fredo, the middle child, was with the Don when the hit happened and is now shell-shocked, terrified, and useless. And Michael, the youngest son, wayward since birth, the only Corleone son who resisted the ways of his father, finds himself drawn into the fray.

When Sollozzo sends word that he wants a truce, Michael is the only member of the Corleone family that Sollozzo trusts not to try to kill him. Together with a crooked Irish cop, Sollozzo arranges a meeting with Michael in a secure Italian restaurant. After smuggling a gun into the restaurant, Michael kills them both. The blood has barely dried on the bistro floor when Michael is put on a boat and shipped to Sicily for his safety.

Later, Sonny gets word that Carlo Rizzi, his sister's husband, is beating her again. Sonny flies off in a fit and heads straight for their apartment, only to be ambushed and brutally murdered at a tollbooth. The Don, wishing there to be no more violence, calls for a meeting of the five families of New York. At the meeting, the Don requests that Michael be allowed to return safely to the United States. To ensure Michael's safety, the Don accedes to the wishes of the other dons and agrees to use his political influence to protect the drug trade.

Meanwhile, in Sicily, Michael falls in love with and marries the beautiful Apollonia. Don Tommasino, charged with the protection of the young Corleone, warns him that his marriage has made his whereabouts known to his father's enemies. Passionately in love, Michael ignores the warning, and a short while later an attempt is made on his life. The bomb meant for him kills Apollonia instead. When Michael regains consciousness, he tells Don Tommasino that he wishes to return home to be with his father and to ascend to the position that's been waiting for him his entire life.

Back in America, Michael marries Kay Adams, his long-time girlfriend. He confesses to her that he's now running his father's empire and vows that within five years the enterprise will be completely legitimate. Before that can happen, however, he has a few loose ends to tie up.

Michael heads to Las Vegas and makes Moe Greene (a wayward member of the Mob) an offer he can't refuse. Moe refuses and is ultimately killed.

Then the Don, joyful since his retirement from the "olive oil business," dies of a heart attack while tending to his tomato garden, and although the death is sudden, Michael's plan is already in motion and the Mob war begins.

Philip Tattaglia is murdered in a motel with his mistress, Don Barzini is killed by a hitman disguised as a cop, and Tessio, one of the Don's most trusted *caporegimes*, is sniffed out as the rat and "taken for a drive." Michael personally visits Carlo and says he knows he was responsible for Sonny's murder. Carlo is strangled to death.

And just like that, with a series of swift and brutal moves, Michael Corleone rises to take over his father's throne and to restore power and respect to the family.

But this, of course, was the last thing he ever wanted.

THE EXORCIST, William Peter Blatty, 1971

Chris MacNeil, divorced single mother and celebrated actress, moves to Washington, D.C., with her daughter, Regan, to finish her latest film. Regan soon grows bored and starts using a Ouija board to play with Captain Howdy, an imaginary friend who finds it amusing to move Regan's furniture around and make things go bump in the night.

Regan's father neglects to call her on her birthday, and Chris believes that's the reason for Regan's sudden shift in mood. Once curious and cheerful, Regan grows sullen, temperamental, and capable of some seriously salty language. Doctors believe she's suffering from a strange form of epilepsy, with symptoms that include speaking in tongues, lifting the bed into the air, and feats of superhuman strength.

Unsatisfied with the diagnosis, Chris reaches out to Father Damien Karras, a handsome young priest who is dejected and full of doubt about his faith. Karras agrees to see Regan, but he warns Chris that the church does not easily hand out permission for exorcisms. He has to make an indisputable case for demonic possession.

When Karras first meets Regan, the child claims to be the devil, impersonates the voice of Burke Dennings—the film director that the demon threw out of Regan's bedroom window to his death—speaks in the voice of Karras's recently deceased mother, then covers him with a stream of projectile vomit. Karras, still unconvinced, decides to record the demon's voice.

After studying the recording, Karras realizes the demon isn't speaking an ancient language but is instead talking backward in English. The following day, he's given the go-ahead by his superiors to begin the exorcism, and to assist him, the church sends Father Lankester Merrin, an elderly priest who has struggled with exorcisms before.

Merrin arrives immediately, prepares Karras, and sets about performing the exorcism. After three days of nonstop exorcising, the men are beset by emotional and physical fatigue. Merrin falls dead of an apparent heart attack, and Karras, enraged by the death of the priest, demands the demon leave Regan and take his body. The demon gladly accepts, and once Karras is fully possessed, he leaps through the window to his death.

JAWS, Peter Benchley, 1974

It's mid-June, and the resort town of Amity is hoping for another prosperous summer catering to the beachgoers from the city when a young woman is killed by a shark attack during a late-night swim.

Police Chief Martin Brody meets with Harry Meadows, editor of the *Amity-Leader,* to issue the beach closure. Meadows insists that he will not run the story of the girl's death, nor will he issue the beach closing. Meadows tells Brody that a number of local businesses have already demanded the *Leader* not run the story for fear of scaring off the tourists Amity so desperately needs.

After the tourists begin arriving, the shark soon attacks again, this time taking the life of a six-year-old boy. As Brody is hosting a press conference regarding the attack, another victim, a sixty-five-year-old man, is claimed.

The next day the *Amity-Leader* admits the three fatalities, including the first victim whose death went unreported. The mother of the young boy storms into Brody's office and blames him for the death of her son. Brody, racked with guilt but sworn to secrecy, accepts full responsibility.

Brody and a fellow officer take a boat to visit Ben Gardner, a fisherman hired to track down the shark, only to find the boat deserted and damaged, with all signs pointing to Gardner's being the fourth of the shark's victims. Back at the police station, Meadows introduces Brody to Matt Hooper, a scientist from the oceanographic institute, and Brody realizes that the only way to return the town to normalcy is to kill the shark.

Brody learns of a shark hunter named Quint, and when Brody reaches out to him, Quint agrees to hunt the shark (for the right price, of course), with the help of Brody and Hooper.

Once they're all on the boat, there is no sign of the shark. The second day is even quieter still, until the baited lines are snapped clean. The shark breaches near the boat, and the men try to harpoon it to no avail.

The following day, Hooper brings a steel cage to the marina. At sea, they locate the shark and toss the empty cage into the water. The shark ignores the cage, and Hooper dives right in. The shark then attacks the cage head-on. The shark mangles the cage, squeezes his head inside, and kills Hooper with one vicious bite.

On the third day, Brody and Quint take to the sea by themselves and are immediately attacked by the shark. Quint manages to lodge two harpoons in the shark and tries to run the ropes through a winch in order to drag the shark. Instead, the shark launches itself onto the back of the boat. The boat begins to sink, and as the shark slips back into the water, the rope from the harpoons gets tangled around Quint and drags him down to his death.

The bow of the boat is almost vertical, and Brody grabs a cushion to keep himself afloat. As the boat sinks, the shark heads straight for Brody. Just as the shark is about to attack, the harpoons lodged in its massive body take their toll and the shark dies, mere feet away from Brody.

Brody plunges his head underwater, opens his eyes, and sees that the shark is kept from sinking by the barrels, and Quint's body, still tethered to it, floats just above the shark. Satisfied that the shark is dead, Brody paddles for shore.

THE DEAD ZONE, Stephen King, 1979

Johnny Smith didn't know he had acquired the ability to see the future when he hit his head on a frozen lake in the winter of 1953. And when he and his girlfriend, Sarah Bracknell, take in the carnival in the fall of 1970, he didn't know he was seeing the future then, either, but he was. With his power, strange and uncontrollable, he wins over five hundred dollars on roulette that night at the carnival. It's cause for celebration, except Sarah notices that something isn't right with Johnny and it makes her ill. She blames it on a bad hot dog but needs to go home. Johnny, riding home alone in a cab, gets into a horrific wreck with a pair of drag racers and spends the next four and a half years in a coma.

During that time, his mother develops an unhealthy obsession with Christian fanaticism, Sarah marries another man, Walt Hazlett, and bears his child, and the Castle Rock Strangler (a serial killer) continues to add victims to his growing toll.

As soon as Johnny awakens, his power is fully evident. By touching people, he can see into their future. He warns a nurse that her house is on fire and tells a doctor that his mother, who he presumed was dead, is actually living in California. Stories leak out about Johnny's paranormal powers, and soon the national media arrives.

His mother watches a live interview with her son and is so shocked, she suffers a stroke. Before she dies, she insists that his power is a gift from God and he must, above all else, "heed the voice when it calls."

When it does call, it's in the form of Sheriff George Bannerman from Castle Rock. He and his detectives have exhausted all options, and even though he doesn't completely believe Johnny's brand of hokum, he's willing to try anything to locate the Strangler. And they do, if a bit late.

By the time Johnny and Bannerman locate him, Frank Dodd, trusted officer on the force, is already dead of an apparent suicide—a note tacked around his neck that reads, "I confess."

Soon after, Johnny moves in with Roger Chatsworth, a successful businessman, to tutor his athlete son, Chuck. Johnny enjoys his anonymity, and as a hobby, he begins attending political rallies throughout New Hampshire. Johnny makes it a point to shake hands with each candidate to sneak a glimpse behind the political veneer. But all that changes when he encounters Greg Stillson, a dangerous megalomaniac running for the House of Representatives. When Johnny shakes his hand, he sees visions of a nuclear holocaust.

Johnny feels he has no choice in the matter. He writes two letters, one to his father and one to Sarah, explaining his actions, and sets out to assassinate Greg Stillson. Johnny fails, but in the ensuing chaos, Stillson grabs a small child to use as a human shield. An eyewitness snaps a picture of this outrageous act, effectively crushing any hopes Stillson had of a career in politics. Johnny is shot and killed, but before he dies, he reaches out and touches Stillson's ankle and sees that the world is safe.

THE HUNT FOR RED OCTOBER, Tom Clancy, 1984

It is 1984, the height of the cold war, and Captain First Rank Marko Ramius sets sail from a Soviet submarine station deep in the Arctic. In his charge is the *Red October,* Russia's newest top-secret nuclear submarine. His orders are to perform a two-week training exercise in which the Soviet fleet will attempt to locate him while he avoids detection using the sub's experimental new propulsion system.

Soon after leaving the base, Ramius murders a political officer in his wardroom and replaces the official orders with a set of forged documents. Ramius informs the crew of the horrible "accident" that claimed the *zampolit*'s life and delivers the bogus orders to the crew. Their mission, Ramius explains, is to head to Cuba, the home of their socialist brothers, and avoid detection by American and British ships alike, thereby establishing the dominance of the Russian navy. The crew rallies around this objective, while one crewman, a cook, feels something is amiss with the commander's orders.

Meanwhile, Jack Ryan, an author of naval histories and part-time information analyst, arrives at CIA headquarters with photographs (taken by British agents) of the *Red October.* Ryan requests permission to show these images to an old friend and mentor in order to figure out what the new features on the sub are capable of.

Skip Tyler, Ryan's former teacher at the U.S. Naval Academy, figures the Russians have developed a silent propulsion system similar to a version the United States fumbled with in the 1960s. Ryan relates this information to the CIA and outlines a disastrous scenario where the Russians could use this propulsion system to sneak as close as the continental shelf and attack without warning.

Back in Moscow, a high-ranking political official receives a letter from his nephew Ramius detailing his intentions for the *Red October*. Within a few hours, the Russian navy is ordered to locate the *Red October* and sink it.

Unbeknownst to Ramius, the sonar man for the USS *Dallas*, Sonar Technician Second Class Ronald Jones, has picked up his frequency. Soon after, Jones hears a number of Russian subs speed up in unison, signaling the beginning of a major operation.

The CIA is aware of the activity at sea but is unsure why it is taking place. Ryan deduces that the *Red October* is about to defect. He explains his theory and then advises that the United States welcome her with open arms and that they should keep the *Red October*. There is some dissension among the ranks, but there is also an interest in the possibility of obtaining the experimental submarine.

One of the *Red October*'s chief officers (also involved in the conspiracy) provides the sub's doctor with a series of contaminated radiation badges. The officers immediately begin to check for leaks and determine that most of the systems are working properly.

Meanwhile, Yuri Padorin, a high-ranking Soviet official, faces the members of Moscow's Politburo, the Russian parliament. Padorin assures them that the agent embedded on the *Red October* has strict orders to sink the sub himself should anything go awry.

The USS *Dallas* finally makes contact with the *Red October* and informs the Soviet commander of the plans to help him defect. The *Red October* continues to suffer from a series of "malfunctions," and Ramius announces to his crew that the work of a saboteur is now evident.

Ramius tells his crew that it is much too dangerous to continue to operate the *Red October* and that they must abandon ship. Together with his high-ranking officers, he will scuttle the sub once the crew has been safely transferred.

Meanwhile, as the plan to help the officers of the *Red October* is under way, the helicopter carrying the agents charged with completing the ruse suffers a malfunction and crashes into the sea, leaving no survivors. As a result, Jack Ryan, now aboard a British carrier, is ordered by the president to make direct contact with the *Red October* himself. Ryan boards the *Red October* and begins removing the crew, not realizing that one crew member has suddenly disappeared.

When a gunshot is heard aboard the *Red October,* Ramius and Ryan go to investigate. They find one Russian official dead and an American severely injured. Ramius himself gets shot, but Ryan is able to kill the embedded agent only seconds before he can destroy the ship. The *Ethan Allen,* a dated American sub, is then scuttled and everyone is led to believe that it was the *Red October* that was detonated.

The hunt for the *Red October* is called off, but as the subs are being recalled to port, Soviet Naval Command orders a few submarines to linger behind to possibly recover intelligence on the Americans.

As the *Red October* makes its final attempt to reach an American naval base, Viktor Tupolev, one of Ramius's former students, discovers the *Red October.* Tupolev attempts to destroy the submarine only to be rammed by his former teacher. Its hull ruptured, the sub sinks to the bottom of the sea.

Ramius and his conspirators are welcomed to the United

States, and Jack Ryan is finally able to fly back to his family for the holidays.

THE FIRM, John Grisham, 1991

Mitch McDeere is the one and only Harvard Law School grad that the tax firm of Bendini, Lambert & Locke is interested in hiring. He's young, brilliant, and married (a must), and he was raised in abject poverty, which makes him a perfect combination of talent and appetite. He's already had offers from three of the most prestigious law firms in the country, but the representatives from Bendini, Lambert & Locke make him an offer he can't refuse. With a phenomenal starting salary, the promise of a low-interest mortgage on a home, and a BMW in the color of his choosing, Bendini, Lambert & Locke's offer seems too good to be true. And it is.

Unbeknownst to Mitch and his wife, Abby, the head of security operations for the firm has had them bugged from the moment their plane touched down. The limo is wired, their phones are tapped, and their house is full of listening devices, all in the interest of protecting the firm. It's bad enough that Kozinski and Hodge, two of the firm's lawyers, are already talking to federal agents and some of the firm's more "senior partners" are asking for a contingency plan to silence the men, should they not listen to reason.

Before long, Kozinski and Hodge are killed in a scuba-diving "accident" while on a business trip in Grand Cayman. As a result of the firm's tragic loss, Mitch will have to pick up their slack, and he proves to be every bit the workhorse they hoped for.

During a brief break in his hectic routine, Mitch is approached by Agent Wayne Tarrance, FBI, and the lawyers at the firm press Mitch for details of their conversation. He wisely says little. Still, to be safe, Mitch consults a private investigator named Eddie Lomax, an old friend of his brother's from prison. Mitch asks Lomax to look into other suspicious deaths of the firm's lawyers and to see what he can dig up on Tarrance. Mitch isn't sure whom to trust.

Soon after, Mitch travels to Grand Cayman on company business and is seduced by a local prostitute. Later, he learns that this was a setup by the firm to gain leverage over him. After his visit to the islands, he travels to Washington for a tax conference, and in a clandestine meeting, he's told by FBI agents that the firm is a front for the Morolto family, a large crime syndicate based in Chicago. The FBI, of course, wants him to help take them down.

After much soul-searching, Mitch devises a plan that, if it works, will satisfy the FBI and free him and Abby from the grip of the firm. Together with Abby and Lomax's former secretary ("former," because Lomax has been murdered), Mitch begins to make countless copies of incriminating documents (it's a lot more exciting than it sounds).

He and Abby escape to Panama City Beach, Florida, to meet up with Mitch's brother, Ray, whose release from jail they've stipulated as part of the deal with the FBI. The three hide out in a motel room while the cops, the feds, and the Mob comb every inch of the beach looking for them. Abby sets up a video camera, and Mitch, quoting from the illegal documents, goes about making a deposition that exposes the firm's activities.

By the time he finishes, it has taken Mitch sixteen hours and fourteen cassette tapes, but the evidence needed to convict the Moroltos is finally ready. Mitch puts in a call to the feds, tells them where they can find the tapes, and he and Abby escape to a tiny Caribbean island.

Not long after they're settled, they receive a package of newspaper clippings relating the indictments of over fifty members of Bendini, Lambert & Locke and over thirty members of the Morolto clan. The McDeeres are safe and happy. For now.

THE BRIDGES OF MADISON COUNTY,
Robert James Waller, 1992

It's early August 1965, and Robert Kincaid has been assigned by *National Geographic* to photograph the covered bridges of Madison County, Iowa. An outdoorsman and a well-seasoned traveler, Kincaid is lonely and spiritual, loveless and romantic. He's fifty-two years old and a divorcé.

After a week on the road, Kincaid arrives in Madison County and has no trouble finding six of the bridges. It's the last one, the Roseman Bridge, that proves difficult to locate.

Lost on the backcountry roads, Kincaid comes to the Johnson farmhouse and finds Francesca Johnson sitting on her front porch. As Kincaid asks for directions, she senses something sensual in him. She tells him the bridge isn't far and she'd be happy to show him where it is. Richard, her husband, and their two children are away at the Illinois State Fair and will be gone a week.

After some initial scouting of the bridge, Francesca invites Kincaid to the farmhouse. Francesca soon admits that when she was growing up in Italy and imagined life in America, this Iowa farmland wasn't what she'd had in mind. Kincaid tells her he understands, and sensing the stranger in the pickup truck may already know more about her than anyone else in her life, she asks him to stay for dinner.

As they prepare dinner together, Kincaid waxes poetic about his ex-wife, his job, his travels, and his dining habits. His level of sophistication is a marvel to Francesca, and she, trying to impress him, cracks open the seal on a bottle of brandy she's been saving for years. After Kincaid leaves for the night—he does have to shoot the bridge at dawn—Francesca sneaks out to the Roseman Bridge and tacks a note on it, inviting him back again for supper.

The following night, Kincaid accepts the invitation. He showers while Francesca bathes, and when they reunite in the kitchen, they realize that they have fallen desperately in love with each other. They dance, kiss, and make love, an event so marvelous, Kincaid recites lines of poetry and recalls the sight of dolphins swimming off the coast of Africa.

For the next few days, Kincaid abandons photography and Francesca abandons her chores. Instead, they while away their days together tangled in each other's arms. Inevitably, their conversation turns to the fact that Kincaid will soon leave and Richard will return.

Francesca is the rational one. She says that she can't tame the wild force that is Kincaid, that he must be allowed to roam free. She also admits shame at the thought of humiliating Richard and her children. Both she and Kincaid are heartbroken but recognize that she's right and go their separate ways.

Richard and the children arrive. While Richard and Francesca are driving about town, they pull up behind Kincaid in his truck. Francesca bids the long-haired photographer a private good-bye and begins to cry. Francesca tells Richard she's okay, and Richard, satisfied, tunes in to a livestock report on the radio.

In 1975, Kincaid stops appearing in *National Geographic*. Four years later, Richard passes away. In 1982, Francesca receives a package from lawyers informing her that Kincaid has died. In his will he left her his bracelet, his chain, and the letter she first tacked onto the Roseman Bridge, where he had his ashes spread. Francesca dies in 1989, and she also has her ashes spread at the Roseman Bridge.

Soon after, her children uncover the truth about her relationship with Kincaid. As the novel comes to a close, they sit at the kitchen table in their old home in Madison County, Iowa, absorbing these revelations about their mother and drinking what's left of her special brandy.

The Da Vinci Code, Dan Brown, 2003

Jacques Saunière, head curator at the Louvre in Paris, is murdered in the middle of the night by Silas, an albino monk searching for a powerful secret. In his final moments, Saunière realizes that if he dies, the truth will die with him, so he scribbles out an elaborate set of riddles in his own blood and leaves a message to contact Robert Langdon.

Langdon, an esteemed Harvard symbologist, arrives at the scene and is met by Sophie Neveu, a French cop and cryptographer. She warns him that the police are trying to pin the murder on him, and together they divert the authorities and are left alone inside the Louvre to study the clues. It turns out that Saunière was Sophie's grandfather. She loved him dearly but hadn't spoken to him in years, not since she had witnessed him engaged in some sort of mysterious sexual ritual.

Langdon and Sophie flee from the Louvre with an item they discovered during their search, a key that bears the initials of the Priory of Sion, an elusive organization that Saunière was apparently associated with. Langdon suspects this key is somehow linked to the secret of the Holy Grail. The key leads them to a Swiss depository where they find a coded cryptex, a small combination vault that if forced open will destroy the materials inside. Langdon and Sophie then hijack an armored truck and head straight for the home of Sir Leigh Teabing, the foremost expert on the subject of the Grail.

Teabing explains to Sophie (and to the reader) that the Holy Grail is really a metaphor for Mary Magdalene, the wife of Jesus, the mother of his child. He explains that this is a secret the Catholic Church has been fighting for centuries to suppress. The Priory's job is to protect it. Jacques Saunière, we learn, was the grand master of the Priory, which explains the bizarre sex ritual that Sophie witnessed.

Silas breaks up the conversation but is soon overtaken, bound, and gagged. It's much too dangerous in France, so Teabing advises that they take his private jet to London. On the flight, they decode the cryptex, only to reveal a smaller cryptex. While in a creepy London church, Teabing's manservant, Rémy, frees Silas and the two men kidnap Teabing and steal the cryptex. Turns out Rémy is working for the Teacher, the mastermind behind the entire plot. The Teacher congratulates Rémy with a drink from his flask, and wouldn't you know it, the flask is poisoned. (Actually, it was just peanuts, to which Rémy was allergic.)

Yes, Teabing is the Teacher, and yes, he was responsible for Saunière's death. At their final encounter, Teabing threatens Sophie's life and Langdon threatens to shatter the cryptex. When Langdon tosses it in the air, Teabing stumbles after it.

As he realizes it's empty, he turns to see Langdon holding a piece of papyrus in one hand and a gun in the other. The police rush in and arrest Teabing. By novel's end, Sophie learns she is a direct descendant of Jesus and Mary, and Langdon realizes that the Holy Grail is buried underneath the Louvre's inverted pyramid.

INDEX

HIT LIT

Cracking the Code of the
Twentieth Century's Biggest Bestsellers

James W. Hall

A Reader's Guide

QUESTIONS AND TOPICS
FOR DISCUSSION

1. Are you less likely to read popular novels or more likely? Or does popularity even enter into your selection process for choosing what to read?

2. Why do some books grab you and others don't? There are many possible reasons you might choose to read a particular novel, but what's the number one aspect of a story that reliably and regularly hooks you? Why does it have so much appeal?

3. Which of the novels you've read lately, either popular or literary, contain some of the ingredients detailed in *Hit Lit*?

4. Which of the twelve recurring features do you think is most central to a book's success in general? Which of the twelve is most central to your own reading experience?

5. Can you think of any other features that recur in these twelve novels—or other popular fiction—that aren't noted in *Hit Lit*?

6. Which of the twelve novels that *Hit Lit* examines have you read? Of those you've read, which do you remember most vividly or most fondly? What aspects of that novel stay with you? Are any of these aspects related to one of the twelve recurring features the book describes?

7. What are some of the differences between these commercially successful books of the twentieth century and recent bestsellers, in your opinion?

8. Most of the books on this list of highly successful novels are not written in a literary style. Does that matter? Should it? Do novels that are full of beautiful prose have the same kind of emotional impact on you as those with more unadorned writing? Do you find that the style itself affects how you read a book, or not?

9. When you choose to read a book rather than watch TV or a film, what are some of the factors that go into making that decision?

10. In the "Juicy Parts" section, the author argues that in all these novels there's one sexual episode that is life changing for a character, or somehow crucial to the outcome of the

plot. Can you think of other novels you have read where this is also true? Why do you think this is such a widespread device?

11. One argument *Hit Lit* makes is that a common thread that runs through all these bestsellers is a focus on American values or American characters of various kinds. Do you think American bestsellers challenge conventional American myths and beliefs, or do they pander to the conventional views that Americans have about themselves and their society?

12. Why do we like mavericks as protagonists in fiction? Do these characters succeed because they rebel against convention, or do they eventually succumb to the pressures of normalcy? Take Scout, for instance. Will she always be a rebel, or will she learn to work within the system as Atticus does?

13. Discuss the tension between urban values and rural values Hall points out. Does this same conflict exist in other books you've read lately? Is this part of what some describe as the "Two Americas"?

14. Four of the twelve novels Hall discusses are written by women. How do these novels portray a different vision than the ones written by men? In particular, are women more richly characterized by the female writers, or do men sometimes achieve the same level of dimensionality?

15. When we read books like *Jaws* or *The Godfather* or *The Exorcist*, do you think what we are learning about human nature or the way the world works is different from when we read Khaled Hosseini's *The Kite Runner* or Jonathan Fran-

zen's *The Corrections*? Or do we gain similar insights, regardless of the type of fiction we read?

16. Should students of literature be required to study popular novels as well as the literary classics? Should schools include *Valley of the Dolls, Jaws,* or *The Godfather* in their English curriculum or only books like *To Kill a Mockingbird*? How do you think this would help, or hurt, our understanding of literature?

17. Which of the novels on this list of twelve bestsellers do you think people will be reading a hundred years from now and which won't last? Why?

About the Author

JAMES W. HALL is the author of seventeen novels, four books of poetry, two short-story collections, and a book of essays. He's also the winner of the Edgar and Shamus awards.